Pin Up Dolls and Classic Cars:
A COVID LOVE STORY

Kenny Dupar

This book is for entertainment purposes only, and the views are those of the author and do not necessarily reflect the official policy or position any other agency, organization, employer or company. This is a work of fiction. Any similarity to actual persons or organizations are entirely coincidental. In order to maintain anonymity, in some instances I have changed the names of events and places and may have changed some identifying characteristics.

Book layout by Jim Wornell, jim.wornell@gmail.com.

Edited by Hannah R. Lyon, castlelyonediting@gmail.com.

Pin Up Dolls and Classic Cars/ Kenny Dupar — 1st ed.

ISBN 978-0-578-26868-2

Cover model, HellCath (IG @HellCath) in front of a sweet '57 Buick.

CONTENTS

LIST OF CARS

Chevy Nova

Bel Air

Buick Rivera

Impala

Cadillac Eldorado

Pontiac GTO

Skylark

F-150

Toyota RAV4

'69 Mustang Ragtop

Corvette

Plymouth Road Runner

Maserati

Porsche

Model A Ford

Toyota Tundra

Kia Sportage

Nissan Sentra

Chevy Silverado

Mercury Cougar

Costco Petal Car

Barracuda

1950 Chevrolet 3100 pickup truck

Go Karts

'40 Willys Coupe

'48 Anglia Trio

El Camino

Dodge Challenger

'32 Ford coupe

1967 Rally Sport Z28

Dodge Ram

Thunderbird Sports Roadster

Kaiser Dragon

Regal

LeSabre

Ford Fairlane Crown Vic

Expedition

Explorer

Lincoln-Zephyr Convertible

Continental

Oldsmobile Starfire

Pontiac Bonneville

Honda Civic

Camaro

LIST OF CHARACTERS

	Pin Up name	**Nemesis**
Corrine	*Corrine De Menthe*	Evan
Cory (son)		
Peter		
Audrey	*Holly Hot Rod*	Kaelani
DeMarco (son)		
Tamah (son)		
Mitchell (Uncle)		
Owen		
Ryan		Tiffany
Delmonica (daughter)	*Cherry Nova*	
Johnny (son)		
Jack		
Kimmy	*Serenity Jade*	
Brian		
Donna	*Donna Diva*	
Aleia	*Miss Demeanor*	
Aaron		
Lawrence		
Gary		

Part One

1
Mother's Day

"What's your favorite color, and what does it smell like?"

"My favorite color is black. It smells like the exhaust from racing fuel," Holly Hot Rod replied to the Master of Ceremony's prearranged question.

She posed with one gloved hand high in air, her toothy grin imposing. Her dress had the intensity of a midnight storm. Camera phones pretended to click. She was more powerful than the other Pin Up Dolls. The high slit in her evening gown was like a fleshy, flashing lightning bolt upon a disappearing shadow. Audrey (though no one there used her real name) was the fastest machine at the classic car show that day.

Oh, the gearheads liked her! The genuine applause was filled with loud, male handclaps with a few thundering "yeahs!". She turned wrenches for Boeing and had the gritty confidence mature men want, until they get it. Taught by their dad's example to use Gojo's orange oil and pumice filled soap, everyone was cleaned up real good today. The grease under their fingernails had even been brushed out. Although for some mechanics, oils seeped into the layers of their skin from constant contact. It just leached back after the surface was scrubbed bright.

Holly was crowned Queen of the first pageant of the season after the judges tallied and the popular vote was counted. It was Mother's Day, 2018. The "Brazen Beauties" Pin Up club helped promote the event. She would stay late to clean up, after most from her chapter bailed. Her fiancé waited at home with her underemployed, car-less son. The unlucky man having to work on a Sunday. They both gave her thoughtful cards. And Holly texted her man the happy news after she had hugged practically everyone.

Beautiful women and muscle cars blended in a symbiotic perfection on a partly cloudy day. In the Pacific Northwest the adults were ready to play after a rainy Spring.

Lockdowns hadn't been imposed and COVID had not yet killed.

Corrine De Menthe was asked by the MC if her man was planning anything special for her on Mother's Day. Donna Diva passed out slips of paper with random questions to the Dolls five minutes before the Q&A started. She didn't have time to worry about the emotional impact it could have on a single, boyfriend-less girl. The microphone passed to Corrine. Within the car show's beer garden, a small space was carved out for the interview portion of the pageant.

"Well, you know, I got my special present this morning. . . 'cause, you know. . ." Her lace off-the-shoulder party dress strained to cover her eight-inch oval headlamps. "If Momma ain't happy. . ." Her chest heaved with a dramatic pause. "Then's nobody happy!"

The crowd's assent was unanimous and rowdy. Her real present was a crayon drawing on construction paper.

"But if Daddy ain't happy. . .?" she asked absentmindedly.

Three men lowly replied in unison, "then no one cares," which got some chuckles.

Miss De Menthe added with a wink, "But believe me, my Daddy's happy today."

And that was enough. Slutty responses always proved effective. It was a popularity contest, after all. Corrine cried a little when her son gave her the picture of them together playing with their puppy, and read the unsteadily written, sincere, "I LOVE MY MOM." She almost won Miss Congeniality that mid-May day, but this was only her second year, just "patched in" over the winter and the Chapter president, Miss Diva wasn't yet in a giving mood towards her. Corrine curved perfectly like the fenders of 1939 Deluxe Ford Coupe; she was bulbous and wide, painted in a harmonizing tropical green. She got lots of votes, most of which were counted.

Grills gave wafts of smoking meat to imbue the Americana set. The small brewery hosted this day hoping to make money with Kielbasa and pale ales. Such super spreader events as these were soon to be a relic of the past.

Ginger Honey Bear, Marie Bella Rose, Serenity Jade, and Katastrophic spoke about the pediatric cancer charity the chapter supported, their lives' victories, like personal illness, eldercare, or children with special needs. Defeating wounds like divorce and death were avoided.

Masking her usual, self-serving self, Miss Demeanor pined on and on about how much the "Sisterhood of Pin Up Dolls has meant so much in my life." It was a "soft ball" question pitched by Miss Donna Diva to her long-time friend. Some sisters hated the fact that her dresses were always special ordered, never second hand or personally sewn.

An immigrant girl from the Philippines attended her at a salon the night before, so she could always win best makeup. Another bedazzled ribbon sat across her dainty chest. She was named a Princess many times over but didn't use the title, "Miss", being integral to her name. She never tried very hard at anything and couldn't give a fuck about becoming a queen.

Her son was on the other side of the country. It occurred to her to call her ex, since he'd wait for her to phone before making their five-year-old son talk to his mom. Somehow Aleia found the money to outspend most girls in the Brazen Beauties Pin Up chapter, although she was damn near homeless, a sociable but slippery girl.

Authentic Pin Up chic was pursued with hairdos and many accessories like parasols, handbags, and faux, vintage, clear crystal jewelry. Tattoos were too numerous to be found inauthentic in the 21st century. Body art clashed with sleeveless dresses. Contestants showing up in a ponytail, however, were judged to be unpardonably lazy.

It wasn't about winning awards for many enthusiasts, but the car scene itself. Hundreds/thousands of people came to Issaquah, those who could pronounce Native place names, in order to appreciate what others had built, and lasting friendships were made. Magnificent lowriders and traditional custom rebuilds parked side by side. Imaginations flourished from fresh off the assembly line, glorious, back in the day original styling. Artistic design and attention to detail inspired future builds.

But none could ever surpass the perfect creation of the human form itself. Amazing, awesome friendships welded together, ground down, and Bondo'd to seamlessness, helped men stand strong when family passed away. They enjoyed meeting people because of the cars.

Both Dolls and Gearheads strove toward beauty abstractly, in Washington State. It was something you could almost touch, but fleeting, like a chance for a few hours of recognition.

The Dolls wanted their pictures before, atop, and within a Nova, Bel Air, Rivera, Impala, Eldorado, or a Pontiac GTO. Their owners wiped chrome into glass with micro-cloths.

Pin Ups asked, "Can I touch it?"

The smart boys responded, "Yes, you can. As long as you're wearing your gloves." Don't smudge. Pride outshined sexual tension barely, by a smidge. Owners needlessly related their car's modifications to ladies who had spent months choosing outfits and altering their looks. Ornery curmudgeons scowled and rarely won awards for their cars, or friends.

With baskets full of their business cards tied to candy, Dolls stepped carefully through grass with too high heels. Calves would be sore by the end of the day. Attentive men offered their hands over uneven ground. Many wanted to win a prize but would settle for photographs with racy composition.

Flat red looked orange in the spotty light. Bonnets were fully raised over engines. Backgrounds often sucked as people milled about, other cars or objects getting in the way. Photographers with cell phones spoke clumsy suggestions on maybe how to pose. Get up close. Check the serpentine belt, is it taut? Should you even be under the hood? Are you allowed? Did you jiggle the hoses? Are they all connected good? Did you just get caught being naughty? Could you top off the fluids? Why don't you get behind the wheel? Do you like to go fast? Let's see your pouty face. Check your mirrors. Is someone following you? Is Daddy going to let you drive? How 'bout we hop in the backseat? Can you blow me a kiss?

"Just one?" she might ask.

Even though it was awfully tempting, Ryan didn't buy a delicious porter at the small brewery that hosted the car show with the Carburetor Crackups car club, and Brazen Beauties sponsoring. Forty or so vehicles of all makes had entered. He sat in a folding lawn chair and sipped from cans of Mountain Dew, then used the empties to spit back into while enjoying a dip of Copenhagen mint long cut. He was a car enthusiast, and this was his first show he had entered.

There was no chance he'd have any alcohol before putting his baby to bed. Having poured about 20k into his '70 Nova, he didn't need another drunk driving offense. Eight years ago, they didn't have the "blow and go" but it still cost him over ten grand in court fees and increased insurance. As a reward for such self-control, Ryan planned on getting shitfaced when he got home. His daughter Delmonica and her fiancé wanted pizza for dinner, so they planned to get some pies to go. Eating out would upset his liquid appetizers. It was a good day with zero pressure.

Recently, his buddy Jerry had an ignition interlock device court ordered for a year resulting from his OUI, and it was a real pain in the ass. One morning after drinking heavily, a positive result required a tow to a licensed service shop to reset the computer, and two days away from work and a reported violation to the Motor Vehicle Department. Jerry got another six months tacked onto having a breathalyzer. He stopped by to give well wishes and admire his friend's efforts. That was at least one vote Ryan could count on.

The kids sat with him most of the afternoon. Another gearhead, Jack, sporadically talked details about the rebuild to his future father-in-law. They installed the black door panels in a weekend with only one case of Rainier beer between them. Named for the mountain that dominated the southern sky view of Seattle, it was an inexpensive Pilsner that had its intended effect.

Jack was glad it wasn't his credit card that financed the pursuit of an automotive dream. It would have been less costly to order the whole interior kit and then Craig's List whatever they didn't need. The correct lens for the interior light was on order. Ryan was building it "one piece at a time." Goofing around a previous weekend in the garage, the kid played Johnny Cash's song by that name on his iPhone and got called a "son-of-a-bitch" for the effort. It became their anthem.

"You haven't even met my mom yet, Ryan. She's good looking. You know I came from a broken home, so maybe you could be my new d-aaa-dddy?" he bleated like a sheep. "Not just an in-law, but for reals."

"Like that wouldn't be weird." Ryan swigged a third of a can of Rainier, "That's wrong in too many ways." After a big pause, he added, "That means Delmonica would be your sister and your wife."

"It's happened before." The zone between three and five beers, when men could still somewhat safely work with tools, also corresponded with smack in the middle funniest banter. He's a sick bastard, he thought. And he liked the notion. He continued to consider in his mind: maybe I'll meet his mom at the weddin'? That was a sore subject as there wasn't a definitive date for the nuptials. Soon Ryan's daughter would be on her own, maybe. As far as his family was concerned, he was in charge of jack shit.

A few Pin Ups came by to talk, passing out cards and asking for votes. They traded promises to mark ballots for each other, Ryan entering the Best Chevy category for only $20. Another twenty and he could have shown in the Best Hot Rod or Best Paint. Best interior was a project too far away. Best in Show seemed unattainable.

He thought about joining the Carburetor Crackups. Pretending to be interested in their efforts, he told most of the girls that they had pretty dresses. Most were in their 40's or 50's but beauty knew no age. He was getting a glimmer of how to politic for votes in this world. And for a moment Ryan became embarrassed for wearing just a Motley Crue T-shirt and a ratty pair of sneakers.

"How long have you had your car?" Ginger Honey Bear asked. She accented her cherry-colored hair with pink carnations and cat eyed red frame shades. Everything she wore was pink except the roses and stems on a below the knee rockabilly swing dress.

"I bought it from a guy in Puyallup last year."

"Love the paint job. What kind of orange is it?"

"Actually, it's called Monza red. It took a while for me to find replacement paint that matched the stock color. It's not brilliant but flat, so it can change the look depending on the light."

"Can I touch it?" Her smile and squinty eyes were so playful that it made Ryan want to play, too.

"Do you have pink gloves?" This being his first show, Ryan forgot this time to ask for pictures to be texted right away, before folks blended back into the crowd. There could have been a few he'd print out full size and hang in the garage. A mark of small victories. Something to look at and smile, wondering who was going to give who a ride.

Corrine De Menthe walked Serenity Jade, aka Kimmy, around the car show, showing her the ropes, asking for votes. Kimmy was Ryan's sister-in-law and just recently joined the Chapter as a prospect.

"Where's my brother at?" Ryan asked.

"He's working in Nevada. Still setting up displays at conventions. It's a two week gig this time."

"Is he going to hang out before breaking down?"

"No, they fly the crew to Reno next weekend, in between." She missed her husband and told Miss De Menthe to never fall in love with a traveling man. Not that her advice would soon matter.

Corrine had worked with Ryan distributing Pepsi Products a few years back and they remained very close friends to the annoyance of his then wife Tiffany. Ryan and Corrine endured her job shadowing week while making sure she could drive the rig containing hundreds of cases of soda, always working at a fevered pace.

Jerry called her twice to come and keep Ryan out of jail when he was obnoxiously drunk at local taverns and wanting to fight. With her, Ryan was like an older brother and if he had amorous inclinations, he kept them to himself. Being fifteen years, her senior probably had an effect.

He "licensed" her on the hand truck and reported her required physical attributes. "She's plenty strong." He appreciated a woman willing to work with her back. The wage humping beverages wasn't great, but the overtime added up fast to fat paychecks. Few applicants had the hustle, and laziness meant job security for Ryan. At least these days he could finally spend some money on stuff that brought him pleasure rather than everybody else's essentials, like Amazon delivering car parts. It was Corrine who bugged him until he agreed to bring his baby to the show.

He strapped the over-the-shoulders restraints over his belly and rumbled out of the grassy yard soon after Holly and a 1966 Buick Skylark were said to be the best that day. Del and Jackass (a new pet name) picked up the pies after he gave his daughter fifty bucks for the effort and he rolled slowly enough to enjoy the ride back to his house all alone.

Baby had the whole two car garage. His like-new, used F-150, canary yellow truck took up one side of the driveway. His ex-wife's 2013 Toyota RAV4 sports utility parked it in. No fucking pride in anything, he thought.

The idle propelled his Nova past the car he bought her. Looking inside one would see fast food wrappers and wrinkled clothes. The exterior was a record of inattentive driving with scratches and dents on every panel, a few giving toeholds to rust. At least she put her own gas in it and insured it herself. Her snarky request that the least he could do was change her oils and keep it road-worthy blazed worthy arguments.

Ryan opened the workshop fridge before going inside the house and grabbed a cold one. Tiffany was smoking at the dinner table, watching the Hallmark Channel.

The pleasant glow of the afternoon dimmed quickly. "Mel is bringing me pizza. I suppose you'd want to eat?" Ryan said, but it wasn't an invitation.

"I'm not hungry." She was even fatter than Ryan. At least he groomed his beard and mustache and kept his clothes clean. The old hag had translucent whiskers and permanent stains on her gray sweatpants.

Tidying up the kitchen while throwing away mailers, he asked, "there are credit card offers here. Are you sure you don't want some more?"

This time, first blood was his. It was wickedly fun to bait her. At least he didn't open up her mail, like she did to him, he suspected. His bills wouldn't be missed if thrown away. Her need to know supplanted his need to stay afloat. Several times routine correspondence was lost via the stellar U.S Mail, supposedly. Late fees atop interest made his hands shake. Ryan put nothing past her. The paranoia was but one thing to cloud his judgment?

"Don't be an asshole," she snapped back and put out a butt. Then Tiffany braced to lift her 230-pound frame. "Oh, my knees are creaking today."

There were two boxes of macaroni and cheese in the waste bin since he left for the show. He grinned and mused to himself, I bet she ate a whole stick of butter today. Buy your own glucosamine and chondroitin, bitch, let them joints snap, crackle, and pop. She can answer phones for $20 an hour. Customer service? Her fat ass.

"Hey, why don't you throw away your beer cans before you open another?" Tiffany shot in his direction.

Ryan absorbed the jab without a counter punch, returned to the garage, and turned on the radio to an oldies station playing AC/DC.

She made him seethe in waves. Even though they were divorced, the separation wasn't that long. He had paid for both of their lawyers. Peace was shattered when he found out that his only child and his ex were living in the unheated garage of a family-friend.

She had been granted majority custody but couldn't even put a roof over their heads, even with $1000 a month in child and spousal support. Then, a few months later, a homeless education liaison from the local school district contacted him to establish his daughter's address. Delmonica couldn't provide one, as she and her mother were living in Tiffany's SUV.

He took a swig from a bottle of Jim Beam. "Kissing Jimmy." That's what he called it. It was a package deal, their moving back in, and it removed much of his financial strain. He didn't have to pay Tiffany a grand a month anymore, but now bought her groceries and changed the oil in her car. Jerry asked if taking her back to court was an option. All Ryan could respond with was, "with whose money am I going to do that?"

He woke up the morning after learning how his daughter was living, not remembering how he'd cut his hands and head. Jerry helped piece together the previous night's fight at a local bar. Ryan did that often. Bourbon whiskey affected his memory several ways, first pushing back the idea of his child shivering under blankets, on a cot above an oil-soaked concrete floor, then bringing anger out in waves considering how Delmonica could sleep in a car.

Tiff got his money with the custody and enjoyed vacations and plastic spending sprees for Chinese made Walmart crap. There wasn't much choice but to take both back into the four bedroom, two story house, whose mortgage he met through his own effort, his own sore back, delivering Pepsi products sixty hours a week.

At least his kid could graduate with him in the picture. The deal with the devil was that the bitch was back. All of her shit (worthless possessions) were back from the big storage space she had rented, spreading out her filth like a diseased rat, sniping and back biting at every turn.

Now Delmonica was about to graduate high school four months pregnant. At least Jack wasn't a mean guy. Ryan told him, "If the baby is a girl and you name it Tiffany, I'll kill the entire Goddamn family." It was said with sick humor but may not have been too far from the truth. Especially if Ryan got blackout drunk.

...

Although she looked a bit like a melted candle, Audrey got a big kiss when she finally got back to their double wide. The Queen's crown was readjusted in the carport and the sash was checked for folds, its safety pin keeping everything from being undone.

The porch light flicked on before Audrey was exactly ready and a goateed man with a cowboy hat opened the front door. Exposing his bald spot with a bow, he removed the hat with a sweeping motion, face to the floor, and uttered, "Your Highness!"

Holly Hot Rod had won princess tiaras in the two years she had competed, but this was a huge breakthrough in the land of positive self-esteem.

Oh, she liked that! Owen had asked about her speech and whispered in her ear as she swept inside with a small suitcase and a big swag bag. "You smell like racing fuel," he commented.

A big, toothy grin pulled wider across her face. "I just need a glass of wine and a shower."

"Let me help get you out of your dress."

"Stop, peasant. The wine first."

He tapped his forehead, bowed, and intelligently stopped talking.

The door to her son's room was closed as Audrey walked the six steps of the hall. The "Master" bedroom was choked with dressers and two chairs filled with outfits. Accessories were scattered over and beside the bed as if a rushed tantrum had taken place earlier in the day.

Owen entered and tried to find a place to set the glass down but couldn't immediately find a space large enough. "Here you go," he said and handed her the wine glass. "If you need any help, I'll be playing my guitar." He turned to leave, then remembered his dinner plans. "Do you want a burger, or a foot long? I'm grillin'."

"I haven't eaten all day. But first, you could sit and listen about my day."

"Where? I mean, okay. Where you going to put your crown?" He stood smiling with his hands interlaced, hanging by his silver engraved oval belt buckle. There were never enough places to put all her stuff and he got rattled when it spilled into the rest of the double wide.

Her kid moving in, although he didn't really have that much, wasn't at all a help. Her princess tiaras and sashes were displayed prominently, around battery operated candles and over the bed frame. Owen wondered if there was an anniversary for shacking up. He remembered the commemoration with a special dinner out.

The kid wasn't bad, just lazy. When I was your age. . . popped into his head often. Thirty years earlier he had a BA in music theory and was working in radio, selling advertising and gofer'ing for any other, more established, employees. Owen was used to being poor. His divorce made him poorer still, but another chance at happiness was a good tradeoff.

The pictures were supposed to be the payoff. "Aaron was taking pictures of the girls but look how shitty the angles were." The Queen manipulated her phone to show him. "He's always on a knee looking up." The grills of the cars were more prominent than the Pin Ups.

"Who's Aaron?"

"Miss Diva's husband."

"She's the President of your club? She was the MC?" His questions were ignored as Holly Hotrod was too tired to explain the organizational details again. If she had at all. Instead, she simply handed her phone to Owen. "Yeah, I see that. Did you get some good ones of you being crowned?"

"She sent me some from her phone."

Owen asked her to forward the good ones to him and she agreed.

"How was the station?" she asked him. "Is the garden show still putting you to sleep?"

"I'd rather produce the mortgage show on Saturdays. Sorry, I couldn't be there, babe, for your victory." They exchanged a hug. A kiss. A little ass grabbing. Owen could kick himself for being so dense. There was a sequined, strapless black evening gown to help peel off a girl's body. What a show. He almost missed out. Those great long struts and springs.

He did manage to stammer out, "you got great legs, baby." Then he struggled to refocus. "Are you going to act like a Queen now?"

Always searching for the sexual opening herself, Audrey responded with another hug and said, "Oh, it's going to get worse."

Having the kid added much stress for their young relationship. It was temporary until Demarco could find a place. Fat chance for a part time grocery clerk who had recently spent six months in jail for burglary. Before he got locked up, though, Demarco did manage to impregnate a wretched girl named Kaelani. She gave birth before Demarco was released.

Audrey and Owen brought flowers to the hospital but were prevented from seeing the baby as Mom refused access, stating "they ain't family", enjoying her new-found power to separate, control, and destroy.

Her Samoan brother acted like a bouncer from the Jerry Springer show trying to control a fight that wasn't going to happen, blocking the door with hands ready to push flatly against Owens's chest. In a hospital corridor Audrey was crushed, a bouquet pointed toward the floor. The intended target was brought low. But she did meet her grandson in her own home once Demarco was situated there. She'd be on eggshells with Kaelani, forever fearful of her inexplicable hostility.

The rents were high near the offices of Microsoft, Amazon, Google and Facebook that were in and scattered around the Emerald City, named for Chief Si'ahl. In the sticks with the poor white trash, though, not so much. First, Audrey's ex moved out, then her son, then Owen moved in, then the kid back again. Audrey had lived a lot in the last few years in her rented double wide.

Owen knew enough to never get between a woman and her son. When she got mad that he was smoking pot in his room he agreed with her, but Owen was metaphorically lynched because he'd gotten high with the lad once. If he disagreed with her with anything concerning her twenty-five-year-old, he was wrong. If he was right, he was wrong and if he was wrong, he was wrong. The only thing to do was watch what he said, put his headphones on, strum his guitar, and make dinner for three. There was still a thin chance of getting some "Nana love" this weekend.

...

Corrine went home to an empty, two-bedroom apartment and fed the fish. Her son's father, Evan, had Cory that day, just as he would have Corey for Father's Day; it was just how their trading weekends schedule fell. It felt selfish that she had special plans without her son on Mother's Day. She could have easily argued to have him. Her mother made mention of it when Corrine had called to wish her well.

It was always a battle to change dates, but she hadn't tried, preferring to have fun with new friends. Corrine criticized herself a lot, feeling guilty, not knowing how to protect her child from a hostile and sustained attempt to alienate her from her kid. The constant disrespect sometimes seeped through.

She and Corey had names for the fish but it changed often. "Gekko" was a favorite name from the PJ Masks cartoon series. Changing from white to green to blue depending on the fish's mood, the Chromis scooted around little plastic plants, fake coral, and a diminutive SpongeBob SquarePants pineapple house. Miss Donna Diva asked if the "her man" question was okay only moments prior to the Q&A portion of the pageant. What was she supposed to say? "No, my last date was with a four-year-old"?

Her dress pulled reluctantly off her hips. Little man could zip up and down which would have been a help. Her Pin Up friends helped her pull it together and into her meadow green dress that morning. Corrine was emotionally charged just getting into the shower, feeling so fat and unattractive.

She sobbed a few times while she toweled off but managed to place her new pictures on Facebook. Then she called several girlfriends until finding one who would gab for an hour. Having a pleasant personality worked for her how? The super sweet, fat girl overwhelming aspect of her hadn't much changed since getting her Associates Degree. Just being pathetic had added bitterness.

Corrine caught herself in a "poor me baby" attitude sometimes. But one day she would win a princess tiara and then the tall, glittering crown! Queen De Menthe would be like the Queen of Hearts in Alice in Wonderland and command, "off with their heads!" Corrine was also the funny, super-smart, sweet, fat girl.

...

When she got into the camper, Miss Demeanor tossed her bags onto the queen bed then instantly grabbed her stubby bong from the dinette table. She turned up the thermostat and slid into the elevated pop-out booth. Parked on her friend's property she had to figure her next move soon. Three months' rent free was going to get old. She needed a grand gesture for the Donna.

Though she'd been married four times, there weren't any keepers at the show that day. Maybe she could get another telemarketing job? Aleia hated that. Drinking meant carbs and not fitting into clothes. If only she could score some speed.

The weed relaxed her instantly. Aleia preferred a body buzz cannabis to a head buzz. Today had been so much fun hanging with the dolls. Bringing her one hitter, Lady Ida Delight and she were floating and giggling through the rows of cars. Flirting and getting their pictures taken, it was delightful, getting high in public.

Public Storage boxes filled with little boy art, lots of dresses, shoes, and accessories filled her 8x10 rented space for $99 per month. Late fees added onto her tab for over $250 and Miss Demeanor needed to pay that off in order to move it or keep it there. A few pictures of her four-year-old playing in snow, smiling when kissed by his mom, could be thrown into a dumpster if she didn't pay.

But taking another drag from the bong and a little swig from a cheap pilsner made her plans foggy. Construction paper turkeys made from handprints stared back at her, wishing her well. Cotton balls and sequins stuck by thick streams of Elmer's glue told her how much she was loved. They were beloved since a child had gathered rocks by a stream while camping, and now they became precious treasures in jeopardy of a landfill. Precious cash must be dedicated to preserve a connection to her slipping memories.

A favorite pastime for Aleia was trolling for another sugar daddy via dating sites. Her relationships always ended badly; eventually the bloom fell, leaving a limping stalk. Someone else was always going to pay the mortgage. For her lovers, unencumbered sex was always supplanted by resentment. Dropping out of high school before her foster dad tried to rape her didn't portend well for her academic pursuits, or healthy relationships. Not that she had any of either. She got her GED when she was twenty-five.

Players need not apply to her Plenty of Phish site. Big ballers were fun but would never, ever shack up, or pick up a check, for that matter (outside the first one or two dates). She wasn't made of gold but acting like it helped. Girls usually posted pics with themselves with their lap dogs or cats. Guys liked to post pictures of themselves with animals they'd killed, like big smelly fish or a deer.

Camouflage clothes and boats meant men with less than fatal faults. Aleia placed pictures of herself hiking, camping, and wearing sports jerseys. Always, she was within a crowd of new friends from that year. She lied about her job and only showed photos from many years ago. Glamor shots of her Pin Up pursuits while emphasizing charitable concerns could tempt a church boy. They were easy to hook, sincere, but were ultimately boring, so trusting and in desperate need of a slow, sloppy blowjob. That type of pfishin' could be a lot of fun.

She'd been patched into the Brazen Beauties club for five seasons and saw first-hand how hard her friend worked to keep the organization afloat. When the former treasurer, Morgan Sweet, had moved to Vegas to work a hospitality job, Aleia volunteered to replace her.

All the dues, pageant fees, and purchases for prizes and gifts had to be accounted for, plus outlays for future events, plus the money raised for charity. Getting drunk with Donna on her patio was like an ongoing chapter meeting. Just because Miss Demeanor hardly had any money didn't mean she didn't know how to manage it. And she desperately hoped she wouldn't have to embezzle the funds.

2

XXX Root Beer

"What are you driving?" The proprietor of XXX Root Beer asked almost every customer after taking their order. His hair was slick and black from decades of oil and color. Bilingual, his extended family quickly served those hungry for the low rider double cheeseburger.

Trans fats made it from the deep fryer, through ventilation ducts, then rode the wind to nearby nostrils, eventually tickling brains. His welcome to visitors during the car show was usually the same, but always upbeat. Some grilled and assembled, some pushed mops and took out the trash, some confident enough to announce into the microphone said things like, "CHERRY CHIFFON - SMALL VANILLA MALT," with a Spanish accent.

Cumulus clouds bumped into mountains at 3,000 feet. Salish sea level Seattle was twenty miles to the west. They passed slowly like the line for ice cream floats for current pageant princesses. Relic cash registers rung next to credit card readers. It was a little breezy for girls in dresses. Smarties in pants felt fine. Hairy legged ol' boys in shorts enjoyed the cool on their legs while they sat at long oval tables, shaped like the wooden staves of root beer barrels.

Inside the restaurant the décor was a time capsule. The photographs of celebrities like Jay-Lo, Santana, and the Rolling Stones were featured in prime locations near doors and supporting columns. Coca-Cola napkin holders, along with red and white upholstered booths ran along the walls. Decades of unfamiliar famous people and their autographed pictures were hung, like local bands and politicians.

Signs for products and businesses like Orange Crush and Texaco filled every conceivable space on the walls. The fries were unremarkable, but the shakes were thick; the juice from burgers ran down arms past checker-board paper wrappers. A retro-Bluetooth jukebox changed hues of primary colors and played Elvis, Johnny Cash, and Hank Williams tunes at a respectable volume. The "No Firearms" notice at the door, a red circle and slash over the picture of a handgun, was lost in an optical explosion.

The restaurant was an icon, and large events in the empty lot beside them was a boon. The margins were slim for this Mexican familia. Shutting down for a day was laziness, a week was unthinkable, a month would be catastrophic let alone a year.

DeeDee Dauntless, Mars Cherrie, and Black Lingerie represented another Pin Up girl post from Spokane known as the Atomic Kittens. Dolls were free to enter other club's pageants as long as they met club requirements with pre-meetings and signups.

The girl who captured the most attention had spiderwebs in her hair, a dark greenish skirt, and cobwebby nylons that strained toward her trunk, reminding leering gearheads of the elegant cigar shaped curves of a '53 Cadillac Eldorado, fabulously rich and silky. A lipstick color named "oil slick" highlighted una Latina hermosa. Beautiful Black Lingerie won the prize that day, the tall Queen's crown.

Not everyone had a concealed carry permit who attended the car show, or entered their automotive creation, or dressed to kill. Pin Ups could quickly access their locked firearms from their pickup trucks. Some auto show contestants would certainly protect their investments. Off duty cops would utilize their training and show restraint.

Donna Diva was armed and executed the schedule as the President of the Brazen Beauties club with zeal. She was a multiple awarded Queen bee. Miss Demeanor or Bonnie Bandita would place a bullet through a brain with a calm and steady trigger squeeze. Saving other people's lives would just be an excuse in order to watch a man die. Not having much to lose would be a peril for a potential perp and those who would shoot back. It may have been as safe a public American space as it could be. Threatening adult playtime here was ill-advised.

The troop of pistol packing mamas had their booster club called the "Skull Fuckers" nonetheless. Their motto was "Just the Tip" and they scanned the crowd for scumbags. Their royal mauve and tan bowling shirts had nicknames written on the front and a hideous skull on the back, missing an eye.

Mostly these husbands and boyfriends loaded and unloaded gear like Rock N' Roll roadies and fetched lemonade to keep their loves hydrated. An old man sporting a Santa Claus-like beard had ripped, dirty jeans up the crotch, kept hanging around the Dolls, trying to stammer into conversation. The booster club politely told drunk Grandad to "get lost" and escorted the besotted fool off the premises. Pretending to be Secret Service agents. This task was immeasurably fun and came with wide grins.

The Capital Cruisers hosted the car show but invited two sets of girls for the date. It was like stirring up a hornet's nest. One booking was for charity and one to show off their bikini clad bodies for a fee. The Brazen Beauties Pin Up Dolls were contracted to appear and given an opportunity to solicit donations for their childhood cancer effort.

Between awful high school band sets, they performed a talent show judged by previous pageanters. Luckily, the bikini clad chicks who danced on stage for a local Motley Crue cover band quit the rally quickly due to cool weather. Modesty in pretty dresses prevailed. The Brazen Beauties Pin Up Dolls won the field, then vowed to end their association with the Capital Cruisers. Not from humiliation but from immodest competition; the event organizers violating trademark and good taste by associating the two groups in advertisements.

The pollen count was high with fine yellow powder from spruce, true cedar, and hemlock trees, causing micro clothes to become filthy. Honey berry and sapphire surf bluebeard bushes scented fields where cars parked, usually overwhelmed with exhaust. They perfumed the air far more sweetly than the nape of a lovely woman's neck.

The good times rolled before a people appreciating it not. Flattening the curve referred to a car's suspension.

A 1950 Mercury won best in show at the XXX. It was as iconic as a classic car could be, worthy of veneration. The heavy body glided like a graceful giant pill, formed to shave corners back as far as a designer could. Keeping a Ford a Ford, the engine was upgraded to a 302 and overdrive. The suspension was a Mustang II and the bucket seats in back were modeled from a '64 Thunderbird. The roof was made convertible and necessitated building a spine to keep the car together. Bone white, the cloth top contrasted the Mercury Comet maroon base.

A little girl with butterfly wings was bound with a leash, along with the family puppy dog controlled by her Nana. Her brother sat in the grass for a moment, saying he'd hit his head but couldn't say how or why. With no tears or marks, as soon as it came it was forgotten. Mom had tied her sweatshirt comfortably over her gut and Dad was impatient with the family crawl while inspecting other men's automotive efforts. His pay was slated for a mortgage and diapers, not fun stuff like grownup matchbox cars.

Ships, airplanes, and cars are often referred to in the feminine tense as a matter of affection and importance to those who build, maintain, and polish them. The mathematical beauty of slight curves. The smell of leather. Sometimes designers had swan shaped hood ornaments or winged ladies cutting the air before them.

During the talent portion of the pageant, Dolls lip synced and danced to vintage or favorite songs like the Andrew Sisters' "Chattanooga Choo Choo: "Pardon me, boys, is that the…?" A son of the Boogie Woogie Bugle boy of Company B remembered and approved. His dad, Teddy, had a '40 Chevy truck that he kept running well into the 1960's. It had a long, chrome, Jane Russell like nose making a distinctive air intake opposite a short bed.

The son restored marvelously, in black satin, a 1946 Chevy pickup with the wide mouth grill in tribute and his vote for the singer was as assured as his wife knowing why tears rolled down his face when he heard the World War II era song. Teddy fought in Italy during the war until a bullet passed through the middle of his left hand. It left a stigmata like purple bruise that throbbed from time to time even as the decades passed. He had come home and procreated mightily having seven children, most of whom were well-adjusted to church and the modern economy.

DeeDee Dauntless reminded the forty or so ring of spectators of her military family history. Her Pop Pop had flown missions in Europe, her uncle was an airman in the east China sea during Vietnam, and her son was currently a Marine with fifteen years in uniform and three deployments to Afghanistan. That was cheating, really, being a gaudy crowd pleaser, a beautifully brazen vote getter, she told a story of what motivated folks; an attachment to ancestors admired. The meaning met reality in song and pageant and metal.

Jack got a feel for the hustle during the previous show at the brewery. He made a business card with Ryan in front of his '70 Nova, including the specs on the back. 200 of them cost twenty bucks. When he showed Ryan, his flustered response was, "what am going to do with this?"

"You're not. Oh, I'll give you some. But I'm going to work the crowd. How's anyone going to know who to vote for unless we tell them?"

"They have the ballots at the show. I'll be on that."

"Okay. Let's just say that everybody votes for themselves. And the people who show up who are family and friends vote for the same car in whatever category they're in. But the people who just show up need to know how they should vote. That's where we tell them how they should vote. You know, America. A popularity contest. You're going to be a wiener!"

"And you're a dick," Ryan replied cheerfully.

"But you want to be a wiener, don't you? Why else would you enter a contest? Do you watch what the Dolls do to work the crowd, passing out cards tied to candy? I'll get every one of them to have pictures taken with your car and I'll pass out your card to everybody around. We get ten votes and we're going to be wieners! That's what they want, to get their pictures taken with the cars."

"No, I'm going to be the wiener and you're still a dick. But thanks! You bring them to me then I'll talk them up."

With a smile and nod of agreement, Jack said with a drawl, "riiight."

Mars Cherie made an outfit that looked a little like the pack that the Ghostbusters wore. She had the spray nozzle in her hand and danced to the entire song, which could have been abbreviated as she was out of breath at the end, sweating with her chest heaving under her shiny, silver tank top. Who you gonna call to get a getup like that? The crowd knew: "Ghostbusters!"

Cherry trees dropped their white petals messily in patches around the field. Crabapple trees wafted scents like dryer sheets, strong and fresh, then gone. Or perhaps it was the other way around? In the heat of the day, mid 60's, kids didn't wear their jackets. Parents pulled toddlers in red wagons to avoid the glacial pace of their tiny legs. Automobiles sporadically drove very slowly between the lanes. The sprints of crumb crunchers, in any conceivable direction, were thus avoided.

When it was time to give out the awards for the Pin Up dolls and classic cars, an argument ensued. Queen Diva laid down the law to the organizer and car club president of the Capital Cruisers. "Ladies first. If you announce the car winners first, everyone will split, making a shit ton of noise while I'm trying to give my awards to the Dolls. It's happened before. You gearheads smoke your tires after you've lost and the crowd is gone. So, hey. Just wait. Ladies first."

So, magnanimously, the guys waited and applauded the princesses and then the queen, Black Lingerie. Ryan's Chevy didn't make the cut in the three categories Ryan competed in: best paint, best Chevy, and best muscle car. Jack was suspiciously pissed that his strategy failed until Ryan won Best in Show! There was a plaque commemorating the event with the logo of the car club. Best in Show! How cool. Ryan said little when called before the crowd, stunned and grinning, a little embarrassed at being applauded. Yes, the same jackass who had hung automotive parts with his future father-in-law had figured out and employed a winning strategy to manipulate unsuspecting people. He pondered a career in politics.

The crowd dispersed quickly and cleanly. The sons of the XXX owner made quick work of policing the field of the few errant soda cups and wrappers. Staying open late was already part of the plan, until anyone needing a malt and a burger had a chance to get them and pay for the nostalgia.

The elation dissolved quickly, like instant coffee into hot water as Tiffany's omnipresence crushed the victory. Good news should have been shared with phone calls and texts and electronic posts. By the time Delmonica and Jack arrived at the house, the screaming match was in full throttle.

"Why don't you go fuck your fat girlfriend, Corrine? What the fuck she every saw in you I have no idea." Ryan's ex tried to spoil his friendships too, pretending not to be jealous.

"She actually cares about me, not that you ever lifted a finger to help me. And your disgusting fat fucking cunt that'll never see a dick again. I wouldn't wish you on my worst enemy."

Tiff kept screaming, "You'll always be a loser, 'poor me baby,' piece of shit."

His hands were clenched into fists, shaking. They faced off at other ends of the kitchen table. She made sure she had furniture between them in case Ryan tried to grab her.

Ryan's daughter, instead of needlessly intervening, packed a bag quickly and the two went to the boyfriend's efficiency apartment. Jack was worried they'd come to blows but could only think about getting the hell out of there.

"I'm a piece of shit? And you had our daughter living out of your car? You couldn't take care of a dog, let alone a kid."

Del was afraid of what may happen, Jack was trying to comfort and reassure. This wasn't the first time Ryan tried to throw Tiffany out, maybe the third time physically. The truth was that he never laid a hand upon her, except for twisted arms and unaccounted for bruises.

The pointlessness of being raged upon dangerous fuel. All grievances came to the fore. Everything that reminded him of Tiffany was like twisting a knife in his gut. Anything she had put a hand to reminded him of the agony he felt by her making his house into her home without consent.

He wouldn't have crossed the street to piss on her if her brains were on fire. How he loathed her. Stupid porcelain figurines of animals, mostly dogs, were displayed in a glass standing cabinet. He smashed it to the ground. She used credit cards for wall hangings or throw pillows with pithy sayings like, "you're my sunshine." It made Ryan boil over.

The betrayal and the constant nipping, taking little bites to cause pain and make him sore, made him hyper-sensitive over the frame of two decades of knowing Tiffany. She was putting holes in his financial bucket, constantly, paying for almost nothing herself.

A wife who threw more away out the back door than he could bring in the front door. A constant evil he felt was bent on his destruction. She broke and he couldn't repair everything. Backhanded compliments were always followed by jab, jab, jabbing. Like a wrecking ball swinging, he couldn't get out of the way.

Would this leech ever get ripped from his skin? There was too much rage for one to bear. Tiffany was indifferent and constantly pretended to be the victim, although she wouldn't leave peaceably. That kept placing Ryan in the worst light to friends and family, bad-mouthing, roiling, waiting to set family apart, ostracizing. She didn't care if he lived or died and made that plain at every conceivable moment.

"Get out. Get out, get out!" Ryan began to throw Tiffany's stuff onto the back patio. He wanted her gone, out of his life, again. How many times did he have to break up with this disgusting bitch? Delmonica was going to graduate and have his grandbaby without his ex's influence.

"You're a cancer," he snapped in Tiffany's face. "I'm going to cut you out if you don't leave right now." Ryan was inches from her, like a barroom brawl was about to take shape. Of course, it was happening in less than an hour from coming home a champ. Restraint and judgment left completely.

Ryan had called Jack, but he didn't pick up. He called Corrine but it was fun, fun, bath time for her son. Tiffany called her daughter from her car, screaming about Ryan's threats to kill her. Soon, his friend returned Ryan's call and a serenity entered his mind momentarily.

He didn't express it, but in his mind, he was saying I love you and goodbye at the same time. Corrine tried to cheer him, but it fell flat. The litany of how he'd been screwed by Tiffany was recounted. He couldn't do his usual amount of overtime because his back ached most days. The mortgage plus yellow truck plus baby had become a financially unsustainable shuffle. Corrine called 911 after Ryan said the magic words: "I'm going to kill myself."

Everyone close called everyone else and Corrine dropped her sleepy son off at her sister's at 9PM. By the time she arrived at the house, four squad cars had made a rough cordon of it, rapping on neighbor doors and ordering evacuations. Protocol be damned. Corrine kept calling and crying with Ryan, although the watch commander tried to impose control. The single shot of a firearm reported loudly, and the cops prepared for forced entry, to see the beer cans stacked like trophies on the kitchen table next to a near empty bottle of booze.

Before midnight, the sickening report reverberated for a moment and Corrine gasped. Cops peeked in the windows and soon slammed into the house to begin to secure an individual homicide scene.

The body spilled more than a quart of blood from the top of the head. Ryan had dashed his body to pieces, a sin. She saw it after shouldering her way into the kitchen. The moment the scare hit, Corrine's vision panned in and out from the bloody bits that seeped like crimson stucco into the ceiling, walls, and windows. Ryan's face was turned away toward a corner, but Corrine saw the bleeding hole beneath his chin and his skull cap blown clear off before a cop pushed her out of the house.

Someone would have to clean up the blood and brains tomorrow. Someone hired by the local authorities. Who?

Corrine was back several times before the yellow tape came down, so she could memorialize, and cry. In plain view, she stood on property soon to be in foreclosure, where a man had succumbed to frustration. His besotted mind was unable to build upon a fantastic win.

3

Go Fund Me

Getting the death certificate was vital for Tiffany. Her putrid plan was in continuous development. Speed and decisiveness were needed now. Crocodile tears streamed into social media like a flood. Delmonica cried at the slightest touch or acquaintance's call. Everyone that Tiff knew that Ryan knew heard the news, then hundreds knew about the tragic loss of such a fine man. Of course, there wasn't any mention of alcoholism or violence. The love of his life was devastated. And now, poor thing, she had to manage her husband's affairs and a great big house.

There wouldn't be the "clack clack clack" of a cane shuffling down a rehab's hallway after knee replacement for Ryan. Almost fifteen years of humping soda were over. No need to strive toward retirement anymore. But Tiffany could see a series of paydays, picking off the bones. She'd get the knee replacement instead.

Ryan's brother was traveling out of state, setting up and breaking down convention spaces, when his wife phoned. On Tuesday morning, Delmonica reached out to Kimmy. She'd heard her mother say she'd let everybody in the family know about the loss. She wasn't stunned that Tiffany didn't include her dad's family. "Yesterday, you said you'd let everybody know," Delmonica whimpered like a child.

They were Del's family too, but such consideration made her mother rage. "If you want to, you call 'em. Ain't no kin to me. Never had a kind word for me." Tiffany said it with a gleeful lilt, knowing that it hurt.

"Your niece texted me to call her, so when I did, she told me that her dad was dead! He shot himself, Brian. Your brother's dead." The words hung in space like an iron weight that wouldn't fall. "Brian! Brian did you hear what I said?"

"Yeah. Yeah, I heard." He gently laid down a dinged up twenty-five-foot tape measure at his feet, thinking he saw a quiver in his hand. More like, his eyes were losing focus. "When? How?"

"Sometime this weekend, I guess."

"Sometime?!" His blood pressure shot straight up. "You guess?" Kimmy, his wife, was trying not to cry, startled with his anger. "What the fuck is Delmonica talking about? I'm going to call her now."

"No, don't." She was telling him what to do.

"'Don't'? What the fuck are you talking about?"

"Brian, she was hysterical. You're not going to pump her for information."

His anger spiked for a moment, then, out of nowhere, he remembered his brother's hysterical laughter when the older bro had fired a football like a bullet into the beans and frank of the neighbor kid's junk. It made a "ppuuck" sound, like the nose of the pigskin plugging into a socket.

Why would a hilarious childhood memory invade his shock right now? One chuckle quietly left his lips, then the realization of loss and pressure reformed behind his eyes. Wife and husband didn't speak for half a minute.

"You can look on Facebook," she said, breaking the silence. "Go look at Tiffany's page."

"You look on Tiffany's page! What the. . .?" He paused, trying to pull back. "What does that have to do with anything?"

"Well, for the Go Fund Me."

His soul gasped. Was it possible that the ex would milk the tragedy? "It's up to almost five grand. A lot of people loved your brother."

He wanted to say that he'd take care of the arrangements. But he didn't know about his brother's finances, except that when he was divorcing the cunt, Ryan had tried to borrow money. At the time, Brian was broke and had been thinking to call on him. Their parents were dead. And the realization that he was now all alone in the world sunk in hard. But he had Kimmy.

"I'm sorry, babe. I can get home quick." The roof's reflection off the polished concrete of the near empty convention space made him feel he was walking on the ceiling. He was ranging out in widening circles, away from the small crew building displays.

"Then what?" Kimmy always had the level head. He could sit on the couch getting hotter or keep his job. "Not yet, babe. I'll find out what the fuck."

"I won't call Delmonica."

"Call her tonight, babe." He'd keep working for the mortgage and try to stay afloat. Brian's boss, when informed, assumed Brian would be leaving Nevada for a funeral. The one thing the younger brother was sure of was that Ryan's body or ashes wouldn't be in a church. The only times he and Ryan went into a place of worship was for other people's funerals.

Being a Methodist, Lutheran, or Baptist simply because you thought that was your family's tradition lost meaning generationally. Eventually, the religious preference became N/A, not applicable, nothing. No words could be said in a holy place for Ryan, as Ryan had brought himself into a desert of holy words.

Brian's brain concentrated on his current tasks instead of what was to come. Working helped him cope.

...

Driving to the Medical Examiner's office was a chore at the end of the day. Toward the County Safety building, at the wrong time, twenty miles could mean two hours. Staying jittery, Tiff picked up Del from her retail gig early. It was their second trip out to the office, since Delmonica's birth certificate had to be provided along with an application earlier in the week. The clerk asked if they wanted more than one official copy. It'd only cost another $1.25. Since they were there, why not? Brian could get his own copy of Ryan's Death Certificate when he got back into town. But the runaround was very time consuming, even if you didn't have to stand in line to present your vaccination card.

Fuck him, Tiffany thought. Let him go through all this bullshit with the County. What he'd ever do for me?

It was true that Brian and Kimmy had been merely polite during Thanksgivings, birthday celebrations, and at Christmas time. They never "clicked" into real family. With the sun in her eyes as she drove, she decided that stronger had won. With that piece of paper Tiff could contact Ryan's bank, or her daughter could. She needed to find out how to sell the yellow truck, so she could get something out of it, if possible. GMC Financial needed a stamped copy of the death certificate as well. She had to get her fat ass back to the County's offices to get more official copies. Always on a low boil, five bucks for another four copies turned the temperature up. Cleaning up Ryan's mess was definitely a lot of work.

If someone, not pertaining to her business at hand, asked Tiffany for the death certificate, she amused herself by practicing the response of: "you'll have to go to the County." Adding to someone else's frustration and not lifting one helping finger was like a tasty morsel of food in her mouth. Sweet/salty, their troubles slid down her gullet, leaving her wanting more.

As soon as the police tape came down and Ryan was cleaned off the walls, Tiff's mom moved in. It was a big house with four bedrooms and a finished half basement. Del moved into Jack's efficiency, acquiring a little family at last. He had the money for a down payment on a house, something he'd have to pull the trigger on very soon.

First in, last out. She and Ryan had seen the place together with the realtor twelve years earlier, and Tiffany ensured she was the first through the front door, to see how it felt to her, which was quite fine. Maybe, she thought back then, she'd even fuck him again and have another baby to fill up the place.

Now, however, throwing pictures of Ryan and his personal effects into black, contractor garbage bags felt to his ex like ridding evil spirits from a home. Her mother was unusually spry and energetic, throwing things away and dragging bags to the garage, fixing a room for herself upstairs.

Tiff even lit a few candles and set out potpourri in low glass dishes to freshen the two-story house from man stink. Then she stood back and lit a cigarette in the living room with great satisfaction of a job well done. Or at least, well started.

...

Owen's Sunday was actually Tuesday, and today he wanted to spend time building a potato gun. His backyard fell off quickly into a wooded valley whose ravines extended for miles as if joined to the palm of a giant's hand firmly impressed into the earth. At twilight, the shimmering of porch lights broke in and out, winking through the branches. Totally obscured in the lush summer, distant neighbors' houses were somewhat detailed at Christmastime from lighted decorations. He and his #1 squeeze Audrey had folks living on both sides of their rented double-wide, but the back of the property offered unlimited fields of fire.

The Sunday paper hadn't been picked through. Starting the day at the kitchen table, looking at box scores and drinking from a mug of coffee that read "Hot Stuff" on the side, at a singular moment Owen felt that life was indeed very, very good.

It didn't matter where it came from, as coffee mugs weren't actually purchased but populated cupboards like transients. The little pink hearts suited him perfectly and when Audrey made her appearance from the bathroom to say good morning, Owen turned the mug's message directly toward her path to the cup which he had poured her. It didn't elicit the comment he wished for as Holly Hotrod had barely started her engine.

Darn human beings being so unyielding to impromptu inside jokes.

The Yorkshire Terrier terrorized their Pomeranian with nips and doggy kisses. Better said, Owen was well-aware that they were her dogs. If Owen messed this relationship up then he could lose the girl and the dogs, like a classic Country song. He drifted back to the Pacific Northwest, mostly because his dad was in an assisted living facility in a northern suburb of Seattle.

After making a sideways career move and not having anything or anyone keeping him from what was his then home, moving on seemed like a sensible thing to do. There were too many memories of things that happened in the Midwest city he knew so well, wrapped into his thoughts. It felt constricting.

Like when his little family went to the zoo and a child's balloon got away. Floating slowly, with determination, he'd gazed up at it with a sense of irretrievable loss. "We'll get you another one," he assured the seven-year-old.

"You should have been more careful!" his ex-wife scolded.

He and his daughter watched it, walked forward, and spotted it again, but Mom wanted to keep going. So, they walked on without a glance behind, taking the kid's hand and pulling. Eventually, Owen couldn't find the blue dot blowing away.

Being left behind and forgotten was tough, and Owen was reminded of that fact even harder when he had to drive through his memories every day. The pain of staying was greater than the pain of losing what little he left behind.

Demarco's alarm went off at 8:30 and he left the house fifteen minutes later. He groggily acknowledged the now wired and well caffeinated Owen with a "Hey" as he headed toward the front door. In the older man's mind, he knew it wasn't a good time to be a Chatty Cathy.

"Going to work?" he asked shortly. The paper ruffled as the pages refolded upon themselves.

"Yeah," was Demarco's response. Benito and Chop Chop barked and tussled with Demarco's shoes, wanting their "good morning", which they got with quick reaching down rubs.

"Have a good one." And Audrey's son flashed the peace sign over his shoulder as he left the double wide.

Getting ready for the party scheduled that weekend was the task of the day. There was a decent list ahead of Owen: busting up pallets for firewood, buying several cases of Rainier, crushing the empties left that had accumulated since the last wingding, and buying hamburgers and hot dogs. Owen had some friends to invite. Audrey always had a blanket invite for her Pin Up buddies. At least quarterly they threw a bash.

The toughest part of making a potato gun was the ignition. The gun tube was plumbing PVC and the accelerant hair spray. Too much was as ineffective as too little. It was the spark that counted. There was a romantic connection there somewhere, but Owen kept his mind on the task at hand.

He destroyed two grill lighters before finding one with a flexible wand. He cut grooves into the rigid plastic piping with a hacksaw, epoxy welded a pistol grip from a Super Soaker water gun, and completed the assembly with black duct tape, just like MacGyver inspired him to. He added a 4" x 2" reducer, then a four-inch tube for the gas and a cleanout plug. A ten-pound bag of russets sat nearby, waiting to be used as ammunition. The last consideration was whether to wait until Audrey got home before testing it, just in case there was an explosion, or he accidently lit himself on fire.

Demarco returned after a less than full shift.

"Hey, buddy! Wanna watch me light myself on fire?" Owen had the potato gun across the patio table and motioned to it with a grin.

"What the fuuu…?" The kid's 23-year-old brown-green eyes focused on the gun. "What are you doing with an RPG? You built that?"

Apparently, he knew of rocket propelled grenades. That was a good start. "It's a potato gun," Owen explained, then took a long pull from his Rainer. "I need you to take me to the hospital if after what's about to happen happens."

"Uhh, I think you should wait 'till my mom comes home."

"Sweet Jesus, Mary, and Saint Joseph!" Owen strained an Irish imbibed accent. "Demarco! That's the worst thing I could do." Owen grabbed and pulled at his goatee, smoothing the hairs. He stood up and placed his straw cowboy hat on and started walking toward the fire pit with the can of hairspray in his right hand, his homemade weapon in his left.

Glancing back quickly over his shoulder, he continued, "like I'm going to tell a woman that I'm about to do something really stupid just to hear her tell me that I shouldn't and get pissed off. Then after this prototype works splendidly, she'd still consider me an idiot."

"She wouldn't think that."

Owen sliced a big potato in two and rammed a piece into the two-inch diameter tube with a cut off mop handle, slowly pushing it toward the breech. "She's a woman, isn't she?" he said, giving Demarco a sideways look.

Demarco had a double wide grin and took out his phone. Holding it with two hands extended from his body, he pointed the screen at the firing line. "So, this is my mom's boyfriend," he narrated, prefacing the disaster beforehand. "Owen has built himself a plastic gun and is going to try to shoot a potato across the valley. How much have you been drinking this afternoon, Owen?"

He quickly glanced into the camera, then stated with a straight face, "A lot." That wasn't true, but for insurance purposes, documenting how this impending accident happened may prove important. Workman's compensation, all like that. "Luck be a lady tonight!" And there was the romantic reference.

Unscrewing the end of the gun, Owen shot hair spray for two or three seconds, then screwed the plug back in place fast. He hoisted the thick end up onto his shoulder, where it sat ready to shred Owen's face.

"FIRE IN THE HOLE!" he cried.

Click, click.

"FUCK!"

Click. And then:

Thuuumppp! A potato flew the length of a football field into the wooded expanse.

"BOOYAH, BABY!" Owen whooped.

"I can't believe that worked!" Demarco and Owen laughed and giggled. The builder was too excited to watch the video right away and stuffed more potato down the barrel, sprayed, turned, and aimed. Again came the clicks, then *Thuuumppp.* This time the two pieces diverged about 200 feet out. The report of the explosion wasn't loud. The gun was unwieldy, too; it didn't really kick, but Owen guessed a forward handle would help aim.

"Your turn, your turn!" he insisted, offering the gun to his cameraman. "Keep the video rolling."

Slice, ram, spray, then the weapon went up onto Demarco's shoulder. Owen picked up the phone and they both aimed. "Fire in the hole!" Demarco shouted this time. Click, click, then *Thuuumppp.*

"Shit!" The firer had super elevated the tube, and that time the potato flew higher than away, maybe reaching 300 feet at the top of the arch.

They watched the video after smoking a bowl, the older man placing a beer in Demarco's hand. Male bonding at its finest.

"Don't tell your mother about the weed." It surprised some people that the government would eventually deem the cannabis shops essential. Some were grateful they were.

"'Bout what?" Demarco replied with an innocent face.

"Smart man."

They launched half the bag of Russet potatoes, stoned to the bejesus, right into the palm of a giant's hand.

4
Bombs Away

Another weekend in the summer season and the Bombs Away Car show crowned Miss Donna Diva queen. Her dress impressed as she spent more than a rebuilt manifold for bubblegum colored fabric that she covered with copy catted webs. A big plastic spider complimented her style, crawling delicately over her big boobs. She sold it well. Cloth pink dahlias accented her hairdo, pinned into her big, raven curls heaped in large piles across her head.

Never a lackluster moment, she spent hours meeting everyone, establishing forever friendships with the creator of the Brazen Beauties club, where she'd competed herself. Usually she didn't. It was important to promote other club members to win ribbons and crowns for "best makeup", "most money raised for charity", and "best in talent" besides the runners up.

However, sometimes running the pageant was easier at the littler shows. She'd been on top of her game for several hours. Once bragging that she hadn't been sober since 2004, Donna Diva was usually sipping through the straw protruding from a Big Gulp, 40-ounce plastic cup, filled with Captain Morgan spiced rum and a splash of Diet Coke.

"You can't hold me here!" cried a young mom attending the car show. The baby splayed about the back of the minivan, trying the new trick of rolling over. The hatch was up to enjoy the temperature in the 60's. Momma was yelling in a public space. Less than half his weight, her threatening continued toward a mountain of a silent man.

She was breaking up with him, it seemed, to a casual observer walking near the rows of displayed classic cars. The responsibility for family lay too much one way, it seemed to her. The dirge of physical closeness with a skinny wife measured less, that part of them seemed dead, to him.

He supposed in her heart she had put his picture away, face down in a bottom drawer. Needing attention, too, her Hercules approached his little family trying to be gentle. The tattooed man spit out his dip too late for her not to notice. A spiderweb was inked to his elbow. His mother-in-law was entered in the pageant, and he could see an ugly future, in a dress filled like a sack of potatoes with a matching parasol.

How come his wife blew up his phone when they were apart, just to be instantly cross when together? The angry new mom was constantly swimming upstream, an ever-present ascent toward a man whose verbal communication wilted becoming nonsense.

The two passed each other by like fish too tired to spawn again, unsure if they even recognized each other with the brains of fry. She was like an airman dropping payloads from thirty thousand feet, unable to feel the massive destructive force, the shock waves, and the concussive effect of threatening to leave him. She threatened that he'd never see his baby again unless...

The casual observer felt he had stood too long in one spot, listening; so, he moved on to see the rest of the show. It wasn't his business and he felt like a creep for eavesdropping within a public space, even if the young mother didn't care who heard her weaponizing her child, common in any age. If someone had an old Road Runner on the grounds, he would forget the disturbance.

Donna Diva approached Corrine. "Honey, it's so good to see you." Donna grasped Corrine's fleshy arm at the elbow then let it slide to a hand's grasp. Miss De Menthe wasn't signed up to compete.

"I'm just here to support," Corrine explained.

Donna nodded. "I'm sooo sorry about your friend Ryan."

Corrine began fumbling within her satchel for a hanky, sure the water works were about to come. Tears pooled in her eyes, the pressure turning on fast.

"I spoke with Kimmy," Donna continued. Her husband Brian is. . ." Her speech stumbled for a moment, "was Ryan's brother."

"I knew I shouldn't wear makeup today," Corrine blubbered and big, blobby tears streamed down to her chin. She glanced at Cory, who stayed playing in the grass kicking little pebbles, then examining them. Corrine hadn't worn much makeup in the two weeks since the suicide. Donna hugged her.

"Is she here today?" Corrine asked, referring to Kimmy, aka Serenity Jade.

"No, but she was signed up," Donna replied. "Her husband Brian can't get back to town 'cause he travels for work. Stuff is really messed up, I guess."

Corrine hadn't known that. She padded her cheeks and chin, not wanting her son to see Mommy cry.

"Could you judge with the kiddo here? I really could use you, maybe take your mind off things?"

Corrine's answer was cut off quickly with a mad dash to keep a four-year-old from wandering too far. Donna Diva sometimes needed judges ad hoc, not always knowing who may show up, especially during a national holiday. The Brazen Beauties club had twelve patched-in members and three prospects figuring out the ropes. They were figuring out how to win, adhering to Donna Diva's bylaws and wondering if they really wanted to be a princess as American girls were groomed to do.

"Cory, come back here. Say 'hi' to Donna."

The toddler scrunched his face, looking up at the tarantulas crawling all over her, very unsure. "Hi," he managed to squeak while raising his hand to a halfway wave.

Donna couldn't keep herself from bending down to eye level and grabbing his innocent chin briefly. "Aren't you a cutie?"

Cory looked straight ahead at her big bosoms with shock. Strange, spicy, and sweet aromas flowed from the queen to his little, trusting nose.

Then Donna turned upon her hapless, equally buzzed husband for sitting down instead of setting up the soundboard and speakers like a good little toady. She knew Corrine was too kind to decline helping, unlike her sperm donor.

"Fucking relax!" Aaron drunkenly shouted. "Lawrence is driving the van around now."

Never called "Larry", Donna and her hubby's neighbor was a retired US Army Special Operator. He had a tattoo of flames rising from his neck and tickling his right ear and shaved head. The gentle giant type, he had bad knees and a bad back from jumping out of aircraft boldly. Lawrence knew how to set up the soundboard.

"Well, are you going to at least take pictures, like I'm paying you to do?" Donna Diva wouldn't keep her voice down either. Their kid was nearly grown at nineteen.

Aaron stood up wobbly and grabbed his camera bag, the body and lens costing him almost $3,000. He could afford it as a Union Plumber making $65 an hour. "You never gave me money for nothing!" He was super pissed, and Donna merely looked toward their friend Lawrence, who gave her a wink back.

Some of the Dolls met the military framed show with flourish. It was the last day of a lucky four-day weekend. The Fourth of July had landed on a Thursday. Holly Hot Rod had decided on prints of anchors and pilot's wheels that made a broad border hemming her mock dress whites, with wide lapels and a navy-blue belt to accentuate her waist.

Audrey hugged Corrine. "How's it going, sweetie?" Her concerned, pinched face could see her friend wasn't competing today. Her hair was just in a ponytail, and she wore sandals, not heels.

Miss De Menthe did manage to shimmy into her favorite key lime pedal pushers. After returning Audrey's squeeze, she picked back in the saga where she thought she'd left off. "Big news, for me. Tiffany wants to use the Eagles club in Black Diamond for Ryan's memorial, according to her Facebook page."

Audrey sputtered. "Shit, that'll be weeks and weeks after. . .after it happened."

"Oh, she's been milking the GoFundMe page like a bitch," Corrine snapped bitterly. "Crying about 'expenses', but I know the hall will be nearly free with him being a member and all. I've always tried to be nice, but I know she doesn't like me. Me and Ryan being buddies for years. I just hope I can say my peace at the memorial without tearing into her. It's going to be a pity party for her. Tiffany's mother moved into the house within just a few days of Ryan killing himself."

Owen walked up and said, "Sorry about your friend, Corrine." Audrey had mentioned Corrine's posts about being present when the crime was committed. He wasn't a Facebook type guy, so Owen learned about people's lives slowly, through conversation or not at all. He pressed down his full sandy brown mustache, a nervous habit.

"Thanks, Owen."

Corrine's son Cory collected dandelions in bunches and presented flowers to nearby pretty princesses such as Lola Liberator, Carter Corsair, and Martha Mustang. Owen knelt to eye level to show Cory how to blow the seeds to the wind from fluffy buds, but only after making a wish.

Cory blew but did not say a wish, not understanding the tradition. The ineffective sounding "plleww" that issued from his baby lips was so endearing as to turn a stone heart beating. His pedal car had flames decaled down the sides and a special Pennzoil sticker pasted by the back panel where the gas cap should be.

The kid would be informally entered into the show at the last moment as an extra trophy was without a winner. Taller than him, it was presented as a special prize from the Bombs Away club's afternoon presentation, a special favor to the Donna Diva and the "Brazen Beauties" Pin Up Dolls club. Cory squeezed his horn and the grownups helped him drive straight over pavement. Gravel and grass impeded the movement frequently. Wearing a dark Navy vest and clip on black tie, the fedora wearing tot was a sensation amongst the slight crowd.

A vendor grilled hot dogs nearby, sending smoke unfairly through the assembly of thirty cars and owners, selling chips and ice-cold Coke. Owen couldn't resist, his tummy growling after church, and went over to buy the lad and he lunch. He wore his Skull Fuckers purple bowling style shirt, a frightening, desiccated face missing an eye on the back, with his booster club name, "Haywood" on his shoulder blades.

If you knew the joke, you could ask him, "Hey, would—?" and you'd get the gaudily rude response "—ya' blow me?" If anyone was funny enough to ask.

Mom mildly scolded Holly Hotrod's boyfriend for providing her son a sugary drink on a warm, bright day. If the little un' got the jitterbugs and danced to Elvis singing through the show's spread-out speakers, "Blue Suede Shoes", then Haywood would be the instigator and proud of it. So okay, it was worth the rebuke. But the kid seemed happy, so the gesture went heavenwards with the smoke, a wisp disappearing as soon as it was seen. A little like the over-protectiveness of a mother or the loss of an unhappy man's life.

Greo's Garage in Tacoma hosted many shows and told many tales with the cool cars it always had behind red velvet ropes. Small plaques gave visitors performance and provenance over a gleaming wide checkerboard floor. The owner kept history alive to racers and their Maserati.

They sold orbital polishers and gave Cory a chance to touch the inside components of a Porsche on display, even the engine compartment without a speck of grime. While his mom held a clipboard and helped judge in the adjacent field, Owen was on temporary kid watching duty. He lifted Cory like a plank so he could grab the hoses and touch an engineering marvel. The techs were paid to teach gearheads and recruit new ones to replace those who died…and wipe off any tiny fingerprints.

The casual observer caught sight of Miss Demeanor in a yellow mustard slim fitting dress and was instantly smitten when she gave him her card, professional pictures front and back with a throw away email address just for Pin Up. She seemed like a McDonald's French fry, freckles dangerously exposed to too much sunshine, with a shock of red hair like being dipped in ketchup. To all she was a yummy treat, a woman to be eaten up, tasting like honey in the mouth but turning sour in the stomach. She secured a promised vote. Aleia was easily the most beautiful Doll, and super friendly fun.

The Walmart bought sandals this guy wore placed stripes across his feet after a noon of walking between Rat Rods and classic pickups. He listened and wished for smells and sights like the sweaty skin from a peeled off banana clad Doll, or the distress that held them together, past their antiperspirant or greatly faded Coco Mademoiselle.

When the handsome creep realized he could get cards from the many Pin Up dolls, he made sure to canvass the field. When he asked Corrine for her card, she said she wasn't competing. "But my collection won't be complete unless I get cards from all the 'Brazen Beauties' Dolls." The silver-tongued devil's trick worked.

Couples entered their cars, the hobby being a joint venture. Women hung parts they ordered from dealers advertising in collector car magazines. A few brave men joined Pin Up clubs so they could wear pretty dresses in public. Gender lines blurred in the 21st century to some concern. Girls being gearheads way ahead of boys being beautiful, to most.

Lisa Demure's chrome dome was beet red by the end of the pageant. Even to a casual observer it seemed that one of his sisters would have offered a parasol or the suggestion to accessorize a pretty hat with Lisa's next outfit. Pin Ups had to plan or otherwise feel the scorn of the weather.

The price of the beauty learning curve was high, often being painful like feet in smashingly matching pumps, or the cost of a closet full of shoes. Men generally unaccustomed to taking skin care seriously could see a bad sunburn coming on Lisa's shoulders, too.

Isn't someone going to help that poor man? . . .Girl? . . .Pin Up? must have run through many bystanders' minds.

Lisa gave a rambling, inaudible speech during the introductions that was given greater applause than deserved due the obvious quantity of guts she possessed. Martha Mustang did share some sunblock in the mid-afternoon. Lisa felt gratitude in having made a friend finally. But then again, she wasn't a very chatty person.

Cherry V was an established queen who entered herself and her Rat Rod along with her husband Jessie in contests and pageants. Both professionals earned more than $100k each in the tide of tech economics centered in Seattle. Their Model A Ford had an appropriate amount of rust on the panel's edges, its body painted an old, stock black without a clear coat. A racing number "424" was scrawled in seeming haste along with its name "UNDERTAKER" before and aft of both single doors.

It looked mean, with the visor shading the slim windshield like a professional gambler counting cards. The vertical grille was ready to gulp air and bury any competition. They belonged to several car clubs, and wide, exposed tires gripped both the road and votes alike wherever they entered. She could eat no lean and her husband no fat. Transporting enthusiasts to pre-war days was as easy as Cherry lip synching to her signature song, Vera Lynn's "We'll Meet Again". *"Don't know where. Don't know when. But I know we'll meet again some sunny day."*

For those who had deployed to the recent wars and those who loved them, the song connected generations. Long distance relationships between spouses, parents, and kids testified that good did not always triumph. Some people never came back. Some died in hospitals without family present, buried without funerals out of an abundance of 21st century caution. Heartbreak's tears could roll easily with the sound of a lonely woman's voice.

Owen's Toyota Tundra chromed out Solar Yellow pickup (not to be confused with Canary Yellow) sat under the double wide car cover built into their rented home. It wasn't parked alongside the road with his K-K-K-Kia. Owen simply called them "yellow truck" and "the car that could not die".

For more than a down payment on a home, he had the former painted upon delivery. It screamed, "Look at me!" It was a present to himself after the court approved the marital separation agreement from his toxic wife. Owen needed the reassurance, a makeover. It supplemented his daily traveler, a Signal Red Kia Sportage, that told the world, "This is all I got out of the marriage", minus alimony created as a perpetual lien.

While she drove her 2007 Nissan Sentra back to the doublewide, Owen got a call from Demarco. The silly ring tone that blasted out of his phone was that of a panicked Scotsman telling him to pick up.

"Hey Owen, I picked up another shift at the grocery store. Can I take your Kia?"

Why wouldn't he agree? Not only was the young man hustling, but it meant he wouldn't be home that evening.

Demarco borrowed his mom's car usually but failed to regularly pay his mom for adding him to the insurance. It was a messed-up situation but otherwise the boy wouldn't have wheels to get to his job as a grocery clerk. It was a requirement of his parole, working. Popping hot was another violation, indication of his getting stoned with friends.

In the car shuffle, therefore, "Yellow Truck" became Owen's daily traveler with the requisite risk of door dings and scrapes as he couldn't always park away from other cars. So, Audrey was added to his insurance at additional cost, and she drove the Kia. If it got another ding or scrape no one could have seen the difference.

"Babe, the kid needs to drive the Kia tonight," Owen explained. "You drive this thing and I'll enjoy Yellow Truck."

"I don't want you paying to insure him."

Owen didn't respond with, *there's a choice?* But instead, he offered, "We got to end this car rodeo. We'll figure it out." Which meant Owen would eventually sell Demarco the car for a dollar, and he'd pay the insurance himself.

"You're a good man, Owen. I'm so lucky to have you." A compliment like that was worth a million miles.

They enjoyed an adult beverage on their deck, which faced a lush valley before hills and mountains. For the second time in two days, Audrey was silhouetted against a soon to be setting sun with all its car colors. The fuzzy fine hairs on her ears struck Owen and he gingerly grabbed his girl and kissed her left, fleshy helix rim. "You have beautiful ears."

"Stop it." She still hadn't disassembled from being Pin Up ready. "I smell like a goat." And she squirmed away. Owen did notice she was a little ripe. "Why do you always get horny after a show?"

"I'm always horny for you, baby." He smiled. "Let me kiss your ears." And Owen reached out his hands when Audrey grinned. Her eyes squinted nearly shut with laugh lines folding at the corners in such a darling way. They were two candidates for a happy quarantine.

With the kid absent there was no need to hush moans. He dropped his drawers and grabbed fresh clothes, getting excited, of course, while standing in the buff before her highness. "You girls get yourselves all dolled up, then act surprised when it has its desired effect."

Through tremendous strength of will, after a day in the sun, Owen jumped into the shower and was out in five minutes to make way for the queen's bath. He started dinner, nervous they wouldn't have time before he got cock blocked. But more delicious smells, tastes, and sights awaited

Owen before he could finish making his signature hamburger patties, squishing and turning the spices into cold ground beef. Audrey was back in the bedroom more quickly than anticipated, a fast toilette.

"Alexa, play Diana Krall." Owen's head snapped like a dog hearing a kibble bag opening. The jazz pianist softly sang of love.

Creeping into the master, he whispered, "Are you ready?"

"I was born ready," Holly Hot Rod said.

5
JCPenney

"We have a remodel at a JCPenney coming up soon. You did one in Kansas City, right?"

Peter had never met his immediate supervisor who was asking the question. It was somewhat weird, even for a traveling man.

"Well yeah, I did the salon inside a JCPenney, in KC, and I did that Talbot's in Houston. So retail, no problem." He had recently finished a three-week double shift job at a jewelry store in Duluth. It dumped eight inches of snow the night after he arrived from Wisconsin, so he'd experienced no early spring in Northern Minnesota and a chance to see the sights (as they may be). Duluth was a gritty shipping town built on high bluffs, the first port for iron ore and coal from America's mountains and plains to Lake Superior, then the world.

At 8:30PM every evening Peter would be on site prior to the mall's closing to get the subcontractors going. The owner's project manager knew when the work had to be completed for his report card, but not when the new electrical fixtures would arrive. Typical, lousy construction management.

It was a wall covering and carpet job. Making sure that by 10AM the store would open without dust on the display cases and that the floors vacuumed were the prime directives. Remodel while the store was still in operation was the name of the game. Usually, he'd split around midnight and reappear in the morning to clean and take debris to his dumpster. In the afternoon, Peter emailed and took phone calls when necessary. It was a total pain in the ass, messing with his sleep, workout, and beer drinking.

He had a few days off once returning home before the roulette wheel spun once more and the ball found the pocket with his name amongst available traveling superintendents.

One of Frank's biggest jobs at the general contracting company was to get guys with great construction backgrounds who were willing to travel to projects with imminent starts. He was a new hire, whereas Peter had been with the outfit for eight years.

"I need a guy to get to Tukwila to meet Carl out there next Monday. He'll be the PM," meaning project manager.

"Okay." Peter hesitated for a minute. That could be anywhere. "Where's Tukwila?"

"Seattle. Are you interested?"

"Yeah sure. Sweet," the traveling Soup said. "Okay. What's the scope?"

"We're replacing all the carpet in the store. It has three levels. But we have to abate possible asbestos when we demo, so we have to do that third shift."

Peter shuddered.

"So, I'm going to send a guy to babysit the demo guys at night and then you as the main superintendent, will work during the day with the carpet guys and painters. There's also a salon that they want remodeled and a package pickup section."

Though Peter nodded, he wasn't sure what that meant. The Pacific Northwest sounded like another fun adventure and his happiness filled him like the perfect beverage from Starbucks, a Mocha Cookie Crumble Frappuccino with soy and half a shot of Chocolate. Peter thought adding cream to a venti Pike Place was exotic enough, however.

It was Tuesday, so Peter had a full two days to pack a company truck, with tools and clothes for a three-month gig. First things first was to check the route and the weather. It was a three-day drive without any delays, two thousand miles, easy. Driving in rain had to be avoided even if Peter had to leave a day early. Driving a full loaded truck in bad weather through the Sierra Nevada from Reno to San Fran, or snow in Iowa, or the mountains around Chattanooga, Tennessee after the sun went down were hours and moments of terror that could make your belly flop when the ass end wiggled, or the motor petered out.

Peter had been on several long-term missions with this Silverado. It had over 200,000 miles on it, rough and ready. It mirrored his assessment of himself, a few scrapes and dents to prove his thirty-three years on earth had been productive. The idea of travel restrictions in America was absurd.

He was too far away from retirement to even give it a second thought, except to plan for it. He got an associate degree in Construction Management after high school. Being an architect's toady taught him practical construction lessons in a servile and submissive working environment. He was filling plastic cylinders with concrete during a large placement for a theater addition (for later compression tests) when a carpenter foreman he'd been friendly with for a while just asked, "Peter, why do you want to be the architect's bitch? He's a fucking idiot. Why don't you join the union and make more money, pension, health benefits, the whole nine yards?"

So, he looked up what an apprentice would make starting off, and with the insurance it was a pay increase. It was one of the rare crossroads in a lifetime where the blinking sign said, "turn here" and he listened.

About four years later, Peter became a journeyman. His desire for increased responsibility led to running work on the road. His resume got stoked and his lifelong bond with loneliness continued. He hadn't impregnated some bar fly. Not getting laid was an inconvenient truth about Peter.

The Pacific Northwest in late May was a joy, bright and clear every day. It rained in Chicago more than Seattle, so the reputation of gloominess was nowhere to be seen in the early summertime.

Carl pulled into the parking garage soon after Peter did. It was 9AM and the store wouldn't open for an hour. Still when they met Mary, the store manager, she quipped, "you're late," just to bust balls and communicate her continual sense of urgency. She had once been a beauty that had packed on an extra fifty pounds eating fast food while getting the most of her workers for a small JCPenney pension.

With 90,000 square feet of carpet to replace, the store was huge. It was an anchor to a mall called Southcenter in the metro area. After the recon in which the bill payer JCPenney PM attended, it was plain that there was a long "honey do" list that made the defined scope creep into more of an avalanche.

But the customer was willing to pay for what Mary wanted. She had enough seniority with the company to tell anyone how to measure success for the facelift. They wouldn't have a construction superintendent or dedicated resources for probably another five years in the future. Long before then, the department store chain could be belly up, after 118 years, a casualty of a germ.

The maintenance contractor for the area JCPenney stores would do nothing without a work order, and then slowly accomplished tasks in a half-ass manner while incessantly complaining about being overworked, a guy deserving of getting laid off. It was going to be a successful job despite him.

Thank God, thought Peter, when he met Scotty. They called each other from within the store passing each other on the escalators but finally greeting each other. "Man, am I happy to see you!" and the main Superintendent shook his hand. Younger than him, with very little construction experience, another farm boy, Scotty had worked in his family business, mainly raising corn and soybeans. For his Midwestern can-do attitude, babysitting the demo guys became a slam dunk, no worries.

The demo contractor could remove more stained carpet than the store could make available five nights a week. Stuffed with merchandise both on the giant sales floors but also in the back, the hardest part of the whole project was the delicate dance between how much floorspace Mary's staff could clear daily, the demo and asbestos abatement that evening, the carpet guys the next morning placing new material, and the store spreading rolling racks of merchandise as soon as the black vinyl base was adhered around supporting columns, then along walls and fixtures. Like all new construction, once finished it looked great.

The weakest link was the painter from Texas who showed up with two apprentices, (both with little concept of quality), and a contract that greatly underestimated the amount of work to be done. Mary called out every imperfection and Peter, usually a gifted diplomat, chased the painter around with blue masking tape to mark every thin spot, glob, or missed valence behind where display lights were hung. The painter walked out with only three weeks to go from the massive space. He lost his ass, financially, and surely never got his last check.

The hardest part of the day was when the subs left and the laptop closed. The gym membership was with a national chain and sometimes Peter would go and stretch, maybe do a few sets of upper body. There could be a few baby mommas to glance at and inadvertently find a machine nearby. But if he barely had the motivation to go, he was sure that they'd might be struggling, too. And besides, if you could slip in a quick remark to a pretty girl at the gym she probably didn't want to be bugged anyway.

It was the same dilemma no matter where in the country he worked. If he met someone either online or the old-fashioned way through sass and moxy, he was only going to be in town for a few months, tops. So, no relationship there. When he was home between assignments, Peter was a worker bee. To be fair, a local girl should be told that eight months of the year he wouldn't be around. The company would fly him home pretty much whenever he wanted but even short weekends for family birthdays or say Thanksgiving wasn't much time at home at all.

He could go home and take a demotion and try to climb back up the supervisory ladder, (Few wanted to go on the road) and he could find a local girl to love, but being a traveling man was fun, going to new places and meeting new people practically every day. He had finally gotten out of his home state of Wisconsin and started to see the country.

It didn't matter to Peter's father that it was cliché telling his son to "call your mother" before he went on the road. The goal was once a week, on Sundays, if he remembered. After three weeks, a familial pull would make him dial. Rarely did his parents call him, not wanting to interfere because they perceived Peter was always so "busy". It was very Midwest. Somehow it didn't occur to his son that the reason the elder was so insistent that the boy called home was so he could pepper his wife with questions. "Why don't you call Peter if you want to know how he's getting along?"

"No, a boy should call his mother." A habit was more or less established. Her friends were jealous that her son called her. She must be special. That was a proud feeling. Peter liked knowing what he was missing on the farm. Any work he chose away from it certainly would be easier, despite a great increase in commute time.

The building inspectors in FLOR-E-DUH were notoriously uncooperative, racking up fees as fast as they could. The state was filled with the sketchy and the near homeless. The weather in West Palm Beach was literally perfect in January and February.

West Virginia had the most polite people in the USA, with "after you, Ma'am" and "Bless you heart" common public phrases for a people tightly bound by tragedy. The skinny, younger folks with dirty clothes not pushing baskets at the Walmart were the tweakers of meth. Floods, coal mine disasters, and economic lackluster were the norm, along with hollers without electricity.

Kansas City was prosperous, a crossroads of America for the blues, and a terminus for drugs. The Bay Area was gorgeous with people packing San Francisco and San Jose tight, squeezing working families into long, congested drives over bridges. Chicagoland was a flat, featureless mass of humanity where you gladly paid a toll to leave the state. Only the tough prospered there, and no one could survive unsheltered in deep freezes.

When Peter ran his own projects the boss he had never met (Frank, superintendent of the traveling superintendents) would call about once a month to see if he was still alive. The mantra being that if no one was calling him to complain about Peter, he must be doing a good job.

Carl, the Project Manager was sort of a peer sort of not. He held the financial stings but was typically jovial.

Being 2,000 miles away from the home office was peaceful. It was just him and the customer. Carl wouldn't fly back out to Seattle until the very end of the project, three and a half months after the start, a month past the original finish date as JCPenney kept moving the goalposts back. In the end, Mary was happy. Frank gave Peter two weeks off with pay. Carl finally threw him out of Washington State and told him to start driving. A very expensive asset, a traveling superintendent had to bounce quickly.

The ethical ramifications of flirting with JCPenney associates were low, yet Peter hadn't reached out for the forbidden fruit of giving his "all" to the customer. There was a forty-something who ran the Sephora cosmetics section that made his blood boil. And he couldn't wait until the project progressed to the point where he could talk to her about the wonderful things he was about to do.

"You need new carpet and paint in your little office? It's not in the scope but let me see if I can't get it added." It was added and Blondie was appreciative. It was the right thing to do. The Loss Prevention folks were left out of the original plan too, as was the optical department. So, he was just doing his job making sure the pretty girl wasn't the only one outside the facelift.

Going to local bars for dinner seemed pointless. Eating and drinking alone ate up his per diem, and he could always make a stir fry or tacos or spaghetti within the kitchenette. Talking on the phone to old friends became routine. The visit to the Space Needle and the Chihuly Garden of Glass left him agog with improbable colored sculptures. A hike to

Rattlesnake Ridge and a boat tour of the Seattle harbor gave Peter a tiny feel for the city, and its environs were beautiful and lonely.

Sharing space with the homeless at local libraries was uncomfortable. Pot was legal but popping hot meant losing your job and having a black mark with the union, and while forgiving, he worked too hard not to have to hang drywall every day or build concrete parking garages as a career.

On Father's Day, Peter called his dad. The conversation was short and included complaints about arthritis along with details about the farm. Senior remembered a short stint in Seattle while in the Navy. They brought a boat from San Diego to be de-commissioned at the Puget Sound Naval Shipyard at Bremerton. When Peter's dad found a subject pleasant it was usual for him to give details. He liked to describe how Seattle had lots of floating houses in its twenty-five-mile-long urban Lake Washington. Peter wasn't home for Mother's Day, either. Being on the road was a mixed bag.

There was another glass museum in Tacoma, just down the road. Dale Chihuly made teams of glass blowers creating giant rainbow lotuses. Sculptures soared fifteen feet high, impossible feats that were gaspingly beautiful to see. He stopped for chowder along Ruston Way to peer at the harbor, watching a ball game at the bar.

Sometimes Peter would strike up a conversation with someone other than the bartender. The weekends were for exploration, to get out of the Extended Stay gloom. While filling up with gas, he saw a flier for the 21st annual South Tacoma classic car show and street fair for the Sunday of the fourth of July weekend.

The painters wanted to work Friday, the fifth of July, and probably that Saturday, too. Scotty played it well; after the demo guys were done on Wednesday, he flew back to go shuck corn, then back on Sunday to start up again. Peter didn't need the hassle of traveling and telling Carl the painters wanted to keep up and that he'd be there to make sure they progressed where they needed to. It showed commitment to the job, not going home. And it saved the project money. He didn't socialize with his subcontractors, either, as it would eventually undermine his authority in case someone made a mistake and he had to call them out for re-work.

He spent the holiday in the movie theater watching Spiderman and "Once Upon a Time in Hollywood" by Quentin Tarantino, which was excellent. Then he opted to get drunk in the room rather than find some park, spread out a blanket, and admire the fireworks show by himself. That would be strange even for Quentin.

Peter made sure the painters were good/no issues/having clear direction, early on Friday, and the same for Saturday. The loneliness became tedious. He needed a hobby.

The car show was at a fancy dealership. The street fair was a mile away. He had just started walking the grounds when he watched a woman flip out hard on her husband. He circled back to listen to the verbal thrashing the big guy was getting, trying to be casual. But the fellow kept quiet, smart enough to know that if he started yelling the disturbance could blow up. The little kid got agitated at Mom's rant and Peter moved on. Show over.

Making his way to the tent with the two dozen trophies, he saw a banner for the car club but also another tent with a half a dozen girls all dressed up in patriotic themes. Peter got a ballot to vote for his favorite cars and there was an entry for his favorite Pin Up girl. Passing out calling cards to passersby and the gearheads, they looked for pictures with classic cars and asked for votes shamelessly. A little kid in a fedora, vest, and clip on tie struggled with his pedal car, making everybody smile at the irresistible power of cuteness.

Donna Diva looked over Peter like she was about to gut a fish.

He read her card. "Do your lovers survive?" he asked.

Her tits spilled out of her dress just enough to cover her half-dollar-sized nipples. She hoarsely barked, "Well, look at my husband there, sitting down, not taking pictures like he's supposed to." Her voice was loud enough to make sure Aaron heard. Donna Diva turned her cheek back and batted her long lashes, bearing down, staring her black doll eyes into Peter's soul. "He's about all used up. I'm gonna need another Honey."

She was a hard forty years old. "A young'un. You vote for me, sweetie." Then she turned to play a different song list, fiddling with the sound board. A mountainous man stood just behind her, bearing a flaming tattoo on the right side of his shaved head, looking on ominously.

Peter gave Donna Diva his promise. It was demanded. He backed the winner with his vote.

It felt like a revelation from God. A 1972 two door Mercury Cougar, four barrel at 266hp, didn't compare to Lola Liberator's blue and white polka dotted dress, pearls, and tattooed rose stems reaching from her right foot to a well-muscled calf bearing the buds. The red leather interior of a Pontiac Bonneville didn't have the styling that Holly Hot Rod had. Those were expensive models, out of his league.

He asked Miss Demeanor if he could take her picture next to the rare and sought-after 2013 War Eagle Chopper, her slim build complementing the elongated forks. She seemed like a matchstick with a form fitting mustard yellow dress and sizzling flaming curls. Aleia chatted him up, finding out where he worked and what he did.

Being from out of town didn't come up and Peter didn't volunteer. She was the kind of very pretty girl who didn't act like she knew it. Now he had to see how many cards he could collect, but Miss Demeanor's was the most prized. Even the most beautiful women in the world needed boyfriends. But how to get close? Should he reach out through her Pin Up Doll Facebook page?

Cory pedaled up toward Peter, with Corrine following close behind. "Is he entered in the car show? Bet he'd win." There weren't too many girls in their 20's doing the Pin Up thing.

"Cory, don't drive into people."

"It's hard to steer and pedal at the same time," Peter said. The boy squinted upward, displaying two missing upper front teeth. His mother had perfectly clear skin, a canvas for what looked like prison tattoos or someone practicing/not charging for shabby looking pistols pointed inwards on both collar bones. Corrine had pale blue eyes behind cat-eye glasses.

He knew she was a Pin Up since she was gabbing with all the girls but didn't make the connection she wasn't "bringing it" today, not at all Pin Up ready. He didn't consider her footwear (sandals), too astounded by all the details.

"Do you have a card? I came for the car show, but the whole Pin Up thing is fantastic. I'm not really a car guy, but it's fun to see beautiful things. I got the Donna Diva, Miss Demeanor, Holly Hot Rod. It's like baseball cards."

"I don't think so. Not on me. I'm not entered today. I'm judging instead." Corrine had a clipboard with at least a dozen pages.

"Is it hard?"

"Is what hard?"

"Judging."

"It can be."

"Too bad you don't have a card. My collection won't be complete unless I get cards from all the pretty girls." And Peter had found an obsession to fill his waking mind and bring color to his boredom.

He stayed to watch the award presentations. The kid got a trophy after all. Peter clapped loudly. It was too cute, even for a construction guy. He got Corrine De Menthe's card through perseverance. He said he'd vote for her next time.

Lawrence broke down the tent quickly. Donna Diva asked Corrine, "Who's the guy that stuck around?"

"Peter."

Donna Diva could size up men fast. She smiled at Corrine. "Looks like that one could be trouble."

...

Serenity Jade, aka Kimmy showed up at the same time as Corrine. Both ladies were alone. Although by the next party at Audrey's place, Corrine would bring Peter, a traveling man. And Brian would be back in town for a memorial service.

The Pomeranian and Yorkie were excited by all the new people smells. "Get down Ginger!" Holly Hotrod scolded her pup climbing up Miss De Menthe's freshly shaved and lavender lotioned legs.

"Chop Chop smells my lotion. Or is this Benito?" The hostess with the mostest was setting out a veggie tray bought from the grocery store. No chop, chop, chopping this time.

"It's Ginger Snap and Lucy." Her tipsy boyfriend was setting up the soundboard in preparation for karaoke. It was already loud enough for all to hear. "Dammit, Owen. Stop telling people the wrong names of MY dogs!"

Reflexively, the slightly tipsy Owen denied, "I didn't", but then glanced at Corrine's smirk, and cried, "Stop causing trouble!"

"My middle name is trouble," proffered Miss De Menthe.

Audrey took a few steps forward and asked her #1 squeeze, "Are you lying to me?"

"No." But the gig was up. "I mean, yes." Then he pressed a button and a song called, "I'm A Blues Man" started to play a little too loud.

"You're lucky!"

"I know," said Audrey. Owen wasn't a perfect man. Not complete. But he was perfect for her. Five days a week he'd tell her, "I love you, babe."

Both of them knew how easily love could slip into silence.

Owen, a man with good smarts, confided boisterously to Corrine, "The pups must smell your perfume. Hey, you shaved your legs!"

"Do you know what happens, Owen, when a woman shaves her legs and doesn't get laid?" asked Corrine. Audrey smirked.

"Uhh. . .no. I can't help with that."

"A unicorn dies."

"There aren't unicorns anymore."

"Exactly." And the self-deprecating joke fell upon the spirit of the sweet, funny, smart fat girl. "Why Benito?"

"It's not Benito. It's Lucy." Audrey wasn't sober either and began playing along, slightly.

"Like Benito Mussolini. The Italian dictator. The Yorkie terrorizes Chop Chop."

"Who's that? I'm the victim of a public education, Owen. Is he in a boy band, Mussolini?"

"No, like World War Two?"

"I was too young to be in that."

"Her name is Lucy." And Audrey left them to their idiocy just as Demarco and a buddy came through the screen of the sliding glass door. She turned to meet her son's friend and was glad he had him over.

Corrine, always the instigator, appreciating that the young guys weren't sober either, asked Demarco what the names of his mother's dogs were. The party stopped immediately to listen.

"Uhh, Chop Chop and Benito."

Owen yelled, "My man!"

Audrey turned and swore, "Fuck me running!"

Thuuumppp, Thuuumppp, Thuuumppp! The potato gun was a hit by the fire pit. Holly Hot Rod had a committed, fun-loving man. She wondered if they were more scared than in love, fearful of not having a plan. She wanted to fly away from all encumbrances of love relationships and responsibilities. She wanted to be alone sometimes.

Holly wanted no one close, no one in her rented double wide. No fifteen guests milling around, using her toilets. In a perfect world, she was by herself. There was no son dependent on her wage. Indifferent. Done. But she pushed these depressing thoughts back for the sake of her guests. She was never alone, not even when she slept. Not never. It pressed upon her like an old-fashioned gin, crushing until it achieved lifelessness.

Kimmy, aka Serenity Jade, found Audrey still in the kitchen. "Your Majesty! How does it feel? I'm only ever gonna be a princess." And she made a frowny face.

"It took me a long time to put it together. The outfits, the presentation, talent shows. You know Corrine through your husband?" She said, changing the subject. She thought she remembered but wasn't sure. Kimmy was holding her red solo cup filled now halfway with tap beer from the iced quarter barrel on the porch.

"She worked with Ryan for a while. His brother, Brian, is my husband. Corrine was my sponsor into the Chapter."

"Oh yeah, that's right." So it was her brother-in-law who shot himself. "I saw the Go Fund Me page. I'm really sorry for your family's loss." Audrey hugged her Pin Up sister and was hugged back. "You want something stronger than that piss water my boy toy has out on the porch?"

"Like what?"

"I'll make some Black Russians." Vodka and Kahlua, she explained, the coffee flavored liqueur.

"Yummy!" Kimmy agreed and dumped her beer into the sink. "You didn't give money to that Go Fund Me site for Ryan, did you?"

Holly got two highball glasses out of the cabinet and grabbed a bottle of Stolichnaya. "Well, not much."

"Don't forward it to anyone. Ryan's ex-wife's out to scam as much money as possible. Right after he died, she went on a two-week vacation with her mom, daughter, and future son-in-law."

"The one who's pregnant?" Queen Hot Rod had the proportions down perfectly and handed Kimmy the glass with a perfectly measured cocktail.

"Delmonica's the one I feel sorry for. The fucking leech, Tiffany, is all crying and carrying on. It's horrible. Had to be in charge of everything. Now, the kids have bought a house, and she's moved in with them. Supposedly, just until the baby is born. Maybe longer. To help out."

"Sounds like the service is going to be a nightmare." She made a face like stepping in dog shit with heels on. The hostess hated funerals and hoped she wouldn't be obliged to go to Ryan's.

6

The Rockford Peaches

In a salute to the movie "A League of Their Own" President Donna Diva organized a Sunday afternoon outing at the Seattle Mariners baseball stadium. The naming rights were either a telecom giant or an insurance company, depending on the year. She drove with Lawrence. Arron brought Aleia, aka Miss Demeanor, which seemed an odd arrangement.

On a non-premium day in late July, as another doleful team came to town, the Mariners gave a group discount for the already cheap upper concourse, three hundred level tickets, high up on the right field line. An announcement appeared some time on the jumbotron during the game for Donna Diva's promotional club pictures, plus a few beans for pediatric cancer was the supposed deal.

A twirl dress throwback to the women's baseball leagues during the war years, the Dolls had to spend ninety bucks each just for the flamingo-colored uniforms, candy red belts, and cap. The logos were stitched on hat and chest alike. Socks weren't included. Calves were saved exertion with white sneakers. The Dolls' hobby could get pricey quickly, especially if worn but once. Wedding dresses were much more easily found on Craig's List.

Alterations were pricey, especially when only few knew the long-lost art of sewing. Gearheads not mechanics matched the same predicament. It was a matter of scale, but still the pride of doing the thing yourself, and developing a skill to be boasted upon and shown off, ended up paying dividends.

The Mariners baseball club wasn't very interested in promoting the Brazen Beauties Pin Up Dolls and Donna Diva kept the schedule of events mysterious. Stumbling to get everyone in the stadium wound her drunk ass up. Getting mean fast was a hallmark of hers, especially with her hubby, Aaron, who left in the third inning to follow his dry mouth to a bar closer to home. A perfectly groomed rabble followed her inside the engineering marvel.

More than ten gals and their significant others found their seats by the second inning after stopping for group pictures before the bronze statue of Ken Griffey Jr. Herding cats ineffectively, Donna Diva stopped for a brew before bringing the gang to their seats. Honey Lemon Drop, Mini Mimosa, and Serenity Jade waited impatiently for their fearful leader, but when the iPhones were raised, they posed with their baseball mitts seemingly ready to catch a foul ball.

Focusing on the game, Owen tried not to listen to Audrey's and Corrine's hours-long gabfest. He was pissed that he missed the first pitch due to Donna Diva's dithering, not to mention the National Anthem where he would have held his tattered cowboy hat over his heart. To ban the fans from the national game would be to postpone baseball itself.

The girls paid attention only when the fellas got excited. They shouted collectively as a baseball was hit out of the infield by the offending team. Serenity Jade's yelling, "You guys suck!" made Owen wince. It wasn't very nice to badger the home team, four hundred feet from home plate. Kimmy was right, of course.

Throughout the game she continued to echo loud, slight derivations of, "you guys suck," like adding "donkey dicks" at the end. That, at least, made Owen chuckle.

"This is stupid. Lawrence, let's go to a bar. Fuck this shit, man." Aaron was slurring only slightly, the mark of a professional drunk. He may have realized that he needed to drive now or never. Or perhaps he could stop drinking, which wasn't going to happen, so therefore he was going to leave. The fact that if Lawrence went with, the girls would be stranded, never entered his mind.

"No, I'm good, man. I love the ballpark," replied the happily retired soldier.

His buddy sneered in the opposite direction, toward Donna, who was watching him from two rows up, sitting with Miss Demeanor.

"Would you fuck Lawrence?" Donna asked her friend.

"You can have scary man all you want." Their gaze was zoned high above the diamond, oblivious to what was happening on the field. "What does he do, anyway…besides you?" She smiled and gave Donna a playful nudge in her side.

"I'd fuck 'im. Ohh yeah. Gotta be better than old whiskey dick."

"He's around all the time," Aleia pointed out. "Does he have a job?"

"He gets a disability from the VA. He only lives a few blocks from us."

"He lives alone?" Aleia asked, eyebrows raised.

"No, with his mom," Aaron's wife stopped talking when whiskey dick got up and stepped clumsily toward the concrete stairs. Lawrence got up, too.

Aleia remarked, "How cute, they're going to the bathroom together."

Whiskey dick headed down the stairs slowly, keeping firm hold of the railing, saying nothing.

"Are you going to hold his pecker for him?" Donna called after them.

"I was thinking about it, but I didn't bring my tweezers," Lawrence snapped back, beaming at the girls. "Do you want anything?" He winked at Donna, proud of himself. It was a good slam.

"Not right now, maybe later."

The boys rocketed into the concourse to pee.

Miss Demeanor exclaimed, "He's sweet on you! How precious. What did you do, spray love potion number nine on him? Does he have a big cock? He obviously doesn't have money."

"Don't know about that yet."

When Lawrence returned with three more beers and handed them to the girls, he reported, "Aaron split. Said he was bored. I'll take us home."

Miss Demeanor moved over one seat so Lawrence could be in between. "There, now we can both share him," she said with her best sugary voice. She sipped her beer, placing it in the cup holder, then flirtatiously grabbed his meaty upper arm and briefly placed her head on his shoulder. She glanced at the Diva, who also had her meat hooks on Lawrence.

She hissed, "I told you I don't share."

Lawrence giggled. "I love the ballpark!"

The starting pitchers for both teams were doing well and there were few hits and few runners on base, making things boring for non-baseball fans.

From a few rows down and over, Corrine turned toward Audrey. "Have you gotten a chance to see your grandson recently? Is Tamah a Samoan name?" Corrine scrunched her brows, knowing her friend was hurting.

"Oh, since I posted his pictures on my Facebook page, Demarco got to have him for a weekend, 'cause the bitch wanted to go get drunk in Vegas."

"That was at your place? Obviously?"

"Yeah, I got a little bassinet from my 'buy nothing group'," Audrey shared candidly. "It's fun playing Grandma. I bought lots of baby clothes from Walmart."

Owen heard that and could have added a lot more items to the shopping list: diapers, a diaper twisty pail, wipes, a baby changing table that he assembled, not to mention formula, bottles, and nipples. But the domestic yoke felt fine to him, especially as he got to hold the littlun' sometimes.

The $300 spree was paid by his Pin Up with a good job. A sense of gratitude for another chance for family was confirmed by his full emotional support. Besides, the child slept almost continuously. But when he could peer into the tiniest and clearest eyes ever, all foreseeable sacrifice on his small part was written in contract upon his heart.

"Is that what you call her now, 'the bitch'?" Corrine put her over-priced pilsner into the cup holder.

Audrey was sipping a beer as well, enjoying this delightful day at the ballpark. "Demarco goes to see the baby all the time. Tamah is a beautiful boy."

"The kid's going to have great looks. Black, white, Asian."

"He's got a huge head." The grandma sighed.

Corrine hadn't said anything but could see from the posted pictures that Tamah was a melon head baby. Something about Pacific Island people, maybe? But that was racist, right? The ninety-five percentile of baby craniums? She checked those thoughts at the door.

Owen caught that last part. "That baby has a big ol' coconut."

The women looked at him expectantly, hoping he would share more.

"Probably play football without needing a helmet," he chuckled.

Corrine giggled and Audrey exclaimed, "Ohhh!" Making a pouty face she added, "I love my bubble head grand baby!" That produced big smiles for both listeners.

After a quick 5-4-3 double play ending the Mariner's inning, Corrine asked, "What do you think about your girlfriend being a Nana, Owen?"

"She's the most beautiful Nana in the world," he declared and kissed the Queen on her cheek. The beer made him somewhat smooth in that instance.

Audrey asked, "Is that the beer talking, or you?"

"That's all me, baby." He stood up. "That reminds me, I'm ready for another. You girls still nursing your beers? You want the nachos in the Mariner's helmet thing? We could wash it out and put it on Tamah. No, never mind. . .it wouldn't fit." He did say the baby's name correctly with the accent on the second syllable, "Ta-ma'". And the jibe was digested with ease.

"Stop it," Audrey said with a smile, shaking her head. "I'm fine. Maybe later you can get me something."

Corrine chimed in, "She wants a footlong."

"I got one of those," Owen laughed and wiggled his eyebrows.

"Don't encourage him."

"Yeah, I don't need encouragement," Owen admitted and checked out the baseball situation on the scoreboard with a quick glance. Then he looked down at the funny girl. "You good Miss De Menthe?"

"I'm good, thanks."

Like most instances when one gets up for a bathroom break or to grab drinks, Owen was about to miss the most scoring of the game in one inning. And not by the home team. He bought the girls more beer anyway since he was feeling fine, like being dished up a fat grapefruit over the plate with the footlong quip.

Taking another sip from a warming brew, Corrine thought about how to better advise her surrogate Sis. "Eventually Demarco will need a parenting plan with her. So he can see his son by himself. Like, regular." The women had been over this territory before. Audrey was living it with her.

"How did you do it again with Man-cub?" Audrey asked. She was obliging, having chosen not to remember all the salient details. This slam was of Corrine's impregnator, the baby daddy that gave her Cory, then proceeded to make life as difficult as possible for her for the past four years. "Has Demarco established paternity, or was his name on the birth certificate? He'll need a good lawyer. Not like mine."

Corrine shot her a frightening glance. "I thought that maybe he wasn't, but when he got out of jail there was never any question to him. And you can see the resemblance. Even for a baby. His name is on Tamah's birth certificate."

"Then he has to petition the court. That was one of the first things Evan's family fucking hit me with when I left their fucked-up house. Getting a good lawyer is going to be key. Mine was shocked that Evan would lie about me. She didn't fight."

Audrey recalled how Corrine had followed her sister to the big city from Yakima. Or "Crack-ya-ma", as the elitist, western Washingtonians denigrated rural communities with big drug problems, although they were just like their own.

Having to do something after high school, Corrine buckled down and tolerated living with Mom and Dad for two more years in the hardscrabble town, earning an associate degree in Communications. Big Sister had paved the way and pushed her to apply to the Boeing subsidiary she worked for.

She moved to Seattle and got a job humping soda. That's when she met Ryan. After more reminders and less than gentle pushes, she eventually sailed her way through the interview process and was hired as a logistics specialist in their distribution services division for seventeen bucks an hour, with benefits. Soon she was introduced to Audrey. They had met during a company sponsored charity event years ago, providing diapers to luckless moms.

It was no surprise when her parents filed for divorce as soon as the nest was clear. It was her father who left, doing the paperwork himself.

He was an unhappy man who deserved better than a sour, angry woman who drank wine every day of her life. The bottles accumulated in the recycling to crash and clink loudly when it got picked up. It seemed so sad to waste so many years. Everyone in that family lived separate lives except for the occasional dinner out to celebrate a birthday.

Big Sister moved abroad with her sailor husband, then eventually moved back, and Corrine cleaved to Audrey like a lifeline, a new Big Sis. It had always been a mentoring relationship. Feeling really appreciated, Audrey even got little sister into Pin Up. Owen had to share his love, and that was fine by him. Holly Hotrod had a big heart. And now Corrine was eager to provide perspective from her own tragic tale, experience from a no fooling, now grown-up grown up.

Corrine met Evan after moving to the city of Renton, Boeing's base. He was tall and handsome, with a lean, hard body who liked to party. A really good fuck, too; in fact, the best she'd ever had. He possessed little intelligence and less integrity, content to stock grocery shelves part time and pretend to be an amateur tattoo artist. This was her Baby-Daddy. Even a criminal record would have demonstrated some ambition from Evan. His father had been collecting a check for an on the job back injury for nearly twenty years and his mom was paid by the state as his sole caretaker.

Having a big house and new cars seemed odd to Corrine as she and Evan moved into his parents' living room when Cory was born. Corrine spent a few months living with her in-laws, but it seemed that no one ever left the house. Evan even used his new father status to bag out of shifts at work.

She went back to full time work pushing aircraft parts across the country just to get away. The influence of that level of lazy was like a gravitational pull, and she knew she'd be living in hell unless she broke away. His child support was $250 a month after the court agreed to the parenting plan.

Evan got Cory on Tuesday night, all day Wednesday, then returned him Thursday night and had him every other weekend. He was the epitome of drama, the one who had refused to allow Corrine's mom into the hospital room after the kid was born. A seemingly current, common cruelty; purposeful separation of family, weaponizing parenting.

Through Cory's toddler years, the stress provided by her impregnator and the demands of ensuring the supply chain hummed, whether she got paid for the overtime or not, started to grind upon Corrine. She began getting achy, joint pain like early onset arthritis, unexplained rashes would appear and remain for months on her back and legs, and she wore a slight pink butterfly on her face in the springtime which was intolerant of any makeup.

Evan sensed a vulnerability to criticize her forgetfulness, while he contributed very little. The dermatologist finally referred her to a rheumatologist that diagnosed her with Lupus. Now the co-pays added to her expenses, but although there was no cure, the young woman was determined to fight the autoimmune disease.

She was informed that she might live a full life and avoid kidney damage if she was very careful, fully employed, and insured. The fear of changing jobs and being told her Lupus was a pre-existing condition jabbed at Corrine in vulnerable moments. She told Evan this in a desperate attempt for mercy, who dutifully searched the internet to learn its possible genetic origin, only to slash at her when her fatigue prevented her from picking up her son at the appointed time, which dug into his drinking time with friends.

"You probably got Lupus from your drunk mother," was his nasty response.

Cory's worldview was shaped by movement between beds and different toys. He always slept in Mom's room but had his own room at Grandma's. Evan said he was his best friend. That no one could ever love him as much as Daddy. It was tough getting presents right before Cory had to leave to go with Corrine. The grownups would argue about coats and shoes. The food was different, as were the rules, as was bed and bath-time. Sometimes his mother would read him books; his father watched a lot of TV.

"Mom says you can't take the new Velociraptor with you, buddy."

"How come?" the tot would ask.

"Because she's mean to you. But don't tell her that."

Frequently, Corrine would get mad at Evan for new "owies", red marks and bruises left for her to discover without warning or decent explanation. "Cory got hurt today playing outside," was too little of a parental courtesy for him. Evan probably didn't know about the injury himself, or once his son reported it, was told it wasn't important.

It was neglect and complete lack of supervision while Dad played video games pretending to be a warrior killing people. All the Mountain Dew and sugary cereal he wanted was at Grandma's. A dentist was horrified at the state of his baby teeth and had to pull his two upper front incisors from rot. Corrine forced Evan to take him so he could listen to his son cry. The adult teeth probably would not emerge until Cory was ten.

There was no good will between Cory's parents. Evan would push her buttons and she'd take the bait. Per their parenting agreement, consent had to be given even to take the child out of the county, let alone the state. Planning a trip to Yakima was like being held hostage.

In cycles like a cat playing with a mouse, it was great fun for Evan to torment until Corrine stopped getting upset. Thanksgiving a few years ago had been punctuated with threats to call the sheriff, to Evan's great glee. It was hard for Corrine to stop her mind hating when it was time to go to sleep. Messing with her motherly instinct was most painful, which was Evan's strategy all along, to inflict pain like he felt upon her rejection.

"We could all live together, but Mommy doesn't want us to be a family." It was routine for the boy to hear this when it was time to leave. Evan's still thinking there was a chance for reconciliation was testimony to his mountain of stupidity and thrill of revenge.

Cory's upset was all Mom's fault, a lying theme to be reiterated over many years until it would become a basic truth.

TAKE ME OUT TO THE BALL GAME.

TAKE ME OUT WITH THE CROWD.

BUY ME SOME PEANUTS AND CRACKER JACK,

I DON'T CARE IF I NEVER GET BACK.

LET ME ROOT, ROOT, ROOT FOR SE-AT-TILL.

IF THEY DON'T WIN IT'S A SHAME.

FOR IT'S ONE, TWO, THREE STRIKES, YOU'RE OUT

AT THE OLD BALL GAME.

The Pin Ups swayed, arms around each other's waists, saluting with beer cups. Miss Demeanor twisted during the following clip of "Johnny Be Good" then "Mustang Sally", holding Donna Diva's hand, her ride back. She screamed the loudest amongst the Dolls when the "Brazen Beauties — Pediatric Cancer" thanks appeared on the Jumbotron, as she hoped to ingratiate, in suckling fashion, herself to her drunk benefactor: the one who let her live in a decent trailer for free. Now Treasurer, the red-haired vixen now had the all-important account and routing numbers with a balance of nearly five thousand dollars. It was the result of several years of membership dues and backyard raffles.

The Mariners lost a not-so-close game, their starter giving up five runs in the fourth inning. It was an awesome sight as the retractable roof rolled swiftly over right field to cover the diamond and cantilevered over the third base line.

When the threesome arrived at the double wide, in a beautiful mountain rimmed working-class town, one hour north of the big city, it was assumed Aaron had passed out in all his clothes, as his truck was haphazardly parked on the gravel driveway. How he'd get up to drive to a plumbing job in a few hours was a mystery.

In the meantime, Donna, Aleia, and Lawrence made mixed drinks and howled on the patio at their boorish cuts on the only one who still brought in a regular paycheck. Miss Demeanor remembered her patron's warning and announced she was going to bed, got into the trailer adjacent to the double wide, and hit her stubby bong twice.

Donna sought to mate and she succeeded.

7
Plenty of Phish

Skillful navigation through the disingenuous waters of online dating had taken time for Peter to develop. Creating an attractive profile seemed like the commonsense first step, as the designers led the uninitiated toward. Years into the effort of finding someone to love, it still made Peter shake his head upon seeing profiles with only one picture, no pictures, blurry- sideways pictures, or pictures next to toilet partitions within public accommodations.

Women complained sometimes about men showing off the animals they'd killed, not wanting to hunt or fish with these men, who were doing the things they enjoyed. Lonely girls showed off their dogs and cats, with whom they had devoted affection. Getting girls talking by asking the name of their pet had a slim chance of getting a response.

In the cut-throat realm of online dating, it was the women who had most of the power. Despite clever introductions and jokes, Peter's few sentence messages rarely met with replies. Even then, after a few chats, "ghosting" was normal. It was an abrupt tactic to dismiss without a reason given. No explanations, no regrets, just a full up flight reaction at the smallest twitch of discomfort or whiff of danger. Unless a girl initiated the chatting process, there was little chance of a date.

Since most attention spans are inordinately short it seemed to Peter that having a series of good photos in his profile was extremely important. Many women made the mistake of only taking pictures of themselves or exclusively frowning. Being sullen wouldn't a shy mate make. The easiest deception was posting personal pics from long, long ago, from a place far, far away.

Sorting out the most recent wasn't too hard to discriminate. Vacation pictures were perfectly acceptable. They demonstrated riches, profile smiles, and good times, as well as a desire for adventure. His hiking in the Grand Tetons of Wyoming was picture perfect. Traveling companions were often desired for day trips. Posting pics with friends and family became hyper-critical as it showed that other human beings could stand to be around you, that you had basic relationship skills.

People shifted into a "forever" mode as distrust among the living as to who was sick prevailed. When the weather got colder and "where to go meet?" became as tough as it gets, culture shifted, becoming even more insular and fearful.

"Dick pics" online and solicitations from prostitutes, invitations to go to another site were red flags for scams. Plenty of Phish policed the site for criminal and lewd presentations.

Peter's interests were plagiarized from those of women's profiles he liked. Because he was transient, he didn't have the gear to go camping or take bike rides, but he liked to hike, and in the PNW there were trails and sights aplenty. Many girls presented themselves as a well-rounded, loving person where family always came first. Those of Peter's age almost always had kids.

All the women wanted a best friend, probably their last love. All of them also had battle scars, sometimes on the outside, too, as broken relationships and violence abounded. It was a level of complexity not unknown to him, as he'd dated girls with children. Infants and toddlers would usually take moms out of the dating pool for years.

The thought of an instant family wasn't repellant if playing catch outside as in the offing. Peter remembered Grandad letting his sisters makeup his face with hand me down cosmetics. One picture became the centerpiece of several albums, while another one was made into a Christmas ornament. Becoming a girl-daddy seemed homey, even. Being in his early 30's and working on the road, his default interest was getting laid, which he knew, no matter where he was or what he was doing, wasn't going to get him very far.

The dum dum's who wrote very little about their interests or wouldn't say what they did for a living would often challenge the reader with, "just ask me". Women who said they were sarcastic or were proud that they had no filter probably meant they were a bitch. Smart girls typically would provide a picture of themselves with no makeup on purpose.

Hot chicks who sent "Hi there" messages were probably whores, and more than likely had skimpy, philosophical profiles or claimed to be a "professional". Those who most certainly would be neglectful of a good man were abundant but hid very well. Those who reported drinking socially lied sometimes and those who said they didn't drink at all swam in the smallest eddies of the stream.

Comedy clubs, concerts, sporting events, fine dining, and anything else that required expendable income was money well spent to Peter. Education, like age, were gray areas in the vicious plenteous sea of fish. "Some College" could mean anything, although there was a glass ceiling where his associate degree wasn't going to penetrate; no panty dropping opportunities there.

Staying within the middle-class pond without associating with the bottom feeding embarrassing stupid wasn't easy. A girl who presented her appealing physical side obviously knew how to take care of herself. A pretty dress, a shapely form, a bit of cleavage respectfully shown demonstrated the desire to attract. Many said they were down to earth or had no time for drama. There are lots of lazy fish in the sea too, who thought "Hey there" in a message was poetry.

Those who said they were "a few extra pounds" were the gold standard for truthfulness, having healthy appetites and perspectives. Honesty betrayed most online seekers' approach. But making sure at least one pic was a full body shot was important.

Peter was "Christian-Other" and the non-religious could be discouraged. One boon of travel was the required exploration for Sunday services, exposures to different varieties of approach. Another fantastic difficulty presiding within the will of God was the substantial longsuffering of a recent convert. Finding a girl with spiritual interest, plus being horny was the final nail in the romantic coffin while on the road. Peter could find congress, but didn't want to debase someone's daughter, or someone's sister.

When Peter appeared in a new zip code, traveling the country with a hammer, he'd change his location and drop his line. Being in a new pond seemed to generate instant activity with two, maybe three girls willing to message back and forth. Then his numbers dwindled to none upon knowing that he was from out of town. He was doomed.

That was until he saw a resemblance between a pretty girl's profile and one of his Pin Up cards. It was the pistol tattoos that left no doubt, although her name, Corrine, was nowhere mentioned in her profile, so he began his message to her through the dating site:

"Dear time2Bme, I think I met you during the Tacoma classic car show."

It was a magnificent opening line. She had some Pin Up shots in the photo array, enough to make his blood boil. Although heavy, her "few extra pounds" went greatly but proportionally to her breasts. He admired her brown curls piled atop her head, cat-eyeglasses, and yellow brick road colored dress as she rested on the pavement beside a 1939 Lincoln Zephyr, her tangerine waist belt infused into the car's bright paint reflecting into a sunny afternoon. The next line was critical and in the time it took to drink a beer Peter was logged out and he had to start over.

"Your son certainly deserved his trophy. I'm new to the PNW. What's your favorite Rom-Com? Will you be in another Pin Up contest soon? I'd like to vote for you!"

Into the ether of the World Wide Web a longingness went at the speed of light. It was the best cast he'd made in months, but it would probably be met with the stillness of a pond without ripples.

Now was the pins and needles part of dating online where the message was either unread for weeks, read with no reply, or deleted with a malicious rejection that etched one's skin from thin to thick. The platform required a person's participation, or not. And Peter waited for a nibble.

The effects of social media produced a hormonal rush that society deemed important, in other words immediate. The waiting was exquisitely painful. JCPenney didn't open until 10AM, which gave the carpet guys and he a few hours to bring thousand-pound rolls of carpet up escalators prior to the mall opening and placing them into an empty store near the entrance of the second level. He kept checking the P.O.P. site for a response, disappointed each time there wasn't. The job was progressing without too much trauma, and for a thrill-less man like Peter, nothing was exciting or new anymore.

Cory woke up before his mother and stumbled the few feet from his "big boy bed" into her bed, acting like a twitchy alarm. The best little man snuggles warmed her more than the comforter and the worries of work slid away. A sweet boy, he began singing just because and smirking bleary eyed Corrine checked her phone, then got herself going, making sure the kiddo's eating and pooping, brushing, and dressing was in concert with her caffeinating and lunch making, makeup-ing and driving. She waited a full half hour after getting to work to see if what she had written was read. She checked his profile. Peter wasn't a gargoyle. Where was the lie? He was a man, after all. She thought about responding but waited until break, needlessly.

"Ha! Little man loves his trophy." And she clicked the SEND MESSAGE button.

They were like bees conveying the location of nectar, head to head, antennae feeling excitedly, flurrying with myriads of touches and with a jubilant dance just beginning.

The reel WHIZZED, the rod bowed, and he was shocked with a bell exclaiming that something jumped into the inbox. FISH ON! Peter's heart pounded; the adrenaline rushed as the prudent parts of his brain pumped the brakes. He waited until the evening until responding with a greater effort than building in an occupied retail space. Why hadn't she answered his questions? It took many beers to compose a response, and a maturity to wait that usually is a hallmark of an older man.

That Tuesday afternoon, little man's dad picked him up from day care at 2:30. She called Cory after work, drank two glasses of inexpensive Chardonnay, then ate two gas station bean burritos she picked up along the way. Taking a lavender bubble bath, Corrine wondered almost aloud with a groan how strong man hands would feel massaging her neck and shoulders, thumbs digging into her lower back, finding her stress points as she tingled. Coconut oil rubbed into her while linen scented candles thrust shadows into corners of the bathroom, Spanish guitar music carving out the rhythm.

The next weekend Evan had Cory, and having a new, nice boyfriend was barely conceivable. The warming lubricant and a spritz of Dior's Sauvage cologne upon her wrist inhaled at just that special moment of relief. She was a grown woman having her toys that pretended a loving, strong, mature, masculine presence, just for fun.

Then she spread her legs under the covers, finding the cold spots with her feet. Then fluttered mightily, falling into a very deep sleep.

Peter waited a full day and a half before replying on the platform, "I love seeing you Pin Up Dolls and the classic cars. When's the next show?"

...

Miss Demeanor didn't like trading messages on P.O.P. too long before offering her phone number to text to. A happy fish with a heart to boot probably wouldn't blow up her phone. Although, that did happen from time to time when she chose unwisely. Then angry and profane reactions typically cut big ballers and the poor boys short.

Finding guys to help her out took time. Aleia was a cheap date. What she wanted was the innocence of the new relationship which included living together and screwing often. She had to get her stuff out of storage quickly, and that meant paying the arrears. The little mementos from her son must not be lost into a landfill.

If she didn't contact her second husband, who parented their son, he wouldn't threaten to file with the court for full custody. Paralegal girlfriends of hers doubted that Washington State wouldn't grant some custody to her, but that meant having a stable job and place to live, not the camper of some friend in "Hicksville" almost three thousand miles away.

He had de-facto full custody already, and if she called to talk to her kid, she'd hear phrases like "child abandonment" and "court costs". Aleia would have to get her shit together, otherwise she'd never get to see her boy. Maybe if she pleaded well enough, she would talk to the little guy on his birthday or at Christmas. She hated that son-of-a-bitch #2 making her grovel like she was dirt.

The 2011 Honda Civic she removed from marriage number three kept running and the ride was relatively smooth. Finding gearheads to help her maintain it was relatively simple. She couldn't afford not having wheels. Putting in ten bucks of gas at a time was humiliating. The last of her unemployment benefits were going to run out soon. Buying brake pads wouldn't break her, but Aleia knew how to barter for free labor. She'd dropped the insurance when she'd gotten herself fired from the previous bullshit job selling vacation timeshares.

"My baby just keeps running, but now when I brake, I hear a squeal and it pulls to the right." She stood taller than the owner of the 1970, 440 'Cuda. And she may have been a smidge older.

He had asked her previously if she liked muscle cars as she traipsed through the car show giving away her cards tied to candy canes. "The Barracuda destroys the Camaro. Is yours a six or a four barrel?" Miss Demeanor had spoken to lots of gearheads and actually paid attention when they described their cars. Asking men about their passions was the easiest way to get them to do what she wanted. Plus benefits.

She knew her little Civic needed new brakes; Aleia just didn't want to pay for them or making sure her alignment was tuned in either. Once a man was on his back, on his wheeled creeper under her car, who knew what he may recommend? To keep it on the road? She'd tell him back at his shop/garage, "I don't have a lot of money to spend right now." That was always the truth. But she'd buy beer and maybe a fifth of Tennessee Whiskey when a gearhead guy was working for her, if that's what he liked. Anything he liked to make it happen.

"What shade of yellow is this? It almost matches my dress."

"It's a Citron Twist."

"That wasn't a stock color, was it?" She took off her pumps, holding them dangling from straps by her left shoulder. She looked right through his sunglasses, hers creeping down her little ski slope nose, unafraid of getting her feet dirty.

"No, but Chrysler offered it."

"I like the bucket seats. Would you like to take my picture with your car? Maybe I could pretend to drive?" This was somewhat forward, but her agenda had to be kept. Watching her slim form, shapely B-cups, and hugging ass getting in and getting out was the highlight of gearhead's month. Miss Demeanor asked for his vote and to send the pictures to the throwaway Gmail account on her card.

"You're a pro. Would needing new brake pads cause my car to come out of alignment?"

He was a full-time mechanic and quickly answered, "I suppose it could. We would check your alignment when the wheels were off." He had a goatee and easily smiled, having a nice early thirties build of a man who worked hard. Miss D was sure he'd check her alignment. "How's your tire wear?"

"I looked at that once, but I can't tell."

"I could check it out," he offered, "if you got time."

"Thanks, maybe after I win the queen's tiara." Miss Demeanor stuffed more cards into his shirt pocket. "Tell your friends to vote for me," she reminded him, then gave his chest a gentle pat.

The following weekend, Aleia drove the Honda to his place. She knew where she wanted to go, so there wasn't a reason to hurry. She posted some of his pictures to her Facebook page then friended him. After a few messages, a Saturday afternoon date was secured. It seemed safe enough to ask him for his phone number, just to text the address. When he called her, she made sure the game plan was to go to a parts store and that she would buy the brake pads, if that were what they were going to do.

"Are you sure your wife isn't going to get pissed when I come over?" she asked.

Donna knew her plans and coached her well: "Make sure he checks it all over. A free mechanic is worth his weight in gold."

"Ain't nothin' free, girl!" Aleia had replied. "You know that!"

The Diva just grinned, "Well, then at least get your kicks."

The gearhead was all business. He didn't even live with his mom. He owned a three-bedroom rambler that needed major home improvements. Obviously, carpentry wasn't his bag. When he had the front wheels off, she said she had to pee. Just enough time to look for pictures of other women, but this was bachelor territory. It probably never occurred to him to buy a plant or rip down the wood paneling in the living room.

There wasn't a sign of female presence in the bathroom cupboards or drawers. No lotions or emergency lip gloss, no shower puff loofah or hair conditioner in the bath. Either gearhead was slick or he didn't have a girlfriend. It was "virgin" territory, no telltale signs of a marauding bitch wolf. Just Gojo and a Lava soap at every sink.

As Aleia stepped down into the spacious heated garage she was asked, "You know you have a hundred and ninety-one thousand miles on your car? When did you last replace the brake pads?" The front was resting on stands and now the tail end was jacked up, its wheels off.

"Ummm..."

"That's okay. We're going to replace all four."

"What about the rotors?"

She is so pretty, he thought. And she knows what's going on.

"Those need to be replaced, too," he admitted. "It's time. Sorry."

"Could they be resurfaced?"

God, she looked good in those jeans. She wore a white tank top without a bra, covered by a purple plaid button down, long sleeve shirt.

Her response surprised him. "I do have a buddy who has a lathe but how soon do you want this done, Aleia?"

She hesitated.

"Look, pretty girl, yesterday I checked the auto parts store around the corner. They have what we need to keep you going. Cost you about a hundred and twenty-five bucks." He wasn't going to pay.

"Front and rear?" she asked next. "Rotors and pads?"

She was great! "Yeah," he agreed. The gearhead was grinning from ear to ear.

"What about the calipers?"

"They're fine. How do you know all this?"

"The internet." And she showed him the screen on her phone.

He started to wash his hands in the garage sink. "Are we doing this thing, or what?" It was refreshing when a man acted with confidence.

"Let's go." This was becoming a fun date, despite the cost.

At the auto parts store they found his pre-order quickly. Aleia put it on a credit card. Her date bought an oil filter, an air filter, and some other stuff, like nitrile gloves and Loctite. Auto parts never became items that people tried to hoard.

"So you don't get too much grease on your pretty hands," he explained. "I'm not doing this by myself." Gearhead had an agenda too, and that was to get as close to her as possible.

They worked together replacing the parts. He wore the thin gloves, too, conscientious of the always seeping oils and replaced the gloves several times when they tore. He did the same with her gloves, too, when she forgot. Many times they worked shoulder to shoulder touching hands, forearms, and thighs repeatedly as they moved stubborn bolts and then knocked them back tight with adhesive. Only country music could fit such a scene, and when they were almost finished Miss Demeanor asked, "do you have any beer in that frig?"

It was a dumb question as the refrigerator was in a man's garage. Before there could come an answer, the door was open. Pabst Blue Ribbon was perfect, tasting good to working people. Aleia's new boyfriend (he didn't know that was his title yet) changed the oil and replaced the air filter. He had gallon jugs on shelves, buying in bulk.

"Why don't you get cleaned up? I'm going to the grocery store and get us some dinner," she announced, and he thought that was fine. She returned with a big deli pizza and an orange flowering houseplant. And he thought that was fine, too.

While the oven heated up they talked loosely about past personal history. Aleia asked deeper questions, to burrow within. The gearhead was unable to stop talking.

They made out for a while before she left. He was a good kisser. He smelled and tasted like coconut shampoo and a Marlboro Red all mixed with the garlic in the pizza. His hands stayed upon her waist although they didn't want to.

The last thing he said to her before she pulled out of his driveway was, "we need to talk about your tires."

Miss Demeanor was smitten.

"Let me know if your car wants to drift!" he called to the rolled down window frame.

She blew him a kiss with her right hand as the Civic pulled forward. They had forgotten to check the alignment. He desperately wanted to see her again but was very slow to figure out how.

When she rolled back to Donna's on fumes, she opened her back porch screen and gingerly walked inside calling, "Hello? Anybody home?"

Aaron's bedroom door was closed but the radio was playing AC/DC through his stereo. She decided to text her friend.

Where are you?

Aleia was so excited to tell her about her wonderful afternoon. The evening was still young, with pale sunlight still streaming into the valleys, not yet blocked by the nearby mountains.

The text replied immediately: **Where are you?**

In your living room.

Then she ambled toward the camper, meeting Donna coming out the door and down the three steps quickly. Aleia stopped. "What's going on?" she asked with a playful lilt in her voice.

When they passed each other, Donna had a scared look on her face. "Is Aaron awake?"

"I don't know." That was a weird question to be asked. There was no more an expectation of privacy with living in the camper. The timer went off for her to move the fuck out.

Miss Demeanor had a few pieces of pizza in a plastic bag upon her wrist as she twisted the doorknob, knowing instinctively her patron had been screwing on her bed. She stepped inside, quickly followed by the Queen Bee.

The same station was playing on the radio; in fact, it was the end of the same song, "You Shook Me All Night Long." Her eyes immediately inspected her disheveled comforter. This was going to take some tact. It was Donna's (more like Aaron's) camper after all. She was just a long-term guest/squatter. A few seconds passed in silence.

They both looked so guilty. Aleia diplomatically placed the pizza and her handbag down, then asked Lawrence, moving her face close to his, "Lawrence, why are you sweating?"

"Ha!" roared Donna Diva, immediately forgiven, it seemed to her.

Unconsciously he wiped his face with his hand. "I'm not sweating," the former Special Operator calmly said.

"Can I put away my stuff now?" Aleia asked the camper. She was going to change all the bedding before crashing. Again, all that laundry would go in Donna's washer and dryer, paid for by the husband made a cuckold. Aaron would be the last to know about the affair, of course.

"Come on, sweetie," Donna said and held out her hand. Big, scary man took it and was directed out the door.

Donna took a long swing from her PBR sixteen ounce can and smirked at her friend.

Like a dog lucky for scraps, Aleia asked, "Am I going to find used rubbers someplace?"

"You would have…"

Like the slut she was, Miss Demeanor interrupted, "Is it bigger than Whiskey Dick's?"

"Oh yeah."

"Well, I had a wonderful day! Got a brake job. And he lives alone."

"Not a blow job?"

"Get out, you tramp!" And Aleia sat down alone, perfecting her demeanor before continuing the party on Donna's patio.

It was then she resolved to take from the "Brazen Beauties" club all that she was owed for this offense. And because her coffers had become dangerously low, and she was effectively being kicked out. Her mistress would use her key as she pleased.

Within a minute Donna's son showed up and more mixed drinks with spiced rum were made for his mom, Lawrence, his fiancé, and himself. Aleia sipped on a harder cider. Everything seemed so normal until Aaron popped his head out the sliding glass door, smiling, looking confused, obviously still drunk after his nap.

"What's going on?"

And everyone stopped talking.

8

South Sound Sally

When Corrine decided it was time to run the gauntlet, her memory banks were full of what to keep an eye out for. Costco sold little bottles of hand sanitizer she knew she wanted. Wiping down the handle of the shopping cart with an antibacterial, disposable cloth was as routine for her as it was for Cory to form his hands together into a little bowl when Mommy flipped out the bottle of jelly.

"Rub," she commanded and squirted some onto his skin. Thus, they had pre-pandemic habits built into their trips outside the house. Adding a mask was like slipping on an old shoe for her, since protecting her compromised immune system was now written into her DNA, perhaps as Lupus was.

Cheesecake was another thing to look for. Bulk items like mac n' cheese, paper products, snack bars, forty-eight-ounce bottles of mayonnaise, and double boxes of Captain Crunch too, were on her mental checklist. Through experimentation they found what they liked and stuck to it. She bought veggies for her diet, but they sometimes went to waste.

Supplements were a budgeted item. The fish oil, multivitamins, and things like D, C, and zinc were abundant and cheap. Prednisone helped as an anti-inflammatory. Corrine was betting the glucosamine/chondroitin supplements would protect her joints from deteriorating rapidly for $40 per month.

Costco didn't always have elderberry, echinacea, turmeric, or ginkgo biloba (for memory). Cory got Flintstone chewables, although he liked the dinosaur gummies better because they were dinosaurs. Her doctor had her on hydroxychloroquine, a prescription she could fill at Costco while getting prescription cat-eyeglasses and getting her tires changed. When other people panicked at shutdowns and bought shit paper and spray disinfectant, Corrine simply added to her prodigious hoarding stock of anti-inflammatories and supplements.

The greeter checked her membership card. He didn't have to enforce the government mandated 25% max capacity restrictions yet, that would wrap the queue around the building in any weather.

"Are we gonna get the pizza first?" the sweet lad asked. It was a perfect Friday night date.

"Ohhh yeah!" Corrine replied. They usually did. For less than $3.00 a slice it was the best bargain in town, and pretty damn good. Finding an open table in this whirl of humanity wasn't too easy.

"There's no use shopping on an empty stomach!" Cory proclaimed and he padded his tummy as he watched his mother sweep bits of refuse onto the ground with a handful of napkins.

"Hey! That's my line," Mommy beamed at her precocious little boy. "Do you want to try the samples today?"

The massive white warehouse was churning with noisy people talking and carts squeaking. Ringing sounds echoed into the high, exposed ceilings as goods crashed together in carts. Signs hanging from the joists advertised new products, special membership bonuses, and more. There was activity everywhere.

"Cory. . ." He was chewing his pizza and paying attention to anything other than his mother. "Earth to Cory?" she tried in a playful tone. Still no reaction. "Cory!"

His head snapped back around to meet her gaze. "What?"

"Are you going to try the samples today?"

"I don't think I'll be hungry anymore." Going on five, her son's brain was growing fast, too.

"Eat your pizza. It's brain food." And Corrine bubbled with love, wiping his little chin and pushing his hair to one side.

Pre-schoolers were germ factories and his academic day concluded with Cory strapped into his car seat, forming his hands into a bowl like Mommy taught him. Next came a cold squirt of gel, then the command, "rub", which he dutifully did while singing the happy birthday song to make sure he did it good.

Saturday morning was an extension of a late evening. The petticoat was three layers of white tulle fabric making a crinoline hoopless underskirt. Miss Corrine De Menthe was going pink for the South Sound Sally pageant, who co-sponsored the Pediatric Brain Tumor Foundation and their charity Car Show for Kids.

The floofiness helped hide her hips and buttocks in plain sight. Motorcycles, trucks, and all classes of cars by the hundreds would be there to raise money. Months before she found an inexpensive pink, XL, past-the-knee length dress with roses. Their leafy stems were plastered all over to the slight sleeve and plunging neckline. The waist was tight and her boobs didn't want to fit without wanting to explode.

Although Kimmy (aka Serenity Jade) was a better seamstress than Holly Hot Rod, the three had congregated at Audrey's, since she had a better sewing machine. Owen watched for a moment then went out to his little shop to do anything else.

Corrine brought the hard cider and a vintage white lace collar she bought off the internet, but as soon as she showed it to Kimmy, worried tears formed behind her eyes. Could she pull this off without looking stupid?

"Oh, this is going to work fine!" Kimmy reassured her. She was already wearing her Western motif dress.

The pressure behind Corrine's eyes skidded like pumping brakes.

"Well, put the dress on, girl! Let's see them boobs." Holly Hotrod decided to change into her outfit, too, as she needed opinions on the choice of complementary shoes. She was going Japanese!

Corrine De Menthe's pink strappy pumps and gloves perfectly matched her dress, but the spilling out boobs were the issue that the seamstress quickly put to rest. Once it was back on, the women admired the dress with the new lacey/racy collar that covered most of her more than ample bosom.

Holly Hotrod asked, "You said that new guy Peter was going to meet you there Saturday?"

As pageants got closer, so did the metamorphosis quicken unto their Pin Up Doll alter egos.

"Yeah, I'm pretty sure."

"He doesn't stand a chance," remarked Serenity Jade.

"Don't settle. The boys are going to be buzzing around you like bees," Holly pointed out.

"But will they find the Honey Pot?" Serenity mused.

The Pin Ups were laughing when Owen came back in to use the facilities after drinking two Rainiers. "You girls playing dress up?"

That was the wrong question to ask.

"Get out of here!" his wife berated him.

"Go on, git!" Miss De Menthe piled on.

"This is girl time!" Miss Jade was all fired up, just like at the ballpark.

Quickly doubling back and closing the sliding glass door, Owen pissed against his workshop, giggling somewhat for the relief, protected from view by the trees and bushes in full growth on a mid-week August evening.

After only three hours of sleep, Miss De Menthe dragged her ass to the kitchen for some green tea (this had replaced coffee for its medicinal qualities — and having less caffeine). She had only three hours to do her makeup, hair, and then squeeze back into her dress. Hopefully, little man would be up and she could get him ready for another wasted weekend with his bastard father.

The faux pearl strand and imitation flowers for her big, curled hairdo were picked out weeks ago. This was the only thing that didn't simply keep her alive, that she spent her money on herself. But that was wrong; Pin Up kept her alive, too. She didn't have to practice a speech, but she did buy a cheap, adjustable hula hoop and practiced outside their apartment door, much to the delight of Cory who practiced at her side, and the curiosity of a Labrador pup, bought as the best birthday present to a boy ever.

While the puppy was a lot of work, and involved picking up poop and continuous expenses, she knew that her ex could never match the gesture. It was like shoving a ram rod up his ass. The hula hoop contest was indeed a thing, and although she'd never win, she didn't want to embarrass herself. It conditioned her core a little. The Pin Up doll turned on her speaker to stream some R&B once the danger passed of waking Cory too early. With her makeup and hair satisfactory, she would need little man to zip her up.

Finally, after letting Cassie (like Lassie) outside on her tether, she finally picked up their pup and threw her atop the sleepyhead. She watched the two littlun's act clumsily together on the bed.

"She peed, now you have to. Come on, we have to leave in forty-five minutes." For Miss De Menthe, that really meant an hour and a half until wheels were rolling. But she had to feed them all, pack at least one change of clothes, get the Radio Flier red toy wagon into the truck with the coolers, and get the pup settled into her wire crate.

Next, she made sure soft rock was playing so Cassie didn't get scared being home alone, packed the kid, and bought ice. It was time to chill the six dozen bottles of water with ribbons and cards tied to their necks. And her name was written on red duct tape wrapped around each lukewarm plastic bottle shoved into cold, and drive to Evan's early enough so that she wouldn't miss Donna Diva's deadline to sign in at 10AM.

"I didn't know you were coming so early," said her impregnator's mom. It was 9:15 and she looked like she hadn't had her cup of coffee.

Kissing the pup three times was part of a goodbye ritual before she was crated. When Cory walked away carrying his big boy backpack. "Hi Granma," he said. "Bye mom," was all he piped before disappearing to go watch TV, probably all day long, was also routine. So much for "I love you" or "you look great" or "good luck." But she got loves all the time, truth be told.

"My, aren't you all dolled up? Do you have time to come in?" She bet she didn't from Corrine's hurried pace and slight perspiration on her upper lip.

"No thanks. I got to fly. Tell Evan that I need Cory's shoes back on Sunday when I come to pick him up. There must be three other pairs of his shoes here."

It was true. The boy arrived dressed and was returned often barefoot or without the hat, gloves, socks, a sweatshirt or the coat Cory came with.

"Oh. Well, okay. You look really good. My, you certainly spend a lot of money on clothes." The idiot fell into her own double meaning.

Miss De Menthe smiled, fondly thinking about how he left her part-time grocery clerk son high n' dry. "My job's going great, and my outfit is actually really cheap. I did the alterations myself." Her left hand fluttered about the lace collar. "Well, goodbye."

"Good luck with your. . .your thing." And her never to be, never employed mother-in-law closed the front door to their family's two-story house.

...

The treasurer of the "Brazen Beauties" Pin Up Club collected fifty bucks for girls who weren't pre-registered. It was thirty-five for girls who'd paid before. Some paid in cash, much to the delight of Miss Demeanor. Miss De Menthe got there with ten minutes to spare.

Donna Diva gave her the near to touching bow/hug that big boobed women performed, while saying, "Girl! You're sweating like a whore in church!" It was going to be a warm day, which fit in well with Corrine's plan.

"I was afraid to be late for sign in," Corrine explained with short breath.

It seemed quaint to the Queen that a novice would be flustered by the rules.

Looking at her treasurer, Donna Diva replied, "I'm sure we'd let slide a few who may come late." Of course, she would. Aleia looked at her abusive patron with the all-knowing stare of a bored kitty cat.

The folks who ran the whole show had ballots that listed the names of the Dolls to decide who became the "the People's Choice." But who became the crown queen for the day, or Miss Hula Honey, or Miss Classy Chassis, or Miss Delectable Delight, was within the purview of the president, her judges, and how she decided to tally the votes and scores.

Those who didn't sign up in advance weren't on the ballot. Even Donna understood that life got in the way. To stay in good standing with the club, a member had to attend at least six events throughout the year. That could include any regular meeting or sponsored event.

About the only contest with fair scales was the hula hoop contest, as the winners of assigned heats competed until the doll with the most rockin' bodies clearly outlasted every other girl. Seemingly frivolous, the exhibition was a crowd pleaser as the gearheads liked watching experienced females rotate their hips in tight little circles without stopping.

Miss South Sound Sally was the biggest show of the year. Over twenty Pin Ups would be competing, not including the club officers. There were some big hitters, including previous Queens with entourages of family and friends that could secure about ten votes just to start.

Peter arrived on time and purchased a single ballot for ten bucks. It was a rigid process for the car club where in one line he paid and got a slip of paper and a program. In another line, he handed in his slip and received a ballot. Right away, he was instructed that only ballots turned in by 3PM would be counted.

There were lots of categories for the vehicles, most of them starting with the word "best", as in: Best in Show, Most Liked, People's Choice, Sponsor's Choice, Best Ford, Muscle Car, Trickiest Truck, Hot Rod, Best Paint, GM Performance, All Original Chevrolet, Low Rider, Original Mustang, Vintage Camaro, Best Chevelle, Best Pro-Touring, Rat Rod, Engine, Exotic, and Custom. Plus, there were the motorcycles that included categories like: Best Freestyle, Best Custom Street, Cruiser, Off Road, Sport Touring and Chopper.

To this dizzying end, these beautiful, complex machines were placed in a communalistic relationship temporarily with much more beautiful and complex organisms called Lola Liberator, Katastrophic, Marie Bella Rose, Ginger Honey Bear, and Carter Corsair. From clubs as far away as Portland and Boise came real heavy hitters such the dreaded Violet Villainess, Cherry Chiffon, and Daisy Lane.

All of the above were super sweet, dainty politicians who'd slit your throat just for the princess tiara from another club. Prospects like Wanda Woodworthy, Miss Amanda, or Charlotte Sinclair knew they should watch, step lightly, and learn how to lose with grace.

Nasty rumors got started from the upper strata and spread amongst the gearheads and public alike. One heard overt racism such as, "Cherry Chiffon drives a Nissan" or transgender stereotypes as in, "I thought she used to be a dude. Look at her Adam's Apple." In packs they circled like bitch wolves and criticized each other's accessories, especially shoes that didn't quite match.

Questioning a girl's sluttiness would instantly boomerang. Better still to whisper, "That girl's colder than a witch's titty."

"So lazy! Her makeup looks like it was painted with a roller."

"She didn't even shave her legs!"

The local girls tried to help those still trying to outfit themselves with bobby pins, emergency rouge and eyeliner, maybe the removal of sheer stockings on a hot day or adding base to rashes caused by a particular disease.

The gearheads' bonnets were raised above their engines and Peter took a bearing between his own automotive dreams and a dream girl.

He texted: **I'm here trying to find you and the vintage Camaros.**

Looking for a girl dressed in pink with roses and their leafy stems amongst hundreds of gearheads and onlookers seemed like a needle in a haystack proposition amongst the cars.

Corrine De Menthe pulled her red vintage toy wagon with cold water bottles one row over, with her thick legs working beneath her crinoline pink dress, shopping for votes.

"Hey!" was what Peter wanted to shout, but instead made his way obliquely into her path. Then he spotted what he thought was a late 70's Z28. It was painted a dark pink, like bubblegum. It had a tubular roll cage to make it "Pro Street." The owner was shadowing Peter.

He asked him, "When did you put the Rat motor in?"

The big block V8 replaced an '83 small block Z28. The owner explained his desire to race with the improved specs he achieved with better torque to revolutions per minute. Peter had a '68 Plymouth Road Runner, back home, in a shed. He just wanted to keep his running, not having the passion to modify for a race he'd never run. Peter guessed the owner raced a few times, but just knowing what the build could do was the satisfaction. Where had the girl gone?

Being so stupid, he now ignored a 1941 Chevrolet De Luxe Business Coupe with its Ocean Blue hood having red pinstriped, chromed louvered sides. She couldn't have gotten too far pulling the wagon and yucking it up with everyone who responded to, "Hi there. Would you like a cold bottle of water?"

He continued down the row she'd been in, but no Corrine. He took a right, then another right back to the '77 Camaro, then doubled back again. How could he have been so stupid? Just as his desperate gamble was about to pay off with an actual face to face, Peter started chasing shiny objects instead and now he was lost.

Whether it was the orangish '70 Nova or the pretty girl with the floofy flowered dress that caught his attention first became an inside joke between the pageant couples in the months to follow. There was a gaggle of people surrounding Corrine, who seemed a natural center of attention. They all seemed to know her pretty well. Not wanting to interrupt, but also not wanting to slink away like a junior high school boy, Peter waited quietly to one side like a foreign lieutenant awaiting to introduce himself in court.

"Nobody cares when you register your car," Jack was explaining to Miss De Menthe.

Delmonica was past eight months pregnant and rolled out of her lawn chair onto her hands and knees. "Don't nobody help me up!" It was said with an eighteen-year-old's humor.

Peter instinctively flinched. Her fiancé just watched as Owen grabbed her hand and a belt loop of her stretchy paternity jeans. With a steady pull, he righted the overturned ship with baby on board.

"Girl! You're about to pop!" said the goateed man. He was tall, wearing a white straw cowboy hat, and transition eyeglasses that still showed his eyes through purple lenses. An instantly likable person.

"Thanks, Owen. Good to see there's still some gentlemen around. I want to give my fake cousin a hug."

Delmonica and Corrine swayed a bit together. Then she said, "I know it's not ours, but I wanted to honor my dad one more time. They worked on it so hard." Her face got pinched and she had to wipe beneath her eyes.

"I only helped Ryan sometimes," Jack said as he handed his girl a clean, folded, paisley handkerchief.

"No, you did a lot."

Audrey, aka Holly Hotrod, added softly, "We're all so sorry about your dad."

Owen saw Serenity Jade walking over with her husband Brian and announced: "Oh, here comes trouble!"

Miss Hotrod hit her husband with her black, grass flower folding fan. "Be nice." She was wearing a maid's kimono costume, with a wide top skirt bow sash, immense bell-shaped sleeves, which were black with a dainty floral pattern. Holly painted her eyes in the Geisha style.

Owen turned and bent over a little, showing his fanny. "Hit me now!" he whimpered, and she did. Twice with the fan, whack, whack.

Brian walked straight up to Delmonica, his niece, and cried, "I'm sorry, baby." Now they both were crying, which made Corrine start to cry.

What the fuck have I walked into? thought Peter. He made a little circle around the group where people were both laughing and crying, not knowing what to do. All he could manage as an outsider was to distance his orbit somewhat from the drama.

Through tear-spotted catty glasses, Corrine looked over and somewhat recognized Peter from his pictures on Plenty of Pfish. "Oh, hi. I thought that was you." In the emotionally charged atmosphere she gave him a hug, although this was the first time they had met. Which he thought was weird.

"Everybody, this is Peter."

Brian had composed himself somewhat and gave him a firm handshake. "Pleased to meet you. I'm Brian."

"Thanks, Brian." *So all these people are Corrine's family?* he thought, gazing at the wide range of personalities around him.

Jack asked in his typical jackassery, "And why are you here, Peter?"

"I think I'm her date."

Owen stared for a moment with a straight face. "What? You think? What, you just follow her here from the bus stop?"

His wife added, "No. I've seen him before at the car shows, following the Dolls around."

Serenity Jade chimed in, "I've seen him, too. All inconspicuous like."

This was going sideways fast. Were these people joking or was he about to get the shit kicked out of him? Peter really wasn't sure.

"How long have you been stalking me, Peter? If that's your real name?" Corrine got into his personal space, obviously amused at the worried expression he was wearing.

"Uhh. . .only for a little while?" he answered weakly.

Delmonica and Brian were completely confused. They hadn't seen each other since her father/his brother had died.

Jack continued the inquisition as Miss De Menthe stood next to him, taking his hand, smiling. "Are you here for the girls or the cars?"

Why is she holding my hand? Peter asked himself. *Are the men about to rush at me, and my "date" is holding me so I can't run?* There was a long pause.

"Uhh, both, I guess."

Corrine dropped his hand and placed hers on her hips, staring, trying not to smirk.

Owen said, "Boy, we need to talk," while Holly and Serenity giggled.

"I got a ballot," Peter almost shouted. That was all he could think to say. And he proudly showed Miss De Menthe's family how he'd already voted for her.

"You're so sweet," Corrine said.

"What do you have down for 'All Original Chevrolet'?" asked Jack.

Peter grabbed his pen and looked at his ballot to find the spot blank.

"Write down number one-twenty-four. That's Ryan's Nova."

Then, Holly Hot Rod excitedly told the entourage, "My grand baby is here!" She was staring at her phone, texting her son back, instructing him to find the Pin Up Doll's green striped awnings by the main entrance.

The huge parking lot could hold thousands of spectators for the casino, horse track, and event spaces. And people came and went from all possible approaches. However, there was a corner, closest to the main drag, in which the car show sponsors congregated.

"Come on, Miss De Menthe. You haven't seen Tamah yet." And Owen swept his arm toward the meeting place about 100 yards away. He knew how important it was to his wife that all the girls ooed and awed at the newest member of the family.

Delmonica started waddling as quickly as she could, asking, "how old's the baby?"

The Geisha maid grinned her toothy grin. "Only five months. My son, Demarco brought him."

The group was moving like a glacier. Peter grabbed the handle of Corrine's wagon, staying in the rear with the fellas. Jack left the Nova with its bonnet up and made sure Delmonica hadn't left any valuables behind, grabbing a handbag with unknown contents.

Corrine noticed both gestures and asked her friend, "Do you think Kaelani came with?" She tried to pick up the pace, excited to see the baby at last.

Holly Hot Rod looked at Serenity Jade to explain loudly enough that her son's girlfriend was a wretched person. "She wouldn't even let me see my grandbaby when he was born." That had to sink in emotionally for a moment. "She hates anything to do with Demarco's family. She would never have come along."

Brian heard this report like a portend of Tiffany's influence regarding his niece's child. It was a chilling warning of common cruelty.

Owen spoke to Peter and Jack, just catching Brian's attention. "Now guys, I have to warn you, this boy has the biggest melon you're ever gonna see on a kid. His mother is Samoan."

"Oh, a spam head baby," Peter commented.

"Yes. Exactly. Jack, why are you carrying a purse?"

"Fuck you, Owen," Jack spat back with all affection.

Owen shook that off. "Don't nobody say nuthing about Audrey's bubble-headed grand baby's ginormous head." The entourage soon descended upon Demarco like friendly paparazzi. The young father allowed a strange Japanese woman to pick up his snoozing son, folding her sweeping sleeves around his thin baby blanket. Audrey beamed with pride as she introduced the gathering throng of Dolls to her grandson, Tamah. The estrogen concentration peaked with high pitched cooing, pinching the brains of all males within fifty yards.

Demarco was still wearing the stretchy baby carrier sling, complaining to the women that, "I put him in the stroller 'cause I could feel it in my back. Don't know how you women do it." Was this shameless sucking up to the people who could give him practical advice or was this young man about to cry? Jack shuddered.

Corrine quipped, "we're built to endure pain."

"So you have to get the convertible back carrier." Serenity Jade began to instruct Demarco, and he listened intently like he was taking survival notes in his mind. She gently asked if she could hold baby Tamah, cradling his head with her fingers splayed like a baseball fielder's mitt. "Ohh, he has such a tiny butt."

"Huggies size one," said the proud poppa, avoiding the fear in the eyes of the men watching.

"Do you see your future yet, Jack?" Owen looked over at him. "You'll be carrying around a baby bag next."

Peter chimed in, "I bet that stroller cost 250 bucks."

"Three hundred. I was there when she bought it for him. Plus the bassinet, clothes, diapers, crib. . .it never stops."

"Jesus." Peter's incredulity was body checked by stark reality. The men made up the last ring of admirers but couldn't help noticing the man child's skull. Jesus! It was like the largest pumpkin in the patch.

"You better hope you don't have a bowling ball head baby like that!" Brian exclaimed, truly afraid.

"Fuck all you guys!" Jack shouted. His excited pitch was met with a few, quick, female, disapproving glares. And then, mercifully, the visitation was over.

There were votes to buy and only a short while to do it. After the obligatory conversations about newborn poo and sleeping habits and techniques, the new dad looked for shade. The day was getting hotter, and the Dolls needed to spread out, getting pictures on Rat Rods for promises to vote. By 2PM they had to subject themselves to private interviews with the judges under several awnings the club had popped up.

"Are you going to help Corrine get the popular vote?" Jack asked him before everyone peeled off.

Peter gurgled some kind of response.

Like a wizened old political power broker, Jack advised Peter that "people don't know how they should vote until you tell them. And besides, this is the only way to spend time with her today. This is the date."

Peter thought this young feller just became his best friend, and for the rest of the day he did exactly as he had been instructed. Peter followed Corrine closely, stopping sometimes to admire the cars. Once he asked an owner about the rims of a '34 Ford, so pretty in a fire engine red and spotless 355-inch "Mosch" motor, all chromed out.

Slowly, he began to ask people he passed if they'd voted for a Doll yet, and if not then they should vote for the prettiest girl at the show, Corrine De Menthe. Selling conversation for water, he needed another twenty cards after an hour or so. Corrine was working it, too, simply asking how long the owner or owners (many cars had a couple attached, under an awning beside their baby) had been coming to the Car Show for Kids.

She gave Peter fifty cards after she secured another vote. When he told her she was low on water, Miss De Menthe coyly and coquettishly asked if he would bring the other cooler to the Radio Flier wagon.

After explaining generally where her Toyota Tacoma was and that the bed cover wasn't locked, Peter found it, drained some water to lighten the load, and wheeled the replacement to her. Then he reversed the process, loading up the previous cooler with ribboned water bottles, with Corrine De Menthe written with a Sharpie over red duct tape wrapped around the bottle, and covered it with whatever ice was still left.

As a reward Peter guzzled a bottle and briefly left her to inspect a 1965 Pontiac GTO. Known as "the GOAT", it could hammer 100mph in thirteen seconds. A legendary muscle car, looking long and lean, it was still heavy at 3500lbs. The Gran Turismo Omologato was a potent thoroughbred. Another vote was secured on his ballot.

Miss De Menthe continued like a woman on a mission. She traded sorrowful stories with women who had had sick kids. Pediatric brain cancer meant trying to discern why a child had headaches, their bones ached, or they vomited frequently. The thought of her boy in distress tore Corrine up; however, Cory's pain was more of the emotional variety, of neglect. And a pang of regret ran through her.

They canvassed as much of the crowd as they could, traveling the long rows, with Corrine getting pictures taken by the owners upon request.

A few times Peter tried working up a beer vendor line, saying, "Get your picture with a beautiful Doll heerrah!" She hadn't heard. "Get your free water heerrah! Vote for the prettiest Doll at the show heerrah!"

When she took a modest break, she peered into her phone and exclaimed, "Shit! I got to get over so Aaron will take my car photos."

Peter shoved a big, sugary, fresh squeezed lemonade into her hands. "I don't want you passing out. You're doing great! What car photos?"

The Dolls paid to have Donna Diva's husband take "professional" pictures with a car of their choice, and, of course, the owner's consent. Miss De Menthe convinced a gentleman that if he allowed it, his 1950 Chevrolet 3100 pickup truck would be featured in the Miss South Sound Sally calendar for next year.

It was less a sell than a swap. Corrine sort of knew how to pose, in and out of the bed and over the hood. She stepped out of the driver's seat, lounging before the red painted grill, which complemented the carnations of her dress. It helped the hapless, inebriated photographer set up his light although he hadn't a clue about composition.

"Are you hungry?" Peter asked.

"No. Well, I had a granola bar. I don't want to eat in this dress. It's too hot anyway. Thanks for the lemonade. It hit the spot."

Peter nodded but pressed on, "Do you think you may want to get a bite after the show? How are your feet doing?" There was only an hour left before the personal interview portion began back at the Brazen Beauties Awnings.

"Women's shoes suck," Corrine admitted.

"The pink webbing is going to leave an interesting tan on your feet," he chuckled.

She was going to continue to jabber with this particularly persistent man, but she only had an hour left to solicit. Corrine would meet people from previous shows and Peter would drift toward a powder blue 1957 Bel Air, wondering if the lights mounted in the hood worked or were just reflective.

The proverbial big fuzzy pair of tied together dice hung from the rear-view mirror. The owners were perhaps strolling in admiration or getting a French Dip sandwich from one of several food vendor trucks. The number of the car was in the windshield, along with a hip high storyboard of the Bel Air's provenance and the owner's rebuild from the barn from which it was discovered.

When his "date" had to leave for the interview portion, Peter pulled the wagon to Miss De Menthe's truck, then slowly filled out his ballot. Upon a brilliant observation that would make Jack proud, he saw folks coming toward the Car Show for Kids ballot box.

"Have you picked out a Doll to vote for?"

He must have asked thirty people walking up to push their paper into the slot, old fashioned style. He would consider his vote for best in show, but after they finished campaigning at 2PM.

Some said yes, but they had the wrong answer, which was really too bad. A few even said, "Yeah, I'm voting for Miss De Menthe! You gave me her card two hours ago."

"Good man!" Then, upon a whim, Peter asked the guy, "What made you choose her?"

Whereupon the man leaned in and replied, "cause she's got the biggest tits of any woman here."

Peter turned his head to giggle and could only respond with, "yeah." Well, a vote was a vote and the truth had to eventually be told. So if she got another five votes last minute it was five votes more than she'd had. Peter didn't see her again until the Hula Hoop contest.

Donna Diva ensured that the Dolls would announce their winners before the gearheads. The Car Show for Kids organizers saw the wisdom of a ladies first approach, avoiding squealing tires exiting while their biggest co-sponsor whirled hoops around hips and pronounced the day's princesses and eventually the Queen. So, while a band played their version of Cheap Trick's "I Want You to Want Me", the hundreds strong throng congregated per the invitation of a Master of Ceremonies.

Then Queen Diva took charge with Miss Demeanor acting as her assistant. Addressing the crowd, the first heat of Five Dolls was called to demonstrate the strength of their cores and the cheeky width of their hips.

An outsider, Violet Villainess, won the first heat, making tiny circles and revolving slowly to the heat of the men. A local favorite, Cherry Chiffon, won the second round. Corrine's hula hoop twirled to the ground after two others also failed, a respectful showing. Then, it was a surprising Serenity Jade in the third heat winning, her husband Brian whooping loudly.

And lastly, little Marie Bella Rose out lasted her competition. Now warmed up, the Dolls prepared for the faceoff. Violet won easily. The hoop formed around her like a planet in its orbit about a heavenly body. She showed off after Serenity Jade finally tired, taking another hoop around an ankle and twirled two hulas like the former dancer she was, being awarded a princess crown as Miss Hula Honey.

Best makeup and dress was awarded to Miss Holly Hot Rod. Someone shouted, "Fuck yeah!" Probably Owen. It was another princess tiara for a recent queen.

Another local "Brazen Beauties" member, Katastrophic, won Miss Classy Chassis. Her first princess win.

Then came the title of Miss Delectable Delight, the people's choice, the runner up to the Queen of this day. After the ruffling of papers, adding to the suspense greatly, the president of the co-sponsoring club spoke with true glee into the microphone.

"There's a new princess in the Pin Up world, and to our own, with the most votes from everyone today, she's a real tasty treat: Miss Crème De Menthe!"

Corrine cupped her hands over her face and shook with surprise and glee. Miss Demeanor placed the tiara upon her curls and the genuine applause reached its highest point in the Dolls' presentation. She cried a little and stepped back amongst her friends, multiple hands grasping her shoulders. Serenity Jade and Holly Hot Rod gave her big hugs.

The interview portion of the selection process was secret. The crowns had already been purchased and spreading out the recognition was very important from an organizational point of view. One question asked concerned each Doll's commitment and support of the charity the club donated to.

Only Donna and the treasurer talked to each Doll during the interview. A $750 private donation nearly doubled the club's contribution to the Pediatric Brain Cancer Foundation, and Miss Daisy Lane from Portland was crowned Miss South Sound Sally.

The gearheads peeled out as their cars and motorcycles didn't win their classes. The men spoke later with envy of the winners, like their work was as a rare jewel, expense knowing no bounds. Winning was a sign or symbol of a man who had passed beyond the need for the comfort of a woman, not needing to keep a job or pay his insurance. He could spend his money and work toward happiness as he wished. Many gearheads idled their cars off the grounds going slow, taking their time.

...

The pageant and show broke down quickly. Awnings were stowed and coolers were drained. Corrine was elated and her feet hurt, mightily. Her new beau asked if she knew of a good Italian restaurant nearby and in an exhaustive acceptance the fading Miss De Menthe, a crowned princess for the first time, warned that it, "might be pricey." Then she added, "I can't stay late. I have to let my dog out of her crate. She hasn't been house broken for very long."

Peter, with a thirst and heat from having been in the sun all day, chasing a beautiful and confident woman, replied, "Well, that must mean that it's good."

They met a few blocks away and he thought she'd want the air conditioning rather than the patio beside the road. But Princess De Menthe merely needed to sit alfresco, and as the cool of the nearing evening became a marvelous treat, he tucked in her chair. A princess!

She quickly texted and responded to texts as Peter found the restroom and was reminded of a lesson from Sunday school. Back in his element, Peter ordered a pitcher of icy water, a dark beer, and upon her final decision for a Woo Woo peach cocktail with vodka and a sprig of mint, he asked Corrine if she liked calamari.

It definitely wasn't a cheap date, but this day was getting as good as it just might be.

"Ohh yeah," the princess assented. He ordered muscles, too.

The waiter brought fresh bread with olive oil and balsamic vinegar with garlic and marjoram to dip it into. He tore into it first, hungry, then their glasses filled with ice water, and a pitcher itself.

Alone on the patio, Peter took two cloth napkins from nearby table settings, plunging one into the cold water. He took her left foot, let loose the pink strapped shoe, and slowly washed her sole and ankle coolly. It sent her nerves reeling, the soft tissue back from swelling, tickling marvelously. Then, after a long minute, he carefully dried her foot, blowing on her toes and asking, "How does that feel?"

Everything seemed bittersweet to Corrine at the moment, a loving little boy constantly jostled, spun around and lied to; a tiara flashing fake jewels was the greatest prize she'd ever won; a man she loved as a great friend, left her with a horrifying death scene, a great guy she just met who would never stay long enough to love.

"Now order something worthy of a princess. Not like the shrimp scampi. I'll probably get the sea bass." Her right foot was itchingly next as Corrine wasn't shy by offering it, the shoe already dismissed.

"Who is the guy with the goatee? The tall guy with the cowboy hat."

"You mean Owen."

"Yeah! He's the one married to the Japanese woman. Hot Rod. . .something?"

Like de-masking at the costume ball, at only the right moment did Peter get to know who these women were with the fashioned new identities. Who was Corrine De Menthe? There were a thousand stupid questions he wanted to ask her. The serious ones would come soon enough, no need to rush.

Corrine sat barefoot as the appetizers were vanquished. The last two muscles in white wine and garlic sauce were argued over, both in favor of the other getting the last taste. They both liked the sauce that came with the calamari: an olive oil base with roasted red pepper, basil, and red wine, not to mention more garlic and black pepper.

The waiter served Corrine her Dungeness crab and scallops while Peter picked the Cioppino, which was a tomato-based seafood stew with scallops, salmon, halibut, clams, and shrimp with fresh thyme and roasted garlic.

"Save room for the tiramisu. And please don't be one of these girls who doesn't get a desert but then I do and then I decide to share out of guilt."

Playing the coquette again, Corrine leaned forward, careful not to get her boobs in her food. "You wouldn't share with me?"

Wiping his mouth, buying time, Peter gentlemanly asked her how her dinner was, specifically the scallops. "When I find my scallops in the stew, I'll share those with you. Don't like them. They have the consistency of pencil erasures." He met her eyes with his and slowly said, "But I won't share my tiramisu, you're on your own." He paused and with all seriousness asked his date, "So, who is Corrine De Menthe?"

Although she playfully glared at him, he had to ask about her alter-ego. "Ever have a grasshopper before?"

"You mean like eating a bug?" He knew she meant the drink.

"Nooo. Like the dessert cocktail, with mint and chocolate. Very sweet and creamy, like me." Having Crème de Menthe as an ingredient went without saying so.

The tiara had now become a little crooked on her curls. She kept the Miss Delectable Delight sash on, across her huge chest during their fantastic meal. It lunged toward him with every deep breath she took. Her fashioned identity was flirtier than when the dress came off.

"So, you are Miss Delectable Delight now?"

"Only when I wear the sash."

Peter sipped his second beer. "Can I wear your tiara?"

Corrine asked, "Are you a princess?"

"No."

"Does that answer your question?" The girl was quick.

They talked about her son. He reiterated his transient circumstance. She told him she was twenty-nine, while he was thirty-two.

Tiramisu, a crème brulee tart with strawberries and blueberries, strong coffee, and a grasshopper (they both had some sips) topped off a celebratory meal for a brand-new princess. Corrine had brought up Ryan's suicide as Peter was curious about how Delmonica was her "fake cousin" and he had commented about how cool the '70 Chevy Nova was. She omitted being present when he put the barrel of the weapon under his chin.

The waiter brought the check and Peter slipped his debit card into the protector without looking at the bill. Instead, he kept his gaze on Corrine and asked her, "What are you doing tomorrow?" He guessed correctly that the kid handoff wouldn't happen until Sunday evening and that she might be free. "When's the last time you saw a non-kid movie? We could catch a matinee. You pick the flick." It was unimagined that a theater would be closed.

"I don't know what's going on yet tomorrow. . ." she replied.

But that was a fib. She would sleep as late as the pup would allow before nuzzling her awake. Cassie was big enough now to jump up onto her bed. She had taken Cory to see "The Incredibles 2", "Paddington 2" and the new "Grinch" movie with Benedict Cumberbatch starring.

She could say she'd be enjoying the peace and quiet, but after cleaning the house after her tornado of getting pageant ready and arranging her princess tiara and "Miss Delectable Delight" sash on her dresser and headboard, missing her little man terrible would set in before noon as it usually did. That's when she worried under what circumstances her child made his elfish way through Evan's parent's messy house. She bought the original Grinch movie at Costco and Cory watched it going on twenty times without any loss of thrill.

Peter tipped high, rounding up as he did and quickly handed the protector back to the waiter. It was essential this worker was appreciated.

He was somewhat deflated that his attempt at a second date had seemingly missed the mark. Perhaps it was too much, too soon, and seemed like a desperation move. Peter held her hand up and removed her chair slightly as the princess arose, excusing herself while she availed herself of the lady's room.

It's never going to amount to anything, no pressure, Corrine thought. It'd been a long time since she had been embraced and kissed.

The poor forlorn fool perked up when she asked, now on the sidewalk. "What're your plans tomorrow?"

"The Sunday paper, finding service somewhere…" He paused, looking at her in a cheeky way. "Buying us the big tub of popcorn."

"I'll buy the popcorn," she said.

Nothing like this had ever happened to her before. A passionate man. A fabulous win. After the meal they departed without even a kiss. Her body felt like jelly.

He fretted since Seattle wasn't his home. In a few months, he'd be sent away from a really cool chick. Peter pointed the nose of the company truck toward the Extended Stay.

9
The Eagles Club

Paula Kasdorf practically ran the Eagles Club in Black Diamond. She sat at the end of the bar and waited on the few retirees to filter throughout the day. If they wanted a burger or chicken tenders or a pizza she would shuffle behind the bar using her cane until needing both hands. She washed them in the three-compartment sink, leaning her bulk into the stainless steel, rolled rim edge.

Cooking with a microwave was cheating, but if members dared complain, they knew from experience at previous club meetings that their grousing would be met with an angry, "Well, then, you get your fat, wrinkled ass behind the bar!"

Meetings were fun, and Paula did okay with tips. It was voted to pay part time employees slightly more than minimum wage. She was also the manager of all social events.

If a non-member stumbled in looking for a brew on a hot summer day, they would pay full price (like a normal bar) and could fill out a membership application, writing an address down on the back, just in order to get served.

Maybe Paula would send an applicant a flier, and maybe she wouldn't. Maybe she'd give you the member discount if she liked the way you looked. Scumbags and tweakers got lousy service. The small tappers were only a buck for a cold Rainer. She just hoped she didn't have to fuck with the beer barrels, as her knees were as shot as her hips. God forbid some townie wanted a Guinness.

The Eagles Club supported food pantries and putting shoes on poor kids. Since Ryan had been a long-time member, Tiffany requested a break on the price of the hall. Paula got that phone call two days after he died.

Dialing Corrine, her geographical mother Paula related an awkward conversation. "Hi, honey. Long time no talk." She didn't know if her surrogate daughter knew this Tiffany person. Although she and Ryan came in frequently, back in the days they humped Pepsi together, Paula couldn't remember Ryan ever coming in with any other girl but Corrine. It was as if they had both adopted her.

"Sure, I know the bitch. What does she want? Rent the hall for nothing?" Corrine was busy at work making the logistical chain move aerospace parts as seamlessly as possible. Getting a call from "Ma" anytime was a treat. Paula didn't text and wasn't a chatty Cathy in the evenings. It was always best to go see her. She and Paula taught Cory about giving and compassion as he hauled small bags of canned goods into the hall when the Eagles had a food drive.

Paula was sort of shocked by Tiffany's request, but also sort of not. "Well, she wanted to know about the member benefits, since he'd died." Her voice was a bit gravelly, and she exhaled the smoke within her lungs. With so few customers, she often smoked at the end of the bar nearest a window. It was better than going outside and missing an opportunity to keep the tappers coming.

"I knew he shot himself from guys coming in," Paula continued. "I'm sorry, babe."

"When did you talk to her?" Corrine asked.

"She called again today. Sort of forgot about it. His only daughter is almost eighteen anyway. So no benefits. She tried to argue about getting the club to help with funeral expenses, getting really pushy."

"So what did you tell her?" Corrine stopped reading email, her attention at full peak now.

"I told her the club doesn't do that. Then she came back with she knew that veterans and firefighters who died got help, so why not Ryan? It was a big pity party, and the woe-is me drama about family and how she has no money. Eventually I had to cut her off and told her she could book the hall in two weeks, on a Saturday for 250 bucks. Otherwise, it'd be another month. Unless she wanted to do it during the week. That's half the usual. And then right away she wanted to put her Go Fund Me info on our website, so I guess I'll get the tech guy to do that today."

"Did you get a deposit?" Corrine questioned worriedly. "She won't pay unless you make her."

"Shit, I forgot," Paula sighed. "Just wanted to get the fuck off of the phone."

"Hey Ma, I'm buried here at work. Let's touch base again soon."

"You go, darlin'. Talk soon." After flipping her phone closed, Paula waddled up to a member and, without being asked, got him another cold one, turned around, and went outside to smoke another cigarette. In her mind, she practiced the phone conversation with Tiffany, the one she was going to have in a few minutes.

It was time to demand a deposit of $125 to hold the date. She bet that the poor woman would stiff the charitable organization out of the balance. But Paula could wring her titty now, before she got nothing but embarrassment from the rest of the Eagles Club Aerie.

Corrine called her back quickly, to warn about the Go Fund Me thing; she suspected that Tiffany would pillage any money that came into it. And more possibly bring embarrassment to the club. Of course, Corrine was a member, too.

...

Date number two didn't allow for a play for second base. She kissed him herself before leaving the bar he liked to frequent. The white halter tank top was tied around Miss Demeanor's slight neck. The boys could see glances of her pierced navel as she moved about, sizing up angles, and bringing her body down to the table.

Two chrome rails punctured her in-ee bellybutton and was held by two stainless bulbs in a vertical stroke. She swam her way past her date like a shark, demonstrating the different bridging styles: open, closed, rail, elevated, and mechanical, as she practiced her stop shots with other men who wanted to play.

It was just enough to show off in front of his friends. Aleia had learned how to handle men using her beauty. There were none to come to her defense when she was coming to age in north Georgia. Aleia left the accent behind and got as far as she could away, to the Pacific Northwest.

Her cut off jean shorts and desert colored Jamie cowgirl boots completed the ensemble. After the brake job date, hanging out merely at his place wasn't on her agenda; using his truck and his back was. She won a few games then said she was bored and preferred to get a little drunk with her new beau.

The bar food was okay, but the Pin Up never opened her wallet. This one was a gentleman. Hustling for her supper had always kept her skinny, paying for shelter being her primary goal. She lost track of most relations, they coming in and out of jail or rehab.

When the hook was set, or typically the boy just swallowed it, the excitement invariably led to questions about plans for tomorrow.

"I told you, silly, I'm moving my junk from my old storage."

Aleia had paid the arrears in cash and only had a week to vacate the eight by ten space.

Several pageant contestants weren't recorded as having paid, although they actually had. In the attendance log they were given credit for participation. It was doubtful that the befuddled Donna would cross reference. The receipt for a cash deposit into the Dolls' account was made the day after South Sound Sally.

Cash helped to persuade the manager of the You-Store-It to remove his secondary lock as she plopped down over 300 bucks. The only satisfaction was telling the fuck that she'd have her stuff out in a week.

"Okay, good." It was really a favor to him. She didn't need to be snarky about it.

It was damn near seventy-five miles from one storage container to the next. "I'm going to have to throw some of my crap away, like an old TV." They packed her Civic, then Aleia decided what she no longer needed, like old bedding and the cutest baby clothes. While the boyfriend moved new junk into the bed of his truck he asked where they were going to throw it.

"I'll show you." And after a big hug and a thank you, Miss Demeanor led him to the dumpster at an Assisted Living facility two blocks away that she had scoped out earlier. Before he even had the chance to object, she jumped out, opened the black cover of the dumpster, and threw a box into it.

They both lifted the TV out, followed by more boxes and an old bassinet. Jumping back in after less than a minute, he pulled out smartly and she excitedly exclaimed, "Our first crime!" smiling ear to ear.

Aleia gripped his shoulder with glee, sliding over and resting her head on his chest only for a moment. She only gave him a kiss on his cheek. God, she wanted to grab his cock out of his jeans and find out! Girls always look, denim hiding possibilities.

Without ever having the true comfort of a woman, her gearhead worked all day toward a storage bin, then followed her to a trailer where another man still paid a bank note. A stop for a fifth of whiskey and a frozen pizza and the two new lovers had their pathetic space.

As the A.C. engaged, Aleia couldn't help bringing out pictures of her son from portfolios and cry just a little, showing off proudly to her new friend. She told him how her other "friend" would come into the trailer unannounced (the truth) and that she paid rent to stay there (a lie). Injustices sought pity, perhaps.

He was superstitious and thought to leave, but brushed his teeth with his finger, gargled, peed, and came back out before some blues mojo that Aleia had stirred up. She placed the oven to bake. They both smoked from the stubby bong and giggled and giggled. Taking off her top while making out was so easy. In the middle of the song, the base singer asked, "somebody help me? Tell me, baby, what you want me to do."

They both heard the next lyric, but Miss Demeanor repeated it.

She made him hard as nails without much coaxing. All it took was some rubbing before unbuttoning and unzipping. Miss Demeanor's conquest relaxed, then requested, "take off my boots."

He played her like a violin, like the skilled tradesman that he was. The pressure built, tasting like the warm water of a freshwater lake jumped into headfirst. They bounced about into different positions, the trailer itself squeaked on its springs.

...

"I have a buddy who wants to volunteer to bring the stuff to the food pantry," Corrine informed Paula. "You said the club's ready for another haul?"

It was an ongoing task at this Aerie of the Eagles, or the high nest of a bird of prey, to give back to the community. Members accumulated a pantry worth of dry and canned goods until the space needed to be cleared out and brought to a local food bank.

Men told their wives, "I'm going to drop off a donation at the club," which actually meant he'd place a jumbo pack of diapers on a shelf then bask in the good karma while having a few brews with Paula and whomever else was donating.

Boredom made Peter a bit bold, and when Corrine said that she and Cory were going to help out at the Eagles Club he volunteered his truck and his back. He was all for good karma anyway, and also getting to spend time with her two weekends in a row. Meeting the kid was a bonus. Peter liked kids. Playing with cousins ten years younger than him was fun at family gatherings, not an obligation. As a grown man he had enough brains to realize building with Legos on the floor brought him back to being seven. But you needed a kid to have the excuse to do it; otherwise, it'd be weird, a grown man playing with Legos.

"Yeah, we're starting to overflow." Ma took the last few drags off her cigarette while asking Corrine about the little one. Paula snuffed it out with the end of her cane and limped back inside.

"He's going to drive me nuts if I have to watch 'Toy Story' one more time." She waited until after Paula's husky laugh turned into gasping, rasping coughs, to continue. "He loves to help. What time can we show up on Saturday?"

"Oh, I guess I'll open around ten. There's a lot of stuff. I'll get some more people over to help." The matron of the Black Diamond Aerie was either at the club or in her trailer a mile away. At sixty-six, she'd be sunk without Medicare and Social Security. While her husband was still alive, taking care of the house and property was doable, but when he was confined to a wheelchair after getting a foot amputated at the VA due to infections in his toes, the place became too much.

She could drive him to appointments, but the last surgery to amputate above the knee landed him in rehab from which he never left, just straight to hospice in another wing. So, she sold everything and consolidated, not needing much around her anymore except the members of the Eagle's Club. She didn't own the land under the trailer she bought out right. Their home had been paid off a dozen years before. Her son lived in Daytona. Three thousand miles away, he'd call her on her birthday.

Recognizing Peter's company truck, Corrine pulled alongside and pushed the button for the passenger's window to roll down. Big drops of rain ran off the glass from the seal, and she said to Peter, "good thing we both have caps. I'm gonna put my ass end up toward the back door."

Wearing a big smile, he responded with, "sounds good." Why did she say that? he thought. Calling Dr. Freud.

She got the jumpy puppy on her leash before releasing her son. Cory ambled out quickly to glom onto his dog, who was too busy sniffing a cacophony of smells, none pleasant or foul for her. They just told a wet, worldly story of old pee getting washed away and plants that were open to the rare summer shower. She ignored her little best friend, too excited to find the perfect place to poo.

"Who's more trouble?" Peter asked.

"My son listens to me, so I guess the dog." The leash wrapped around a tree and the creature was stuck. Corrine had to unwrap the leash at the loop. "Come on, Stup-o," she laughed affectionately.

Without waiting, Peter introduced himself. The kid was looking at him with one eye squinting closed like he was looking at the sun. "Hi, Cory. I'm Peter." And he put his fist out and the kid gave him a bump. "What's the name of your dog?"

"Cassie." The boy had straight straw brown hair and full lips, much like his mother.

"Sounds like Lassie. You ever hear about a famous dog named Lassie?"

"No." Average in height for his age and thin, his jeans had a stretchable waistband to facilitate going. An innovation the grown man wish he could duplicate. Cory's little blue plaid shirt had a fifth of the material needed to cover Peter's upper body. He was jealous of the Velcro strapped sneakers as well, anything to make life easier.

"Yeah, why would you? You're almost five, right? Your mom told me."

The boy sort of shrugged when Corrine chimed in, "Cory, go show Peter where the food is." They turned to leave the sprinkles outside. None too soon, as she was about to cover her hand with a bag to pick up after her pet, something of a private moment. That had occurred to Peter as well. Watching a pretty girl pick up poo kind of killed the dream.

Cory strode in with an easy confidence since he'd done this before. "Hi Grandma Paula," the imp waved when he saw her from thirty feet away. She ambled quickly to the affable kid, turning on the pantry light. She was excited to see Cory. And who was the young man with him?

There was a lot of stuff, folded up boxes that had several layers of old tape on them. This was going to take a while. When Paula got closer Peter introduced himself as Corrine's friend.

"Where's the tape, Grandma Paula? We have to make the boxes?" He really didn't like her kissing him because she smelled smokey. But she did anyway.

"Where's your mom?"

"Outside with Cassie."

"Lassie? Oh, she brought the dog. We don't allow pets in here."

Looking through a few cabinets she found packing and duct tape while Corrine came in alone, leaving her brown Labradoodle in the truck, hopefully not chewing on something in nervousness.

All business, Peter asked Cory how they should make the boxes. The young man started to give directions on how to do it. He'd hold the box together and Peter would put the first piece of tape on. Then he'd pull the next piece out and rip it, handing it to the kid, 'cause putting the tape down was the fun part. The stickiness of it on little hands overcame Cory a few times, but he got better.

Peter said patiently, "keep practicing, kid." And Cory got the hang of keeping the tape straight and not sticking to itself. In fact, Peter referred to him as "kid" throughout the morning.

Corrine watched the boys prepare and asked Paula how she was doing, since she looked pretty haggard. "Don't know which hurts more, the hip or my knee. My doctor said I should get a knee replacement."

"Are you going to?"

"When am I going to do that? Be on my back for two months."

"I'd help you out, Ma. You know that."

Paula had held her hand when she left her bozo impregnator, when she was diagnosed with Lupus, and she voted for her at pageants. She knew Corrine would help. But Paula hated the idea of being a burden. The Eagles would help for sure, as good as men could. Corrine tried to convince her more, but money didn't grow on trees and she needed to continue to work.

"How many people did Tiffany say were going to be here for Ryan's memorial?"

"Said she's bringing stuff for a hundred, with the potluck, hopefully. The Go Fund Me she said would pay for the food."

"Say, not to interrupt, but I think we're ready to start putting stuff into the boxes." Peter glanced back into the walk-in pantry. "What do you think, kid?"

"There's a lot of stuff." He said. Probably two trips worth with both trucks. The young transient man had nothing worthwhile to do other than this. It was some work in order to deserve an early brew. Paula usually took a short glass to sip on along with the first "customer" of the day.

"Is there anything we shouldn't take?" The short answer was no. Peter put boxes on the floor and Cory filled them with everything he could reach. "Don't make it too heavy, kid."

The kid didn't quite understand, but Corrine got into the flow with them packing and Peter humping it into the trucks. The splatter of great big drops soaked his weathered ballcap. The second trip went faster as they had fewer boxes to fill. The community food pantry gave them more used boxes to return with. In three hours, the Eagles Club larder was as emptied as it was gonna get.

Peter gave Cory a little first bump after his mom strapped him in. They had their own shopping to do.

The tot waved to Peter and said, "see you later, kid." Peter smirked. Cory was funny just like his mother.

He was about to leave, the motor started, when he realized he wanted to have a brew with Paula. She pumped him for information and slowly he learned a lot about Corrine.

...

The mere idea of attending Ryan's memorial was repellant to Peter. Not exactly third date type material. He'd already inserted himself into Corrine's life with big strides. It sounded like the proverbial shit show with a room full of mourning strangers.

The big hall got stuffy in a hurry as the exterior doors were propped open, but there weren't fans to push air along in the Pacific Northwest's pragmatic approach to air conditioning. The commercial stove and ovens raised the temperature along with a throng of folks. Most of them filed past Tiffany, who'd helped slightly along with Delmonica to make picture laden storyboards of a man's life. She was playing the part of a grieving widow holding out a begging bag. There was a prominent display advertising the Go Fund Me site. The serving table was forty feet long with multiple crock pots plugged into surge protectors.

It was Evan's weekend to have Cory. His mom commiserated with fellow Club members. Garbage cans overflowed with paper plates and bowls of half-eaten chili and the remnants of veggie platters. Holly Hot Rod came to support her friend, leaving Demarco and Owen to tend to an infant while watching college football. Serenity Jade, aka Kimmy, held her husband's hand fast until he picked up the microphone to begin the memorial after the working-class feast.

Brian spoke slowly, nervously, thanking everyone for attending, trying not to allow his voice to quiver although it did through the fantastic strain. He mentioned Ryan's only child Delmonica, and how much her dad had loved her.

Both of their parents were dead. He sounded like a man alone in his grief. How Ryan would have loved being a grandpa. The loss of a man defeated reverberated amongst the Eagles and their spouses, until overcome, Brian lost the ability to speak. Tiffany rescued the thread and the microphone, thanking Ryan's brother, a man she never liked.

She asked for donations and if anyone else would like to speak. Two or three people entered the queue to include Jack, Delmonica's now husband.

Without script, several friends related short remembrances. Some were even funny.

"He used to call me Jackass when we worked on the Nova," he began. Jack showed off Ryan's winning plaque. "I wish he could have been at the courthouse when I married his daughter." His suicide was like embracing the burner of a hot stove with the flat on your hand. Everyone's ignorance of pain was palpable. The truth brushed beneath remembrances.

Corrine took the microphone while placing Ryan's Carhartt brown, very worn coat over her shoulders. "Ryan adopted me when I first came into town." She turned toward Tiffany. "I took this coat the day after he died to remember him by. He wore it every day we humped Pepsi." The mock widow wasn't going to get everything Ryan found valuable. The statement placed Corrine at the violent place. "He showed me the ropes and brought me to this Eagles club."

Members stirred in appreciation. "I was never his girlfriend. He was more like a big brother. I will remember him always. He had his faults, but he took care of those he loved."

Another dig at the imposter Tiffany. The bar room brawls became excused. The coat was one thing that the bitch wasn't going to get. "When I told him that I had Lupus, Ryan called me every other day to see if I was alright. When Paula encouraged me when I wanted to do Pin Up, Ryan encouraged me, too. Delmonica, my heart goes out to you. Your dad was awesome. A man I will always love. I am keeping the coat, no matter what anybody says. It'll keep me warm in remembrance." The crowd clapped for a long time. Some were certain that enemies had been provoked.

Paula clapped loud. Ryan was her friend, too. She knew how his end was inflamed.

10
Escape Room

The air tasted like a chalky haze during those midsummer weeks. Ill-managed undergrowth caused forest fires in California, combined with those of the Pacific Northwest, making it feel like one was breathing through a surgical mask.

If only a storm would come and knock the smoke from the atmosphere and send the carbon cycling back into the ocean. That might ease temporary human discomfort. Temps reached the 80s in Seattle, maybe touching ninety to remind everyone that summer yet swayed dry. The sunsets at the Extended Stay, and sunrises at JCPenney (one mile away), were a spectacular, fiery red through a hot fog. They allowed Peter to peer into the sun for more than a moment.

Chasing the painters around pointing out lousy work and adapting to the manager's Honey Do List became routine. The schedule slipped with added demands. When Peter would be ordered back to his family's farm in central Wisconsin, back to his prized guernsey goat Braveheart, was unknown. The budget was the bailiwick of project managers; he kept his hours as close to forty as possible, while avoiding free overtime as much as he could. The afternoons, evenings, and weekends were a lonesome warfare. Exploration by himself was dull until he had to pursue a girl, no matter what the recriminations from a life without plan.

Breaking into Corrine's life wasn't going to be easy. He wondered if he even should. Peter didn't pray about it but made sure that Sunday service was sacrosanct on the road, just to keep himself feeling properly grounded in a truth.

"Just wanting to hang out with someone," was an uneasy lie. But she returned his phone calls sometimes, in the evenings. He tried to remember previous tidbits, not slurring his words after consuming a six-pack or smoking a bowl. The real goal was trying not to reveal that he knew about her struggles with Lupus and an evil ex, info from her surrogate mother Paula.

Smart, funny, and she'd been run through the wringer. Corrine had an alter ego and had been hung out to dry. Her friend committing suicide before her was a depth of knowledge, weighty responsibility. That kind of hurt did not confuse Peter, but instead piqued his curiosity and helped him endure the effort to get closer. He was strangely unafraid.

And the kid was cute. An automatic family? With a pup, too? Playing catch, picking up poop, and reading to a young cousin nestled beside him were things Peter had done happily before. With exception to poop.

Her schedule was crammed. So why was she giving him the time of day? He came clean on the next dinner date the following weekend about what Paula had told him, between pageants, when the boy was with his dad.

Peter didn't really think about the need to be loved, except getting that Corrine received such from her "little man". His need to love someone superseded caution and practical circumstance. It was clearly the way a man may think, both generous and self-serving simultaneously.

He peered into a slightly subdued sun, conscious of others' struggles but focused mainly upon his own.

...

The management of the radio station where Owen worked planned a team building exercise for their employees. The corporation that owned it and a few other stations within the same building had sponsored seminars to lead leaders to such ends, along with topics like conflict de-escalation, identity tolerance, and resilience. These things were stuff to ponder, perception becoming reality, paths out of escape rooms, but mostly concrete ideas to assist improving work environments, an honorable mission.

It was the general manager for the Seattle based conglomerate who had the budget to wile away a half-day of pay for her employees to play, and maybe learn something. But it was sketchy. The hardest part was scheduling, in order to maximize participation. Non-participation meant not towing the company line, a potential black mark upon an annual review instead of a check mark for being a good cog within the machine, or otherwise a discordant note.

It seemed like bullshit to some, but at the end of the day, the escape room had lessons to be learned. Juvenile resentment for what most felt was a "waste of time" was typically changed to optimism and a positive end of exercise review for the company that crafted expensively a notion for a team, a soft competition.

On the appointed day, radio engineers (like Owen), ad women, receptionists, on-air personalities, interns, and senior staff met at an address in downtown Seattle, a neighborhood called South Lake Union. After gathering personnel into a classroom and a brief PowerPoint overview, the teams were imprisoned temporarily within very tight partitions, overfilling to eliminate private space, an antithesis of social distancing for effect. Competitive lines between radio stations were drawn, and quickly Owen and his co-workers were forced into narrow pathways like the confines of an old-fashioned phone booth stuffed with coeds.

Within fake fashioned stone walls, recorded audio directed an immediate puzzle. Stuffed participants tried not to touch each other while shuffling between touch screens and drawers to be opened for clues. Books on bookshelves were props that needed to be removed before a door opened past a tiny vestibule that was now filled with ten people breathing in viruses and luncheon breath.

Onto another small maze, Owen and his co-workers faced stations and wired props like battle axes and floating lights to work together. The time limit was one hour and the team that escaped first won. There was a way out. There was a solution. One room led to another. But time was running out. What if you had to pee?

The team had to rely on the competence of each other. No one could get through this alone. Everybody focused. Unmerited favor only, would relieve the tension, and spring forth the exit door. At the end of an hour? Owen's team couldn't conclude the clues within the compressed dioramas fast enough, and the experience was over.

A wrap up after bathroom breaks attempted to draw out past simple experience, to establish a team building takeaway. Those thought to be idiots showed themselves to be insightful. Funny people were cohesive. Everyone was glad to be unconfined. Connected people got a beer together afterward, while others afraid of traffic immediately spilt.

...

Club 309 Mercer, in South Lake Union, was a popular place for people of color; a few "white" girls of European descent, whose boyfriends only had one dance move, got left home. Demarco didn't need old man Owen to chime in, "always go where the girls go," when he had asked his mother to watch Tamah so he could go out with his friends that night.

It wasn't a needed vote, but a simple assent that fell into instant silence. The young man was working, paying a little rent, and was respectful of her house rules, mostly. Since getting out of the County Jail, he'd seemingly reconciled enough with the woman he knocked up, Kaelani, with monetary support. Demarco wasn't perfect, but he was trying, a true sign of repentance not unnoticed by Audrey. Going out late was but a slight violation of his parole, and a big trust/ opportunity to love a tiny life personally.

Putting the baby down was easy at an infant's age. Demarco fed and changed his son before his friend picked him up, rubbing his son's back until Tamah was fast asleep by 7PM.

A big crowd gathered outside the nightclub doors near closing time. Bouncers mostly kept the peace. Twenty or so party goers mingled boisterously, figuring out what was next. Guys and Dolls playfully argued, some too buzzed and relying on reluctant rides. One couple was kissing, mock tough guys were fighting, and girls were still flirting with fellas they may see again. They churned together still on a dance floor in their youngish minds with the musical beat barely audible outside the club.

The rhythm was disturbed by a single wheel gun's shot from an angry man. The bullet crashed just below Demarco's left cheek bone and exited out the back of his neck. A strange angle, but his head was down, laughing at someone's joke. The shockwave and loud report sent the crowd running in a panic like a compressed spring, leaving an empty ring around Demarco, his heart still pumping blood. The murderer was never identified.

The cops showed up just before the ambulance seven minutes later. Those still present wouldn't aid the half-hearted investigation. Unconscious, Demarco would never be asked about his last regret, even if he had thought to have one at twenty-one years of age.

The caller ID said "Unidentified" the first time it buzzed Audrey's cell phone on the bed stand. The second time she squinted at the smartphone screen, five minutes later. "Hello," she answered groggily.

"THIS IS THIS THE KING COUNTY SHERIFF'S DEPARTMENT. IS THIS AUDREY...?"

"It is," she croaked, still gaining consciousness.

"MA'AM, IS YOUR SON DEMARCO...?"

"He is."

"MA'AM, YOUR SON HAS BEEN INVOLVED IN A SHOOTING IN SOUTH LAKE UNION AND HAS BEEN TRANSPORTED TO..."

The name of the hospital etched itself permanently into her mind.

"What? What happened? What's going on?" Owen stirred beside her, not quite completely awake. It was 2 AM.

"MA'AM, WE'RE ASKING YOU TO CONTACT THE HOSPITAL RIGHT AWAY. I CAN GIVE YOU THE EMERGENCY ROOM NUMBER WHEN YOU'RE READY."

Audrey's feet hit the floor. "Did he shoot someone? Is he under arrest?"

Owen snapped into wakefulness hearing this. The baby monitor was quite still.

"MA'AM, YOUR SON HAS BEEN INJURED. HE'S NOT UNDER ARREST. DO YOU WANT ME TO GIVE YOU THE PHONE NUMBER OF THE EMERGENCY ROOM WHERE HE HAS BEEN TRANSPORTED?"

"Wait. Wait. Yes." Audrey slipped from the bed, turned on the overhead light, then sped to the kitchen to find a post-it note and pen. Her boyfriend slipped on shorts and was behind her in only five seconds to hear her say, "Okay, I'm here. What's the number?"

Owen croaked, "Babe, what's going on?" He reached out with a hand to touch her shoulder. She drew away, repulsively, an act he'd feel for weeks to come when he tried to contact her.

"What's the number? What's the number?"

All she knew was that Demarco was dying. An argument ensued. Owen stayed with the baby. His love drove off into the city to claim a corpse. Ninety minutes later, she picked up his second call, hysterical. "He's dead! My only son is dead!"

"Wait, sweetie," Owen insisted, barely understanding her words. "Wait!"

"He's dead, Owen. He's dead!"

"What? What?" In the intervening conversation, unanswerable questions passed between the two, until a nurse and a deputy intervened. Three more phone calls occurred before 6AM Sunday, before Owen's imploring for her to come home sank in and Audrey drove like a zombie.

Tamah stirred, pooped his diaper, and Owen cooed while holding baby ankles, wiping, tears falling from his nose. The youngster was awake, ready for the day. Owen would call in sick in a few minutes. But before that, he held the child closely singing "Hotel California" as a lullaby. But the infant wanted to eat, so to soothe him Owen prepared a bottle quickly. From observation, he adequately, soothingly, for a moment even successfully, made it happen.

Audrey parked erratically without pause. The moment she got inside, she clutched her grandson from the bassinet, although the kid laid peaceably. Bringing Tamah to her, Owen sort of grabbed her shoulder just to have his woman pull away yet again. "Did he eat?"

Owen stepped back and replied, "Yeah. Absolutely. He's dry."

With that she turned toward her man, baby in her neck, deepening circles beneath her eyes. Exhaustion was prevalent and she kept crying, which made the baby cry, too.

"Let me take him," Owen suggested. "You're upset."

"UPSET?" Audrey shouted in the doublewide. "MY SON IS DEAD!"

The dogs cowered.

"Let me call someone." Owen pulled the baby away. "Sit! Drink some water! There's no reason to yell." His frustration reared ugly for a moment. His voice pitched, too, and Tamah kept whimpering. He sat on the couch and rocked the child. All Audrey could do was watch.

Audrey wouldn't sit beside him. She took the baby back, then sat in the same place he'd warmed as he nervously began to pace. Owen toasted some English muffins, spread butter and black berry jam onto them, and presented the plate to his love with a tall glass of orange juice, stating forcefully, "we need you to say in the game. Take the nourishment."

Corrine's VM picked up, then Owen texted her in all caps: "EMERGENCY. DEATH IN THE FAMILY. PLEASE CALL AUDREY. HURRY". Surely, Kaelani would be calling soon. Why Corrine was the only one he contacted then was a mystery, though also instinctual. He was by himself with a woman beside herself, getting stonier by the moment, not answering, unable to respond to basic questions like, "give me the baby", "go to the bathroom", and "refresh yourself." Her glare was like peering into a casket.

He put on the radio and instantly Audrey shouted, "Turn that shit off!"

The silence felt like the core the bullet bore through Demarco's brain. The dogs needed to go outside, and Owen felt reprieve in that moment just to let them go pee and poop in the early morning light.

He stepped out from the screen door and prayed. He was plenty scared and told the Creator Being that he didn't understand what was happening, asking Her to be with his woman right now. What had been a little family, a chance for redemption, was a rotten floor he'd fallen through, again. Tears rolled down his cheeks and he followed an instruction, sat beside his woman, and let his sadness flow vigorously, silently.

Until Audrey said quietly, "you should let the dogs in."

Her cell phone rang and Owen picked it up, walking into the bedroom to share the awful news. Corrine had wheels spinning toward Audrey in twenty minutes, unencumbered by little man that weekend, making a mental note to break a date with Peter to see a movie.

Kaelani called Audrey for the first time, stating she was enroute to get her son. Demarco's death was a footnote in an abbreviated conversation.

Corrine barely knocked then entered the home she knew so well to see forlorn faces freshly and continuously wiped with Kleenex. Nobody wanted Audrey and Owen then, but she did. She placed herself so as to peer into pure baby brown eyes when the Devil came moments later to claim a life.

They all stood as Owen opened the door. Tamah's mother barged into their home exclaiming, "Where's my kid?"

She swooped the child from Audrey's arms, her big Samoan brother filling the doorway. He softly threatened Owen, who took a step, with an outstretched palm. "Don't do it man."

His heart was breaking, too. Demarco was like a brother to him. Kaelani was gone, out of the driveway in less than two minutes with the child they wouldn't see again until the funeral. And then, probably never again. Audrey's existence was an outside threat to a bitter and angry young woman who would keep all of her son's love to herself, as was her due. Audrey deserved to be punished; a mother shouldn't outlive her child. The fat, new ignorant mom gleamed with satisfaction to ruin.

An emptiness stared at the closed front door. Owen broke down first in the silence, which brought the women into hysteria, witnessing a man on his knees broken to pieces, like a sword suddenly withdrawn from a pierced gut. They closed together, shouting profanities within tight walls. The pups cowered more.

Like an escape room, Audrey found herself in a cell of despair, locked down. This time it wasn't of her own construction…or was it? She had let Demarco go out that night. She could have prevented his death but didn't because she wanted to play Grammy for an evening. The tiny hands and soft, baby skin were now taken away, just as memories of her now dead son as a child.

Aspects similar to rooms of a house under constant construction had mirrored her building of a life, until a wrecking ball swung. She had moved between a great job and a great man; she even had an alter ego that was now a queen, loved by friends and pets. Now it was all a rented vesture unto meaninglessness.

Audrey heard the "CLUNK" of the sliding, jail door within her mind, and she was imprisoned in grief. She favored the rot of depression spreading throughout her edifice, a mildew, her fault. The sorrow crowded all things out, wantonly destructive, firing at will. Audrey stepped into the cell, shaking because she thought she must. It was the reckoning of all accounts, judgment, like being weighed in the balance and found wanting, a writing on a wall producing a fear that loosened bowels.

Staying focused, looking for clues, solving puzzles, and fellowship would help her get out. Audrey knew she'd also have to admit that she couldn't find her way out on her own. There was a way out from the escape room of her only child's murder and the forever loss of her infant grandson. That night would be the last time Audrey would ever be trusted with such responsibility. The bassinette stayed in the small second bedroom for months after her son was killed, until Owen tasked himself to move it from where his young friend had laid his head as well, a necessary impediment for release from Audrey's barred prison cell. Something she couldn't do herself.

But that empty room always remained. And she passed it every day, usually several times a day. The passage of time helped a little, until she saw other people's little kids. The design of remembrance never passed away. It would always be a bottomless well of sadness. The black spots of depression would never, ever, be soothed nor scratched completely.

...

A few days later, Corrine got word that her away from home mom, Paula, was found dead in her trailer. A heart attack, it was presumed. Another funeral through the Eagles Club began to be planned. She was now locked into her own escape room. Her little boy was affected by her crying, not knowing what to do except to hug and kiss and let her alone for thirty seconds at a time. Her crying was making little man want to start crying because he was afraid for Mommy.

Peter called to console her soon after Demarco's death, only to be shocked by yet another loss in the young woman's life. His thought was to listen attentively, and ask sincere questions when Corrine paused enough. To buoy tremendous grief, to ask about her son and her pup, to remind perhaps other rooms were full of blessings. Mostly, Princess De Menthe avoided, choosing to complain about her job as a way to avoid talking about the worst. But he pressed on.

"You must be in some kind of shock," Peter suggested one night.

"Yeah, maybe. Going to work today was helpful to stop thinking about things."

"Paula didn't seem to be in the best of health. She was what? Mid-sixties?"

"Still too young to die."

"To be sure." Corrine's boyfriend didn't know how this would impact them. Probably, the sorrow would give her a reason to call things quits, then he'd go back to Wisconsin wondering what could have been. Peter didn't want to say the wrong thing. So, instead, he offered some advice.

"I imagine that it's going to take time to process all this. Are you talking to your girlfriends and such?"

"Yeah, but I still have to take care of little man. And he doesn't like seeing Mommy cry."

That put a lump in his throat, but he had to ask about Audrey. At two earth-shattering events Corrine was present: Ryan's suicide and the forcible retrieval of Audrey's grandchild. How could anything good sprout from the given circumstances? All this tragedy would have to affect her somehow.

She still had to provide and protect her child. Corrine still had to go to work. He thought she'd still continue doing Pin Up as a means to allow an alter-ego to pretend the pain into nothingness. That would at least still keep the human connections with her girlfriends and social safety circle, because she was that smart. But would she still want or need some strange man? Peter had his doubts. Her emotional cup was full, and he wanted to put some ice cubes in it. Would something overflow? Could another bad thing happen?

So, like a silly man, he interrupted the flow by asking, "Have you ever castrated a goat before?"

She had been crying, wiping away streaming tears. Peter had heard wavering in her voice for the last ten minutes. Now, Corrine answered softly, questioning, "No. . .what?"

"Castrating goats."

"You castrate goats?"

"Absolutely. At my family farm in Wisconsin I was known as The Castrator." It was a half-lie but made for a good story. "It's like a superhero name. A superpower!"

"Cutting off nuts?"

"Exactly. I'm a pro nut cutter-offer. Kind of like Mariano Rivera from the Yankees, in baseball. . .the closer?"

"You're confusing me. What does that have to do with what's been going on with me?"

"Nothing," he replied without pause, "but as a friend who has been hearing about the tragedies you've been through in the last couple of days, I thought you might like to smile thinking about boy goats getting their nuts sliced. And it's pretty painless, really."

"Go on."

"So, thinking about something completely different, like goat herding. I know about that, tragedy less so. Except for some stuff."

Corrine quipped, "I want to hire you."

"To do what?"

"Cut's someone's balls off, Superhero!" Was there going to be money involved now?

"Do you remember when I cooled your feet off at the restaurant?" Peter was still on the make.

"Yeahh…" He had changed the tone masterfully from grief to frivolity.

After a very long pause, Corrine picked up the thread and asked, "So how do you emasculate a goat?"

"First of all," Peter continued, relieved, "since only the she-goats produce milk, which we make into the best cheese in the world, you don't need but a few bucks around to make new baby goats. Make sense?"

"Sure," she garbled. "How do you stitch the nut sack?"

"You're getting ahead of me. And the answer is glue, not stitches."

"So you Superglue the he-goats nut sacks after you slice 'em?"

"I get you're a city girl so won't understand this."

"I'm from Yakima…"

"Is that in the United States? Anyway, you have to slice at just the right time, when the joey is about a month old."

"Who is Joey?"

"The point is, that you don't want to slice and dice them too late, like at two months. It's really no big deal."

"What do you do with the nuts?"

"Eat 'em."

"Ahhhuuugghhh!"

"No, seriously, we got pan fried goat nuts, nut gumbo, nut scampi, roasted nuts, nut pancakes. Goat nut jelly is a delicacy in Japan. Big money!"

Corrine guffawed. "You're lying to me. There's no such thing!"

"But...I ain't lying when I say I want to see you again!"

11

Lightning in a Bottle

Capturing electricity with a kite in a lightning storm, using a string, a key, and a copper wire within a glass jar helped make him famous worldwide. Some of that was a bit untrue, except for the physics. Benny F. had dozens of patents under his workaholic genius credulity before he became America's ambassador to France during the War of American Independence, entertaining royals with his static electric amusements.

The lightning rod, Poor John's Almanac, and the Franklin stove all bore evidence to his practical genius; as well as coining the technical term "battery" for electrical storage, from artillery formation. Although he greatly suffered from gout, it didn't keep him from being known as a lady's man in Europe and a Founder in the USA.

But his personal life became shambles. His one son amputated himself from him, due to politics. His poorly cared for, tethered wife was always estranged into their old age.

Yet, Benjamin Franklin caught lightning in a bottle, they say. He was an inspiration to the scientifically, curiously minded, and to young 'ins who sought after each other from the sorrowful stratosphere.

...

In her dream she was girl maybe five years old. She walked through the gate that separated her inattentive home from the big meadow and left it wide open. Right away, something caught Corrine's attention: it was a cat crawling through the grass toward her. He stopped behind a tree, then peered partially behind it. It was her good friend Peter, pretending to hide.

Her father had warned Corrine against dangerous animals coming from the forest, but she wasn't afraid of this one.

Nearby, a little sparrow and a duck were arguing about whether birds should swim. A wolf rushed from the forest toward the pond where they sat. Corrine watched in horror as the sparrow sprung into the air, calling, "Run, everyone run!"

Peter yelled to Corrine to climb up the tree with him. "We will be safe here," he promised. She followed.

The duck ran but was caught before she could reach the gate. Corrine sat near to the cat on a branch, while the wolf circled below, looking up at the pair with hungry eyes. Flying much higher than the stone wall surrounding Corrine and her father's house, the sparrow circled around the wolf's head, diving and snapping viciously. What a clever tease, and the wolf couldn't do anything about it! It could only watch the sparrow carefully, hoping she'd get too close.

Corrine and the cat took their chance: together, they jumped from the tree and tied the wolf's tail together, around the trunk. He was too busy with the sparrow to notice.

Just then, hunters came out of the woods, shooting as they went.

"Don't shoot," Corrine insisted. "We've already caught the wolf. Let's put him in the zoo."

Her dream changed to a triumphant procession. Corrine marched at the head, followed by the sparrow and the cat. The hunters were next, with the manacled wolf trailing behind.

Father, however, was not pleased. Discontented, he demanded," Well, why hasn't Peter killed the wolf?"

But the sparrow flew by, saying, "What fine fellows we are for defeating the wolf."

They could all hear the squawking of the duck, who had been swallowed alive.

After that, Corrine's cheeks became bright red. Father said it was punishment for leaving the gate wide open and tempting a dangerous animal from the forest.

...

Paula's trailer would have to be detailed or something. It smelled sickly smokey to Corrine's nose upon arrival. There was no law that said she couldn't smoke inside her own home. Corrine had to beg an emergency, leaving of her kid for a few hours with shit heel Evan. Being an early Tuesday evening, he graciously allowed the interruption from video games. It wasn't as if her impregnator would lose pay. Asking why, Evan told Corrine that she should leave it to the dead woman's family. That she was always doing "stupid" things.

She brought contractor debris bags but found a tidy place with lots of picture frames of people she didn't know. They looked like anyone you might find attending a car show or having a membership to a civic organization. The Eagle's club president merely said the door was probably unlocked.

Could it be that Paula had no family locally to call for help? Where were her keys? Corrine investigated the vacant space, feeling poorly that she had never visited her "surrogate" Mom's home before. But perhaps it could never have been, due to mean circumstances and a lack of an invitation.

She couldn't help thinking of her dream. Was Paula the duck? Whom or what was the wolf supposed to represent? Death itself? Corrine emptied the ice box into a black bag she was using to dump garbage and perishables. Was Peter a lurking cat? Would she sit on a branch with him?

Who'd sell Paula's car, trailer, and meager possessions? She separated foodstuffs that could still be had by her. A food bank wouldn't sort things, and that which may rot was destined for the dumpster at her apartment complex. Corrine wished she could chuck her last few weeks into a dumpster, although she knew that three deaths in such succession must leave a mark, like a heavy gate closing.

She made a cursory search for an address book and found one. She found a cell phone without a charge, too. Why was this traveling man calling her in the evenings, asking how she was? Peter was trouble, just like Donna Diva said. Her mind was in a whirl of anguish and in need of protection.

He probably just wanted to get into her pants, she distrustfully thought, then remembered his continued kindness. But why would he? Could there be anguish other than hers? Losing Paula suddenly was the icing on a shitty cake. It seemed to Miss Corrine that she was the only one to take a bite.

She found a battery charger for the Android phone and hoped to find help. After a few minutes sitting on Paula's bed and staring down the length of the trailer, stupefied as to what to do next, she thought that maybe it would be okay if she did something for herself. More than she allowed now.

Corrine's self-imposed mission to eulogize before the Eagles would take an extraordinary effort. Her employer required increasingly more time, with no raise, until she felt like she might burst. She doubted anyone else would bother with Paula's things, like throwing away perishables before they grew mold and searching for an address book. She tried a few times to start a speech, but the words weren't coming easily without tears, a "no no" in public speaking.

That night she couldn't stop thinking about Peter. In her dream, he'd approached almost unnoticeably through the long grass of empathy. How she wanted a boyfriend. And he peered at her, pretending to hide. Soon, he'd be gone to slice he-goat nuts back in Wisconsin to make nut scampi, or so he said. The dude was funny, though, and persistent, but in a thoughtful way. Trusting a man had always been a mistake in her experience. Maybe she should screw him silly; it had been a long time since she'd had the "real deal".

Audrey was a basket case, and Corrine's emotional bucket seemed to be emptying fast. Why was someone like Peter trying to patch the holes as the leaks kept appearing? She glanced down at the screen of her own phone and noticed she'd missed several calls while she'd been working. She didn't remember placing her phone on mute.

"Hey Corrine, this is Owen," her voicemail played. He'd never left a message before. "I just wanted to thank you for talking with Audrey every day. I owe you a lot." The mustachioed man with the silver belt buckle who shot potatoes from a homemade launcher paused in the recording. "We still don't know when or if there's going to be a memorial service for Demarco. I miss that guy. Anyway, there's been nothing but crickets from the Samoan gang." With another pregnant pause, Corrine could tell he needed to hurry before he spoke too long. "Audrey hasn't been to work since, but I've been going in, like regular. Well, I hope you're well. I know you've had another loss. I'm very sorry. Please call me if I can do anything." The man sounded scared.

Another VM shouted: "Hey look, I don't know if I can pick up little guy on Saturday morning. Might go fishing in Idaho with a bud this weekend instead of takin' him. Since I covered you last minute yesterday you get it. I'll let you know what I decide." Click.

Evan, a half-man, who had had his dick inside Corrine, was, in fact, now her nemesis. Her impregnator was an inescapable agent of her emotional demise...if she let him.

The President of the Eagles club recorded, "Hey lady, did you get over to Paula's? I have a phone number for her son but thought it might be better if you called him. His name is Cristin, his number is (904)123-1750. Let me know. We can still have a service here if you can set it up. Don't know much about Paula's family. Let me know." Another click sounded, and she shuddered.

Corrine picked up little guy from the expensive pre-school day care, buckled him up, and drove back to their two bedroom. Nuggets and French fries were prepared. Next came the spastic bath/naked time for the lad that only a single mom could spend an hour and a half cleaning up after, guffawing at the silliness. Corrine listened to her messages again, then became sullen. Cory made it all better, with snuggles and telling her, "I love you Mommy," after the end of the bedtime book.

There were so many competing demands coming in. One, however, actually made her smile: "Hey, Corrine. Just checking in. Do you like slasher movies? I don't. Maybe we could see something like a romantic date movie. When you're free? Sometime. This is Peter." He was so dumb. And he didn't even try to kiss her the last time they went to the movies.

Naturally, she called him right back. "Hi, Peter. Are you busy?"

The young man talked her ear off. She listened to him recount tall tales about how he swam mountains and climbed seas. While he spoke, she envisioned the two of them tying a wolf's tail around a tree without even getting a scratch.

Peter didn't know why he did what he did, except that loneliness sucked. He crept forward because it seemed gentlemanly. Sometimes he stopped just to adjust his gaze toward her feminine form. Corrine became so fragile so fast, like the dropping petals of a dried-out bouquet. He knew being gentle was key, because he was something of a good man.

But who was he fooling? He'd be recalled as soon as the gig at JCPenney was successfully completed. They'd give him a week off, then send him to another part of the country, where he'd start again from another Extended Stay. The PNW felt fine. And he played, liking to be playful, pretending to hide even though in plain sight. But while they were on the phone that day, he decided that on the next date he'd kiss Corrine no matter what. Peter ensured she picked out the movie, not being too opinionated or handsy.

The soda machine was 21st century type with a display where you could pick hundreds of flavors. The big soda cup that "allowed" refills cost almost eight bucks. She liked the root beer, while he preferred the Cherry Vanilla Coke. Pete insisted on seeing the previews (so as to suggest another date). The theater darkened and Corrine grabbed his hand in expectation as Pete had nervously placed it on her knee. Drinking lots of soda meant at least one pee break for both during the show. They both whispered desperately into each other's ears when they returned, "what did I miss, what did I miss?" Having someone to love could have been the refrain.

It was time. It had to happen. Peter had to act. Several times they looked at each other while getting settled in. They shared the popcorn as the new Romcom played. There was even kissing in the movie! Peter's brain was on fire until he turned and lifted her chin. His strong, left arm was about her shoulders, pulling her gently toward him. He worried about his breath, having applied Cherry Chapstick just to be sure and, miraculously, she kissed him back.

Corrine could resist falling in love easily when she focused on the help Paula's son Christin was asking for. Later, she was able to find the contact information for the property manager, the President of the Eagles Club, and the local funeral home. Cristin drove a truck in Florida and was probably going to struggle with the expenses.

Another date night and Corrine and Peter went go-karting. It was a bit spendy at ninety bucks for two races. A guy with only one leg crashed into Corrine's kart, destined to leave a big, purple bruise. The karts were super-fast around the little indoor track. They received memorial thin gators to wear inside the racing helmets. She chose blue, him red.

Peter allowed others to pass him, trying to never apply the brakes, getting the hang of sliding the ass end around the hairpin turns, while his knees had nowhere to rest. She alternated the brake and gas, getting faster with every lap.

During their second race it was just the two of them. When Princess De Menthe spun out, he went by in a blur. But when he couldn't see her on the track, Peter looked back quickly and saw her right behind him trying to pass. After a few laps he let her by to see if he could pass her! Several more laps ensued until they wrecked, with him pushing her back end sideways till she collided with the guardrail. So much for being a gentleman.

The following Wednesday, late afternoon after work, Princess De Menthe wanted to go ax throwing. Twenty-five bucks apiece for an hour. She paid, not wanting her friend to think she wouldn't. The 250 bucks a month she got in child support was a pittance, and when Evan turned twenty-five, she vowed to take him back to court. Maybe the judge would increase the payment to $500 a month, but on a part time grocery clerk's wage? She doubted it.

Each lane was separated by chain link fencing. A bullseye was painted over pine boards, with lots of splinters and sawdust on the floor. The young girl with the multiple tattoos demonstrated the basic throwing techniques:

The double handed over the head was the base. It wasn't like throwing a baseball across one's body, but instead the movement was vertical and plumb to the earth. One revolution and the semi-sharp axes would stick into chewed up mounted planks. There were even leagues, supposedly. But this establishment was dry, probably to the requirement of the owner's lawyers.

Princess De Menthe stuck the overhead throw, with her dominant hand on top, then the single hand, then she switched to the overhand with her left hand on top, sticking the ax into the bullseye, followed by the left single handed. Meanwhile, Peter clunked it again and again, sometimes making it stick somewhere.

Corrine asked the one employee for increased complexity, where she nailed the double ax overhead and then threw an ax in each hand, scoring most of the time. She felt sorry for showing up her beau. . .kind of.

"Don't know why you're having problems," Corrine said with a wink. "I'm doin' it even with big boobs getting in the way!"

"Don't remind me," Peter responded. "That's not helping my concentration."

"Twawanda!" she screamed, sticking two axes with two separate hand throws simultaneously, repeatedly. Peter was mortified, bouncing another ax handle against the wood wall. She needed a victory. The fact that he sucked at this didn't help, the male ego as fragile as it is.

Gratefully, the hour rented concluded. "We should do this again!" was responded with, "Let's go get a burger."

Corrine became a better friend than ever to Audrey. Having a man pursue her made her feel attractive. Maybe she was an even better mom, too; she was definitely less grouchy and weepy, even relieved a bit from anguish. She went to church service again, with Peter, as was his devotion.

When would he give her a really passionate kiss? Right before he left? She'd stick her meat hooks into him if given the chance, with lovey-dovey handwritten notes exuding Pin Up Doll sexy glamor shots she'd pay for. But maybe just getting laid right now while everything else was shit was all she could expect. Falling in love was at the perfect moment where two people who hoped to, not needed to, couldn't help to fall in love.

The next date was at the Seattle Zoo on a lazy, bright afternoon. They fed goats at the petting farm and gawked in the aviary. Peter kissed her while she chomped a hot dog, stating she had a bit of mustard on the corner of her mouth. When asked which was her favorite animal, Corrine said the giraffes, and he said the funky fluorescent sea horses in the aquarium.

She drove them back to the Extended Stay after a wonderful afternoon. It became the first place they made love, although it wasn't very fancy.

Jazz played on the Bluetooth speaker, with light still coming through the shades. Peter marveled at the amazing strength of the underwire of her bra. When Corrine opened her eyes from kissing, he was looking straight through her. Always, twinkling, she thought she saw stars, but she wasn't going to make the first move. That was the boy's job.

The pines shadows moved across the windows and them, an excellent mood light just before a sunset, atop a very used bedspread. He attended her feet again, removing her shoes, moisturizing, and finding where skin rubbed raw. Knuckles kneaded into her soles.

Peter pulled her toes, cracking two or three. Moving up her legs as her jeans barely allowed, he stretched her calves, pointing her toes then pushing them back like an amateur masseuse. The coconut oil, calming her calves, was much better than the restaurant. She remembered how her feet ached, then tingled. "How often have you done this?"

The studio musicians drew the bows of their violins at first quietly, then increased intensity before Etta James began with a restrained force:

"At laaast. . ." holding the note longingly, with strength.

"My love has come alongg. . ." The violins drew like a teeter totter. The bass established itself singularly.

"My lonely days are over. . ." Now her tone was pleading.

"And life is like a song!" It all became a singing, harmonized shout.

She sang conclusively, with the hips and hops of the strings following her journeywoman voice. The bass reverberated in rhythm with the thumping of Corrine's pulse as he brought her hips to his, pulling strongly. Princess De Menthe swayed her hips, too, feeling how excited he was. Like a roll of Lifesavers in his front pants pocket multiplied by ten.

He asked her to turn onto her tummy, and shoulder rubs with strong carpenter man-hands ensued. Peter ran his fingers through her hair, placed their tips on her scalp, rubbing hard and then more gently on her temples and the base of her skull, squeezing. He pulled hair strands like big finger combs for minutes, relaxing her until Corrine began to purr.

"Let's get your top off so I can do your back." It was a none-too-subtle trick that she complied with immediately. Peter pulled her hips close to the edge of the bed so he could get the proper leverage without having to straddle her backside. At least not yet.

"Where on your back do you hold your stress?" He kissed her ears, then her neck, inhaling her hours old "Flower Bomb" perfume, growling, nuzzling, once or twice feigning a bite. "You're top heavy, so I'm guessing your lower back." And his thumbs began to dig past her waistline.

Exasperated, Corrine's man soon declared, "Well, this bra strap is just getting in the way," and it snapped open with a force like cutting the ribbon on a present. But what was the next move? He was afraid he was putting her to sleep until Princess De Menthe rolled toward the center of the bed and reached for the top button of Peter's jeans.

"My turn," she said. Laying on her side, her breasts ballooned forth. "Is that a roll of Lifesavers in your pocket, or are you just happy to see me?"

Lifesavers? Her nipples were the size of half dollars. "You ever been to Texas, sweetie?"

"Ummm. . ." No whitey tightys tonight. His stylish unders were unceremoniously thrown on the floor to be scrounged for later in low light, along with all other cast-off clothing, mixed up momentarily when picked up.

"Alexa, play Kool and the Gang." The playlist was updated twice more.

Just a step from the kitchenette, they found hot water for a washcloth and ice water to slake their thirst. Corrine twitched all over. Peter was brimming with confidence.

They embraced, very satisfied and relieved. Legs and arms locked like loving wrestlers. Kissing continuously, wondrously stupefied, both knew they were just taking a time out.

…

She didn't want to ask when his job at JCPenney would be over. Peter said that the end date was pushed out by a month, whatever that meant. Corrine told him about her ex, Evan. He told her about the scant relationships he'd had, kind of, barely, being embarrassed, being laid only a time or two.

Her work was a mix between plodding along and being given more responsibility for the same scant pay. Peter told her funny stories from the store, like when a shoplifter stole an associate's walkie talkie and harassed the staff for half a day, sending them on goose chases to find the make-believe homeless guy pooping in the middle of the Men's department, or calling the manager by name, telling her that mall security had caught hooligans outside the north entrance.

It seemed to her that he never had a long relationship, which was true. He looked up Lupus and was shocked to learn only 80% lived longer than fifteen years even with modern care. Lupus in Latin meant the wolf's bite, since it made girl's faces turn red. Peter and the wolf battled for a young woman's life.

…

The project manager knew that the painters were threatening to walk off the job. The sub of the subcontractor had bid sight unseen, and as the scope leaped ahead of expectations, the point of losing money came quickly to he who held the brush.

The Chuck-it whipped the tennis ball three times farther than a man could throw. Corrine's pup would run herself until the chucker was tired. Cory tried, but almost five was an in-between age, where running and throwing were still iffy. JCPenney's honey do list was long, but they were willing to pay for Peter's expertise and "git it done!"

There was that Midwest attitude. The two lines of effort, between falling in love and the bill payer's desire, met at the intersection of passing the final building inspection, which closed the permit, ending everything.

"I'm going to send you another Superintendent to help close things up. It's no reflection on you, but we gotta get out of there," the PM spurted out on the phone the following afternoon.

SHIT! They were racing to the finish when he'd found a girl who remembered everything he said, who liked what he liked, and finished his sentences when he paused. It began to form an iron rod where his backbone was. Indeed, things were starting to make emotional sense.

"Did you find another contractor to finish the paint?" Peter asked.

"Yeah, well I got a guy who owes me a call back. I'm going to send Gary your contact info. He's worked for me all over the country. Just want to get this one wrapped up. He'll be your helping hand to get all the little shit done. He's got time between jobs."

Obviously, the project manager had the money to fly a Super out, with all expenses. The budget was good, but things would wrap up fast with a pro coming in, who probably worked really fast and to quality.

Corrine wrote him little love notes and hid them in his wallet and pockets. Peter helped to landscape outside her little patio, where he and Corey had fun, hands in the dirt. Immediately upon finding the surprise sentences, he'd text back an Emoji with hearts for eyes. So sweet it'd make you sick.

It was almost six AM when Gary called. Peter was just walking to the store from a mall's parking garage. "Hey, Pete. I guess I'm coming out by you."

"Hey, Gary. Good to hear from you. I'm not sure why you're coming out, but this is going to be an absolutely no pressure gig. When are you flying? Ever been to Seattle?"

"No, been to Portland. The PM just wants to wrap this up. What should I bring?"

"I got all the hand tools we'll need, don't need much." Peter laughed enthusiastically, "This is going to be like a vacation for you. I've already got everything squared away, no landmines." Man to man, he added, "Lots of pretty girls out here. Where you going to stay? When you flying?"

Corrine invited him to dinners of mac n' cheese and take-out Sushi for them. After bath time little man gave him hugs before story time with Mom. He watched the ESPN highlights for an hour and ate leftover French fries and chicken nuggets, drinking a pilsner.

Once or twice, Corrine woke him up afterward, pouring a glass of wine for herself and snuggling with big man. Once or twice he left without making love, bittersweet having found a girl "Att laaast!" Their love had come along. Simultaneously, they were like small craft moored together temporarily in a small harbor before rough seas began again. They knew they'd cut their ties before breaking up, each afraid of shipwreck, being dashed to pieces. Which one of them would blink and risk the little they had?

When Gary hit the ground there wasn't going to be any running. Peter gave him the tour of the huge, three floor department store. The carpet guys had only another five thousand square feet to place of the 90,000 contracted.

"There's no rush," Peter explained. "I'm going to need you to take your time. This back dressing room popped up last minute, and it's pretty messed up. Let's go take a look."

Gary was sixty, tan, with a buzz cut, square jaw, and thirty-four-inch waist. A solid man, he worked for GM for thirty years building cars. Moving from Michigan to Missouri, he now traveled the country performing feats of retail magic for a general contractor from Wisconsin. It was a Thursday morning when he showed up.

"Do you have any plans for the weekend?" Peter asked.

"Uhh, no. I don't know where anything is. I guess I was going to go downtown to check that out." Peter looked amused and curious, playtime seemingly more important than the punch list.

"Hey, I could use your help." Peter's eyes began to twinkle. "I've found the honey hole of all time, of good-looking middle-aged chicks. Have you ever heard of Pin Up dolls?" There was another pageant this weekend. "You like classic car shows, don't you, Gary?"

"I like girls more."

The plan began to unveil itself. There was some light demo to do in the dressing room, too.

12

Black Diamond

Arranging Demarco's funeral service was like an emotional dumpster fire, nasty in every way. Although they had lived together for years, Owen didn't know his love's PIN to unlock her phone. Several times Audrey had to answer calls, as either the Sheriff's office or the hospital needed authorization to do something. The funeral home needed a deposit. Three grand wasn't but a thing for Owen, compared to his love staying in bed, having to be prompted to eat and get cleaned up.

He talked to her boss and screened her calls until she snatched her phone away in a huff days later. She had a Rolodex where he found the name of Demarco's father. It occurred to him to ask Audrey his name on day two of the new normal. He didn't want to leave a voicemail with the news, so two days passed before the man picked up the call directly.

Not knowing if any relationship existed between the two men, the awkward silences as Owen passed along what happened made him believe there wasn't much of one between son and father.

When girlfriends called Audrey, he'd peek in on her. "I'm awake. What is it?" came forth strongly, and he asked if she wanted to talk to so and so.

After listening to a hospital social worker's distressed message about Kaelani's demand for information, Owen called her back and got the tenor of their oppressor again. "Yes, you can tell her where we had the body taken to."

What were the family's desires? The strange question was asked by a permanently sympathetic man. When he stepped out of the house, Owen left her phone on the dresser, on vibrate. Surely, she couldn't be sleeping half her days away. No, there wasn't a burial plot. This was going to get expensive quick.

Contacting Kaelani after her despicable act in his own home was the worst thing to swallow. He had to call her. It was a necessary consideration. A date needed to be picked out so people could plan. Demarco's father was out of state, for instance. A brief voicemail did nothing. A text brought out a savage response:

"WTF you planning my man's funeral. My family got this. I'm going to call there and tell them to not do nothing 'till we decide, bitch, mother fucker!"

Luckily, the next morning a lifeline of sorts was thrown across bows. Kaelani's brother Mitchell called him. "Hey, is this Owen?"

"Yeah."

"I saw you when we came to get my nephew, Tamah."

"That was fucked up." Owen's blood pressure rose really fast.

"Yeah, bro. That was fucked up. My sis is like a powder keg, bro."

Owen started to replay the invasion in his mind.

"Thanks for taking care of Demarco. That's a good place. I've seen the ads on TV."

"What's your name?"

"Mitchell. Call me Mitch."

He must be one of those gentle giant types. "Hey man, I can't deal with your sister and I'm paying so far for this." He caught himself too late in frustration. Why wasn't his love pushing the buttons? Maybe because her child was murdered, her grandson snatched away, her life collapsing in no small part due to the undue hostility of Mitchell's family. "You know we're not rich people!" Owen's tone was too excited, the loss of peace too much. This man might become an ally. "Sorry, dude, I mean Mitchell,

Mitch. This has been a lot to process. Audrey has been down for the count since everything happened."

"Audrey. Yeah. I didn't know her name." He paused to swallow, continuing, "Tell her, when she's feeling better, that Demarco was part of our family. Everyone's been crying over here." A big tear rolled down his big cheek then another. "I visited him when he was in jail a few times. He was a good dude."

"How long did he know Kay-lane-ay?"

"Kaelani. . .dude." Owen made him laugh accidently. "That's some funny shit."

"Yeah, well, I'm Anglo."

"Sure." Still amused, Mitch added, "they knew each other in High School, but never went out 'till after I guess."

"Dude, the funeral director called me 'cause your sister tore his ass up."

"Fuck that, man. What you're doing is golden. We'll pitch in as we can. But we need a date for the funeral itself, right? That's the biggest thing now. Where's the cemetery? Is it local?"

"Dude! You tell me. God, I'm glad you called. I've been over here handling everything, taking a vacation week, trying to make the girl get out of bed. I don't. . ." Good men have always seemed to be able to communicate directly, quickly, to each other in times of great stress, without regret.

"She's afraid she'll never see the baby again, right?"

"Christ! Yeah. After you guys were here."

"That ain't gonna happen. You tell Audrey that."

They talked about dates a week or two away and agreed to talk again the next day. Perhaps Owen had a temporary partner, or maybe he was being taken for a ride. Providing hope to his love was a double-edged sword that could swing toward lies and treachery. In the meantime, another seven large was required before another decision was directed to the funeral home. It was easier for him to make financial decisions than his love to escape from stupor.

Cremation was going to be a lot cheaper. He called Mitch but texting was the only way he'd communicate. Voicemails weren't returned. That first week he allowed Audrey to wallow. Then facing the prospect that he'd have to return to work, sure as shit she wasn't going to stay in bed. He started by being nice or not so nice by opening the shades and windows. Miss pissy pants was scolded a time or two.

"We're going for a walk. Get dressed. Your muscles are going to atrophy, and I don't feel like washing your bed sores. Get up. I'm not playing." Her man acted assured.

Once around the block, then the other direction so the sights were different, Owen told her about his conversations with Mitchell.

"Do you believe him?" she asked through emotional exhaustion. Some houses were neatly groomed, while others had old cars parked on overgrown grass.

"He might want to assure you'll see Tamah, but it's not his call. I don't know."

"It's bullshit. After the funeral I'll never see my grandson again." Some homes had pretty flowering trees and vegetable gardens, others had peeling paint and shingles infused with moss.

Owen tried to spin her toward him for a hug, but she raised her arms and kept walking. She wore big-lensed sunglasses although it was a cloudy day, and the wind gusts strong. It would rain again soon.

"I was going to say. . ." He could feel his anger percolating. "You don't know that. But I doubt it's possible to reason with that ignorant bitch. She's hurting, too."

"Well, she doesn't have to take it out on me." Then she stopped and turned. "She's hurting? She wasn't nice to Demarco either." Audrey pointed a finger at his face. "Don't take her side. Ever!"

"Fine! Fuck. All I'm saying is that the stupid bitch has the emotional development of a four-year-old."

Owen had to change the difficult conversation by stating, "Demarco's father called and asked about a date. Other people, too. I'm going back to work starting Sunday. It's going to be hard to orchestrate the service by myself."

"I told you I'd pay you back," she said. That wasn't the point. Audrey had to function again. Go to work, talk to friends, go grocery shopping. When they would marry after this tragedy was held in abeyance. Owen's speech asking, with a big fat engagement ring, turned from fancy to a conceit.

"The Samoans aren't cooperative. They're going to be pissed no matter what. Do you care if Demarco gets cremated?"

"What are we going to do? Divide the ashes?" The vulgar thought stopped Owen in his tracks.

"Christ sakes." Owen had to nearly shout into the wind, "You'll want to visit his grave. They can't take that away from you." Now Audrey stopped walking and turned to hug her boyfriend/ husband. Big tears left a patch on his jacket.

Friday morning was the decision point. He told her as he stirred her oatmeal that he was going to the funeral home to complete the plan. Audrey replied, "We'll go together." The hall, the plot, the casket, grave marker, flowers etc. were almost another 8K. She wrote the check. There would be no vacation that year, and another year with the same crappy car.

She asked him how much he had paid thus far. Owen replied firmly that the initial payment was on him. "Demarco was my friend, too." He said.

When he got home, he wrote a long text to Mitch giving him the details and asking if they were going to make a picture board, or perhaps they could collaborate and show pictures on a monitor with photos of Demarco and family, shuffling continuously. The response was less than encouraging. "I'm going to start finding pictures to put into a loop, babe, for the service."

She made herself a Black Russian and went to bed without brushing her teeth.

The men were able to talk on Sunday afternoon after Owen produced several radio shows from realtors, financial planners, and gardeners. Mitchell's family wouldn't eat with their side, as they would have a big bar-b-que Samoan style to celebrate Demarco's life and the child that was now within their clan. Owen suggested they could collaborate, maybe rent a park space? Mitch was adamant that that wasn't going to happen. It was a foreboding sign.

Kaelani wasn't going to let anyone hold the baby, Tamah, when the day came. Audrey was too upset to talk to anyone, past a few words. Owen had her in a bear hug until he got up to say a few things. He even mentioned the potato gun. Many Pin Up Dolls came to support. The crowd of over fifty were a collection of colors, swan to truffle, to chestnut, to seashell.

A tall, lean man in his late fifties came to the podium. "My name is James, and I'm Demarco's father." He wore a new suit, off the rack, and it seemed uncomfortable to him. "Time just seems to keep slipping by so fast. I wasn't around a lot for him when he was growing up. Now, his casket is closed, and I'm not ever gonna be able to talk to him, make up for lost time some more. And a killer goes free!" He let out a mighty exacerbated, "HUMMPFF."

Demarco's father seemed more preacher than part-time handyman at that moment, more disappointed in himself than anyone else. "Time keeps slipping by so fast. I have good memories when he was little, with his mom and me. And it all gets washed away so fast. I believe this young man had turned a corner, that he was going to make right. He cared about

Key-laney and Tam-mah. He was a good man. We talked and wrote some letters when he was away. Guess he had time to think about this old bag of bones."

He made himself laugh; tears pressured behind his eyes. "Now, I see I have a grandson. Maybe, I'll meet him again someday." James knew the score with Kaelani, too. "So, I say goodbye to my son. He just slipped away so fast. That can happen, then you got nothing."

Audrey's mother couldn't believe she had to be satisfied with only viewing her great-grandson, from a distance. Infuriated at eighty-two years of age, she said repeatedly at the double wide reception, "That fat bitch is going to ruin that child." Many families congregated because of tragedy.

Demarco's father spoke to Audrey a little, ate a little, then left, being the ultimate outsider. He wasn't going to be in his grandson's life either, it appeared. Besides updated contact information, the only thing he accomplished was affirming his belief that he'd wasted the time he could have had with his son.

The only contribution from their side was a gaudy collage and a family minister.

Surprising himself, Mitch got up from his seat immediately following the eulogy and violently took Tamah from his sister with angry muffled words. He brought the grandbaby to Audrey, placing the boy in her arms. Then he kneeled beside her, his big paw on her shoulder. No one would interrupt the moment as he prayed over them, asking for everyone's divine protection.

Owen wept, his right hand gently over the baby's crown. Tamah's brown eyes were so clear, with specks of hazel, gazing into a wondering, wailing world. The big man had to rise after thirty seconds, taking Tamah back up within his pounding chest.

Audrey pleaded, "No. . ." Her arms now cradled her stomach, her gasping sobs crashed crisply like gunshots.

...

Black Diamond was a twisty series of roads away from the city. Gary held his phone as the GPS directed the route through farm fields and stands of forest, and when confident for a mile or two, he set the phone beside his Starbucks Venti Pike Place with cream.

Over knolls, in the sight of mountains, past an Eagles Club post where another funeral service was being planned, his rented Buick moved away from the Puget Sound to a small town (Gary avoided driving non-GM cars). This dude Peter was right about this short assignment feeling more like a vacation.

His old man expectations bubbled. They went to Home Depot together to buy 2x2 diffusers, duct tape, toggles, and base, just to shoot the shit and slow down the pace of production. It felt more like a road trip. He was forty-five minutes late on his day two, to Peter's great amusement. But now was the weekend. Saturday morning, an old Veterans of Foreign Wars club building seemed the first in a short main street in Black Diamond.

He texted. Then he walked in. He felt lost amongst the girls setting up diligently for the immediate pageant starting in forty-five minutes. Peter greeted him. "Is it too early to drink?" The bar was open, and filthy Bloody Marys were being produced. "My girlfriend and I brought the sound system. She's the hot one in the black, stretchy pants. Beware of Donna Diva. Hey Hon, this is Gary. Gary, this is Corrine De Menthe."

They sat down, trying to stay out of trouble. Men were in the definite minority amongst ladies doing their best to receive recognition amongst themselves, before all motored the mile to the car show grounds. "That girl over there is Serenity Jade. There's Carter Corsair, and Ginger Honey Bear."

Donna was getting really loaded already, handling the mic like a cock to the cheers and jeers of her sisters. How the pageant was detached from the classic car show with its pretty grandstand was a drunken administrative folly, not lost on the seriously minded in the club. These women had placed their all to compete in expensive outfits, shoes sometimes costing more than tires.

After every Doll had her chance to answer a private question before her mates, Donna Diva, Miss Demeanor, and Serenity Jade hid to tally their marks. The annual charity totals for pediatric cancer were tallied, too. Gary was beaming at the sites and stuck to sipping beer. Peter injected himself into pictures with Dolls, kissing girls on their cheeks with Corrine De Menthe's approval. Once she shouted, "He's coming home with me," to cheeky laughter.

Not to be undone, Miss Demeanor asked Peter the name of his friend. Lots of pictures were snapped with both she and Donna Diva sitting on his lap, the other kissing his tan cheek. The spontaneous female affection melted Gary. This solid bull smiled ear to ear and had to agree with his superintendent pal that indeed this was the Pfishin' honey hole. Aleia needed a new man since her mechanic dumped her impoverished ass. She wasn't going to let go of this hard man for many months. She never knew who might end up becoming husband number five.

The sashes and tiaras were presented at the Veterans of Foreign Wars. Katastrophic was crowned Queen. Her Pin Up name was contrasted sharply with her 1950's chic. She could have walked off a television set of the era, the prettiest white lady you've ever seen, with her baby blue, white polka dot dress, tastefully hemmed below the knee, and keen blue eyes.

Her Highness had a faux pearl necklace about her throat with little tattooed birds flying up her collarbone, a rose tattoo wrapped down a silky-smooth calf and around her toes. They were nuzzled into snow white pumps. A cut off lace sweater wrapped her sturdy shoulders and partially covered her ample bosom, with just a hint of cleavage. Big blonde curls held a cherry red carnation to match her fingernails and lipstick.

Pearl bracelets on her wrists hid very recent ligature marks. Her Pin Up name fit her, like a forest fire quickly racing through your pretty mountain town. But Katastrophic dressed deceptively, lulling efforts to evacuate, like watching billowy clouds tumble slowly through a bright blue sky suddenly noxious with choking black smoke.

Reconvening at the car show a mile away, pockets of Dolls, some with their fellas, stepped gingerly through the uneven grass. Gary more than once held Miss Demeanor to navigate treacherous spots between the rows of about 200 cars. She grabbed his meaty upper arm for balance. From then on, when he spied trouble ahead, he held out his gentlemanly hand.

But the trouble wasn't along the ground. It was the diminutive redhead with green Irish eyes in the bright floral dress. A tattoo with her son's name was written in long hand on her left wrist.

Queen Diva's hapless amateur photographer, cuckold husband, was promised to take pseudo-glamour shots with the Pageant Queen spread over cars of her choice (and the de facto permission of owners), all for free. Composition wasn't Aaron's strong suit. Lawrence helped his friend by humping lights and regularly his wife. Neither was perception apparently, which was strange for someone who endeavored toward an artistic advocation.

There weren't votes to vie for at the show. The girls were free to just get some pictures with cool cars and chat with friends. When Peter and Gary found ballots, he explained to his new friend how typically the Pin Up club was paired with the show, but weirdly not this time. The auto club hosted a gamut of projects from a '34 Chevy, '40 Willys, and '48 Anglia trio to '67 Chevelles, '70 El Caminos, and '72 Dodge Challengers.

Peter thought he could pick up some insights from the "King of GM", but Gary's interest lay elsewhere. Even the Queen of Black Diamond, Katastrophic, gave Gary the "big eye." The day was turning into an adult playground. And the boys asked the girls if they wanted some lemonade.

Miss Demeanor let her new friend amble away, but not too far, before she circled behind him. Gary was asking the owner of a '69 Camaro about his car's specs. It was an incredible streeter, sporting 18x15 solid aluminum wheels with Michelin "bigs", a 427 rat motor, a custom moly-tube Pro stock chassis roll cage, and shaved door handles. Gary guessed correctly that the color was a GM "code 29" blue, which looked black from twenty feet away. She stood beside him, sipping through the straw, drawing it up and down, making it squeal, vying for attention.

Corrine came with, feeling a little jealous of the attention her man wasn't paying her. Placing her hand around his waist, Princess De Menthe rested her head on Peter's shoulder for a moment.

"Hey, can I get some pictures of your car?" Gary asked enthusiastically to the owner. The hydraulic flip front U shaped bonnet was raised over the engine.

Peter interrupted, "What he means to say is that he wants to get pictures of the beautiful girl with the beautiful car."

"Ahh, you're so sweet, Peter!" He placed his hand out to hold Miss Demeanor's lemonade.

"He's new. He doesn't get it yet."

The owner quipped, "Yeah, sure. Knock yourself out."

"You should take her pictures, babe. Have her pose for you." There was a rock song playing nearby. Peter nodded his head along with the beat, looking at Gary with a wry smile. The singer repeated, "All she wants to do is dance."

Miss Demeanor pulled pink gloves from her little purse, stood behind the Camaro's tail, and rubbed the back quarter panel toward her hips, her tongue just meeting her top lip. This was going to be a clinic.

"Rub that spoiler, girl." Corrine was taking pics quickly. Occasionally, the wanna-be model looked in Gary's direction with a naughty smile. Strutting toward the passenger window, she placed her forearms on the door, poking her face just inside, pretending to engage the driver. Miss Demeanor was lean, her backside tight, her legs spread shoulder width apart.

She asked the owner, "can I touch your engine?" She pulled gently and inquired, "What's this?" Stroking chrome, she asked, "How does this feel?" And she laughed a sailor's laugh. "Can I get inside? Will you help me?"

Miss Demeanor squealed a little as the strange man pulled her knees up and over the structural steel wrapped in gray velour. She checked the mirrors, touched up her lipstick in the vanity mirror, then played with the gear selector and throttle, wanting to go fast! She shook her head as if the wind were violently whipping through her fiery red hair.

Corrine must have taken seventy-five shots, when she exclaimed, "Jesus, Aleia, I think I'm getting turned on!"

The men just stood stunned and giggled. But Gary had enough presence of mind to take a few pictures with his phone, staying behind Corrine, trying to replicate the same angles. The Camaro's owner, not to be outdone, after lifting the young lady out, roared it to life for dramatic effect.

He let down the hood as the hydraulics gently lowered it around the towering blower, twin Holleys, and custom headers. He wanted to get some snaps himself of the now pensive girl, afraid to get too close. She gave him her Pin Up card, her picture behind cartoon prison bars and a throwaway Facebook address on the back.

After the Camaro stopped tingling, Miss Demeanor wanted to go find Queen Katastrophic. Donna texted that they were about to do her shoot with a '32 Ford coupe, another rat rod.

Brian and Serenity Jade were watching, too. Lawrence had set up the umbrella light and schlepped the battery over to power it. Katastrophic knew how to pose relatively well. The vehicle was straw yellow, extremely cool; however, it was surrounded by other taller cars and tents. Her "glamor" shots would have other people in the frame. Aaron was a lousy photographer, but still relied upon for the snaps for the yearly calendar, which was the club's biggest single money maker, besides dues and fees. The club's meager finances boasted several thousand dollars still.

"Sorry, I haven't called you since the baby shower," Serenity (aka Kimmy) apologized to Corrine. They finally had a chance to speak alone after the pageant. "What a shit show."

"I wouldn't have known about it, if it wasn't for you." Corrine was appreciative of getting an invite of sorts.

"Delmonica said she didn't 'unfriend' me from Facebook, but sure as shit, the day she posted the date, I was ghosted. That cunt Tiffany is fucking with all her shit. I mean, Delmonica is exhausted with the baby so she can't really defend herself, but from her own mother? Now, she is going to move in with the kids, trying to get Ryan's house sold before foreclosure."

"I didn't know that. What the fuck is Jack doing? I can't talk to him. What about Brian? Can't he step in to sort out the money stuff?" Corrine was very agitated.

"Without a will, it has to go to probate. Tiffany's all over it, and Brian's, like, never home. He keeps going to the courthouse for all the paperwork. Besides, whatever is left over should go to Delmonica." Without saying it both women worried that little would be left of Ryan's money after all accounts are settled.

"And what can anyone say to her? Your mother is evil? I think Jack knows that but they're so young and still believe her bullshit. Tiffany is filing for disability, too. Brian is in town maybe one week a month. He went over to see his niece. Said Tiffany wouldn't stay out of his space until he left."

"I can't believe Jack was able to get into that house. It's pretty nice," Corrine added. Women rolled in most of the afternoon, to see the baby. Either housewarming or baby stuff were appropriate gifts. Corrine brought powder blue onesies, a slightly used stroller, and a mega pack of teeny diapers. The dogs were excited with so many visitors. Delmonica held the baby, mostly, but let her Auntie Kimmy and Corrine hold the tike, too. Tiffany tried to hold court, continuously bringing up the awful mess their beloved Ryan had left behind. And how she was working diligently to right the ship of state.

"Now that poor young man will have a mother-in-law living with him before they even get hitched." Shifting to other God-awful developments, Kimmy continued, "I've talked to Audrey, trying to coax Holly Hot Rod to come out today to play but she just said she didn't feel like being pretty right now. I should have taken the day off to go to her son's funeral. I feel shitty about that, but the timing with work was the worst it could have been."

"Talk about a shit show." Corrine paused, trying not to cry. "It was. . .it was the saddest thing I've ever seen, watching that big Samoan bastard rip the baby from Audrey. She was inconsolable. Like she'd never see the baby again. The mother, Kaelani, is like Tiffany, or my ex, Evan, who weaponizes the kids to damage adults. Like it's a kick controlling folks. So destructive. Hard to say what they care about." This cruelty was commonly human.

"It certainly isn't the children," Kimmy agreed.

"Now, I'm planning for Paula's service. Her son barely has the money to fly out. Everything's been like on remote control, and I'm his legs. I even picked up her ashes and brought them to the Eagle's club for safe keeping." She gulped, trying to catch her breath. "I've even been calling her old friends letting them know what's happened."

"Ahh girl, shouldn't her son be doing that?"

"Yeah, I guess, but I have her address book with her contacts in them. Don't ask. It's just another fucked up detail in my life." Said Corrine.

"Well, you have a new boyfriend. That's great, right?"

Corrine wanted to share the detail that he'd be leaving soon. What was she supposed to say? That he had a big dick. "It's just so confusing, the good with the bad."

Gary was like a kid in a candy store. Gawking at Motorcraft builds, he had a 1967 Rally Sport Z28 in a garage built just for it, in Missouri. Separate from the divorce settlement agreement, it had languished beneath a tarp. Men who threw off encumbrances, like women, and saving for retirement, thoughtfully, displayed all they had, working toward recognition.

Riding fast in a machine you built was a thrill like none other. His heartbeat was fast for two reasons on this marvelously hot, sunny day. Looking at Miss Demeanor, he said, "I'm going back to the Camaro. I want to ask that guy about the suspension." She looked confused. "Are you okay, Aleia? You look like you're going to melt."

"It's really hot."

"Some of the dolls have parasols."

"I know, I forgot."

"Let's get you into some shade."

"No, you go talk guy stuff. I'll be okay."

"Are you sure?" A strange thought entered his mind and before his brain could check for appropriateness the words flowed out, "Listen to me, will you? I'm acting like we're on a date already." The spontaneous quip was clever and she genuinely smiled.

"What are you building back in Missouri?"

"How did you know about that?"

Miss Demeanor laughed. "I can read your mind, Gary."

"What am I thinking about now?" The funny man straightened up and said before she could reply, he added, "I'm sorry, Aleia, that was dirty."

She laughed again. "Find out about the transmission, too, funny man. And check out the stereo. It's an original GM. Just like you."

He grinned and stumbled, like he had to force his legs to move away from the hot, smart girl.

She was the kind of girl who seemed to have an itch he was eager to scratch. She liked him, but why? Everyone seemed to be out for themselves always. Miss Demeanor was too fast, too quick; wanting a home without thought of her own provision. The work she would provide wasn't any work at all.

Donna Diva acknowledged that the Dolls were sweating to death and the car club didn't really support her club's efforts anyway, so their forever fearful leader announced that those who wanted their pictures taken should drive over to Ginger Honey Bear's house. It was in the neighborhood, meaning five miles away. It was a relatively successful herding of cats via the dreaded group text.

Corrine told Peter, who texted his new pal, "Gary, party's moving." The exchange of messages with the address was easier than the drive winding through mature woods, up and down past farm fields, several lefts, and then some rights to a shady lane with ten cars descending quickly on a pretty little house on a big lot.

Aaron took some pics, Corrine watched a joint get passed around, and in less than an hour another caravan sought a local roadside restaurant another five miles away. After their burgers, Peter told Gary he was taking Princess De Menthe home. The girls were pretty sweaty, and it was time to get his love cooled off. He and Aleia sat together holding hands.

He asked Gary, "Are you going to be okay by yourself?" He looked at Aleia and added, "Take care of him, he's shy."

"Didn't know that, thanks."

"Monday. Don't be late."

Gary smiled and sang, "Okaayy." Pretending to be put off by being reminded of his tardiness the day before. "You bet, boss." And he shook his hand in a vise-like grip, grinning all the while.

Corrine hugged Kimmy (aka Serenity Jade) and her husband Brian. "Let's go see Audrey together. Like, just barge right in."

"Tomorrow's not too soon," said Kim. "Call Owen."

13
Party at Owen's

The Project Manager of the JCPenney project wanted Peter out of Washington state, pronto. He was expensive and the Honey Do list had to wrap up. He flew out unexpectedly on a Tuesday and along with their client's bill payer, and the store manager, they agreed on a very short punch list, or in other words, things still to do.

The salon was complete, as was the carpet and new online product pickup station. The flooring remediation was complete. 110 yards of leftover carpet could either be added to attic stock or used in the back of house to beautify the staff offices or employee meeting spaces. The municipal final building permit was signed off. The contract for $785,000 was satisfied. The extras were agreed upon in principle.

In ten days, the company truck had to be rolling back to Wisconsin to return power tools to inventory. Then, Peter would be available for another assignment, someplace in the USA. Future employment drove the present, for now. A seed was dying within the earth in order to be replaced by something else, a natural germination; that was a concept a farmer's son grasped readily.

Gary helped demo the carpet in the Loss Prevention Office and swapped water-stained ceiling tiles by the dozens from a heavy, ungainly, twelve-foot ladder. He replaced the chair rail in the photo shop using the finish nailer his pal had transported 2000 miles. He told Peter something to make it clear he was glad he came out to help.

Aleia and he had gone shopping the day after meeting at Black Diamond. There was a carousel in the mall, and she rode a fancy horse undulating up and down. He held her, to ensure her safety, inside the ring of gaudy sea creatures and dolphins, standing beside her with one hand around her waist. Her hands grasped the brass pole over his other hand so that he couldn't move away. Gary tried not to get dizzy as her calf stroked up and down, a devious prelude. It made him pause for some seconds after she withdrew.

Aleia laughed as the music faded, hopping off, watching if he could walk straight. He ended up staying weeks after the company F150 crossed the Cascades back to the Midwest. It was a carousel ride Peter would replicate a few months later with Corrine. Wonderful, sexy ideas like that should be repeated.

Before Black Diamond, Corrine had a date with her man in Tacoma, known as the "Paris of the Pacific Northwest." Whenever she didn't have her son, they went to the movies, or they cooked together. It seemed that she pined for Peter. In succession she'd witnessed a suicide, consoled the inconsolable, and searched for lost relatives of a dead friend.

He read books with Corey and giggled. Her dog loved Peter. Cassie wanted to poop and chase a chucked tennis ball at the moment of seeing him. He played on the swings and chased, playing hide and go seek. Even when his breath grew stale, she wanted to kiss him; he was just a big kid.

He wasn't afraid of her Lupus, even as her cheeks blossomed red with stress, her joints ached, and she felt tired all the time. He filled her up in many ways. Could it be? On Sundays, Peter went to church. Yet he had lied to her. She wanted to sit on a sturdy tree branch with him. He was going to run away and never come back.

Then there was Paula, who she had not yet eulogized. He was there just then. Why was Peter present when all this loss happened, at her lowest ebb? When the ocean ran out, he was searching for sea creatures on the beach, with a shovel and bucket ready to build. He was here right now, for now. But soon he'd be taken away, like everyone else, pulled away in an inescapable undertow.

Taking her to the little promenade at the port city, just after they shared muscles steamed open in a garlicky, wine sauce and sourdough bread dipped in olive oil and balsamic vinegar, he told her of a piece of man's wisdom that his grandfather had told him about women. "Sometimes a man can see a good thing in the face, and not even know it." Peter wasn't going to make such a mistake.

"I just wanted to tell you that I have fallen in love with you." It was the worst and best thing he could have said.

Corrine leaned forward a bit to ease the awkwardness and he kissed her well. She didn't respond just then, stunned, reserving judgment.

Then the waiter brought out calamari with a zesty marinara sauce. The natural light began to dim behind the Puget Sound.

...

"Hi, Donna. This is Owen, Audrey's boyfriend." It was the Monday after the pageant. There was plenty of time to react, if he had a good partner who was audacious and sneaky. He usually took Monday off, since he typically produced radio shows on Sunday, like realtors and investor groups hawking their wares.

"Oh, hi, Owen. I remember you. We sure do miss your wife. How's she doing?" It was a none too subtle, playful jab from a previous party conversation, where Donna Diva proclaimed that three and a half years of being her "boyfriend" was long enough and that now it was time for him to "buy the cow." Or did he plan on getting the milk for free for the rest of his unnatural life?

Donna swallowed hard. She had fucked up, forgotten a sister.

"She's slowly coming around. I wish Holly Hot Rod could have come out to Black Diamond. We live so close. Say, I need your help." Holly Hot Rod seemed like a thing parked in a shed with a canvas tarp thrown over it haphazardly, like nobody cared. Many Dolls had called her since the funeral, he guessed, but aside from Corine and Kimmy, it didn't seem like much.

"What's that, sweetie?" Donna hadn't really worked for years, sucking off of a back injury she sustained at an Amazon processing plant. It was before noon; she could still be modestly productive before happy hour began at 3PM.

"I've decided that instead of getting Audrey to slowly climb back to life, that life should come back to her. In other words, I could use your prodigious management skills to rally the Dolls to my house, as soon as possible, like even this coming Saturday. I don't have the contact info, although I'm not beyond breaking into her phone, if I could."

Oh, this was delicious. What were sisters for? "Woo, this could be really cool! Like a surprise party."

"Well, yeah. Just tell people to show up any time after 4 o'clock. I'll have what we need. You know, just pop in and then stay till whenever. I'll have a bonfire, karaoke, the whole nine." Meaning beer and Bar-B-Que. "But they can't tell Audrey they're coming, obviously. This has to be on the QT, hush hush. Please don't group text this. That's a sure-fire way of accidently looping her in, ya know? I'm going to try and get some of her Co-workers to come over, too, and our neighbors." Owen didn't have to worry about his neighbors calling the Department of Health and Safety about illegal social gatherings. He had partied with them long before the Governor's emergency edicts.

Slightly pausing, he shifted gears, not meaning to emphasize but doing so anyway. "She needs a lot of love right now. She's going to work, but she's not taking care of herself. I want to shake things up like pronto. If she finds out, she'll tear my ass and stop the whole thing."

Donna lived an hour north of the city, Owen an hour south. But for the sisterhood... "We're in!" She'd have to figure out the transportation piece, and see if her lug husband, Aaron, wanted to come. Regardless, she'd bring big man Lawrence as the designated driver. If drunky pants wanted to stay home, then she and Lawrence could get room.

"I'll call it an emergency club meeting or something." Every Doll had to attend at least six planned events per year to remain in good standing or "patched in".

"Wonderful." Owen was so very relieved. "Would you let me know how many may come, or whatever? You know, by like Saturday morning, just a guess?"

He felt like a thin line between the normal space where grownups operate in and experiencing a slow-moving train wreck. Audrey's family wasn't close, his non-existent. His love didn't want to do anything. Watching a movie together was an accomplishment.

Audrey was drinking Black Russians with a vengeance. He was doing everything alone these days, even making and eating dinner. If he came out onto the porch to admire the view with her, she'd go inside. All offers to run errands were answered by, "I don't care. You go." She didn't want to garden or go to the lake with friends.

"I look like shit" and "I feel like shit" were the answers to, "How are you doing, babe?" If he rubbed her back there was zero response, the same with kisses. When he tried to hold hands, she withdrew.

If he closed the door to what had been Demarco's room, it would immediately be opened as if a ghost wanted out or a mother wanted to anguish more. After this game repeated itself three times, Owen retreated.

Silently, Audrey was drifting away.

"We need to get her back, Donna. I'm not kidding. I don't know how to anymore."

That stabbed at her little black heart. She had only left messages since Demarco's service. Not nearly enough.

"I'm calling out the cavalry," she said. It was time to fire up the troops!

Through text, and only through text, was the mustachioed man with the big silver belt buckle able to dangle a carrot. Demarco had provided some money to Kaelani when he was working. Owen bet she wasn't working herself, just taking care of Tamah. He met with Mitchell, buying him lunch.

Even though it was coarse bribery, it seemed like the best, last resort. He needed a win, a way forward before discussing this with Audrey. A check for $500 was folded neatly in his front jeans pocket. He wanted to know how Samoan Bar-B-Que was different, offering an open invitation to his own the coming Saturday.

The Samoans roasted a whole pig and the aunties put out traditional fare like breadfruit, taro, and grilled fish. From this he was able to pump more information from Mitch, telling him briefly about Audrey's small family. Sliding the check across the table, Owen asked him to let him know if the baby needed anything.

"I'd like to text her in a few days. Do you think that'd be okay?" The power of the purse could lure Kaelani in. It was an expensive gambit. One that would eventually prove profitable. It was a double-edged sword, though, where a bribe could quickly become extortion. Audrey wouldn't know what he was attempting unless it was successful. Owen's desperation had found its full measure.

There was a refrigerator/ freezer in a big shed he'd built. Another small one stored the mower, landscaping tools, empty pots, and bags of garden soil. The one where the clandestine frankfurters and burgers, and quarter barrel on ice were hidden under a dusty tarp was exposed to detection for half a day. If Audrey walked directly through the car park and opened the frig to spot a veggie tray, dips, macaroni and potato salad, bags of snacks and buns, the shit was going to hit the proverbial fan. Potatoes and six cans of hairspray wouldn't be extraordinary, however.

She did walk her dogs, and seemed a little more chipper, having one amusing story from work to tell. Owen was afraid of what was going to happen. Her man suggested they grill, hang out, and just watch a movie. But he was very nervous. Audrey storming into the house while he was napping to televised golf, shouting, "Why the fuck is there a huge cake in my frig?" wouldn't start their Saturday evening well.

Through the sliding glass door, he kept watch on the shed. By five o'clock he was getting really nervous, where were the Dolls? Then, just as it should be time to start preparing din dins, Serenity Jade descended with Brian, the advanced guard.

"Hi, Kimmy! Come on in. Brian. Let's go get a beer." He left the double wide with gusto, getting out of the way.

"Sorry for the pop in," Kimmy began as she hugged her friend. "We really can't stay long. How you doing, girl?" She gave Audrey a grin. "Hey, it's been ages since we had a Black Russian. Do you have the fixin's?"

"The fixin's?" Audrey smirked. Kimmy was wearing a cute party dress with a bow around her waistline. Audrey wore a sweatshirt with the logo of a state college football team. "I got two bottles of Kahlua and Smirnoff, so yeah."

Their neighbor, Bill, knocked on the other screen door, with a present in his hand. "Helloo," he cooed. Almost eighty, a retired Master Chief from the Navy, he led with a smooth lie: "I remember you telling me that you like naughty garden gnomes."

Owen chuckled as he opened the box wrapped in plain brown paper, to be discreet. The eight-inch-high elf looked behind himself, disgusted and red faced. Facing a tree trunk, both of his hands secured his privilege.

"He's peeing!" Kimmy cried.

The pups wanted to smell everyone, even the gnome, getting very excited.

Audrey, however, raised one eyebrow as she looked down at the little creature. "When did I ever tell you I like naughty garden gnomes?"

"It must be the dementia, then," The Master Chief complained with a smile. "Hey, Black Russian night, can I?"

People began to congregate beneath the carport. Lawrence let himself in off of the deck with a bottle of good vodka in his hands. "I need to pee," he announced.

Owen was trying to hide behind a growing crowd. His behavior became increasingly suspicious. He kissed Donna. Katastrophic was behind Queen Diva with her mate. After parking on the street, she found Holly Hot Rod, another queen.

"Your man said you needed some loves," she revealed, hugging the now-clued-in, in-promptu hostess.

The mustachioed man with the silver belt buckle scurried in quickly, unwrapping the veggies and dip, opening chips, and dumping them into bowls, then playing AC/DC from his phone to the sound system about the deck. Head down, he rushed back outside without saying a word, not making eye contact, like some tall humble servant.

After Black Russian number two, Audrey absented herself to put on mascara, some quick foundation, and brush through her hair. She replaced the sweatshirt with a pretty blouse. She'd let herself go mightily, having probably gained ten pounds on her skinny frame.

She flipped on the Karaoke machine in the living room and stated with reverence, "OWEN, I NEED TO TALK TO YOU!"

Everyone present paused in their conversations, glancing around for the man in question. Without hesitation, Owen looked up to the porch roof and responded loudly, "YES, GOD?"

Audrey heard that. Their guests laughed. He felt pretty loose, having had four beers. She stepped out onto the porch.

"Can't talk now, babe," he said quickly. "Gotta start the grille." He avoided her gaze; he had held his pee to avoid going inside. But he glanced quickly at his love, giving her a kiss on the cheek, still nervous.

Audrey placed her arm around his waist while Owen tried to light the grill. "Leave me be, woman! People want to eat!" Then turned and exclaimed, "Why are you surprised? Everybody loves you." He leaned close and added in a whisper, "especially me." She kissed him back. "Are you mad?"

"Do I look mad?"

"No, you look beautiful." Then Owen handed her the spatula and sprinted inside to use the can.

Miss Demeanor and Gary took a break from screwing to be social, although not much past that would sprout between them.

Peter and Corrine arrived around six. She was lucky, barely able to get a sitter for Corey. Her ex would probably blow that all out of proportion.

What a smash! When Owen wasn't cooking or loading the potato gun, he told everyone: "Go tell Audrey how much you love her." And he wasn't kidding.

Twenty more folks stopped by to make amends for letting Miss Holly Hot Rod out of their sight. Cherry V, a very popular queen, appeared in short order to support another queen.

A co-worker confirmed a really dumb thing that Audrey's boss had done. During a team birthday party in the breakroom, he struggled to open up a bag of chips, with his subordinates suggesting the littlest woman in the office help. This over encouragement caused the boss to tear the bag nearly in two, spraying Fritos about like a bomb went off. Another bomb was ticking too.

"He's going away, when?" Audrey asked Corrine.

"When's the job is done. Probably next week," she confided.

"Three deaths in succession, and now your beau's about to leave you?" Audrey had had too much time to think, to observe, from a very lonely place. "I'm sorry."

"Maybe week after next." It was only Audrey that Corrine would confide in. "Peter told me he loves me! What am I supposed to do now?"

She became stern before a scrunched-up face. "Don't you dare cry." It seemed mean. "Then you're going to make me cry." They hugged for a long moment, jabbing at their eyes with tissues so no one would see. "So, what are you going to do?"

"I don't' know." But the womenfolk thought they knew. Audrey told Donna, who told two girls, who told other two girls. Within minutes, like lightning amongst the buzzed dolls, the same question was on each of their lips: Peter and Corrine were in love, and he was leaving her because he had to? It didn't make sense.

Like the blowup Flamingo costumes that the party goers slid into, watching peoplebirds dance and attempt to mate on the lawn was nonsensical, but hysterical. The pair had long, pink necks and heads with beaks, with an inflatable doughnut body that the inebriated (usually couples) stepped into, past the pink legs and into the giant overshoes.

The grownups put their hands in little wings and tried to entertain, maybe try a little ass-grabbing. Owen, forever the host, had the air compressor at the ready. When Donna Diva and Lawrence had their turn, it was obvious to everyone watching that they were fucking each other. She pecked the flamingo bill at his pecker, then spun around, raising her tail feathers high. They bumped into each other until the end of the song. It probably wouldn't have mattered even if her husband Aaron had been there.

"Gary says you're leaving! It's so sad." He may have made a play for Miss Demeanor, if he could have gotten close enough.

Peter stammered, "Well, I have to. It's the end of the job. I'm getting kicked out of Washington state." The dumb joke resounded untrue.

Serenity Jade asked if he'd come back. "You know, Corrine has never had a good man. Never really had the chance. We love you, Peter."

THUMP. The hair spray ignited, sending a half a russet into the valley. Mount Rainier still retained snow in late August. In the dimming light it disappeared like a memory of something sad. And many times more, THUMP THUMP, everyone who wanted a turn got one.

"It had to be you

It had to be you

I wandered around

And finally found

A somebody who,

Could make me be true

Could make me be blue

Or even be glad

Just to be sad, thinking of you.

Some others I've seen

Might never be mean

Might never be cross

Or try to be boss

But they wouldn't do,

Boy nobody else

Gave me a thrill

With all your faults

I love you still,

It had to be you

Wonderful you

It had to be you."

Brian reproduced Harry Connick Jr. wonderfully in karaoke. Who knew?

Broken up pallets kept the fire pit going. Corrine had a few Black Russians and her demonstration as a flamingo was filthy. She and Peter kept bumping with the inflatables in forecast of sending the sitter home, making sure the little guy slept soundly.

He'd paced himself with tappers, eating two dogs. It was time to get Corrine home and Peter made his way to Audrey to thank her for the party, not knowing what else to say. She beamed, drunk with well wishes.

Owen hugged him. "Just remember, partner, you never know what you got till it's gone." It was a song lyric somewhere. And profound. Of course, he was in on the game. Owen was a hugging man. Somewhere, although he hardly knew him, it felt like a loss, driving away. He was a good man, Peter knew that.

Donna said it best, telling Peter, "You should stay with us, in the Pacific Northwest." The firepit warmed backs until partiers sat in chairs to feel the warmth. "When will you ever fall in love again, Peter?" Her voice sounded like a squawking duck with a rasping, smoking cough. But it rang true.

He turned Corrine's elbow toward the truck for twenty minutes. Katastrophic called, "Goodbye, Peter!" It was echoed from the party goers. Gary kept silent, knowing he would see his "boss" next week.

Audrey placed her arm around her man's waist as the new lovers left, snuggling her own guy.

"What da' think? Will he come back?" asked Owen.

"Hope so." Audrey rested her head upon his shoulder. "I have."

...

The Project Manager of the JCPenney project knew it'd be wrapped up before the end of the week. Driving over the weekend could be time and a half/double time. It was easier to simply pay Peter for the following week, too, both forty-hour weeks on the timecards. There was an incentive to get home, with thanks for a job well done.

Shuffling aircraft parts across the country was getting busier and busier. Corrine became so adept at her job that they gave her a person to train.

Shelly was a little younger than her, a former supply specialist in the Marine Corps, fresh from active duty. She was used to performing work immediately, and needing more, though it took time for her to civilianize. After the two-week job shadowing, Shelly forthrightly started calling herself Corrine's minion. It didn't take but six months before she was as productive as she, kind of.

Hard work was rewarded with more hard work as Corrine was given another trainee/ minion. Her job had morphed into a supervisory role and she had it so noted at her annual review. She asked her boss what she could do to get promoted. More school was the answer in short. Make the two-year associate's degree into a business degree.

He challenged her to create a plan. "No one is going to manage your career except for you. You're young, you're just getting started."

"I think I should get a step increase because I'm supervising two people."

"Show me a plan on what your continued education would look like. How could that benefit the company? You know Boeing gives educational assistance to employees sometimes. Maybe we could submit something. No promises." Times were good, and talented, hardworking young folks were rare, so he gave her the raise. In three months, she submitted that detailed plan.

Now a man had thrown everything into a tizzy. They had one last weekend together, then on Monday it'd be wheels spinning. She maintained that she wasn't going to let him go seeing her all weepy, clutching, and needy. A thunderstruck idea came over her.

She called Kimmy. "Hey, Miss Jade, remember your offer to borrow your cabin for a weekend?"

"Are you going to take him to the island?" Oh, what a great idea she thought. Super beautiful and romantic. "Do you want it for this weekend?" Kimmy was super excited for her friend. "I can drop you the key anytime."

"If it's okay," Corrine insisted. "Only if you weren't going. I was thinking maybe Friday through Sunday."

"No one's going to be out there," Kimmy interrupted. "It's better that people go out there, keep the pipes from rusting you know."

Princess De Menthe was bursting. "Thanks so much. This is going to be our last weekend together until who knows, and I want it to be super special. I'll wash the sheets, don't worry."

"It'll be so beautiful out there. Three days? You may even get out of the cabin!"

Fifteen minutes later she called Peter. "Hey baby, I'm thinking about taking Friday off. You want to go to paradise? When can you get your truck packed up?"

The Silverado had a standard eight-foot box, with a cap that had small side compartments. In all, like Peter had said, every square inch would be packed with tools and a few personal items, like a cheap printer that wouldn't die despite being rattled several times between California and Wisconsin. A seven-foot ladder, drywall cart, air compressor, miter box, nail guns, hand tools, and more. He had to fill the dumpster and leave the store in good shape. Rolls of carpet, gallons of properly labeled paint (date, Sherwin Williams number, and gloss), plus a bounty of adhesives, tape, and sundry hardware in a big cabinet where he'd had his office for over four months.

"Where's paradise? Yeah, I can make that happen. You're drivin' then."

Corrine was almost gushing. "Kimmy has a cabin on McNeil Island. It's gorgeous out there. Let me figure out the rest and I'll call you back."

They still weren't at the trading, "Love you, babe" part of their relationship. Peter talked about love in general ways. She was committed but wanted him to swallow the hook deep into his gut and come back. Admitting such was an additional vulnerability Corrine hadn't spare emotion for, not anymore, not for anyone. Peter would have to tie up the wolf's tail or not.

Gary was going to get paid his forty no matter what, when Peter stopped working simply meant sooner happy happy fun time with Miss Demeanor.

Evan answered his cell that Tuesday morning directly. That was lucky. "I'm working Friday afternoon, so I don't know." Her ex was never sure.

"I could drop Cory off with your mom, like before noon."

"How come? You got plans for the weekend? Like with your new boyfriend?" His eyes glinted, wanting information so he could turn it against her. Like, "Mommy wants to spend time with her new boyfriend more than you" type of venom. When Cory mentioned Peter for the first time, her ex dug hard into the tot, even getting Grandma in on the cause of finding useful details.

Lots of those questions made the child bewildered, like never seeing people's faces because they wore a mask, their feelings hidden, a kind of emotional retardation. Planting seeds of doubt such as, "I don't know if that's a good idea," when all Cory said was that he played on the swings with Peter. But Corrine had seen this movie before.

"Okay, well, I'll call her to let her know."

Snarkily, Evan replied, "She's right here, but I don't know what she has planned."

"Quid pro quo, I've adjusted my schedule. Remember last month when you didn't get him on Friday night, because you wanted to go drinking with a buddy?"

"What does that mean?"

"This for that. I help you, you help me. Forget it." God, he was so stupid. The best way to deal with Evan was simply to treat him as an adult would a petulant child. "Put Sharon on the phone."

"No! I'll let her know."

"Put her on the phone, now!" Corrine didn't usually take such a strident tone, but this could be Peter and her last weekend together. Her ex didn't pick up on the importance, just that he'd scolded.

It was fine dropping Corey off in the morning. Evan was going to be like a ship anchor chained to her ass until Corey was all grown up, and probably beyond that, if she lived that long. But Corrine was smart enough to realize that this storm would pass, and that she did take good care of herself.

Everything about the ferry was exciting. The risk of not getting on board meant not getting to be alone, together again. Peter didn't want to ask about the particulars of the "cabin" as if it could be like a yurt, where they'd have to buy diesel to run the single naked bulb suspended over the squeaky, twin bed. Screen doors would keep most bugs out and deaden air flow, keeping the atmosphere sticky.

It was coming! Everyone was so nonchalant, though. He felt like the Labradoodle who stuck her head out of the truck window. The ferry made a huge arch toward its dock, taking an improbable angle. The south Salish Sea was calm on a toasty afternoon. Cars began to zoom off. Corrine had paid at the kiosk. Once parked toe to heel in four rows, they decided quickly to go to the observation deck above the cars.

Without bow or stern, the powerful boat could hold maybe eighty cars and trucks. The shoreline shrank until it appeared like a model railroad set at the scale you couldn't see people, just their houses and the train that sped just above the beach. The narrow bridge at Tacoma could just be seen spanning the Sound.

Corrine told him how excited she was to spend this awesome weekend together, hugging and placing her face on his chest. The view, the girl wrapped around him, the forward motion of the boat, the sun's heat beat back by moderate winds, invisible, not seeing from where it came or where it went. Everything seemed uncertain in that moment seventy feet above the sea bottom, to Peter.

"I want to see the ferry dock."

"How old are you?" He merely held up his hand and splayed his fingers. "I better not end up with two children."

For a moment Corrine cringed that she may have said the wrong thing, but her man grinned and went forward to feel the diesel engine's drive the screws hard toward the pier gates, sloshing the water powerfully, it pushing back against the momentum of the boat. In order, they drove off into a wooded, hilly, playland for those who worked really hard, and got really lucky finding such a peaceful haven. Even to a non-Buddhist it felt like Zen, being fully alive, appreciative.

"It's a house!" The fluffy Muppet was crying. She was so ready to get out and explore the smells exploding in her brain. Around two small lakes within McNeil Island people built homes by the hundreds. The winter population was maybe a thousand souls. During the summer, it was many times that. First, they had to play house. Corrine got the kitchen set up with the few groceries she brought. Then they could love, go for a little hike, visiting beaches, the Labradoodle fetching tennis balls chucked into the Sound, then sticks thrown into the lake, in order to wash her off. . .mostly.

The lovebirds stopped by the one store on the island. It sold gas, DVDs, a few foodstuffs, construction materials, alcohol, and had a swell café and deli. One could indeed live here year-round, with maybe a monthly Costco trip to the mainland. Kimmy and Brian bought their two-bedroom gem in foreclosure and stuck another 30K into it. It had an open concept roof line that harbored space for an office above the kitchen and bunk beds above the second bedroom.

The master and dining area opened onto the deck where deer ran through the yard. Cassie would go nuts if she detected them. He cooked meat with fire while she set the table. They watched a movie, fell asleep, then dragged themselves to bed to make love and fall into a deep, satisfying spell; the windows stayed open as the island was always cooler. Gentle breezes wafted in until Corrine got too chilly.

On Saturday they lounged, walked the dog, then went to the deli for super sandwiches and smoothies. Hit the beach, swam in the lake, visited a cousin of Corrine's and her family and clan of half shod kids and dogs running wild on a wooded lot. Her husband, about Peter's age, was drinking whiskey and building a long dog run for his pooches, chasing the kids from time to time. He politely declined the offer of whiskey, as drinking booze on a warm afternoon would probably mean an impromptu nap before supper time.

Another friend, who worked at the deli came over for beverages that evening. Peter barbequed chicken this time. He told her his description of wooing Corrine was like trying to capture lightning in a bottle. The three of them got a little drunk and then after she left there wasn't any happy happy fun time as settling into clean sheets, the crickets chirping, and the fan blowing low. Their cuddle transformed into deep sleep, dreams of what could be, or terrors of what had been.

Bacon sizzled. Corrine found it frozen into almost an icicle in Kimmy's freezer.

"Good boys get bacon," she said.

"What about bad boys?" Peter asked. Her hands moved over his pajama pants. "Tell me about Texas."

Neither wished to frame the ending scene. What would they say when that last moment came? Not some inane bullshit promise or "how much you mean to me?" junk.

There were two Christian services on the island, it being Sunday.

Cassie cried to be let out, but she couldn't stop barking after scampering deer, making her human mother scold and call her back before they could leave for the service.

Peter asked her to take an island tour, of the richy-rich houses and the get-a-longs, just to tempt a private ambition of what could be. There were lots of homes that would list toward a million bucks. They even looked through an open house, with a very odd layout and wide views of the southern portion of the Puget Sound. Kimmy and Brian lent them a slice of paradise. Maybe they could do it, too, perhaps. Why not them? Couldn't they have something themselves, they pretended.

Corrine was sold. She tried to figure the next steps. Peter had a pretty good skill set. His woman was an earner, ambitious, and just getting started. Were they going to roll the dice? Who would shoot first? Peter told himself he shouldn't cry when it came time to say goodbye. He later realized that wouldn't have been possible the moment Corrine broke down.

She called Sharon, asking her to take Corey to daycare Monday morning, buying one more night. Their rhythm beat to conclusion, then they showered together, kisses and tears blending. In the early morning hours Corrine dropped him off by the company truck outside the Extended Stay. There were big, lumpy tears; he couldn't help it. Love letters were tucked inside his overnight bag to find, along with a pair of perfumed undies, just for laughs. The route reminded Peter of his home far away.

"Don't forget about me," she implored. The wolf, her Lupus, would keep her unloved. Corrine knew it would be so.

"I couldn't if I tried." It was a silly song lyric that came in the moment.

Both Corrine and Peter doubted what he may do.

They kissed goodbye. She chewed Trident, and he tasted like a cup of Americano with cream.

Peter settled the bill, checking out after many months. He made sure the room was now empty, forgetting nothing.

Wheels spun East.

It wasn't until traversing the mountains near Laramie, Wyoming that Peter felt and understood that he wasn't motoring home, but was actually moving away from it, away from her, decidedly so.

Part Two

14

The Birth of Cherry Nova

Having a baby had twisted Delmonica's frame, like getting side swiped, rear ended, or having a head on collision simultaneously. Her eighteen-year-old body might not ever run the same again. Off the showroom floor she'd been flawless. Her impregnator, Jackass (pet name) hadn't even gotten a scratch in the baby making process, while an engine block violently left its compartment through her front grille.

From then on, little things went awry. She was tired all the time, losing pressure, like a right front tire, but not the other ones. Her idle was disrupted by heartburn, no matter what she put in the tank. There was now a tear in the back seat upholstery, probably from something sharp. Delmonica cried a few times just thinking about her condition, not knowing what breast feeding would do to her once-perfect boobs.

Her boyfriend had qualified for a home loan, so their little family had their own space, kinda. But the days of the free test drives were over. Jackass was going to buy "as is." She loved him tremendously. He paid the bills, as best he could, paying the minimum balance some months, humping soda, gobbling up the overtime, taking care of his new family, the way Ryan tried to show him before he gave up in an angry stop.

It was Jack who wanted to name their son, Ryan, after D's father, who had recently passed away. But since his omnipresent mother-in-law had taken the third bedroom in the little Ranch home and hated his fateful father-in-law with a passion, Delmonica suggested that they name the baby John, after him, with the middle name becoming Ryan.

Her mother would be furious, which was her insane usual, but less so than having to refer to the tiny tot by the hateful name Tiffany continuously disparaged. It was an argument Del preferred not to have continuously for the overlap of their lives. It was what she directed to the nurse when they filled out the birth certificate application.

Tiffany later objected in terror, but Delmonica responded like a Roman Governor: "What I have written I have written." Jack was often relieved by her leadership when he faltered, when he lost faith in what might happen, his lovely was sure.

Tiffany was putting Ryan's affairs in her order. But as his nearest kin and only child, Delmonica became the beneficiary through probate. The estate was more like a pail with many holes in it. She observed what little water it held being siphoned off, after finally sleeping a whole night through.

Her uncle Brian called Del sometimes and came over to the new house when he wasn't on the road, working, to see little Johnny. A firestorm erupted as Brian wanted to get some of his brother's effects as mementos. He wanted to see if there was anything that Ryan had kept from his parents, pictures, and such. But his ex-sister-in-law had immediately sold what could be sold to Goodwill for pennies and burned whatever remained.

A bonfire was more therapeutic than simply putting stuff in the trash. The only answer given her was that Tiffany was the only one who was getting Ryan's house ready for sale. If Brian cared, Delmonica was told, he should have cleared out the house himself. Her mother was hostile to all of Ryan's relatives and friends and demonstrated this even more openly than before his suicide.

But there was one thing that Delmonica wanted. It was the 1970 Chevy Nova, painted a flat Monza red, which took an orange hue in the sunshine.

"We have to sell that to pay off his credit cards. You don't understand," Tiff told her daughter. "You've been flat on your back with the baby, and I've had to make the decisions." Anything that reminded her of Ryan had to be gotten rid of. Seeing it in their garage would be too much, even if Jack had it under a cover.

"Use the Go Fund Me money for that." The apple hadn't fallen far from the tree. Delmonica baited her.

Seething, Tiff erupted with, "I used that money to drive your worthless father into the ground." The truthful pun slipped out unintentionally.

"How much did you skim off the top for the vacation to Montana?" The charge echoed like a bomb exploding in a canyon. "If you had any money then why are you living here for free? Why aren't you doing your customer service gig?"

The responding lie had been prepared: "I quit, so I could take care of you!" Her uber fat frame rippled in fear. "The car has to go!" Wheezing, she added, "so I can pay your father's bills." Tiffany smoked almost a pack a day, and was never pleasant to be around, even if one couldn't smell her deceit.

The baby was stirring because of the shouts coming from the living room. The kid still slept most of the day. "Tell me, Mom, how did my father write checks for your bills after he died, like your last month's rent? I can show you online, right now."

Delmonica paused the attack, momentarily, moving towards the baby's room so Tiff couldn't try to pick him up as a shield. "And I ordered checks in my name from that account, so don't try forging my signature, or sort through my fucking mail anymore!"

Del had the proof, like opened envelopes from the attorney ad litem. She had direct contact with the realtor, too. A fighter, Delmonica was back on her feet, having been knocked down. Although there wasn't much in equity in the big, two story, 2500 square foot, four bedroom, two and a half bath house. It had appreciated a lot in twelve years, everyone suspected. The second mortgage was for only about 30K, and it probably paid for the Nova.

Always the martyr, Tiffany said, "I did what I had to for you." There was always a shred of truth within Tiffany's multitude of deceptions and outright lies, just enough to rationalize hurting whomever, in the moment of her constant need.

Delmonica picked up little Johnny, returning to the living room, just able to turn down the intensity. "Look, Mom, I do appreciate you getting the ball rolling after the tragedy. I know you don't see it that way, but I do." The double meanings were truthful, powerful, and shrewd.

Sometimes the newborn would open his baby blues for a few moments. She turned his face to the new Grandma. "He has eyes like you. I bet he turns out to be a little scoundrel, too." That pleased Tiffany well and brought the temperature down. However, now that Del had the upper hand, and knew that she had to use it quickly or not at all, she pressed, "Jack and I appreciate you being here, but you're going to have to make a plan." Meaning get the fuck out. "This wasn't ever going to be forever, all of us in this house." She placed the baby into the new Granny's arms. "Here, you take him. I have to get to the bathroom."

Del turned on the fan, leaned upon the vanity, and smiled into the mirror. That was a bitch move, she thought. Her Mommy should be proud.

If there was a capital gain from the sale of her house, she planned to buy rings for both of them and propose to Jack, setting things straight, correctly in their orbit, gravitating toward each other, planning a reception, and a justice of the peace. He was so awesome, as a lover, taking her to pleasurable places.

It seemed so clear what Delmonica wanted to do. Until she reappeared and took her baby back. The most private, dear, and boring moments were under constant surveillance and judgment. Like binge watching a TV series in the middle of the day without regret or having competition to change a diaper or attend to a single whimper. Two women could not occupy one nest.

...

"If I wanted to do Pin Up, how would I get started?"

When Kimmy answered the phone call from Delmonica, she was worried something might be wrong. "Huh?" she stammered. "You want to do what?"

"You know, be like your Pin Up character, Serenity Jade. Wear the outfits, be in the pageants?"

She'd be the youngest in the club by far. But Kimmy could mentor her, be her sponsor! This was the best news in months, like telling girlfriends that such and such was going to have a baby. "Well, yeah, you can do that. There's only one more car show this season, I think. But there's other stuff we do. Why do you want to? Would you want to join the Brazen Beauties Pin Up Dolls?

Del thought for a moment. She hadn't really thought about being in a club with mostly older women. And she said just that.

"Everyone's older than you, Del." Then Kimmy laughed. Del, too. "What brought this on? Why are you interested?"

"Well, the times I went with my dad and Jack, it was super fun. I was like a blimp and all the girls had on their pretty party dresses and such. The guys have their cars, always talking about the next build. I don't know. Seems like I want to build something from myself. Someone really fun. How did you pick out your name? Serenity Jade?"

It was a ritual amongst Pin Ups to ask that question of each other. It defined or summarized who you wanted to transform yourself into, like an elevator speech. If men asked, the answer should be quick and clever.

Miss Jade said, "Jade is my birthstone, and I like how it brings out the green in my eyes. A Pisces knows things from deep within and can tell if something is good or bad. And I like the peaceful aspect. Serenity doesn't imply weakness to me, but strength."

"That's cool," Delmonica said truthfully.

"Do you have any idea who you want to be?" It sounded like an invitation to play pretend.

"Oh, yeah. I already figured out a name." Then Del just stopped talking.

"Well. Are you going to tell me?"

"What do you think about 'Cherry Nova?' Does it sound dumb?"

"Holy shit! Like Ryan's car. That is so cool. Like a tribute to your dad! Oh, that's so touching. Is that what you were thinking?" Miss Jade gushed. "And it's red like cherries. Is that it?"

Miss Nova considered. "No. Well, I guess so. But really it sounds really bad ass. Instead of Chevy it's Cherry, like a play on words."

"It could be Shelly Nova?" But that idea fell flat.

Del was going for what was beautiful, sexy, and hot. In perfect condition, like she very recently was, and wanted to have back.

"So, what do we do next? Can I get into a pageant?"

Miss Jade spoke apprehensively, "We'll have to talk to the Donna Diva."

"Oh, come on, there's no such person. Is there?"

"She's the President. But it should be cool. I'll be your sponsor. Bringing in new prospects is like a feather in my cap. Maybe you're the spark I need. You'll have to register for the event, and it's not discounted for non-club members. Probably be about fifty bucks."

Delmonica asked her, "How often do you feel like you're Serenity Jade? And I always wanted to ask if you've ever won a tiara or something."

Kimmy frowned on the phone. "No, not yet." Miss Jade hadn't a princess tiara and there was nothing tranquil about that. Sponsoring Cherry Nova was going to be a reboot, and she'd make it happen. "But that's a really good question. I guess I slip into her when I'm feeling…ohh, I don't know, unsure or anxious. A lot of times I forget I created her. But it's always fun! Get on your horse, we're going shopping."

"I'm not going to have a lot of money to spend."

"You don't need a lot. And let's not take Tiffany."

"Oh, fuck no. Let's bring Corrine, and then…"

Miss Jade interrupted, so excited, "Let me be the one to call her, pleaassee?"

...

She'd forget about the time difference and call just before a farm boy's bedtime. She teased him about milking the goats, asking if the teats excited him. Corrine liked trying to get him worked up, so he'd dream about her. Peter at first forgot about the time difference and called while she was hustling to get Cory to day care and herself to work.

He'd leave a voicemail, or maybe a text to say that he had called and was thinking of her. Then the day came that they didn't talk directly. Young lovers trying to keep a tenuous two thousand miles cord from getting a burr or an abrasion was going to be tough.

From the stationary store Corrine bought pretty peach paper and envelopes. She sent her love notes perfumed to the high heaven. Soon after he started on the road, Peter let his lease lapse from the nearest big city where he had started his construction career. His folks let him keep his old room and he paid for storage in the closest town.

He had everything he needed to set up an apartment quickly, whenever the need arose again. The tradeoff was free labor. But he could do everything on the farm, and liked it, but didn't relish the idea of staking the rest of his life in sleepy, industrious, central Wisconsin. Corrine's letters found their intended target: Peter's mother. She was obviously playing for keeps, all in, dirty pool.

When her third letter arrived in his third week back on the farm, Peter was wrapping hay rolls with white plastic, making giant marshmallows, feeling hot and dusty. Out with the regular hired hands, this was where the work was that day. Sometimes, Peter would operate the air conditioned, 165K John Deere Tractor. His mom left the peach envelope on the top of the mail and her husband found it first, remarking that something smelled sweet. Now they both knew her name. Peter had mentioned meeting a girl in Seattle.

"What is she like?" Mom wanted to ask.

"When are you going back?" Dad would like to know, a big, wry smile on his weathered face.

Instead of opening the perfumed letter from his love, he listened to his voicemail. The prosperous farm paid a lot for an internet hotspot, the family typically kept their smartphones on the big kitchen island. They grabbed a numbered Motorola from the changing station when on property. Peter's company was sending him to Chicago to remodel a diamond store in a suburban mall. This month-long assignment was as close to a death sentence as one could get, working in Chicagoland second/third shift and living out of a suitcase in the cock-a-roach motel next to the mall. . .without actually dying, of course.

Being on the road could be wonderful and it could be dreadful. As a traveling Superintendent, he'd made a big jump professionally. In the nearest big city, he'd probably have to be a worker bee for a while, reestablish himself, in order to get off the road, and stay close to his family and old friends. And now he saw the peach envelope right on top of the rest of the mail. Peter's mom was quite the comedian.

She sold her son the farm's 2013 Silverado for one dollar. Peter sold his 2008 Dodge Ram to a guy, who knew a guy, who worked the farm, for $1,500. Beatrice then bought another F150 as a business deduction, although she still got the chrome package 'cause she wanted to show off their prosperity when she went to town, or when she went to her bible study classes at the United Methodist church. Peter's mom supported the sparsely attended congregation, every year almost to the tune of a chrome package. "Don't get mud on the chrome" was a saying between them meaning, "You work too hard."

His company would pay for four nights lodging each week. That was the deal. If you didn't get out of town by two in the afternoon, Chicago traffic was as bad as anywhere. 250 miles one way. Super! The subcontractors didn't like working nights either.

The month after the Chicago gig, Peter hung drywall with a crew only seventy-five miles from the farm. Lots of windshield time, and weeks of unemployment between gigs. Construction slowed down near to deer hunting, too.

Peter spoke to Gary once, after he had gone back to Missouri, but not for very long. He was still "seeing" Aleia, but of course had no intention of moving anywhere.

Peter felt like he had become completely disconnected since leaving the Pacific Northwest, unplugged, losing a charge.

...

"Do you think I could be a princess?" Delmonica had her head on his chest. They'd gone to bed early, soon after Jack had some supper and held little Johnny briefly. He didn't get home until after seven PM. If they didn't share the living room flat screen, then maybe they'd have a private conversation wherever in their new house they wanted.

"Do you think I could be a princess?" Once again, she asked.

The correct answer was obviously, yes, but he garbled something unintelligible in the fuzzy glowing tiredness of the post cuddle, "Eyedon if uawannato."

The baby monitor stayed silent. "What was that? I think I will make a very good princess."

After a really long pause, her fiancé managed to ask why.

"No, dum dum, like, I'm going to be a Pin Up Doll and win a tiara. Then I'll be a princess, and you'll have to treat me like I'm a princess." Jack was unfortunately regaining some consciousness and began to rub the arm that lay across his chest. "Kimmy, you know Serenity Jade said that I could probably get in on the next pageant in a couple of weeks."

"At a car show?"

"Yeah, I guess so. Kimmy wasn't sure, but it will be so much fun, don't you think?" It meant that he and junior would be solo for most of the day. It was kinda scary, kinda not.

"I don't suppose your mom would come to help with the baby? Which is fine. Wait, you're going to do Pin Up? So, what's your name, then?" Jack asked, a little snarky.

"Cherry Nova!"

"Oh, that's cool. I'm proud of you babe. Trying new stuff."

"We're keeping the Nova, by the way."

"I thought that we..."

"And I told my mom that she has to move out. I can't deal with her hovering around all the time. I got this mom thing."

Jack was still freaked out by the cost of baby stuff, the required overtime, credit card balances, and hopefully making ends meet, which they weren't. However, Miss Nova wanted to screw again, and he couldn't complain about that.

...

That Thanksgiving was Corrine's turn to take Cory to Yakima, to see her parents. When would he fly back? The peach scented letters were mailed intermittently, then stopped, in. "I love you" degenerated to an emoji.

15
Paula's Service

Calling complete strangers to tell God awful news had lasted a full two weeks. Corrine tried doing it during her lunch break or while parked temporarily at the daycare. It was always going in blind and by the time she got through the "G's" and began hoping that no one would pick up she knew that she'd failed.

Paula, as a normal person, never deleted her contacts. Transferring the list to new phones over years became a time constrained, herculean task. Usually, people didn't recall Paula, or barely remembered who Paula was, if she actually talked to a human person. Like the guy who cut her grass ten years ago, now a grown man. He was sorry to hear about her passing. He had called Corrine back after a strange voicemail.

After twenty some calls, she found a woman in Portland who was interested in attending the service, but then her motherly instinct took hold, and she FEDEX'd the address book to Cristin in Daytona. He could deal with it. She had her own son to raise. She tried to bench herself, but she still attended the Eagles Club meetings to help get the word out about Paula's service. Few members used social media. Could Facebook finally become beneficial after a person died?

Somewhere between being able to feed himself and do all kinds of big boy stuff like using the remote and reading books with mom, Cory listened to what the grown-up people said and tried to talk to them about it. He asked Paula if she liked having "all the tappers?" Because everybody kept asking her for them.

Big people laughed when he said things like that, but he didn't know why. It was fun making big people laugh. His big friend Peter moved away, like sometimes his friends at daycare did too. Cory had a "girlfriend" in the daycare, or that's what her mom told his mom. He heard them say that a couple times. But then his girlfriend stopped coming. All Corrine could do was tell him that she had moved away.

"How come everybody moves away?" he'd asked her, then he sulked gloomily toward the oversized Legos. That pinched her heart hard. Cory's friend Paula had moved away, too.

It was bitter to watch a child experience loss. It was a different kind of cry. A sad cry, not like priorities and completing demands of a grownup that didn't mean a thing to Cory. He began to sense that big people had important things to do that had nothing to do with him. Sometimes he felt that he got in the way of grownups doing important things and had to take care of himself, be quiet, and just stay inside the house watching TV. Unless it was okay to go outside, if Grandma Sharon said it was okay.

With Peter gone and the pageant season nearly done, Corrine reflected on her being a good mommy or not? It was as if she didn't have the space to reason if she had been neglectful of her little guy. Only one funeral service left, and she would be past the most turbulent life storm so far.

What hadn't they been doing that used to be fun? Bubble bath time had become letting the kid squirt the stuff in and giving him privacy. Which, to Cory, felt like being left alone, which was okay, too, sometimes. But it was always better when mom splashed and played.

Her house really needed a big clean. The clutter filled every corner. Cassie's big tail spilled things, toppled stacks over, wagging all the time in anticipation of loves. Cory'd yell, trying to get her in trouble, wanting to tease Mommy about their messy home.

The dog was the most consistent element in their lives, always with licks and wanting to play. Corrine tried to make it home to let Cassie outside at midday but work often squeezed lunchtime out. The kid's room was a wreck; she'd been too tired to force her son to help her clean it. Clean clothes stayed in laundry baskets. She kept telling Corey that one day all their stuff was going to the Goodwill. Just to see if it made Mom laugh, the lad petted Cassie and told her loudly that they weren't ever going to take her to the Goodwill! He thought it was like when they brought food to the poor people pantry.

For his effort he got a kiss. "You're a sweet boy."

"Cassie won't move away, right, Mom?"

It made her want to cry, a flutter behind her eyes. She petted the contented, huge pup and lied a little bit, or a lot: "Nope. Not ever." Trying to explain what death was, that evening, to a child needing reassurance had to wait. To be honest, Corrine wasn't sure why people had died, or moved away.

...

Queen Holly Hot Rod was early. Serenity Jade drove with Delmonica. Princess De Menthe met them late at the Mall's Brew Haus. A transformation of fantasy began after singular adult beverages or club soda. One true Queen, one Princess, and a sponsor seemed kind of old fashioned to Del, or maybe that was the point. Except for Corrine, the other women were old enough to be her mom, but she thought it best to think of them now as sisters. The established Pin Ups were more excited than the youngin'.

"So, what's the look you're going for?" asked Queen Hot Rod. "Who are you?" It was a bit over the top. But Miss Nova kept pace, knowing that Donna Diva had sanctioned her attempt to become a Prospect.

"I'm Cherry Nova, and I'm the fastest girl here."

"Ohh, I like that." Then the Queen added, "I think you should avoid the straight up slut thing," and, "You're not the sweet girl, sorry." Those critiques were exchanged and morphed a girl's alter ego.

"I could have done the working girl shtick, but it wasn't my calling," Holly Hot Rod admitted. "I want to be glamorous. Like an old time movie star."

Corinne De Menthe confided in a hushed tone, "I chose liqueur, 'cause it makes me quicker." That got laughs and smiles from her sisters. "And it was a clever play on words. And I like green. And boys."

"So, what might you be going for, Miss Nova?" pestered the Queen. "Who do you want to be?"

"Well, I'm open to suggestions, kind of. The Nova was my dad's, and I'm going to keep it, no matter what. But I just had my baby and it kind of destroyed my body, so I want to feel sexy again."

Serenity piped in, "I like my niece's can-do attitude. What about the Rosie the Riveter routine?" It wasn't usual, but a young vivacious girl could sell it. And popularity was all about sales.

"Cherry, do you work on the cars, like a mechanic?" Princess De Menthe asked although she didn't think so. The names role playing could get confusing but if they were going to pretend the time was now.

"Ohh, fuck no. I mean, I guess I know some stuff. It's Jack who works on cars."

Holly cut to the chase: "Yeah, but could you fake it?"

"Let's put her in fancy overalls, her hair tied up somehow with a red bandanna. Red nails, cherry red lipstick, a smear of fake grease on one cheek. Make her walk around with a monkey wrench. Real tough like."

"A monkey wrench, Corrine?" asked Miss Nova. "Now who doesn't know about cars? That's for plumbers."

"How do you know that?"

"'Cause, I'm Cherry Nova, and I work for a living." It seemed like a worthy tagline, so the girls settled up with the barmaid and paired up, Serenity and Cherry, then Corrine and Cherry, looking first for the sexy overalls. Old Navy had washed rid hole denim style ones. And the group texting began. Miss Jade pulled a short short version and held it up to Miss Hot Rod, "Is this too Daisy Duke?"

The youngest prospect ever asked, "Who's Daisy Duke?"

Serenity put the skimpy overalls back with a sigh. "Google the Dukes of Hazzard." Although the Nova did look a little like the "General Lee" 1969 Charger, but definitely not the nose. The building of Miss Cherry Nova's first Pin Up outfit continued for some hours, with the other girls buying stuff for themselves as well.

"It's going to be the last pageant of the season," said Holly, "so it'll probably be too cold to be wearing short shorts, even if her ass could handle it."

Excited children with pink shorts and black curly hair, like muffin tops, ran too far ahead for wandering families and then sprinted back to their mother's calls. . .sometimes. Asian fathers kept a stricter line, scolding in unamerican, American speech. But Holly had a hole in her pocket and was prepared to spend a fortune on anything she wanted.

"The only thing I regret is that my husband isn't here to hold my bags and give me his credit card." Miss Hot Rod was in rare form, allowable in a Queen. However, as a leader, she knew that it was important to crack the ice, and that the new mom might be skittish, most certainly being money poor.

"First, we need to buy acceptable underwear. It's been a while, and what I got has shit stains." Her Boeing wage and recent calamities made her raw. These Pin Ups were a bold lot. The question they had was whether Miss Nova was too.

Victoria's Secret spun the girls around. Coconut Craze was a splash. Serenity found some drawers, buying a few sexy ones for the young mom to impress her hard-working man. "What, can't your Auntie buy you something other than diapers? What about your butt?" The logic was hard to argue with.

Corrine told Cherry, "We're so excited, so you should be, too. Just go with it. We're buying you your first outfit."

"It's a tradition," added Holly. It hadn't been but it officially was now.

What kind of shoes would go with the denim? Cherry had to be able to get under a car if necessary. In Nordstroms Holly found a nice pair of suede boots with a zipper on the side. "What's your shoe size?"

It was a good match. But Cherry balked at the price at $185. "I can't let you do that, Holly."

In a delicious abuse of power, the Queen merely stated that she felt guilty about not getting her anything for her baby shower and that she was pulling rank. She bought the shoes.

Cherry bought a tight red tank top and a red Paisley bandana, to be half pulled out of her back pocket to concentrate men's eyes to her shapely ass. Without question Miss Nova finally had her mind right. Her new sisters wanted her to play dress up, to see where the build had gone so far. The overalls were very forgiving with different buttons and adjustable straps.

Serenity asked her to take down one strap. "What do you think, Miss Nova?"

"I have mom boobs now." And she sounded dejected. But the Queen announced that they were now going bra shopping, which nobody liked doing. Corrine bagged out, needing to pick up Cory from his dad's.

Jack was at home, where he babied his son by himself: he was introducing Johnny to baseball on TV and taking a nap when he did. He hoped Del got lots of stuff; she deserved it.

It was a lovely Sunday afternoon. So much seemed brand new and fearful.

...

Corrine was going to make the unofficial keynote speech for a member's service again. She was nervous, not sure what the tenor of the speech should be. What did Paula's dying mean? Anything?

Paula's son had brought his wife and two little kids to the Eagle club's memorial, in the PNW. There was a big crowd in the hall, flowing toward the bar. They listened to testimony amongst her friends they didn't know. Cory stood still as a good boy would. Cristin's kids were more like squirmy wormies, having met but not remembering Grandma.

Corrine didn't know what to say until she imagined her dead friend memorializing her own son. What might Paula say to Cristin?

"Hi, guys. For those of you who don't know me, I'm Corrine. I've been a member here for a couple of years. Paula was a member here, with her husband for over thirty. She was like a mom to me when I moved out here, listening to my sad bullshit at the bar." That got some laughs. "Sorry, kids. You have to put your hands over your ears around here sometimes." Cory was amazed with his mom holding everyone's attention with the microphone.

"I'm sure a lot of us can tell some funny stories about Paula, and I hope you will. I just wanted to say that we spent some money on this plaque, for Paula, which will be behind the bar where she served practically everyone who came here, and absolutely everybody who is in the Eagles Club." It was a small rectangle that memorialized Paula as Everybody's Mom. "She was always here, 'cause she loved being here with all of us. Her husband died and Paula moved right down the street, because this was where she was loved. I loved her. Has she just moved on without us? I hope so. She did so much for the club, spearheading the food pantry and all social events. She helped me plan our friend Ryan's service just a few months ago," She scrunched her face hard, but tears came out anyway.

Cory wanted to run to her, but Kimmy held him in his seat and said to him softly, "Your Mommy's just sad for a minute, because she's talking about Paula."

"Who died?"

"Yes."

Corrine continued. "Paula talked about her son Cristin sometimes, now he's here."

She didn't know what kind of a relationship they had, really. So, she was on thin ice. Corrine spoke about what she knew, the way she felt as a mom.

"I know that Paula loved her little man as much as a mother could. You want to protect your kids from every hurt, big and small. Hopefully, they'll confide in you, and as a mom you can help them sort things out. Well, that's what Paula did for me. So, Cristin, just know that Paula was loved so much here, in this club. Now your children probably won't remember this day, but they'll remember how you hold them. Thanks." She wiped away tears again and said, "Okay, who's next?" She stared down a regular named Dave. She waved the microphone at him.

"Oh hell," he reluctantly came forward and took the mike. "Thanks, Corrine. I really didn't want to have to follow that." And that got a few chuckles. "I don't know if I loved Paula. Never really thought about it that way." The crowd was amused. "Over all the years, and I come in every once in a while."

"You're here at the bar every day!" someone interrupted. The gang liked that.

"Okay, so I knew Paula pretty good, but I'll tell you now that when I came in this club, I never got a free beer out of her, not once. I'd be like, 'Hey Paula, I'm a club member, and the beer in that barrel is the club's beer, so why do I have to pay every time? Why do you have to be so nickel and dime?' And she shot right back, 'it's only seventy-five cent tappers, you cheap bastard!'"

Folks laughed and Cristin chimed in loudly, "Now that was my mom!"

Corey was right, he noticed. Tappers were funny!

"For years after that when I came in it was always, 'how's it going cheap bastard?'" There were more laughs. "Because of children being present I won't repeat the pet name I had for her."

Eagle Club faithfuls began to line up to roast their dearly departed friend. Getting a little emotional, Dave finished with, "I don't think I was in love with her, but I'll miss her."

...

He knew he could only text Mitch, hitting him up for another Monday lunch. His texts to Kaelani went unanswered. Owen spent some mornings looking out over the valley from his back porch, letting the dogs out, wondering how to connive a way to get a visit with the infant and Tamah's grandmother.

Audrey felt she was doing better, drinking fewer Black Russians, keeping Demarco's door closed. Ordinary, pleasant things tugged at her elbow like sunshine and friendships. The pithy condolences from coworkers were annoying and were responded to with, "thanks for saying that."

These grated upon her desire to smash into bridge abutments. Demarco was the only child she'd ever have and the future tried to vanish before her except that she kept waking up in the morning. About a month after her son's murder, strangely, her first waking thought was to cook dinner for Owen. Perhaps it was a "thank you" for his feeding her when she could barely move.

Her mom's dad liked to tease her, calling her a "sass a' frass" for her willful and funny nature. That grandpa was departed, too, and childhood remembrances stirred thoughts of the eternal, but it was nothing substantial. Soon the normal playfulness on the job found a way for Audrey finding amusing things to tell Owen about.

When she told him about her wicked abuse of power, buying Chevy Nova an expensive pair of boots, she felt like tinder needing a spark. Audrey even bought sexy knickers for herself but hadn't yet shared. It was almost like first dating, with the boy afraid to make the first move. Owen didn't push; however, she knew his balls were blue. Things needed to click soon.

The $500 bribe seemed to have no effect, although it was cashed. The effort had to be encased about the baby. When Owen texted Kaelani asking if she needed anything for Tamah, there was no response. Like the sound of one hand clapping, he imagined the giant's palm and the slight ridges pushing to the east like fingers, silently. She was sodden from emotional outburst, unlearned. Kaelani's clan were a very proud people. Family obviously meant a lot to them. And family did things for each other.

Something overt needed to happen. Like, perhaps, bringing over a present. Not a gift certificate to the local grocery, or a pallet full of diapers, but something practical. Going further without his love's awareness was too dicey. Maybe even counter-productive, too much out on a limb. Before he went to work, Owen would sip his tea, early in the mornings and wonder about the timing of exposing the vicious wound, the black spot that none could scratch or soothe, desperate to help find an escape for his love.

Anyone who has tried to secure a car seat knows the task is difficult and nasty. Every vehicle seems different, the event timed, blindly hands place themselves into inexplicable goo and crunchies. The child and seat are passed like a baton during a relay race. The older kids get, the worse conditions become.

American law dictated that children be strapped down like stock car drivers, to avoid becoming a ten-to-fifty-pound bag of bones bouncing around a car's interior during a rollover. American culture also dictated that driving with your kid meant moms become like stewardesses on airplanes and toddlers become more like adults sitting at a lunch counter.

Unsure, tiny hands hold juice pouches, Cheerios, gummies, and anything else that could encrust or adhere to a buckle or a latch. The noxious stink of half-chewed, petrified chicken McNuggets, food wrappers, and fries underneath the passenger seat were as ubiquitous in the cars of parents of small children, as stained and re-stained upholstery from upchucking, bundles of joy. Nose blind grownups rushed from one appointment to the next.

So, in Owen's thinking, a $200 brand new car seat, infant size, would necessarily be useful; he would just be taking care of family, of course, popping in on a Saturday afternoon, just to say "hi." Whatever shitty, used car seat Kaelani was using could be the spare, or placed in vehicle #2.

Audrey got home before her man and made some stir fry with shaved beef, broccoli, and Kung Pao sauce over ginger rice. It was a neat surprise. Maybe they would go for a walk after dinner, holding hands; she'd like that. Maybe they'd watch a movie, something romantic. She'd stare at his lips when a couple kissed on screen until he was trained that every time the actors smooched, so should they.

But during their meal, Owen began: "I've been doing a lot of thinking about Tamah, and I've texted his uncle Mitch a few times."

She knew they'd talked before the funeral. It wasn't supposed to be a serious moment and Audrey was confused and about to get mad until a pall draped over her, fading to black. "I think about him all the time. Not a day goes by that I don't. . ." It was cliché but true. She put down her fork and Owen rubbed her shoulder. "What does Mitch have to say?" she asked tentatively.

"Not a lot. I think these Samoans are very proud, very family-oriented people. Anyway, He's the only lifeline that I can see. And he's cool. It took a lot for him to do what he did at the funeral in front of his family. Especially with that jackass sister he has."

"I don't know, Owen, if I could ever talk to that woman, after she stormed into my house and ripped that baby from me."

He began to eat some more; it was very tasty. "I'm sorry to bring this up during dinner, but there is never going to be a good time. . .but I have an idea."

She took a bite, too.

"This is really good by the way. Thanks. I really like the shaved steak."

"What's your idea?" she asked, annoyed. Audrey's effort now seemed to be for naught.

"That stupid bitch did what she did to hurt you, case closed. She's an angry person." But then he considered, adding, "or maybe very afraid."

Audrey was being forced to recall the worst day of her life. "The way she clutched Tamah whenever one of my relatives or friends wanted to see the baby. . .I will always remember that ugly glare, like we were the enemy. She wouldn't let James hold his grandson, either." Tears began to well into her eyes. She was done eating, done with everything again.

"I know. Perhaps we could. . ." The idea of helping James get to meet Tamah was really getting over the tips of his skis. "This chow is really good. Anyway, I'm thinking about, we, us, making a gesture, just to see if we can't get some dialog started. I want to take a car seat over to where they live. Just be as friendly as can be." Owen pushed around the last of the stir fry onto his fork using his thumb and forefinger.

"Use your knife, peasant." He looked up at her. She was a sassy queen even when made sad. "You'd be wasting your money."

"Maybe. Probably. But I want to see you hold the baby again." He held her hand after wiping them in a napkin, and that thought pushed many tears toward her chin. "And shit, they're poor. Kaelani won't say no to a gift. I doubt she'd be a bitch and say, 'I already got one, asshole.'"

"How do you know where she lives?" She daubed her face.

"Facebook got me close, and then I found her looking up her phone. Google. Her brother Mitch lives there, too. You know it's in Kent."

"Yeah, I remember Demarco saying that."

"Maybe we could look through Demarco's stuff. Maybe there would be something in his room, something of his she'd enjoy having. You know, like a peace offering, a picture."

"You think that I should give that piece of shit a present? What the fuck?" Her volume ratcheted up fast.

"No. That's not wha—"

"You want me to pack up his stuff. You're sick of looking at it, is that it?" Her blood pressure spiked.

Owen retreated quickly. "You do what you want. He lived in that room for a lot of years. This is your house. Eventually, if you want to make it into a spare bedroom again, like it was when he was gone, that's up to you. When you're ready." The lease was in her name, but they shared their finances with equity.

Fuming, she couldn't look at him. He'd ripped off a scab for no reason, none at all.

"You're a little too slick for your own good, Owen," at which Audrey put her dogs on their leashes and took off out the door. He cleaned up. The stir fry was good, especially since his love prepared it. He was focused on a result less than a method and was starting to stumble.

The offensive launch wasn't a complete loss. He hoped he wasn't wasting his time, or money, or hurting his gal needlessly.

He was going to marry that girl someday. Or at least ask her. So many storms had roiled their boat, mainly dealing with Demarco. His petty thug attitude was fixed with a nine-month hitch inside jail.

Owen's kids still didn't want to have much to do with him, having embarked on lives of their own, still bitter about their parents' breakup. Audrey was now his only family, and the thought of losing another person forever filled Owen with dread. Placing himself in her shoes stretched him mightily. If one of his kids died young, he'd be the one scrambling. That was his escape room, his unreachable black spot.

If he could make this happen with Tamah, things might settle down enough for him and Audrey to really focus on themselves. But it was a fool's gambit. People never, ever acted like you think they might, and the stormy Salish sea never became calm.

Saturday morning couldn't come quickly enough. As a Senior Producer, he negotiated for at least half the weekend off from the radio station. Audrey knew what he was doing when he told her he was going to Target if she wanted to come. She didn't. Owen came back home, brought inside the usual staples like TP, other sundry items, and groceries, too.

After he put them away, he told her, "I've texted Mitch and Kaelani that I'm coming over to give them something for the baby. I'm leaving before either pitches a fit. Would you like to come? I could use a wing woman." After a dramatic pause, he added, "Aren't you curious at least about where they live?"

Kent was working people mostly, where immigrants sought starts in America. It was big and square, filled with industrial parks and more than one hundred thousand people.

"Who knows? Worst case we say hi to whichever relation is present, drop it off, and split. It'd be good for them to see you. You never know."

Audrey wasn't happy. She felt manipulated. "Okay, fine. Let's do this. Give me five to get ready." On the way there she quipped, "I feel like we're giving into terrorists." Owen could have said something snappy, but just let it pass.

Their hearts beat faster as they passed the little yards separated by four foot high inexpensive, diamond mesh, steel fencing. Like their neighborhood, some yards were immaculately groomed, some overgrown eyesores where renters wouldn't, and old folks couldn't, maintain them. The address of their nemesis was like most, in between calling the city to complain and being listed in "Better Homes and Gardens." Kids played on the street, riding scooters, chasing each other, screaming, "Come here, come here!" Dogs wagged their tails, barking, saying something close to "Hi, hi, hi!"

"I'll find out if this is it," said Owen, the moment he put the truck in park. He shut the engine off, leaving the keys in. "Don't ditch me if there's shots fired."

And he bounded up to the front door before Audrey had a chance for her own snappy remark, "Yeah. Okay."

Owen quickly came back to the truck, opened the back driver's door, and grabbed the big box from a perforated side handle. To his love he merely said, "It's show time."

"What's happening?" Audrey asked, getting out of the F-150.

"She's in there. We hit the mark. Let's not make this an over blown thing. Stay cool." And his pace geared down from fifth to second, just above idle.

"Hey, Kaelani. Sorry for the pop in. I've been texting Mitch. Just wanted to drop something off for the baby." His tone carried a normalcy and strange, slow, calm, betraying the intrusion. And that seemed fitting.

She stood just inside the door barefoot, wearing hot pink shorts, her big gut barely covered by a lime green tank top. Kaelani had her hair in a bun and wore no makeup. A pretty girl, not quite twenty-five.

"Yeah. Okay. . ." she softly stammered.

"We didn't know what you might need, but this is brand new."

"Hi, Kaelani," Audrey chirped.

"Hi," she replied. A dog, three doors down, was barking at some kids. She looked at the big box. "That's cool, thanks. The one we have was 'gently used' as they say. Thanks," Kaelani spoke more elegantly than Audrey and Owen thought she would.

Her sister, who had opened the door when the mustachioed man, wearing a silver belt buckle and a yellowing cowboy hat had knocked, came behind them carrying the sleepy boy.

Her heart leapt like she'd been shocked with paddles trying to save her life. Audrey instinctively cooed.

"He just woke up."

Kaelani scolded her older sister mildly, "You shouldn't get him up."

A child of three or four years mysteriously appeared at her mother's leg as she responded, "Oh, it was time he got up. He has to look around and see people."

"Who's this?" Owen had taken off his hat under the shade of the little porch, and beamed at the little girl saying, his graying, thin hair matted down, "Hi, I'm Owen." His hat was held over his heart.

"Lorelei, can you say hi?" But the shy girl buried her face into mama. Then she asked Tamah, bouncing his little eyes open, "Can you see your grandma? Can you see?"

Audrey placed both hands over her mouth in a prayer pose, something she never did.

"Oh, cool! Another car seat. Is that the kind that can be adjusted both ways, forward and back when the kid gets older?"

Shit! A pop quiz. He wasn't ready for that. "Um well. . .yeah, I think so. It's up to, I think, like, twenty-five pounds." He paused, continuing to stumble. "Is Mitch around? I'd like to say hey."

Kaelani was a bit bewildered. "No, he lives up the street. I live here with my sister and her husband."

"That's good to be around family like that." Audrey's voice trembled ever so slightly and quietly.

"We need to get going, other errands to do. Sorry again for the pop in. We just wanted to drop this off."

"Here, take your kid." And Tamah was unceremoniously dumped into Kaelani's arms by an experienced mom. She extended her hand to

Audrey, shaking it. "Thanks so much. It's a big help. Don't be strangers." Tamah's little arms splayed out, his hands raised in teeny fists.

"I'm sorry, but I don't remember your name?"

"Julia. I know, I forget, too. Audrey and. . .?"

"Owen."

"Thanks, guys. Really."

Something must have made Kaelani's heart grow three times that day and she waved her son's hand in bye bye, saying herself in a hushed manner, "bye bye."

In an unusual move, Owen opened up the truck's passenger door for her and Audrey plunged in. "Oh my God, my knees are shaking." And he got in, starting the truck. "Let's get out of here before something else weird happens."

"That was amazing," she said. It was so amazing.

16
The Blue Ox

When Corrine told Peter about the last pageant of the season, he had already booked a flight west in his heart. The birth of Cherry Nova was a fantastic epilogue to a tragic story. It was good to know that Audrey was with the girls shopping, resuming life. Malls were places he knew and enjoyed well. He asked Corrine if the one they went to had a carousel, but he wouldn't say why he wanted to know, being coy.

So full of questions, Corrine was sure something was up. Dates, locations, and she kept answering: yes, she was going to do it, no she hadn't figured out what she was going to wear, no it fell on her weekend to have Cory, yes, she could try to get Evan to swap a weekend. Why? Corey had come to pageants with her before, remember? Now she was being the playful one.

Well, maybe he could take a long weekend. That would be fine if she didn't have a date already. She wasn't going to tolerate an indecisive man. That poked the bull. And the plan was placed in concrete. She hoped she'd get the horns. The mountain couldn't come to Muhammad, Muhammad would. . .or the irresistible force had to see the immovable object, it was confusing. Peter felt sick all the time. She could take a long weekend, too. Travelocity felt like taking a helpful spoonful of medicine.

If he didn't act, their time together would simply drift away; silent spans ending it, deflated like a party balloon rising away, like an unmeaning whim. Why the hell would she come to Central Wisconsin? That would have to wait for another long weekend and sure as shit not in the winter, which began at Thanksgiving and lasted until the end of April.

Peter had to see her again; otherwise, how he felt about everything would be untrue. If he had misled her, Peter did so openly. It wasn't his intention to fall in love with someone. He was simply tired of being alone. She made him feel wanted, and that pulled him back like a magnet. Corrine liked Peter a lot. But she had her doubts. Maybe he was some wishy-washy great guy, who entered her life only for a season, then crumpled in the field when the weather got frigid. Were consecutive losses making her desperate? Not thinking about the abstract unsure was harder than focusing on the desire for what she wanted.

The sexy glamor shots Princess De Menthe sent him made the attraction spike. She wore a black lace bodysuit and matching stockings, crawling over a white faux fur bedspread, naked behind a rose, lacey parasol, modeling as Santa's helper, the fur lined jacket unbuttoned, enough to see. . . Those made him feel very agitated, worse, actually. It was trickery. He felt like his tail was tied around a tree, or a person he had gladly tied himself to.

Peter had made a huge mess. He didn't know how to clean it up. The loneliness of the road made him do it, he rationalized. He wasn't worried about what came next, or how the Pin Ups would react to him coming back to visit (although he could vaguely hear their voices already). He was purposefully painting himself into a corner. He wondered when Corrine's lease was up.

There were only five drive-in movie theaters left in the state of Washington, one of which was named for Paul Bunyan's sidekick Babe. In the '40s and '50s it was a super popular cartoon feature and statues across America bore their fame. It was as natural as the girl next door thinking the boy next door was handsome, that the owners of the Blue Ox drive-in sponsor a car show. Oak Harbor, Whidbey Island was as pretty as a picture postcard. Commemorating lumberjacking and forestry in general were usual here.

Mountains poked out of the Salish sea to be served by ferries and the slimmest of roads at low tide. Mysterious coves, deadly cliffs, smooth stone beaches, and at one place a famous bridge, supported by island tops a mile above the ocean, called Deception Pass, was built like a stomach-dropping roller coaster. The Brazen Beauties Pin Up Doll club, not to be outdone, co-hosted with a pageant Donna Diva brilliantly called, "Starlight with the Stars."

After the day's festivities, ticket holders would watch Gilda, starring Rita Hayworth; Laura starring Gene Tierney; and Sunset Blvd., starring Gloria Swanson in a trifecta of film noir. The Pin Ups were to dress up like glamor queens from a time when the backseat of a car on a Saturday night was for many, the "first time." And generations beyond that, too.

It didn't have to be spelled out for Owen, and he made reservations for two evenings at a local hotel for a pretty penny. Texting with Peter, Ryan, and Brian, he hoped to get the roadies for Princess De Menthe, Miss Cherry Nova, and Miss Serenity Jade to also book rooms. There was no reason to hustle after the show awards to get onto a ferry just to drive two hours home when you could make out during a movie, fumble with buttons, hooks, and zippers and stay overnight.

The Dolls would be cold, their feet pinched after a day of being glam. Peter told Owen about his Jesus trick of washing his girl's feet after she wore heels all day. He thought it was genius (well, of course), applying the technique himself, but with hot water instead. Dolls and gearheads understood the notion of "fogging up the windows." Poor Cherry Nova and Ryan's steamy play time was now severely restricted by their son's nap time.

When Queen Hot Rod discussed plans for the afterparty of the "Starlight with the Stars" pageant with her man, Owen was adamant that the "Donna" needn't know. He professed, "if you don't want to be with someone, that's fine. But don't include me." Meaning he had no zero tolerance for the clueless cuckold pathetically alcoholic adventures in his presence, nor would have it. And the Dolls agreed, keeping mum through their own cross talk.

Whidbey Island didn't lack for affluent people. Because of its relative remoteness, property values were high and development slow. Because of its relative remoteness, the Old Goat Car Club wasn't expecting much more than seventy-five entrants. And yes, in the 21st century they let nannies compete too, but they were adamantly against changing the name, even for the very young under sixty.

The historic rain tables showed the chances for showers were unlikely. Still, it was dicey; bad weather had ruined the show before. The ferry ride from Mukilteo to Clinton was a fabulous twenty minutes of fog, saying goodbye to the mainland to slithering green humpbacked beaches, as long as you got on board with your hot rod in time.

Owners got nervous being in such close proximity to other people's daily drivers. The clear reason why those with fancy cars always parked in the back of lots where there was tons of space. Being an early bird, being first in line, making reservations on a weekend were all good ideas. The car guys didn't go upstairs to see the views but stayed with Baby to ensure some dumb dumb didn't scratch or even touch, even think of touching the precious, the girls temporarily second.

The hardest part was finding a suitable evening gown, or not. October pageants meant rain and shivering. Princess De Menthe liked the idea of checking in, getting into a hot shower after the pageant, then returning for the drive-in movies. It was the impregnator's weekend with Cory and a neighbor lady promised to let Cassie out of her crate, do the basics, hopefully let her run a bit, then put her back in her crate where the pooch felt safe.

The 1950's teeny tiny waist thing wasn't a thing anymore, gratefully. Surviving into middle age in America in the 21st century meant an allowance for bigger dress sizes. Could she change into an evening gown to wow her friends after the pageant? Peter, like a fool, said he liked the idea until weeks later, realized the complexity of its removal.

But first Princess De Menthe found an Audrey Hepburn Polka dot party dress that had cherries, pale leaves, and slight golden flowers in an XXL, airy and light. At least she wasn't going to have to worry about sweating. The black collar and matching belt and buttons were sure to pop. For only thirty dollars! She could really accessorize now: a new, lacey antiqued parasol and closed toe bridal pumps with Mary Jane lace.

The block heel was important for uneven surfaces, like an old parking lot. She made a mental note to call Miss Nova about shoes and bringing a black pea coat. Not stumbling and falling, not getting a skinned knee, not ruining your only pair of stockings, not bleeding, not crying, not shivering in front of the public were all important stuff to consider if you did Pin Up, to be a princess, to become a star.

Next was an evening gown. Tea length and backless, it was the color of sage and had matching sequins embroidered in grand swirls along the bodice, size fourteen in case it had to be taken in. With a new little purse and matching shoes her outfit costs were about the same as the room. Peter wished he'd had his Road Runner to enter. The combined smells of Armor All and Chanel's Coco Mademoiselle was enough to make a grown man drive into a bollard.

Of course, Missy Cherry Nova was bringing it with a 1950s silky pink party dress. The fitted bodice and waist was a little too small, which didn't help with her nerves. Ryan needed a little solder retrofit in order to ensure the car seat, thus little Johnny, was secured. She got mad when her husband called their son, "his little criminal."

"Just look at my boy. He's gonna be a jail breaker!" And he pretended to eat one of the tot's hands, making yummy sounds and little Johnny smiled and gurgled, hoping Dad had smuggled a hacksaw blade in the diaper bag.

"I'm going to show off me and the baby. I know Corrine is on the boat. Come say hi to Peter." He didn't want to leave the Nova; it gleamed under layers of wax. It wasn't entered. There was no time for that, as his girl was damned if she wasn't going to get a Princess Tiara even if she had to pull it off some undeserving girl's curls. He was on total Dad patrol today.

Navigating the stairs to the decks above the cars, while one of two diesel engines violently shook the vessel, cranking out 3,000 HP leaving the port and swinging sharply into the sailing lane, Miss Nova plopped down the baby carrier before trying to ascend in fabulous, pink wedding shoes with twisting straps and stilettos. She exclaimed, "take the prisoner!" Slowly, she climbed the stairs, tightly holding the banister, stepping at an angle. She smartly left the baby bag for him, too. Ryan closed the gap quickly from behind, just in case she lost control, her new mom full hips swinging with the pitching ship.

"I told you about the heels," Princess De Menthe almost scolded the apprentice Doll. "You look amazing! How long did it take you to do your makeup this morning?"

She was bleary eyed, trying to grasp the forested landscape rushing past at twenty knots. "I don't really remember going to bed and getting up."

Of course, she had to coo at the baby. "That kid's damn cute." Peter pulled himself inside the seated deck, gob smacked by the islands in the distance. He'd just found where they wanted to live and be buried. Honey sugar baby had told him the Nova's were aboard. The men did the fist bump fake out, handshake start/hesitate thing, ending with a near miss knuckle bump.

"Cute kid. Little Johnny." Peter smiled, thinking about a thousand little Johnny jokes.

"Yeah," Ryan began. "He's my smooth criminal. Like Michael Jackson." After a pause, he added, "Hey, Corrine. So, there's two kids playing in the snow: a little girl and little Johnny. The little girl makes a snowman, but little Johnny tells her that she really made a snow woman instead. She asks, 'Why? What's the difference between a snow man and a snow woman?' And little Johnny says, 'SNOWBALLS!' Get it? Snowballs?"

Corrine guffawed and Peter smiled broadly.

"This is why my husband wanted to name him John. So people can make stupid jokes about him." Miss Nova was proud they'd gotten to the courthouse, just themselves, making everything legal. So was Jack.

"So little Johnny gets sent to the principal's office." Miss Nova glared at Peter, but it was too late. Congratulations were in order; however, levity intervened. "He asked the young man what his name was and he said, 'J-J-J JA….J-JA JOHN…JA JOHNNY.' 'Oh, I see,' said the principal. 'You have a stutter.' And little Johnny responded, 'No, my dad does, and the guy who registered my name was an a Son-of-a-Bitch."

Miss Cherry Nova smirked at that. She was sure she was going to hear them all; she didn't see that coming while daydreaming about motherhood.

Ryan placed the baby carrier on a table and they settled in for a few minutes before the PA system announced that people should return to their cars. The Pin Ups got approving looks from fellow travelers. One old goat asked if they were going to the car show. There were other Dolls from unfamiliar clubs also being glamorous on the ferry. The ship swung wide again and shook as the huge aft diesel engine idled, and its twin pushed forward against the dock's rubberized pilings, spewing the sea toward the shore.

They split up, getting to their own rides, but all passed a '62 Thunderbird Sports Roadster at the bottom of the stairs. The two-seat convertible was a rarity. The burgundy seats held a couple in their 70s. The scalloped headrests rose audaciously from the tonneau cover which had been the space for the four-seater. Either a 300 or 340 HP V-8 gave the little bird plenty of power. Her baby was a special white, like eggnog. The wife drove. Maybe hubby was just happy to feel the wind in his face one more time. Chrome wire wheels with triple ear spinner hubs dazzled onlookers as it drove off the ferry and toward the drive-in, forty miles away north, through the gangly Whidbey Island.

While waiting for their turns a Kaiser Dragon passed, leading a procession that drew the ferry crew to the rails to watch the show. The large, heavy, Chevy Bel Air Impala delivered a smooth, Turboglide, imperious ride over the ramps onto land. Its Fathom Blue Metallic stock color, scaly trim before the rear wheels and falling fins seemed like a creature coming out of the sea.

A 1954 Buick Skylark, another convertible, was preceded by a Regal and followed by a LeSabre. A '56 Ford Fairlane Crown Vic. was escorted by an Expedition and an Explorer.

A postwar Maize yellow Lincoln Continental had the top down. A prewar, Volanta Coach Maroon painted, Lincoln-Zephyr Convertible glided by, past Ryan's Nova, past Brian's Oldsmobile Starfire. Miss Serenity Jade was aboard ship but in the rush the girls forgot to text their whereabouts.

Upon getting to the Blue Ox, the Dolls found Queen Donna Diva setting up the pop-up tents, or rather, directing her men, Aaron and Lawrence to do it. There were tables to set up and be filled with her formidable purse collection. Outfits and their accessorizing jewelry were purchased by many gals attending the event and Doll wannabe's. A few sales were checks. The Square was a new method for plastic. Miss Demeanor already had the cash box out, registering Dolls who were both in and out of the Chapter, making money.

There was an ATM at a Walgreens not far away she told them, cash being queen. Having a little help from Peter to hump the big, forty-pound speakers to where the Miss Diva wanted the "stage" section of the parking lot was appreciated. She wasn't used to her new pumps yet. Peter felt briefly like a roadie. His girlfriend set up the sound equipment in no time. She was a very important Doll.

Every pageant was a little different, but typically the ballot for car categories, like Best Ford, Best MOPAR, Best Paint, etc. included the Pin Up People's Choice Award. It was the popularity contest for the Dolls and could weigh heavily for who may be crowned Queen. They had numbers assigned, shared with the folks administering the car show.

There was a 9 AM deadline for registration. What exactly was in the queen's 40oz Big Gulp, only her men knew. Princess Corrine brought five empty laundry baskets for the talent portion of the pageant, which this time was called, "Stupid Human Tricks". It was Serenity Jade's suggestion from the year's organizational meeting in January.

While the women folk, including Miss Lisa Demure, signed in, chatted, and sized up the competition and offered help to complete makeup or dress behind a screen, the gearheads busied themselves with removing ocean splatters and variable dust and pollen with gloved chamois.

Donna Diva using leadership skills hitherto drunkenly unknown, gently suggested for her Dolls to befriend a potential prospect, Lisa. She was a fifty-six-year-old, bald as a billiard ball, man who had the guts to dress like a woman in public, again. She showed an undeniable chutzpah wanting into a sisterhood. The queen felt that how the Dolls treated the least of them reflected upon all of them.

And besides, the "Brazen Beauties" club wouldn't survive very long unless any Miss could become a Princess, maybe a Queen. Attendance and social advancement were paramount to club survival. This sinner knew something about mercy, needing much herself.

Queen Hot Rod told the fellas that Miss Demure felt that no one liked her and within one minute they descended, asking her what her stupid human trick was, what she going to do? Good boys being worthy boys.

"Glad to see you have a parasol today." It was white lace. Her wide brim hat was festooned with daisies.

"Last time we saw you, you got a lot of sun." The men's sensitivity was on display. "Not much chance of that today with overcast skies. It's pretty, though."

"Okay. Thanks," was all she could muster out. But a moment later, she shot, "I'm going to use a blowgun and a mousetrap to eat a marshmallow."

Whaaat?

Owen wondered what his legs would look like shaved.

"What's your number? We'll tell people to vote for you." Peter was trying too hard.

"Sixty-nine," Miss Demure said.

"Really?"

"No," Lisa laughed. "I'm twenty-nine."

So she had a sense of humor.

"–Years old?"

"Sure, tell everybody that." And they all smiled and laughed together.

Brian wasn't smiling, however. For the first time he entered his car. Miss Serenity Jade needed to win a tiara. If he had to choose which of them got the recognition it was a slam dunk.

For three years competing, a little lumpy, she found herself at sixty-one, and also ran. From Cadillac to Chevrolet to clunker, he loved her, and his car. Best Oldsmobile, that was his category. Bomb shaped fenders, he loved polishing them. And always came back to her when he came off the road. V-8 rocket, 394-cubic inch, redesigned chassis, ultraclean, between suspension up over his shoulders. Horsepower was higher than ever. Top of the line, Starfire. Snazzy interior, genuine leather buckets, with power adjustment, they looked forward to movie night, too. A slight drizzle made Brian scowl.

The Starfire '61 dazzled on bright days like this with polished chrome and brushed aluminum appliques down the sides. It was another convertible on display. The Salish Sea in the little town's harbor two miles away kept the temp below sixty. It could get a little chilly tonight and Brian had placed two plaid wool blankets in the trunk in anticipation for snuggles.

Miss Serenity Jade realized her best shot of finally winning a tiara was through makeup. She'd had professional help once before but had practiced enough to do it herself and she spent the money for the best products. Working at a hair salon helped with the research. When Brian joked that he used some of her eyelid moisturizer on his feet, she replied that the tiny jar only cost ninety dollars and she would order another from his credit card. It was never an issue again.

Luckily for her she had perfect, full lips, plump on the bottom with defined, heart-like curves on the top. Her husband found her very kissable when she applied fire engine red to them, but then it was "back off, Buster" for him. A girl at the mall threaded her eyebrows toward the corners of her eyes so she could draw highly inquisitive, sharp curves.

She Botoxed the little furrows on her forehead and the crow's feet. Under eye cream helped with the bagginess. Miss Jade matched her skin tone perfectly and bought colored contacts to dazzle. She changed eyeshadow during the pageant for fun, Hot Glam being a favorite. At the Brazen Beauties Pin Up club, if you were trying, you'd have your moment in the clouds, because it was a sisterhood after all.

The Pin Up Doll field was small today, totally only seven (not including Queen Diva and Miss Demeanor). Mars Cherie wore a blue gingham halter knee length dress with solid navy lines round the hem and halter. A wide band around her waist showed off an incredible twenty-four-inch waist. Some ladies murmured that she lacked the ideal thirty-six in both bust and hips, but her appeal was obvious. From pockets shaped like hearts she handed out butterscotch candies with her name written on a patriotic ribbon. She was the one to beat.

Once the registration was over, Miss Demeanor secured the lockbox in her boyfriend's Mustang. Her mechanic and she were back together. In fact, she moved in with him. Aleia took another telemarketing job, trying to get people to donate to the firefighter's association with her super friendly voice, or with great desperation asking if they knew that their car's warranty was about to expire.

The hours really sucked, with lots of weekend and evening work. She had a youngish (twenty-five years less than Gary), hard-working man who sported a thin beard, trimming it once a week. He kept his hair short on the sides and back and used some gel to style it on the weekends.

His pale blue eyes had seen a woman who didn't have a job and few prospects. Although he wasn't busy, he said he was, then stopped answering her texts, making excuses. She got the point; besides her hot bod, Aleia wasn't bringing much to the table. She had a good heart, Aleia told herself, because if she hadn't, how could she feel such grief thinking about her little boy all the way across the country? Her mechanic texted her out of the blue, like a single moth to a flame.

Both Princesses wore their tiaras and hung onto their men tightly when the couples came face to face. Corrine to not lose her man to the most beautiful Doll, Aleia to ensure this one wouldn't run away. It was a bit of a shock, a bit not, seeing her with another man. Not mentioning Gary was a given, but Miss Demeanor still was uncomfortable; it was going to be a short exchange after quick introductions. Then Peter asked if he had a favorite car in the show yet?

"Yeah, mine."

Super jealous, Peter excitedly asked what he had entered. He completely forgot the woman who he had had a huge crush on, and who had had a fling with his good friend; so fickle were men.

"I have a '65 Mustang ragtop."

"Where is it? You got time? That's so cool. They made a million of those, instant classic." 600,000 actually. Peter was eager to impress his new friend.

"Sure, yeah," the mechanic waved his hand in a general direction and Peter noticed his deep baritone. "It's over there." He wore cowboy boots and a John Deere baseball cap. It was another convertible, and the girls got left in the dust without a glance back.

"Your boyfriend just stole my boyfriend," they argued between themselves.

Other manufacturers tried to respond with "pony cars" of their own, a compliment itself. The stock color was an Arcadian blue, like a powder blue. The varied package options for the 'Stang varied a lot. Miss Demeanor's stud's version had a four-speed manual 260/overhead valve V-8, power steering and brakes, black leather bucket seats, and bench in the back.

It had a luggage rack on the trunk but not the accent stripes and special moldings Peter had seen on other Mustangs. The bonnet was up and folks were already coming over to take a look. Standing like a pretty sentry most of the afternoon, posing for pictures, Miss Demeanor asked for folks to vote for her man's car, not for herself like a car show model, and guarded the cash.

Corrine followed the boys as they wandered off to see another build, citing specs and flexing testosterone. Finally, she asked her man to get the radio flier out; it was time to sell. That snapped Peter back.

"Wow. What a man crush!" She beamed at him.

That was offensive. Peter was putting the cooler full of cold bottles of water into the wagon. "What are you talking about? No, I don't."

"Then why did you watch him walk away just now?"

"No, I didn't." But he guessed he did. "Jealous?"

"Just make sure you don't get lost tonight during the movies." That jogged his memory that when he went for more ice and water today, he intended to also get a little bottle of booze. Getting Corrine De Menthe tipsy would be a throwback/lucky move. If it worked. If it didn't put her to sleep.

As he began to follow her, pulling the wagon, his Princess turned around and asked Peter what brand of jeans he was wearing. That was mean. They were just Levi's.

She wore a ruby red, Hepburn style, Rockabilly evening party dress, and carried a red pastel hanky as a safety measure. She intended to drink a glass of Pinot Noir through her nose. Katastrophic chose it because it had a soft, smooth finish. Queen Diva, using Princess De Menthe's microphone, announced the contestants of the Stupid Human Trick contest and it got a really good-sized crowd gathered around the platform in front of the movie screen.

"Do you want a bib, Queen Katastrophic?" Her drunky voice boomed over the speakers.

"Don't need one." She poured a full glass and called out, "This is for pediatric brain cancer!" Amazingly, this Doll was able to cock her head so that even rare dribbles found themselves into her mouth. Her throat seemed to work in many, many tiny swallows. She used her index finger as a dam, the vino draining into a lovely nostril.

The crowd started chanting, "Chug, chug, chug!"

To which Donna Diva hollered, "This ain't a beer bong, you peasants!" And laughed at her own joke.

The Princess took her time, nearly thirty seconds.

All the banter nearly threw her off, but the task was accomplished to great applause. It was wise to have Katastrophic go first. She curtsied like a lady, patting her face, putting a capital "C" in the word Class.

Ginger Honey Bear had brought her kids for a reason. Although she wasn't athletically built per se, her ordeals, she explained, in order to raise five girls, had given her super-human strength. She announced to the crowd that in the name of their club's charity, she would jump rope with two people hanging onto her. Now, her youngest girl (forty-five pounds) got onto her shoulders and Princess Bear rose from a full squat.

Then another little 'un was placed hugging her sister's hips, everything squeezing Mom's head and neck like a balloon about to burst, swinging on her back like a big papoose. Her husband quickly got the rope handles into her hands and stood back.

"Let's see how many she can do, folks."

Audience participation was pure gold. "One, two, three, four. . ." And the Princess found a rhythm, only stopping because the kid on her back was screaming she was about to fall. Hubby swooped in to catch her as she screamed just a little, once more. It was impressive.

Corrine De Menthe balanced five laundry baskets off her chin, claiming that she never put away laundry; her family just had baskets, clean and dirty. Peter didn't say a word as he helped stack them up the way they'd quickly practiced. The trick was to make sure the first one was angled correctly into the second, then the others could be stacked pretty easily. She held her arms out wide and walked around until she lost control, sending the baskets into the nearby crowd.

Miss Demure indeed placed a mousetrap on a slight angle on a folding table. She took a marshmallow out of a baggie, balanced it on the hammer (she modified it, soldering the end of a baby spoon—after all, it was a trick). Then she walked back about ten feet when the Master of Ceremonies stopped her.

With a throaty slur, she asked, "Miss Demure, tell us what you're about to do?"

She explained very briefly, being super nervous, talking to the Master of Ceremony, not the audience. Then she put the blowgun to her lips and exclaimed, "for cancer!" She shot the blow dart perfectly, hitting the catch square. The spring snapped, the force bouncing the base and holding onto the bar. For one second, over a hundred eyeballs watched the fluff ball arch and then land in Miss D's wide-open mouth.

"She shoots, she scores!" There was genuine awe in such a feat of skill. The crowd-o-meter peaked at that instance.

Miss Cherry Nova removed her bra in less than five seconds, from beneath a sweater, for a supposed trick. Marie Bella Rose attempted to dribble five basket balls simultaneously; neither didn't work out too well.

Luckily for the onlookers, Queen Holly Hot Rod was the last trickster of the lot. She came out on stage, set out a small table, and said, "Now, I'm going to need a volunteer." Then she hopped off the stage and grabbed Miss Demeanor's boyfriend from the crowd (because he was the handsomest man at the show), taking him by the hand. She wore a lake blue cocktail party dress. It had a lacey half sleeve, and lace around a V neck with a tasteful hint of cleavage. A tie around her waist and a flowy chiffon hem all made her look like a woman who belonged on an island on a perfect October afternoon.

"Now, I need you to hold this." The Queen handed him a kitchen broom. Then she stepped ten feet away and just stared at him, seductively.

"Uhh," he asked. "Do you want me to do anything else?"

"No," the Queen said, "I just want to look at cha!" Which got lots of laughs, with one female voice loudly screaming "HEY!" Then a moment later a man said, "EASY!"

"Don't let go of that broom." She passed him like he was a piece of meat. Then she said to the crowd, "I need that to get home tonight." She was a dangerous, witchy woman.

Queen Hot Rod narrated while she placed four glasses of water on the table, then a shallow serving tray on top, but sticking out over the table's edge. Then she placed four empty coin wrappers and four eggs on top of them. "Now the trick is to line up the eggs directly under the glasses of water."

The Queen took the broom away from the strapping mechanic, placing her hands over his ever so gently, then stood on the bristles, bending the broom back with tension. Letting go, she hollered, "Tawanda!" It slapped the tray. The coin wrappers tumbled, and three eggs fell into the glasses. The crowd "ahhed" and clapped despite the trick having not fully worked.

Shamefully, she gave the mechanic a big, long hug, turning his back to the crowd and giving his butt a slap.

Miss Jade was a scratch and Princess Demeanor was judging, so once the Stupid Human Tricks were over the crowd was once again reminded to vote for their favorite Doll and to support Pediatric Brain Cancer. They went back to gawk at cars and eat okay burgers and fries from the snack shop.

That day, the Club raised just over $1,500 in donations, almost all of which made it to the charity except for gas money.

Princess Corrine De Menthe and her loving minion worked the crowd well. It was a lukewarm day, and the free cold water for votes strategy/bribery garnered a lot of support. The mechanic didn't win for Best Ford despite dozens of salacious pictures of his girl being taken, posing all over the 'Stang. He appreciated the effort and got many hot pics himself that would serve him well into his old age.

Before the Old Goats named Best in Show, the Dolls had their turn to award and Kimmy, Miss Serenity Jade, won best makeup and her first princess tiara, and that made all the difference to Brian. She was so giddy that more than one gearhead shouted, "Don't cry, you'll ruin your makeup." The fix wasn't in for his Oldsmobile, being unknown to the judges. The applause was all hers.

Princess Demeanor and Queen Diva tallied, then applied weighted mathematics to give the Stupid Human Trick award to now Princess Demure. Lisa was a prospect, and most brave, so upon leadership's consideration that although Katastrophic drinking great wine through her nose (which was much stupider), she wasn't a member of the club, although she did get a few more votes. Queen Holly Hot Rod got the most votes, but Miss Demeanor disqualified her for an obvious reason.

"And now, for the People's Choice and Queen of Whidbey Island Classic Car Show. . ." The large crowd hushed. "Queen Corrine De Menthe!" The Dolls stood in a ring. Princess Demeanor fixed the very tall crown on her curls with combs. She gushed, crying, with everybody clapping. A job well done!

Peter stood back with his phone, taking it all in on video.

Corrine hadn't won anything ever before. Becoming a mom, fighting terrible vicious head winds, being diagnosed with Lupus, knowing her life could be cut short. Working hard for a future, seeing her friend's brains splattered, death tugging at her elbow, having her kid making her laugh, a man following hard behind, had made Corrine falter. Now she wasn't alone, and her tears flowed vociferously, thanking everybody.

Peter hugged her. "Wow. You did it! Your Majesty!"

Watching, Owen tugged at his Queen's waist, saying "I remember that."

Queen Hot Rod asked, "What's that? What do you remember?"

"How happy I was when you figured out how great you are. Becoming a Queen. It showed you how much you're loved. It wasn't a mystery anymore. You're loveable. You're awesome."

As expected, after the Best in Show for the Old Goats was announced, within ten minutes the parking lot was nearly empty. The Trifecta of Donna, Lawrence, and Cuckold packed up and split. The audio equipment was placed into Corrine's bed, then they squirted to the hotel for a spritz and some royal love making. As they couldn't contain themselves.

Lawrence drove Aaron's truck. It was crammed full to the eight-foot cap, while he boozily snoozed in back for the two-and-a-half-hour cruise home. He grasped Donna's hand, giving it a firm squeeze, wishing his girl was his.

Sensing despair, she reassured, "It's not always going to be like this."

The big guy took notice. "It's like he's giving you away. Right in front of him, and he doesn't care." Lawrence was the most sober to drive. "Doesn't that get to you? You don't deserve this."

Her savior from unhappiness made his queen tear up. "We'll figure out how to get me out, together. I love my big man," Donna gushed.

"I'd kiss you," he said. "But I need to keep it on the road."

The now empty camper had become the "go to" spot whenever Aaron was unconscious, or her bed, when he was at work.

The Nova's sought to catch the last ferry. Brian and Kimmy lounged for a bit at the hotel pool, but it was too cold to go in. Eventually they headed back to the drive-in to get under scratchy, wool blankets. Audrey and Owen weren't in a hurry either, getting a nice steak. Later that evening Audrey and Aleia enjoyed White Russians together. She apologized sort of for accosting her boyfriend, her drinks as a peace offering.

"That's okay. You could have won the talent portion, but we disqualified you for lewd acts unbecoming a Pin Up Doll."

Queen Hot Rod didn't know there was such a thing.

Queen Corrine sported a big crown, wearing her evening gown with now a wide titled sash, walking amongst the cars, shaking hands and hugging. Then she finally snuggled into her truck's back seat, the speaker next to an open window, kissing when the actors on the screen kissed.

17
Rolling the Dice

Both Corrine and Peter wondered, in their individual desperations, if the other was making good decisions. Having someone ask how your day was, was brand new and wonderful. Crawling out of a sex desert had profound effects. Memory of hopelessness was recent, along with the relaxation and confidence which comes from finally getting properly laid.

Professionally, they were on similar trajectories, even if just starting off. Peter described themselves like a well paired team of horses. Both were making money and seeking more education and positions of greater responsibility. It was a very practical observation, weary to the dumb and lazy which neither were. One having been teamed with a person content with sitting on the couch refusing to pull.

Retirement was forty years away, maybe sooner if the partners didn't shoot holes into their collective financial buckets. It was his way to forecast their future, an unintentional signal that Corrine picked up on right away. Perhaps that was how her man thought? Peter was like a little kid with her little kid.

Cory had two men he was learning from, his piece of shit father Evan, and his father who had been faking a disability for almost twenty years, staying on pain meds and hardly acknowledging his grandson's presence. It was Corrine's job, so it seemed to her, to protect her cub from the influence of awful men. But she couldn't, legally. It was taking a huge gamble injecting her new lover into their lives, living together. A kind, gentle, intelligent man could make all the difference in her son's life.

Cory's current favorite game to play with Peter was called, "smell my feet," (her man's invention). Starting with socks instead of actual toes, the winner was the one who could most dramatically "pass out" from the nasty effect of inhaling the stink of your opponent's feet. Cassie liked to play along with face kisses and jumping on those rolling on the floor. Another game that Corrine prohibited mightily was Peter's invitation for the dog to "lick my toes", which everyone knew could send her to the vet.

He pulled her hair lightly, combing with his fingers, one arm under her pillow, when she was barely awake. Peter raked her skin, all he could reach without moving much, with the back of his nails, from calf to hip, very slow. The slower the better, elbow to temple, butt cheek to shoulder blade, hoping and excelling in making Corrine tremble, for fifteen minutes at a time.

He clasped her hand and squeezed strongly, kissing her neck and inhaling deeply. His respirations grew quicker, trying not to be rough, then pulling her legs open, his heel drawing barely against Corrine's thigh. Nearing a relaxation coma, Peter's strong leg turned her upon her back, and well. He growled in content, mock-biting her neck.

Few women knew how to love a man. Manly men got re-defined. But Corrine got it. Never leave him be, 'cause he's lonely, like a country song. Tell him that you love him every day. 'Cause a work-a-day man needs to hear it, and there's nothing he won't do when he's in love.

And if a woman is enthusiastic for her man, twisting and turning, the more better, too.

Corrine was impressed with his emotional intelligence. He spoke Kid, had empathy, and liked crayons. Peter pretended not to understand what she meant when she talked like that, her appreciating.

Corrine was dynamic, and had some tough breaks, like Lupus. Mostly she was funny, ya' know, intelligent. More absurd than he, like how'd he'd like to be. She spoke well and professed her love for him repeatedly. It sounded funny, like a tickle to Peter. Could she drive him away by her saying so? She said it a lot. Peter repeated the phrase back to her; it sounded good, he was pretty sure himself.

She wouldn't stop expressing. This guy was the bomb! Why did he care so much? How could she love him so? They didn't talk about the Lupus. How it was doubtful, but possible, the disease could kill her in the next fifteen years. She mentioned her fear once, for full disclosure. Okay, he said. They had been at the cabin. We'll figure it out when it happens, he said, then rolled over and began to faintly snore.

...

They made their way off Whidbey Island, catching an early ferry and were able to pick up Cory from his dad's. The kiddo napped on Sunday afternoon. Trying silence, a scarce breeze cooled through open sunny windows and a single fan. They heard neighbors parking, bringing in groceries and the sound of kids playing near Corrine's apartment, near the playset with swings. They were too excited to play music.

When the sweat absorbed, they made love again. One like a violin, the other like a big bass drum. The hurry was unfounded as Cory slept another hour after they made themselves presentable. Big funny, ha ha. Peter, like a lemon, got squeezed; Corrine pulsated and she glued herself to her man for a short time. Warm bodies met in an afternoon breezy, touching, sweaty foretold an inspiration, hoping. Corrine's everything kept trembling. They waited impatiently for the tap to get hot; he needed a washcloth. One more hot pull, her a quick spritz, crowded together, in a tight space, now sticky, now not.

When the boy awoke, she mothered. And it became clear to Peter, like a shock, that he needed to leave. She had to work, he had to catch a flight the next day. The plan to shop for a Spiderman costume fell flat. Corrine wanted Peter to stay longer but an intrusive feeling pushed him away like an opposing magnet. The boy cleaved to his mom as a four-year-old would.

All of a sudden, he got it: those two were family. What Peter wanted shouldn't impugn upon what a little boy needed. From the outside looking in, was inadequacy. She didn't get what had made Peter so sad, so quickly. That was how Peter described his loneliness; it was like being on the outside looking in. Everybody else was living, doing; he just existed, watching, yet never coming out from the cold.

He split, spent the last few hours at a hotel bar, uncommunicative except through short texts. His abrupt exit didn't make sense to her and Cory hardly had the chance to say, "bye." He said that his flight left earlier than he thought on Monday morning, and it was best they keep their routine, and have their Mommy/son time that night. It was less than graceful. It was a mistake.

...

Without another out-of-town job in the offing, Peter took a position as a foreman doing concrete formwork for his company, with lots more windshield time. His daily traveler was an older Dodge Ram that had plenty of scratches and dents at 125,000 miles. Each week the odometer rolled on another seven hundred fifty miles. Concrete dust and mud trashed it until in a spasm the Shop Vac and Armor All brought it back to a sense or respectability for just him.

A buddy sold him his 1968 Plymouth Roadrunner years earlier for an inflated price. Peter wasn't really a gearhead; he could do some stuff besides maintain it. His buddy really wanted cash for another project and was tired of looking at it. It went to a good home for $10,500. Underbody rust was a major concern. He might have been able to sell it for a modest loss, but for now a young man had a cool car that he could drive to local towns of less than 500 people. He paid too much, but it wasn't about the haggle.

The '68 was a budget muscle car. The standard 383 V-8 had plenty of power. Car people sometimes asked if it had the Hemi engine which Peter had to sadly say no. The rugged four on the floor manual transmission suited him fine; however, the sand and salt of Wisconsin Department of Transportation plows typically meant that Baby had a cover over her Thanksgiving 'till the end of April. The Roadrunner had sharp lines and competed with the GTO and Mustang, holding its own, meant to be driven by a working man.

His father, about once a year, asked when he could have his big Quonset hut back. The sixteen-foot-wide arched steel metal building held more than just Peter's car. But for farmers, everything cost money and they accounted for this, subtracted from his "volunteer" work around the place. Some years Peter could expect $5,000 at Christmas as his share of a profitable business.

Sunfire yellow with a hardtop, Baby looked pale in direct light. The Roadrunner had a "beep beep" horn after its cartoon namesake. It was one of the first production models and was taxicab plain. The hood air intakes were fakes, but the original owner did order power steering and disc brakes. His buddy had rebuilt the engine and took it to 110 MPH with Peter just to show off. He had it reupholstered with faux leather and carpeting, all black. He shouldn't have let himself be talked into it, but at the time, Peter didn't have anything else to spend his money on, like a mortgage or a girlfriend or a kid.

That morning his folks and he attended the United Methodist service in town. Younger Sis was a freshman in college at Eau Claire, studying prerequisites, whatever that was. Big Bro lived in an adjacent town doing logistics for an equipment dealer (and sometimes lending a hand harvesting goat milk). The sermon series was about "rebuilding" and the reference was Nehemiah's rebuilding the walls of Jerusalem.

"If I can get out to the West Coast after this job wraps, I'll have the Roadrunner out by Spring," he told his father.

That evening after supper, Dad quipped to his son, "You think you're getting out of captivity?" He meant the Hebrews returning from Babylon. He inspected his chapped hands and squeezed Vaseline on his palms, spreading it around. It was funny. Instant family in Seattle-land. Is that what you want? Eyes wide open, twenty-eight-year-old man?

Farmers, or goat ranchers, to be fair, often spoke less under stress. Peter's mom didn't ask about Cory, so her son mentioned coloring placemats and jungle gym tag. It was rather pathetic in retrospect.

"Not being in a person's business" was as Mid-Western as having a snow shovel in the mud room. 'Though there were plenty of busy bodies as well, nosy folks.

"So, when are we going to meet this young woman?" didn't have to be asked. Peter's judgment was a reflection on them. It was an obligation he felt that his motives were pure. But men are fools often, and finally blowing a nut skewed many a stud. Dad, having been in Vietnam in the Army, knew about such things.

When union general contractors asked Peter why he had come to the PNW looking for work, he told the truth, "'cause of a girl." That got laughs. It made sense to everyone, especially to those who had gambled and lost.

"That was your first mistake," was replied sometimes.

As long as he came across as a qualified, decent guy to HR reps or Superintendents, it was possible his resume might be read. Not everyone had a heart of stone.

Peter wanted to be his own man. The motivation to drive his Roadrunner west was powerful. While cutting the clear coat that remained, buffing, waxing, polishing the pitted chrome, every scratch and blemish etched into his ego. This motivation paralleled committing to an instant family. Was he foolish? What was most important?

It occurred to Peter that Cory was at the center. With that he pushed the small stack of chips away and pretended, "All in."

The best card ever…where did he get it? It was a peacock spreading its colorful wings like lace, where he sprayed his cologne, her favorite, that she had bought for him. Another like a bridge, opening, with a purple pen was written, "I WILL LOVE YOU FOREVER." Other sediments about sexy lyrics from songs they liked together made wonderful, cheesy love notes.

"Oh, that would be wonderful if you could come to visit during Christmas." It was only a few weeks out and Corrine still hadn't decided what to get him. She had to weigh what was best for Cory.

"Do you have him over the holiday?" Dates were important for flights.

Corrine pushed hard, "What? You want to meet my folks?"

"Never been to Yakima. Yeah, sure."

Momma Bear thought quickly and to herself said, "Listen, Peter, you're great. But I don't know if this is the right thing. You're great, and I love you, and you're great with Cory, but I don't know if you're great for us. You probably are. I don't know. I'm scared."

The boss he'd never met didn't have an assignment for him in the offing when Peter flew to Corrine the day before Christmas. Her lease was up in February, and even though his $50,000 in savings wasn't a mountain of cash, it seemed enough of a stake to go to life's casino. He made the pitch. Corrine had delayed re-upping, just in case she had a chance for the biggest change in circumstance since her son was born. They rolled the dice together.

...

It took two voicemails in the same number of weeks to prompt Gary to call Peter back. As promised, he was hunting coyotes, fox, and snowshoe rabbit in Canada, and was in a small town to reconnect with the grid.

"This is my Christmas gift to myself, brother." It was mid-January and Peter told him about his doings since the JCPenney mission ended, especially his plans to return.

"That's great man. You shouldn't have any trouble finding work out there. Or are you going to base out of Seattle now and still go on the road?"

Peter was as always feeling in the family way. "No", he said. "I wouldn't do that to Corrine. We're just starting off."

"Right, right. She's got a little kid, too, right? Little boy."

"Oh sure, Cory. The kid's a hoot. Really funny. His real dad is a complete piece of shit. I bet when you were thirty you weren't living with your disabled parents playing video games and working part time at the grocery store, getting stoned whenever."

Gary laughed. He was glad to get into a motel room for two nights before going back into the cold. "At that age I was working as much overtime as GM wanted to throw at me. Kept me away from the ex, so that was nice."

Now Peter laughed. "Aleia has a little boy that age, right?"

"Huh? What? How do you know that?" Gary was quickly trying to recall what happened after the two Superintendents parted company.

"Oh, sorry. I ran into Aleia at the last pageant of the year. I was visiting Corrine. Didn't I tell you that I found the greatest Honey-Hole of all time?"

Gary was thinking about how the Dolls loved his chiseled good looks. How he hooked up right away with the hottest babe of the bunch. It made him feel like the coolest friend ever.

"She told me that you went hunting from November until whenever and that she wouldn't be able to get a hold of you. By the way, how's the hunting up there? What are you going for?" Peter really wanted to know about the crazy road trip with Donna Diva and her roadie, Lawrence.

"We were gunning for 'yotes; they pay you for that. Rabbits are good for lunch. We've seen some wolf tracks but haven't seen one yet. My buddy who's Canadian has a wolf tag, but that's going to be tough." Switching gears, he asked him, "How was Miss Demeanor looking at the pageant?"

"Pretty as ever." Peter neglected to say she was with another beau.

"Peter, that chick is one fine piece of ass, and thoroughly fucked in the head." It wasn't normal for men to dish quite this way, but it seemed to Gary that he'd ought to be upfront and explain that although grateful, in his case, the Pacific Northwest wasn't going to produce another romance.

So the idea that Gary may come back to visit was off the table. "It seemed weird that she told me about a road trip and that Donna Diva and that big Special Forces dude were on a vacation together."

"Vacation from hell, dude. I have a '66 Cadillac Eldorado Convertible that I like taking on the road, and the original plan was that I'd pick up Aleia from St. Louis we'd spend a couple of days down where I live toward the Ozarks, then we'd pick up Donna and Lawrence in Nashville and drive to north Georgia, so she could see her kid.

"And they'd fly back to Seattle from Atlanta. But that bitch Donna just kept changing shit. She shows up in St. Louis with her boyfriend, drunk. I never got real alone time with Aleia for like the next ten days. They sat in the back of my caddy drinking while I was driving. Stayed at my house for free for a few days before that. You'd think a house guest could fill up my fridge with beer at least, nothin' doing."

"Did they fuck up the upholstering?" The idea of being captain of the party barge while Baby got stains on the leather made his friend's skin crawl. "How was Aleia?"

"She didn't party like them but smoked a lot of pot that she brought with her. I think she was worried about seeing her son again. She was pretty quiet. And none of those assholes had any money, so everything, gas, meals was on me."

"Gee Gary, I didn't mean to get you all fired up. I guess I won't see you out here anytime too soon," That was supposed to be taken as a joke, and he got it.

"Uhh, no. Probably not. Not talking to Aleia has been good for our relationship." And that got Peter laughing. Since he was on a roll Gary decided to finish the sad tale. "So, when we finally got to Georgia, we all met her kid and her ex-husband number two at a park."

"What do you mean 'number two'?"

"She's been married four times."

"Oh man. The chick isn't even like thirty-five?" It was then that he knew even keel Gary never had any intention of being number five.

"She's a lot older than that, anyway. It was like some supervised bullshit, and I wasn't going to hang out with Donna and Lawrence playing on the swings, so I just cooled it for like three hours, in and out of the caddy. After that she was pretty much a wreck, crying. Anyway, I didn't want to drink with these people at all, those two arguing. It was fucked. So the next day I convinced Aleia that I should put her on a plane back to Seattle and I drove back from Atlanta."

"So obviously, the Queen and her boyfriend went, too."

"The bitch was never sober and could tell I didn't like her. If you want to have a vacation away from your husband, then don't involve me. It was the road trip from hell. I did some gambling in Nashville, so that was fun."

They chatted some more, and Gary reminded Peter that if he ever bought a GM to tell him and he could get him a discount. It was a bennie he got for thirty years of service. It was payback for getting properly laid. Peter wondered if Miss Demeanor had played her cards differently if Gary would have become husband number five. There had been some connection there. His buddy had enough heart to drive her to see her son, but the priorities seemed upside down. What did he know? He was racing to become a role model for a little boy and was plenty confused himself.

18
Gain of Function

The holiday season 2019 was full of great cheer. Little boys made turkeys from drawing around their hands. Aleia got one. It made her cry then filled her with great resolve. Construction paper, the gluey smell of Elmer's, glitter on the coffee table, glitter on the dog's tongue, glitter on someplace strange was omnipresent in the season of giving.

Children made art with macaroni and colored strings and paper plates, buttons, and plastic seashells. Moms displayed these creations in places of great honor, like the refrigerator, using magnets. They were making happy memories and vows to restore relationships. Audrey hoped one day her grandson Tamah would make art for her, too. Little Johnny would probably corner the crayon market, charging high prices.

With fractious families, time management became a push and pull, a power play. Sometimes couples flew all the way to California to see mom. It was better to get out of town. It had been mere months since Demarco was killed and Audrey headed south for turkey day. It was a matter of receiving support, knitting together. She became thankful that Owen made her visit, well after the fact. Perhaps in the new year she could babysit her grandson, Tamah, at the not too pleasant home of his mother, Kaelani.

"How you getting along?"

"I know that…"

"You must feel…"

Those phrases from some members of the family had the emotional intelligence of cranberry jelly out of the can.

"No, you don't know. . ." It was better to let things pass and watch football, being all together again.

When they got back, Owen and she drove a short fifty miles to see his dad in a Kirkland nursing home. The mustachioed man sent cards to his two children and found progress when one of them sent a card back. In long absences the expectation was to brief other family members about your current situation, in summary. For those with memory issues, remembering losses was a sign of mental agility.

Owen's dad remembered that Audrey had her son taken from her and expressed his condolences. It wasn't the first time they had met, of course, but she didn't usually come with her boyfriend on his monthly trips. He'd call first and try to find out what sundry items he needed, like underwear, Doritos, or razor blades. He liked to have a secret stash of Tylenol and once the staff busted Owen for bringing in the contraband.

"It's cliché, but I don't understand why this happens to young people. It's incredibly sad." And for the first time in a few weeks, Audrey cried for her boy right then. Owen's dad looked like he wanted to cry too and hung his head.

After getting back from Cali, the mustachioed man with the silver belt buckle decided to make an honest woman of the queen. She may have thought, "why marry the bull, when you can get the ribeye for free?" That was going to change, hopefully. Her title would make him a royal consort, which had its own appeal, as he would gain influence within the kingdom if she accepted.

The only thing he knew about diamond rings was that he didn't know squat. The thought of going to the jeweler in the shopping mall was like dead air on the radio, an indication that someone didn't have a clue what they were doing. How much to spend? Pushing his cowboy hat back on his head after looking up the American cultural answer to that made him gulp and go outside to the shed to down some cold ones in consolation. It was a good thing that Owen liked cheap beer. He was all alone on this one. And that was the point, wasn't it?

Queen Bee asked if Owen would go with when she dropped off Tamah's Christmas present.

"What do you have in mind? A two-hundred-dollar gift certificate to USA Baby would be good." It was then that her lover man admitted his $500 greasing of the skids prior to the car seat escapade. She let it pass.

"I'd rather buy a bunch of cute clothes and pop in. Maybe with a text asking when?"

"You'd have more face time then."

Audrey replied, "Exactly."

...

For many Americans, being alone on Thanksgiving was merely an annoyance since the tavern was closed. It was easy to become uninvited, unfriended. It took social skills to reciprocate, to invite others over sometimes, too. Or you could move all the way across the county. Her mechanic made half a turkey breast and she made Stove Top Stuffing. Then, they lit some candles. It was cozy, just the two of them.

He said, "I don't usually celebrate the holidays." He didn't try to. The mechanic boyfriend was yet another person whose forgettable family lived far, far away for a reason. He never voluntarily beautified anything in his life, unless it was made of sheet metal. However, he liked the few decorations Aleia put up: spiced pinecones, a wreath for the front door to the apartment, and kid art on the fridge.

She told her little man to send her lots and lots of art. Oh, how she loved it all. Then she thanked her ex vociferously for mailing it. He let her know that he was moving to St. Petersburg, Florida and that she'd get some documents to sign to her PO Box, to allow the boy to move out of state.

The retired US Army Special Operator could feel the exclusion from Miss Donna's table, so he invited her family to his house instead. This shrewd move enabled him to show off his cooking skills. He cheated with stuffing from a box, and gravy from bottles, but made an apple pie from scratch. His mother and Donna's son plus a few other friends watched football. She tried to smooch him, but he pretended to be annoyed, sweating over a hot stove for her and all. The gambit paid off: drunky pants was promised leftovers so therefore could enjoy his peace and quiet at home. Donna had met Lawrence's mom many times. Making their relationship normal was a splendid idea, his web of love being spun around her.

An evil thing was lurking this flu season, starting in October (near as anyone could later tell). The average death count from influenza in America was thirty-six thousand, year to year, season to season. It wasn't really novel as some people already had immunity from Coronavirus, but those ideas were hopeful and didn't sell newspapers fearfully.

Peter was at the family farm the weekend before Thanksgiving to hunt for Bambi's mom. The grunt call was used to lure rutting bucks in toward his stand, but he may have missed that opportunity by the third week in November. The family had a couple of tree stands, built during the summertime and lasting for years. The biggest rack he ever got was a ten pointer when he was fifteen.

His Dad and brother were present, on forty acres of unimproved land his father bought when times were good. Isolated in northern Wisconsin, with a dusting of snow on the ground, being as quiet as he could be was a good, lonely feeling. Drinking too much coffee left him alone with his thoughts and wide awake. He thought about what it was like being five years old. And kept handy an empty wide mouth Gatorade bottle for peeing.

He scanned his sector of fire, knew his distances, where the salt lick had been in the late summer. He scrunched and un-scrunched his toes. If your feet got cold, you were toast.

By the second week of November, there was a warning from The National Center for Medical Intelligence about internal Chinese communications pertaining to a lab in a place called Wuhan. Three researchers were mysteriously hospitalized with COVID-like symptoms.

Thanksgiving on the farm was etched from absolute, traditional, scratch. The turkeys were provided by Peter's dad, from his own muzzle loaded shotgun. Wherever there was turkey, there could be deer, as the skittish loud birds made them feel safe. Peter made two apple pies from a simple recipe he'd perfected. Fifteen guests were planned for. Cranberries came from cranberry bogs fifty miles away.

Sweet potatoes, onions, and carrots came from the half acre garden, raspberries from five-year-old vines, for cobbler. Homemade beer from showoffs. Strawberry/rhubarb ice cream for dessert. Snap beans sautéed with shallots and almonds. Shots of whiskey and schnapps. The Ladies drank Pinot, the boys the cheapest state pilsner for ten bucks a case.

The kids played video games on big screens in the refinished basement of the five-bedroom farmhouse. Teenagers finally found their way to the dairy barn to smoke some ditch-weed. For those lucky enough to stay overnight venison sausage with fresh eggs over easy was for breakfast. Someone was sure to make true buttermilk biscuits.

Neither of Corrine's parents bothered her about how she was getting along with her new beau. Her mother was alone with no prospects and her father's love relationship was younger than Corrine's. Getting Cory to see both during the holidays was always a juggling act.

Evan's first proposal was that he wanted to take a vacation over Christmas, so Corrine could have Cory then, and he all of Thanksgiving.

"Oh really? Where to?" She had a hand on one hip, waiting for the answer. Since he paid nothing to his parents for living in their big house and a whopping $250 a month in support for his son, airline tickets were his greatest expense, besides pot and beer.

"Maybe go to Canada fishing, maybe to San Francisco to see a buddy. I'll sign off for you taking the kid out of the county if you want. Don't you want to go to Crack-i-ma?" It was the same stupid joke he'd uttered twenty times.

Evan was trying to get her upset, roil the pot. But he had just admitted that he didn't have any definitive plans, the idiot.

"Well, that's stupid. Can't believe you have the time." It was her favorite opening shot. It reminded him that a man of so few accomplishments at thirty years of age was not only lazy but also a moron. It made him very mad.

"We have to divide the Holidays according to the marital separation agreement." Painting the obvious to him was also fun. Although, probably counter-productive. She changed subjects to his non-payment for Cory's dental bills. His two front baby teeth had to be pulled because of rot. His father and grandparents gave him soda, candy, and no toothbrush. Hand washing and brushing was optional at his paternal grandparents' house.

To a dutiful parent, a child of five needed to be reminded constantly. Corrine inspected her son's attempts at both, with redo's and praise common. There was a bill for over $1,250 outstanding. "Why don't you use your vacation money on your son's teeth that had to be pulled because of your negligence?" That was a big word for a moron to ruminate on. Corrine's son would have a gap in his smile for many years until his adult front teeth came in.

Festive holiday plans had to wait for another day. She hung up, shaking at the waste of time.

The grand bargain a week later, with her nemesis Evan, was that he got Cory on Thanksgiving Day, while she got the rest of the weekend. In exchange, she got her son on Christmas day, and being a Wednesday, it was simple to let him have a long weekend. Corrine thought she was going to work anyway.

All this planning meant she would be alone for Thanksgiving, but when she called Kimmy about it, there was no question she'd be with the gang, Brian, Delmonica, Ryan, and little Johnny. There might be another friend coming, but Kimmy wasn't sure yet. It wasn't satisfactory to Cory's father, but she stopped mentioning the dental bill issue and he called it a draw.

The few glorious times a bill collector called her looking for Evan, Corrine gleefully gave them his phone number, address, social, mother's maiden name, date of birth, etc. Then she texted him to let him know how she helped.

Delmonica was thriving as a young mom and insisted on hosting. Kimmy told her friend that Tiffany was not going to be there.

"I'd rather volunteer at the soup kitchen than sit at a table with that bitch." Corrine didn't hold back.

"Brian says he'll rip her tits off if he ever sees her again." She let this small excuse for humor settle, then continued, "Tiffany had another relative to bother."

"Good. Say, I haven't pried. I know the house sold. Did Del get anything after all her dad's stuff was settled?"

"The house had appreciated a lot in thirteen years. Del ended up buying out the Nova, after settling all debts and paying the realtor, cleared over a hundred thousand."

"Oh, that's so cool for them. That'll help a lot, I'm sure."

Kimmy smirked to herself and added, "So, of course Tiffany wanted to borrow money. That's after selling every fucking thing in the house."

During the feast, Little Johnny was strapped into a car seat and placed in a chair by Dad. Just a few months old, he gurgled and cried occasionally, keeping with the banter at the table. Jack wiped his son's chin. "Not bad for prison food," he said, taking the bottle from his lips.

Delmonica yelled, "Hey, I made that!" She was irked with the rebel bullshit.

"Sweetheart, it's Thanksgiving. Do we have to talk about your breastmilk?"

The little ridges of canned cranberry jelly were still observable as it lay on its side in a soup bowl. Opening both ends of the can, then gently coaxing the purple ambrosia in one piece onto the serving dish with a loud, slurpy "thurrummpt" was one of Delmonica's specialties since childhood. Her cooking skills plateaued from there.

Brian made a broccoli salad from the deli and Kimmy brought a beautiful pie from the bakery. One of Jack's buddies brought a bag of chips and two six packs for the host. Corrine, not to be outdone, brought a veggie platter, also from the Piggly Wiggly the night before.

Sensing the hostess' frustration, she asked if Jack knew what a self-fulfilling prophecy was. "Maybe your son will start stealing classic cars when he's thirteen just to impress his old man. Then the cops will be like, 'did anybody in the family know that Little Johnny was headed for trouble?' And we'll be all like, 'oh yeah, his dad paved the way for his life of crime since he was in the crib.' And then you're gonna be like, 'Whaaaat?'" That got some laughs.

"So, you're saying you're going to rat out my boy about stealing cars? Is that right, Corrine?" Jack-assed, dead serious.

"Uhh, no. What I was saying was—"

"Just remember, Corrine, snitches get stitches."

Jack's quiet friend pushed some mashed potatoes onto his fork with his thumb (he had tattoos on his hands), looked up, and said, "Prison law."

"Prison law" Ryan echoed! Then he gave his buddy a fist bump. The prophecy ingrained itself deeply into the code of conduct for elementary school.

"Hope you like the mashed potatoes, fellas. Betcha can't guess what the secret ingredient is." Delmonica froze them in their tracks. "They're really good, aren't they? Hope you're not lactose intolerant. Can't get that in prison."

Little Johnny got so agitated at his future being foretold that his father had to take him to go watch football. The baby always settled down watching huge men knock the hell out of each other. Jack's food would get cold but he didn't care. Most of the turkey he roasted was destined for Jack making soup anyway.

They'd stare at the TV screen, spellbound, a bottle's nipple dripping just an inch from little Johnny's mouth. When the appropriate team scored a touchdown, the new dad danced with son in celebration, the baby smiling.

...

When the Centers for Disease Control sampled 7,000 blood donations just into January, from across nine states, they found 106 were positive for Coronavirus antibodies. SARS-CoV-2 was in the U.S. population in the fall of 2019. But nobody knew it, since most infected had no symptoms. And then it was treated like any other flu, successfully.

More than a million people died in the US during the 1889-1890 pandemic, called the "Russian Flu" because of where it originated. The expansion of railroads and oceanic shipping spread it worldwide quickly. Through natural immunity the human coronavirus OC43 then, is now part of what we call "the common cold."

Funny thing about viruses, biologists debate whether they are alive or not and manipulations of their genetic code always leave markers, like an architect's stamp, so they can find them later. Viruses should not kill their hosts quickly. They function better if they spread really fast, then send lots of people to the hospital, not killing the host right away. A gain only useful as a weapon.

19

The Pacific Northwest

Now that the easy part was over, getting a man to travel two thousand miles, fording wild rivers, navigating badlands, climbing through snowy mountain passes just for her, Corrine had to assemble her outfit. There was no way she wanted to greet her man in a hoodie and stained sweatpants. Besides, going through the motions meant she'd have her first Pin Up outfit ready for the spring.

Because she worked damn hard at her job she could afford to buy from the internet and pay for alterations. Perhaps Kimmy would be able to help her out, she hoped. She found a sunflower yellow, knee-length dress and a crinoline wire hoop petticoat, chartreuse pumps, belt, and a sweater for when she got chilly.

All this to complement a living, breathing flower. She reasoned that taking the child to stores and expecting him to be still as she tore through the racks was unreasonable, so therefore, spending money on herself ordering online was saving frustration for them both, and lots of time.

She practiced making big curls with a new jumbo roller hair setter, for her home-colored brunette hair. When they were in place she roared at her son while he was in the bubble bath, and he screamed to make mommy laugh like she really was a monster.

Queen De Menthe told him while they toweled off that Peter was coming for a visit.

"Is he done moving away?" was Cory's first question, then followed by, "Can we get pizza when he comes back?" He had natural timing between the serious and light-hearted to make his mother laugh again. A very subtle appreciation, even if he couldn't weigh it. This marked intelligence often astonished parents recently used to wiping butts and spooning mouthfuls.

She heard him tell Cassie that Peter was coming back, and the Labradoodle seemed excited as well, her big tail still knocking low lying objects like plastic dinosaurs off the coffee table.

Corrine picked up the toys to avoid stepping on them and microwaved Dino-shaped chicken nuggets, turned on a favorite movie for the one thousandth time, then postulated before the half-bath mirror, seeing a chubby, bride of Frankenstein. "Is this really what he wants?" She growled to herself before the mirror, hands like Tyrannosaurus arms.

"Mommy. Cassie is puking!" She wasn't. Stop joking she told him and eat your apple and green beans. He wanted more ketchup. The boy ate only what he felt he needed, smart lad. Her legs felt like a prickly pear, and although Corrine couldn't say exactly what Peter wanted, snuggling with sandpaper certainly wasn't it.

Well, the big day came, as you can't stop slippery time. She fantasized about greeting him at the baggage claim, all dolled up with her sash emblazoned, "Queen of the Stars", her crown resting on big brown curls, her everything shaved smooth, descending an escalator. But the end of the Concourse was fine, too, as she wanted to show off.

She was all dolled up, just for him! She was breathtaking, like a sunflower. Queen De Menthe's pumps were the color of peas, her shoulder wrap sweater like bright pears. And Peter didn't let the moment escape without telling her how beautiful she looked. He wanted to eat her up. But kissing a Pin Up girl is strictly forbidden, except for the lightest lip-kiss imaginable, a necessary concession to over an hour of applying makeup.

Talking to the kid, he asked, "Doesn't your mom look beautiful?" But the lad looked up as if he'd just bit a lemon, wondering what Peter meant.

They went for wood fired pizza as promised. When the server brought

Cory crayons and a colorless, woodland placemat filled with exotic animal shapes, Peter asked for one himself, and the waitress grinned. Two boys together, asking to share, enjoying the company. Corrine was watching them draw, enjoying a red blend, when Peter asked his friend what color he thought his mom's fingernails were: yellow or green? She displayed her hands upon the table.

"Umm. . .Green-yellow, I guess."

"I think they look cool. What do you think?" It was a thoughtful way for him to compliment his girly-girl.

"Uhh, I don't know." And he continued to color. "Are you done with the black crayon, Peter?"

Later, after supper, Peter the grownup said, "Close your eyes, boy, I'm going to give your mamma a smooch." And planted a big kiss on her when they got home, right in front of him. Peter loved Cory's mom too and he was just going to have to get used to it. Cory didn't mind. It made sense. The boy loved her, too. Sharing the feeling with Peter felt good, safe.

Queen De Menthe kissed Peter back, passionately, and it became awkward.

"See you in the morning, kid. Tomorrow's Christmas, ya know." Corrine snapped Cory out of the car seat and the tot ambled toward the apartment door, giving Peter a fist bump. He wanted to be the one who let Cassie out, to jump excitedly that the humans had returned, and needing to pee.

Alone for the first moment since he appeared, she whispered to him, "I love you, Peter."

"I love you, too. See you in the early AM. Text me when I should show up here, for the little guy. To help out." Then he caught himself to say, "I flew all the way across the country to say that. I need you." And that was even better.

Corrine slept very little, reunited but alone. Peter camped at the local Hilton and drank beer almost 'til bar close. The need to wake up early to do her makeup and hair juxtaposed to a quivering need (of which her man had the cure), kept Corrine uncomfortably jumpy most of the night.

...

Being a senior radio producer meant that 24-7 broadcasting was life's blood. Many co-workers had families that needed tending, old hands not so much. At 4AM Owen woke up, caffeinated, for most it was Christmas day, but for radio was Wednesday. The job was easy, playing holiday tunes. Leaving the ring in the velvet box before he left (in the middle of the kitchen table) with a big post-it note saying, "Call me," was a risk.

"Well, the weather outside is frightful, but the fire is so delightful, and since we've no place to go, let it snow, let it snow."

Will you marry me?

"Have yourself a merry little Christmas, let your heart be light, from now on your troubles will be out of sight."

A young, not so long-ago intern was the on-air voice anticipating.

Audrey, blurry eyed before she put her contacts in, nuked two bags of English Breakfast tea before going back to bed, almost too sleepy to squeeze some lemon in, then peed, then laid back down in bed, wishing she could place her cold feet on Owen's thick calves. How wonderful it was, Audrey thought, having a guy who loved her. Even if he volunteered to work on Christmas Day.

She Facebooked, seeing what others had done on Christmas Eve when it occurred to her something she had seen.

Will you marry me? There was a box the size of a microwave on the kitchen table and eventually her curiosity made her swing her feet, once again, onto the carpet and shuffle out of the bedroom. There was a post-it note on the box that read, "OPEN ME," reminiscent of "Alice in Wonderland".

Unwrapped, she missed it before. There was another box and another, clever, like Russian nesting dolls. They had agreed to exchange presents when he got home mid-afternoon. Well, it looked like Owen was being a "Slick Rick" again. When it came to a velvet box that could hold an engagement ring, she saw another post-it that read, "CALL ME."

So, she did. He asked if she'd opened up the last box. Audrey hadn't. He told her to answer the phone then hung up. Her phone rang.

"I'm putting you on the air when this song ends, hold on." She heard the most popular Christmas song ever with Mariah Carey singing, "All I Want For Christmas Is You."

"Wait. . .what?"

"Hey, Audrey, this is Danny, KTZP radio. You there?"

"Yeah, hi. What's Owen doing over there? What's going on?" The intent was to go fast so she didn't have time to think.

"For our listeners, Owen is the producer this morning, bringing you all kinds of Christmas cheer. Audrey, we met at the company KTZP baseball game. You probably don't remember me because I was drinking. Okay. . .so you haven't opened the last box, right?"

"Right."

"Okay, do it now. It isn't often that we get to involve members of staff on the show but being that it's Christmas and it's only me and my producer in the KTZP building, I guess there's no adult supervision to stop us. Audrey, what's in the last box?"

Barely audible, she breathed, "A ring."

"Put the ring on your ring finger, Audrey." Danny gave her a moment. "Is it on?"

"Yes."

"Is it shiny?"

"Yes."

"Owen wants to know if you will marry him. Okay?"

"Okay."

"Wow. That was really un-moving. But it seems like our producer Owen has officially been spoken for. And he can deal with the squealing for joy off air. You really stirred up a lot of excitement, Mr. Producer."

"Can you hear me, babe?" Owen asked off air, muting her.

"I love you, Owen. This is the best Christmas ever." And a little sob came out.

"Ladies and gentlemen, Audrey is nearly hysterical right now thinking about the decision she's just made. Better marry her quick, Mr. Producer, before she changes her mind."

Danny had her back on air after commercials for men's hair growth, a mortgage refinance outfit, and a weight loss program. Audrey was giddy and took revenge for the trick by publicly stating she was going to bankrupt her fiancé with a fancy spring wedding.

...

Once Cory had received his matchbox cars and track, football and NASCAR posters, socks, books about construction equipment like cranes, bulldozers, and dump trucks, Corrine regretfully dropped him off at his non-essential dad.

She had taken Kimmy up on her offer to use their cabin after Christmas, again. She had vacation to burn. Cassie cried a little driving onto the ferry. The puppy expectantly remembered from the smell of salt water how much fun it was to fetch in the lake. . .the cold hose water later, not so much. McNeil Island was a refuge, the most southerly of the many in the Puget Sound.

Brian and Kimmy were happy to have their friends run the water, make sure no squatters or crack heads had somehow broken in. Calling a few friends over for BBQ was the highlight that Friday night. It would take time for his woman's jewelry collection to build. Corrine showed the girls her present, an opal necklace, on Facebook.

The cloudy stone fired into a rainbow of colors if worn next to one's skin. She got him a gift certificate for two deluxe auto detailings and two tickets to the Mariners first weekend of baseball. They made love, played games, hiked, tried to wear out the dog, cooked some great meals together, and Corrine even got drunk one time. It didn't take much. Sunday service was painful for Corrine, but only because of her headache.

And the next day they brought Cory while looking for townhouses. Two bedrooms, two-and-a-half baths, a staircase that turned upon itself, and a one-butt kitchen, in the center of metro Seattle. With a garage across the parking lot for storage and two assigned parking spaces, the rent was doable for a two-income household at $2,100 a month. Cory had his own room next to mom's once again, but this time the five-year-old had to share some attention. Before Corrine took Peter to SEATAC airport they had signed a lease, three months in advance paid, a plan in motion.

"Sometimes parents, I've noticed, ask their children's assent to things, like, 'is it okay if we go shopping for school clothes?' The way my mom did things was through bribery, like, 'Peter, we are going shopping for school clothes. Do you want to pick out your own shirts?' Not hoping that the child agreed with the adult's plans. Does that make sense?" It was pretty late in the game for full disclosure.

Corrine turned around in her seat and looked at her strapped in kid and said, "Corey. Peter is going to be living with us soon and we're going to have a lot of fun."

"Okay," replied the tiny tot. Peter took up the same emotional space as Cassie, good furry friends. Well almost, not quite yet.

...

Nobody noticed the matching necklaces that the two new soulmates wore until Aleia asked the big ex-Soldier if he'd bought the pair. 18kt yellow gold wheat-link, Donna's was a thirty inch, her beau's a twenty-two. Aaron was hosting his Christmas Party and a few couples visited during the day. Her mechanic actually bought matching ugly holiday sweaters with blinking lights, reindeer prancing on a rooftop.

Donna wore her present over a black turtleneck and under a flannel shirt, while Lawrence was bolder, displaying his necklace above his t-shirt's collar. It barely looped down from his big neck. The metal weave was stunning.

Donna's son thought nothing was amiss. Neither did Aaron. It was probably because their boy was more mindful that his fiancé felt comfortable in his parents' house. Presents were exchanged haphazardly, drinking during the middle of the day excused like any other day off. Wearing a Santa cap, the host grilled burgers and hot dogs. It felt more like a BBQ, being a calm fifty degrees outside. Aleia's gift was getting everyone, except for Aaron, really stoned out on the porch.

A union buddy showed up to play some drinking games. It never occurred to him to ask what Aaron got his wife for Christmas. Car payments would most likely be the bitter answer. Donna would say she gave him a blowjob, but he doesn't remember.

Lawrence got pretty drunk with his Brazen Beauties friend. He was lucky and could stumble home, his mother's house a half-mile away. But he gave Donna a big smooch before he left, not worried about having to get up the next day like his host.

...

Many people that Peter met while knocking on doors looking for work said, "Seattle wasn't what it used to be." They were not political statements.

Speeding past the Space Needle up Highway 99 to the East was Lake Washington, the Cascade Mountains, then high desert; to the West, on his left shoulder, was the Puget Sound, the Olympic mountain range, then the Pacific Ocean. Lakes, the Sound, islands, and mountains constricted traffic that rivaled Chicago or Washington DC., but far less furious. It was hard to find where the ghetto was since there wasn't one. Just pockets of poverty intermixed with working class ranch homes the locals called "ramblers."

A carpenter who doesn't have a truck is exactly like a man who doesn't have a set of balls. What good is he? Peter loved his mom who expected him to get out and work and not be a burden on family, thus the sweetheart deal on the pickup. The scrapes along the side of his F-150 where Peter's mom had taken her truck through brush to get to wooded parcels were more signs of productivity than in-attentive driving. Hiring someone with a brand-new truck, for rough work, wasn't smart. His back, his brain, and now his Ford were a package deal to any outfit that wanted to pick him up. The Roadrunner was going to have to wait its turn.

Blue and green branding reflected its being called the Emerald City. All tollways led to the downtown bringing all arteries from three, to two, and then just one lane. The city leaders built their convention center over the central interchange, locking future expansion in concrete. Driving past Boeing field, newcomers caught glimpses of the skyline between big hills that made up the corridor between salt and freshwater. Rows of container gantry cranes taller than a football field was long was next to the home of the Seahawks football club.

It confused Peter on his job search when ancient neighborhoods were referred to like Sodo, Ballard, Rainier Valley, Magnolia, Beacon Hill, Ravenna, and two dozen more. They were established after Chief Si'ahl led his Duwamish people to accommodate and assist white settlers. The local tribes were systematically removed, their agreements with Americans only haphazardly applied, with Federal recognition removed.

In the "roaring" 20's, home building covenants all over the country were established to keep people of color from some districts, keeping them "nice". Not having a monopoly on discrimination, during the Great Depression, President Roosevelt allowed these redlines, so desperate was he to get banks making home loans again.

Likewise, when high tech raised wages, property values were bid up, old buildings were razed, and new construction abounded. The poorer, less equipped people had to leave. Some called this destroyer of "do you remember when" gentrification, casting differences of class, except for the noble, liberal elite.

"Urban camping" became a crisis. Tents were omnipresent under tollways, city employees swept camps sometimes, considered biohazards with untreated human waste. Those who believed that drug addiction wasn't a crime made the rules. Amongst Pike's Place and Pioneer Square the flotsam and jetsam flourished at the water's edge, the gateway to the Pacific washed up the poor white trash.

It drizzled a lot in the winter. But it rained more in Chicago and a true thunderstorm was unknown. When it snowed three inches the metro area became paralyzed since no one had shovels to remove the little blanket from sidewalks before it could melt, then freeze into sheets of ice. The inhabitants had to wait a day or two for the melt. Seattle had fifty plows; Minneapolis had five hundred.

Peter couldn't bring much more than his basic hand and power tools, knapsack, and a big suitcase in the first sortie. He joined the carpenter's union the second week of January and it was predicted he'd have a job within a month. The job search was like really discovering his new town. After a few nibbles, Peter could tell that if he didn't get his Roadrunner now, there was no telling when he might have the time in the future. Corrine told him they'd need to rent a storage space if he wanted the garage.

Boys and their toys. She knew he had the bug to enter his baby into a show, maybe join a car club. A mutualistic need would be unfulfilled until his budget muscle car brought her to a pageant like Cinderella's carriage. It was a five-day trip minimum, from flying, to prep, and then three days driving hard with no weather delays or mountain passes closing in the middle of winter.

A "Best in Paint" could come from a Plymouth 1968 Mist Turquoise to match her namesake color. "You'd better make Momma a lot of money if you're gonna do that," she said. Corrine posing on the hood of his car, making it onto the Brazen Beauties annual calendar was now the holy grail. So, it'd be a few thousand to fix some of the pitting and maintain Baby's undercarriage from rust. That was a task left to a professional for later, he concentrated on the girl variety.

20
No Huggin' No Kissin' No More

Their schedules synced nicely. Corrine played house, placing pictures and pithy sayings on the walls like "May you be in Heaven for an hour before the Devil knows you're dead." If the kid wanted to snuggle with mom in bed or vice versa, Peter made a quick exit.

He got a great job with a great general contractor running work. His old F150 became part of the fleet fetching plywood and drywall. They gave him a gas card for the rental.

Since he had to start his little tenant improvement in the Emerald City's neighborhood called Queen Anne at six, Peter got home first (it was important to get through downtown before 3PM). Cassie was always super excited to see Daddy. It meant pooping and playing chuck-it, chasing a tennis ball as far as a guy could throw it with the extended plastic scoop. The Labradoodle would run herself to death, but by the time he got the mail and picked up her poop, the human was much more ready to retreat inside than she was.

Going to Costco for staples was a lively zoo, mitigated by fab, cheap pizza at the beginning of the onslaught for supplements and jumbo flats. They used her membership card and his debit, to Peter's great satisfaction.

On one weekend when they were childless, lacking wintery ideas, they moseyed to the mall for Valentine presents. Peter wanted to go to a particular one, being that it had a carousel. He told her that he rode horses all the time when he slinked alongside her choice. There was a spotted leopard with a top hat, and a dolphin plunging under the seas.

Chariots and playful frogs didn't go up and down, which wouldn't be nearly as much fun. Corrine wanted to ride the lion with a mane that looked like flames. It hadn't a saddle and got slippery as the pole pumped up and down. The crankshaft rotated forward, the lion then shuddered back, the motion transferred, reciprocating upon her lucky calf. All too soon the music stopped and Corrine hopped off. The carousel came to a full stop before her beau attempted to dismount, saying he was dizzy, not able to walk a straight line.

He was another implant to the most accepting place in the USA. Three grams of heroin or methamphetamine was considered "personal use" and unprosecuted. Building boomed. Those who could swim in these fast currents and pay increasing rents lamented what had been. Those who hadn't family anymore to enable camped, trying to find a place they wouldn't be hassled. Several times, Peter found used syringes at his project's parking garage, to the building engineer's consternation on how someone was getting in.

Almost anyone could become homeless from a great change in circumstance. An injury that kept someone from humping for Amazon, or giving up to addiction, or no longer being able to mooch on someone else to place a roof over one's head (a change of living arrangements or getting kicked out). Those who were recently sleeping in their cars had a year-long window before becoming lost, chronically homeless.

Campers in disrepair parked on city streets anywhere except where politicians lived. Homelessness became a mental disorder itself. When relieving oneself, staying warm in the weeds, and finding food for the belly became a constant/overwhelming drive to self-preserve only. In response, petty crime, like shoplifting less than one thousand dollars, became a human right. The cops hadn't the resources or authority to respond. And retailers just photographed thievery since 9-1-1 became useless.

Peter Googled an evangelical church nearby and went to establish routine and ask the Lord for patience. She too found another person in her space, her bed, annoyed at simple things like unnecessary splatter on the mirror when brushing one's teeth. Cory got a temporary security bracelet when Corrine left him for Sunday school. A time to pray when the kid napped, or maybe he got a little bible lesson or did a craft. Corrine never exercised, just worked and now loved two men, big and little.

He found a tavern nearby that had an outdoor patio for smokers, if he wanted to be sneaky. They said they might join a gym, but it had to have a daycare. He had a physical job and hated the idea of sitting behind a monitor. Peter suggested that she'd have more energy if she exercised more, a contradiction in terms, it would seem. But he had to move and the pull to have his love keep up was aggravating sometimes.

It was just fine that Pin Up would drive some of the weekend schedule. Once, Peter put Corrine on the phone to say hi to his mother. He was playing with Corey and Cassie outside so couldn't hear the conversation, thank God. Meeting her folks in Yakima had been postponed, as they had seen Cory recently the day after Thanksgiving and a getaway to a snowy island for Christmas bumped the introductions. Sooner would be better than later.

These were as important blocks to check as a foundation being placed level. It was a builder's phase in the relationship, a natural progression of events.

The biggest logjam was Corrine's employer requiring extra time. As a single mom, she picked up the kid most days. Evan was never keen to adjust, and it quickly became a wedge to make life more difficult. Peter couldn't pick up Cory. His father said no. The two men did not meet except for early Saturday mornings and waves from inside cars. His father was tall and non-confrontational. Cory's would-be Dad pinched his neck before he ambled out the door. Perhaps the tot could know a strong man needed him back, but a weak one called the shots.

Corrine didn't like it much when Peter stopped by the local tavern after work. Sometimes he'd smell like smoke. Her Lupus flared up in late February and she was tired all the time. She told her boss and took a few days off when just getting across the room felt like landing a jetliner. A red rash appeared like wings over her chest, and her cheeks became like Saint Nick's.

Peter dropped off Cory at daycare and got to work an hour late, but it was no big deal as Peter was running the show, so he said. The big deal was doing all the housework and dog work and most of the childcare as her joints and head ached. Cory had to strip his clothes off himself and then towel off himself at bath time, Peter checking in frequently for three seconds at a time.

Sleeping all day, she kept quiet, keeping the shades drawn. Was this how it was going to be? Her rheumatologist ran a panel. Her lungs were clear, so she didn't have the flu (Corrine always got the shot), and so it was a waiting game until her symptoms got better.

"Are you under an unusual amount of stress?" she asked Corine.

"No. Just the normal. Well, my boyfriend moved in. He's great. Actually, life's been easier," she answered. "Life's good. Until right now."

"You know, sometimes good things produce a lot of stress. Like a wedding."

"Ahhh. Take it easy, doc. He hasn't even met my parents yet."

"Nothing stressful about that." And both women smiled, renewing the prescription to take the very best care of herself, and her hydroxychloroquine.

Cory was a neat little kid and it was fun reading to him. He'd jump right beside Peter as if all grownups should get close and read, showing the pictures. They worked on the alphabet and printing his name. Kids were messy, though. Peter bought placemats and a tablecloth for family dinner, then served spaghetti and meatballs that night, getting frustrated at the marinara stains on the chair seat, carpet, the placemats, but not Cory's hair, which was funny.

When he grumbled the lad grew a little frightened since Peter weighed five or six times more than him and had secret powers like being able to drive a car. He was too little to help much when Peter worked on his car but helped change the oil once. Crawling under the car was something Corrine preferred he not teach her child. And she said so after the fact.

"What if he crawls under a car trying to get something and gets run over?" she asked him with all seriousness.

"Cory, don't ever go under a car unless I'm with you."

"Okay," said the lad.

"You see?" explained Peter. "End of problem." But she took her son's hand and led him away from the "bad man" nonetheless. That pissed him off.

Those kinds of small frustrations were about it at that stage of the game.

Cory wanted Peter to show him about the Roadrunner. Or was it the other way around? Anyway, it was better than being cooped up inside. And he explained what the components were, with the kid standing on a step ladder. Peter even found through Amazon a kid's book about what engines were.

He figured he'd make the boy car crazy. Matchbox racing tracks filled the living room, with Cassie messing up the track with her paws, sniffing things until they disappeared under the couch. Posters of hot rods were purchased for his room. Corey loved riding in Peter's muscle car 'cause it was cool! He added some eye bolts into the sheet metal of the back bench and ensured the car seat was fastened to the car.

Mama Bear wasn't too sure, but eventually they rode around town, all three, in the Roadrunner. Peter gunned the engine, making Cory squeal. Maybe one day he and the lad would be trusted enough to travel all by themselves just 'cause. Little man helped with the drilling and tightening of the bolts for his own car seat! About this time, Cory began to say the s*** word regularly. There were suspects. Peter said he must have picked that up in daycare. The boys watched football for short durations as Cory really wasn't into it. Still, he got a Seahawks t-shirt from Target.

...

The World Health Organization (WHO) declared a Public Health Emergency, from the UN headquarters in New York. By the end of January 2020, South Korea, Britain, Japan, Vietnam, and the US reported person-to-person transmission. There was no test for the new bug, as the symptoms were like any other flu. For severe cases, hospitalization was required.

Nations with weaker health care systems were going to need help. Kenya and Rwanda suspended airline flights from China. A whistleblower, Li Wenliang, a researcher, signed a confession the Communist authorities prepared, then later died. They ordered labs not to publish any info about the disease and destroy all samples. WHO published whatever the Chinese government told them to, at face value.

Miss Demeanor, Aleia, became most broken first. And began a new flight from arrest before the shutdown began in earnest, accidently, luckily. She wasn't producing much income and hated the hours, especially the weekends annoying people to support local firefighters with donations, telemarketing for a mere three dollars an hour over minimum wage, plus incentive pay for "sales."

She dreamt about her son in horrible danger and paid for groceries from time to time. Her mechanic took her out sometimes, but besides Donna who lived a few towns away, Aleia was pretty isolated. It was a devil's bargain for free lodging, heat, and Brazen Beauty. She was able to save money because her rule was to spend her stash hardly ever. A couple of times her mechanic came home, waking her, asking, "who wants to fuck a drunk?"

And she did, a few times, not wanting to confront a man at least ten years her junior. Much too soon, he'd roll over and snore, fresh from the strip club. Aleia thought she was just a hired piece of ass to him, not the marrying kind. It was time to bail, she could tell. He had a robust circle of buds that he liked more than her, liked going drinking out on the town, maybe finding a different girl.

The tests for the SARS-like Coronaviruses were the only one sanctioned by the bewildering and frustrating bureaucratic maze called the Centers of Disease Control. Ignoring best practices around the world, (using surveillance testing to find hotspots) the mandate caused weeks of delay in February. Could children pass the crud along? The CDC's test was a failure. It was always unclear who decided to ignore the recommendations of W-H-O.

How could she get new Whiskey Dick to install a trailer hitch onto her 2011 Honda Civic without raising alarm bells? This man wasn't stupid, just careless. It would be a delicious act of revenge. The parts were going to cost a few hundred bucks. She priced them through Napa but figured her mechanic could get them cheaper. So much the sweeter that he helped at each step until Aleia loaded up the four foot by eight foot U Haul on the way out of town.

"I'm going to buy a tow hitch bar from Napa. There's one for five hundred and change. Is that a good price?"

That got the gearhead going. "No. Why? What are you towing?" flashed through his mind. Calling him at work so she could avoid facial expressions also meant his typing on the shop's plastic covered keyboard was handy. There wouldn't be any, "I'll look it up tomorrow." She was shrewd.

"Maybe Napa could install it for me if you're too busy?" It was a dagger into the heart of a tradesman, suggesting another man would touch the underside of her chassis. In a pre-emptive strike, Miss Demeanor added that in preparation for the next season Donna wanted to stop relying on her boozy husband's pickup to get her Pin Up merchandise plus photo/audio equipment, plus tentage, plus swag bags, sashes, and tiaras to the pageants. "Why don't you just use someone else's truck?"

"Well, the club is going to pay for it, and Donna can get a trailer for cheap. It has to be covered 'cause it's the Pacific Northwest and always rains, silly." They had screwed the evening before, placing him in a good mood, her especially so. "And if they breakup or something stupid like that happens, it's the two of us that's always going to be around."

It was a splendid lie, mixing a half-truth, the obvious innuendo, a misdirected portend, and viciousness. It was such a pleasant seed to plant. She thanked him vigorously many times before she split, getting her rocks off too, many times. It felt good. The satisfying, cumming, real deal feeling, might have to last for more than a little bit.

In early March, the all-powerful Director of the National Institute of Allergic and Infectious Diseases stated that "people should not be walking around with masks" and that "wearing a mask might make people feel a little bit better and it might even block a droplet, but it's not providing the perfect protection that people think that it is."

Despite this admission of truth, quickly everyone was required to wear a mask whenever they passed the threshold of their own home. No consideration for a kindergartener's perception was included within mandates. Adults became like masked thieves to be feared. Recognizing emotion/communication through facial features was dismissed, while not being able to know what a person looked like prevailed.

In late March, panicking and playing "monkey see, monkey do" the Governor declared for Washingtonians to shelter in place, schools close, gyms close, restaurants close, only essential workers were allowed to travel, although no one knew what that meant. It was called "Stay Home – Stay Healthy", which didn't account for mental health.

Politicians had to be seen doing something before the next election. Special Ed kids weren't considered as "going virtual" seemed so chic. It was almost like teaching, appearing to exist but not really. Computers could be used to simulate human relationships.

Aleia's employer gave her equipment so she could work from home. Fortunately, new Whiskey Dick had paid for high-speed internet along with the cable. Her imagined umbilical cord to her child was nearly shorn and snapped at Miss Demeanor's lack of motherhood skills. If she had to betray to survive, it wasn't going to be her kid. She could insure her care again, until she found something better, then she'd mail the computer, monitor, and other stuff back, as long as they paid her to do it.

It was $2,500 bucks for a one-way U-Haul to Florida. Miss Demeanor would need three months' rent at a minimum. Perhaps Felonious Frida could be a new Pin Up name or, Lolita Lamb (as in- on the lamb). Either could explain her childhood molestation in context. Her revenge was sweet and savory. Everything she did she did for family.

A few embezzled grand wasn't much, but everything to Donna Diva. Too bad for her. And the club, and pediatric cancer. It wasn't as if there was going to be a pageant season anyway, Miss Demeanor figured correctly.

People were told to not allow non-family members into their homes, so Lawrence wasn't hanging out all day with Donna anymore. Aaron's work with the big electrical contractor got slow, 40s going to twenty hours per week then to furlough. Donna's comings and goings changed drastically. Her husband vowed to cut his drinking way back. When she asked why now? Aaron responded, "if we're imprisoned in this little house together and only get drunk all the time, someone's going to die and that's probably me. I'll piss you off constantly, not just most of the time." He started to grab his coat, smiling. "I'm going to the garden center at Walmart. Let's do some landscaping. Maybe plant a garden. Two-week emergency shutdown my ass!" He looked at his still pretty wife. "You coming, beautiful?"

...

An epicenter for the evil thing was at a long-term care home in Kirkland. They weren't big on taking precautions like screening people for temperature or asking people if they had been sick with flu-like symptoms. That became ubiquitous. Owen walked right in, not knowing residents and staff were sick because illnesses weren't being reported.

Soon, the only way he would ever see his dad again was through a window. Congestive heart failure and diabetes became co-morbidities and by June when he passed away, COVID was written on the death certificate; there was more money for the hospital from Medicare that way. The illness translated into money: "of COVID" and "with COVID" weren't distinguished. Owen never held his hand when he was dying.

Law enforcement, media, and hospital workers couldn't stay home. Audrey's job making airplane parts for Boeing was essential for now. But their wedding plans got shelved quickly when their honeymoon in Japan was postponed indefinitely, as international travel stopped cold. Canada closed its border with the Pacific Northwest and the disorganized Americans. Public health officials and politicians were frantic to respond, to be seen as doing something. Hospitals were feared to become overwhelmed and most scheduled surgeries and routine procedures were canceled to make room, idling many doctors and nurses.

WHO projected a 3.4% fatality rate, stoking hysteria. But that measured those already hospitalized. Death for all who got infected was actually less than one in a thousand. And the thousand-fold difference between the very old and the very young wasn't publicized.

"Owen's got COVID!" Audrey sent out the group text with a sick-face emoji. He had a high temp and got a test from his primary care provider. It took several days for the results. He was high in the queue because of where he'd been. False negatives added to the confusion.

Of course, he stayed home, but was almost tip top when his infection was confirmed. Health officials warned against using drugs without their approval such as antimalarial chloroquine or hydroxychloroquine. Hospitals didn't have enough ventilators for those with life threatening symptoms. Owen took Tylenol.

"OMG!" were common texted responses and the dinging of incoming messages sounded like wedding bells that now weren't going to sound for them. Was their June wedding going to be postponed, the Dolls wanted to know? Audrey was thinking of a vintage Celtic Medieval wedding gown, with seafoam green and pale aqua blue hues and long lace sleeves.

Protocols were sketchy but Owen being quarantined for two weeks seemed prudent. Then he got retested and waited, exhausting all programming on Netflix. Finally, Audrey was asked the magic question if she'd been exposed to anyone with a known case of COVID and she got sent home.

Lucky for them that they worked for big companies and their sick time wasn't measured in days and they both got paid to stay home and work on ways not to get on each other's nerves. After a week of lockdown, Owen drove his yellow truck to the store for beer and other stuff on the list, dutifully masked and using the new hand sanitizing station at the automatic doors.

Obviously, the State couldn't shut down grocery stores and pot shops. Person to person contact was dicey. Droplets on someone's hands on a can, onto a shelf that someone else picked up and set down into a cart, to the hands of the clerk at the register who touched every item, to your plastic bag seemed like a virus conveyor belt so they mandated large plexiglass sneeze guards just for show.

Stores ran out of shit paper and hair cutting scissors. In the months to come, Owen would get halfway to the doors of the store, before swearing and turning around, having to go back to the yellow truck 'cause he forgot his fucking mask.

There was little chance that Audrey would get to see her grandson Tamah for some months. And things had been going so well.

...

Jack kept humping Pepsi products, but his hours got cut, severely. Folks weren't at their offices chugging sugary drinks. He didn't have the almost twenty years with the company like his deceased father-in-law, Ryan. It would always sting that he wasn't at the wedding or Little Johnny's christening.

Within three weeks of his getting laid off, Delmonica was at a food pantry trying to score free diapers, canned food, and dry goods. She was so ashamed that she stopped attending to her social media, afraid someone might have seen her, withdrawing into her child. Their margin was non-existent, meeting the mortgage too tight. The budget was based on Jack working as hard as he wanted to. Jack cleaned out their good car and started Ubering.

When Tiffany came around it was too late for beggars. Her mother had been hospitalized with the COVID, too. They were now sharing an efficiency and one social security check. Delmonica held the baby on her hip while keeping her mother on the porch. She wouldn't allow her to get too close to Johnny, because no one knew who may get sick and die. COVID's devastating effect on family was more complete than even the weaponization of children known before.

The convention cycle ended unto seeming permanence, business travel not to resume in earnest for a year. Serenity Jade, aka Kimmy, who cut hair, stopped making meager money immediately, too. Their double wide was nearly paid for, but the next six months were dicey. When the shop she worked at resumed in June, her tips were the greatest of her life. Then she worked seventy hours a week.

Real estate wasn't affected by the pandemic and the thought of selling the "cabin" on McNeil Island was considered. Brian tried collecting unemployment, but the telephone lines were always busy. There were no offices to go to anymore.

State employees either worked from home or were furloughed with full pay. In fact, no one who worked for the government got laid off, even if there was no work, like grade schoolteachers.

Jack showed Brian the ropes about Ubering. Although he had W2's and had worked steadily for years, he couldn't complete a jobless claim because the telephonic system crashed.

The Washington State Unemployment office was overwhelmed, soon to be scammed for over one billion dollars from either Nigeria or Russia it was never clear, with no recriminations ever. Kimmy often worked for cash, off the books, so she wasn't even going to bother to apply. The men had to work or go crazy. Brian and Jack would dig ditches before sitting on the couch.

...

Construction guys found the traffic much lighter, as long as they worked on projects for Googlers, Facebookers, or Amazonians. People who never went to Home Depots wiped out dust masks the moment they were stocked. State financed work like light rail was always essential.

The only option for Cory was to stay with his grandparents during the day as his daycare closed. Some places stayed open to service the Essentials' kids, but not his. His father was forced a near full time schedule, as so many grocery clerks called in sick even if they just had the sniffles.

Evan was now on the "front lines" and was soon declared a "hero." The State mandated he got "hazard" pay. It was an 18% increase, making some urban stores unprofitable, adding to food deserts. When Evan's father got the COVID he landed in the hospital for a few days. Lacking private insurance and not needing a ventilator, he got pushed out quick.

The implications for Corrine reached the most dire. Evan understood why he wouldn't be able to see his son like normal, why the parenting plan just got shredded. He was too tired from regular work anyway. Explaining the pandemic to a child was tough. Cory had to cover his face so his grandpa didn't get sick and die. His mom was already sick with the Lupus and he asked her if they were going to move away.

Corrine worked overtime, logistics, shuffling airplane parts for Boeing. Peter soon was furloughed, but not laid off. He was paid full wages until there was no hope that construction would continue. The homeless, destitute ones, who couldn't make it in good times were joined, in short time, by thousands. RVs became highly sought-after sanctuaries on Seattle city streets. Sometimes, the cops, not often, made them drive to the next block.

The governor restricted travel to non-contiguous states with mandatory tests upon re-entry and quarantine. The ferries were still running for now, but the cruise ships anchored for good and the gantry cranes at the Port of Seattle creaked to a standstill.

Thinking quickly, Peter, not wanting to bring the virus home, suggested his love get away. She thought likewise. A real wolf was biting and snapping, so, afraid, Corrine climbed up a tree. Peter looked forward, hiding like a fearful cat, hoping no one could see him. Corrine asked Kimmy if she could escape to the cabin on McNeil Island while she still could.

She took her son, Cassie, and a laptop, so she could continue to work and care for those dependent upon her. Renting a small U-Haul, they packed a few pieces of furniture, the most precious wall hangings, bedding, clothes, and paper products, stuffing her truck, too. Corrine was wearing a mask when they hugged goodbye briefly. Peter assured the boy he'd see him soon and lastly made sure they had the Chuck-it and tennis balls for the pooch. She looked in the side rearview mirrors as she pulled out of the complex, but she couldn't see him anymore. Corrine paid a normal amount of rent for the refuge, in advance.

In Corrine's frightful dream the duck waddled toward the safety of the pond but was grabbed by sharp teeth. The sparrow snapped at the virus. Father was angry that she had left the gate open, passing from home into the dangerous forest of the Great Dire Wolf.

21

Is you Is or Is you Ain't my Baby?

The thing about going "All In" was you could bust, playing Texas hold 'em, Poker. Bluffing with the Creator Being could get called. It did. The pandemic shook out, through a sieve, what wasn't important anymore. Some believed what they were told and became very, very frightened. Others found workarounds.

Work-a-day America shimmied then stalled, losing its idle. In March the stock market crashed 6,400 points, losing a quarter of its value. The unemployment rate reached 20% the American people were told. Peter's E*TRADE account dropped from 47K to $33,000, over a year of savings wiped out on paper. The first week of furlough was like a vacation, but quickly felt like being locked down because there wasn't anything fun to do.

The tender relief for couples like Corrine and her guy got snatched away. Family patterns shifted radically, and stress doubled every week like a geometric curve. Incomes plunged as parents had to stay home with the children. Government borrowing sky-rocketed against future generations' ability to be taxed. Gym rats cleared out what equipment they could find from stores then made online sales boom.

Golf courses closed. Police warned parents who took their children to parks to mask or else. Neighbors reported when mandates weren't followed. Special Ed kids were first on the causality lists, ignored by absent teachers, not able to focus on a monitor screen for five minutes let alone five hours. Fear grew faster than the virus and fed itself like a media addiction, pornographic, filthy, exposed, enriched.

Suicide rates jumped, then jumped off again with adolescent girls. The social development of children was masked like robbers, grownups preferring their own imagined safety, kids couldn't see lips and tongues to learn speech. Amazon deliveries soared and the company grew to become bigger than US steel from a bygone era, plus Standard Oil, plus American Telephone and Telegraph.

...

Having dismissed Valentine's Day weighed heavily on Aaron's heart. He took walks around the neighborhood before supper time, wondering how he let his buddy screw his wife under his nose. Through years of neglectful haze and months of being stabbed in the back, memories appeared like waking up from drinking binges to be the butt of jokes while his brain swam toward more intoxication.

Divorce seemed like a likely route, but then he'd be defeated by his own boozy composition. If he ever dated again, who'd want him? Strangely, he wasn't angry, not even at himself. Donna was also obviously alcoholic too. Her hands would start shaking by 2PM.

He had plenty of money, so ordering out to support local restaurants seemed like the right thing to do. Better to establish a time to put food on the table each night than drinking himself into forever isolation. So Aaron played a game with Donna called, "Do you remember when?" To recall why they liked each other once before, and stopped drinking, almost completely.

...

Despite the social turbulence, essentially, Boeing kept building airplanes. As a huge employer with Defense contracts that wasn't too much of a stretch. The government controlling the population for its own good was as necessary as avoiding protests in the street, unless the gripe was right.

The logistical parts and pieces machine lurched along. Truckers were some of the last to be required to get the jab. Working from her new home was a blessing for Corrine. If only Peter could be with her. Her son was pretty easy going and it took three weeks of absence before Cory said he wanted to see his dad.

She sat, waiting, afraid, next to her lost best friend on the tree branch, the cat, to tie the wolf's tail, but he didn't know how. Weeks, then two months went by. Could she keep a man?

Corine let him eat Lucky Charms most mornings and wore a headset from the time he got up until after supper. Some nights he asked if she was going to take the headset off. And she'd laugh because she forgot; it was almost a part of her face. There was a lot more time to do stuff like run around outside with Cassie now that they weren't rushing around in the car everywhere.

Most of the kids at daycare came and went so often that Cory played around with a new kid every day. He had friends like Everette and Lynn that he wished could come and play on McNeil Island with its scary pine forests. It was easier to drink from the hose than go inside and ask mom for a drink. Hose water tasted better anyway. Cassie thought so too as the boy cupped his hand before her.

When Corrine worried about getting lost in work and not keeping tabs on those two, she told her son that he needed to come inside every once in a while, to let her know he was okay, and go to the bathroom and such. He asked why. "I can go pee outside, just like Cassie."

"How do you know that?"

"Dad showed me." Practical peeing parenting? "You have to kind of hide so nobody can see you."

Corrine had to take a call and merely responded, "that's right." Her baby was getting all growed up.

"Hi, Mom. How you holding up?" Corrine asked. She and Cory had briefly seen her one-bedroom apartment in Yakima after the divorce. Those walls seemed like a white box prison, with few opportunities to venture out. Corrine's mother was pretty freaked and listed all the super spreaders that were still open like grocery stores.

"Oh, you know. Everything is shut down." It was an often refrain. "Is my grandson enjoying the island? I bet it's like a dream for a boy and his dog."

"Nothing we can do. Except we read old books all the time. The library on the island is even shut down." The truth was cable TV was typical caretaking.

"How is Peter doing?" Her question was the sorest spot. The man had moved over a continent. He made her move beneath the sheets. However, life for Corrine was peaceful and her Lupus rosacea was retreating quickly.

"He got furloughed."

"Now he's by himself? I shouldn't say." Her mom whispered.

"We talk sometimes, but it's hard."

The women agreed. Growing apart was easy to do.

"It must be tough with all of you gone all of a sudden." They barely had time to put pictures back on the walls. Perhaps Peter would decorate in the nine more months of the townhouse lease.

She remembered talking to him one evening when he was slurring his words. Corrine asked crossly, "How much have you had to drink?" Which quickly ended the conversation. And the spaces between texts and calls got longer.

Corrine adapted easily, it seemed, taking care of her boy alone, without distraction. Fear became the watchword, but she wasn't, really.

What if she died? Would Peter and she have a kid together? Would Peter be a good Papa for Cory? Did Corrine want to have a baby with Peter to make this so? Her mother didn't have to ask; she asked herself, while the pandemic sun blazed, and her man faded away. Both lovers were headstrong, unwilling to yield completely unto each other.

...

Audrey and Owen weren't going to visit Japan on their honeymoon, a mere five thousand miles away. They did visit their local "Adult Store" a few times, it was judged as "essential". Owen signed up for the "super saver" account to get discounts and surreptitiously entered his fiancé's email on the application. After she figured that trick out, she called him a "scoundrel". They perused scented oils, and odd shaped stretchy things that maybe could be considered competition. Owen's batteries powered nearly non-stop.

Establishing new patterns, losing most others in a society losing itself, brought them closer. They were kissing, making out, fumbling beneath a fuzzy blanket, just like kids at a drive in. Grownups knew last chances came and went, and they figured they could exchange vows before family at home. It seemed that COVID would win otherwise.

Resistance against wretched times was a project, a build, getting up from the canvas after getting knocked down before the count of ten. A thing of beauty like a '61 Chevrolet Corvette convertible with its pearl scalloped sides, a bulbous edged tail, candy red, white wall tires speeding toward a record quarter mile, they would have to create an alternate plan, and soon, for everyone to congregate, on the QT, hush hush.

...

Across the other side of the tracks in Florida was a place Aleia felt normal, shitty, alone, and apprehensive. Ambulance sirens and palmetto bugs inside kitchen cabinets weren't new (the size of a man's thumb — known everywhere else as roaches), but always shiveringly disgusting.

Before she got to Florida and her rented efficiency, Aleia stopped by a half-sister in Georgia. Poor folks got swept up by the COVID same as a flood or a layoff depression or methamphetamine scourge. Their mother was in an assisted living close to Orlando, not doing too well. Aleia was ten years her senior and let everyone in the family know after she moved out at seventeen, that Mom's boyfriend was a lecher and tried to rape her.

All those white trash "Uncles" and friends of the family were getting young girls drunk. It didn't occur to Aleia to mentor her sissy, just flee. Mom couldn't protect or do for herself very much. That relationship went to the scrapheap soon thereafter, something Aleia wanted to confirm. She vowed to drive the four hours from Jacksonville to see her, probably holed up in some inattentive, government rat hole. Her sister's tale of her own rape came out after multiple shots, by a different scumbag.

"You're not gonna cry and get all weirded out when you see the boy." It wasn't a suggestion from husband #2. But it was said in kindness, at the very least, for his son. "He doesn't need his mommy making him feel sad."

"I'm so happy that I'm going to see the two of you."

"No crying?"

"No crying," she promised. But he promised to take them to lunch the weekend of her return.

"I suppose you'll want to visit regularly when you're settled. A boy needs his mom, but let's not get too ahead of ourselves. I'll be nice if you are."

Afterwards she noted, he didn't say there wasn't a chance between them again. There were a lot of "ifs" in her world right now. She had a ton of clothes that no one had seen her in. And there were lots of Pin Up clubs in Florida, oh yeah.

...

Miss Cherry Nova didn't want to admit to herself that she was indeed a "Fertile Myrtle." Delmonica had periods since bearing "Little Johnny", but they suddenly stopped, just before being spotty. Jack wore a glove sometimes. It was important to try family planning, but they failed. An Uber schedule didn't coincide with her riding reverse cowgirl whenever she could/ wanted day or night. The kid slept a lot.

Luckily, Jack got called back to hump Pepsi products and the health insurance clock resumed. Boy, was she super-horny all the time. Being young and fruitful did not surpass those twenty-somethings.

"You can't get me pregnant twice, again," she moaned.

The stars receded from Jack's eyes for a moment.

"Are you?"

"I think so."

She was.

"That's awesome!" It was the right thing to say, though he was acting a little bit. Then a wave of fear ran through him while they kissed and hugged. Jack began wondering about how to be a "girl" daddy after that.

...

Brian didn't like how Kimmy let her friend rent the cabin for a mere $1,000 a month. Of course, it wasn't being used, and the amount Corrine paid covered its mortgage, tax, and insurance for the property, but they could have gotten a few hundred more. The competition for Uber calls meant that it was spotty. Learning the ropes left him sitting in parking lots listening to the COVID fear porn on the radio and left him with too much time to think.

His ass got so tight he could turn a lump of coal into a diamond in about a week, squeezing. He changed the oil himself to save money, anything to save money like baloney sandwiches. Good thing the restaurants were closed because the price of taking his wife out would be too dear. There hadn't been time for Corrine to sign a lease, and broaching the subject was like committing an act of betrayal.

The thought of celebrating birthdays made Brian nauseous. Buying presents? How about just trying to find shit paper in the stores? How this was changing him was scary. He had to find another gig other than the convention display circuit. That travel pay was good. Being home all the time was another change. Kimmy got on his nerves fast by just breathing, and Brian knew his negativity was contagious.

Maybe he should find Jesus? But he was sure that sort of disrespect was part of the problem. What a fool he was. He'd swallow a gunshot if he had a gun. Men were much better at suicide, successful, planning. His brother gave up. At least Brian didn't drink much. What were the jobs that nobody wanted to do? The President of the United States sent him a check for twelve hundred dollars so he bought a case of beer, Rainier, a good, cheap, local Pilsner to celebrate. He paid the minimums on their three credit cards and part of their main mortgage with it; Kimmy even had a few brews with him. She always was a good sport, a swell egg.

...

Either online or on one of her surreptitious trips to the mainland, Corrine had submitted a change of address, so important stuff for her stopped. That left just the junk mail to remind him that his girl was gone. She took her pithy sayings off the walls, as well as the few pictures, land and seascapes. The bare white walls seemed like penance for being such a damned fool.

He asked Corrine one time for the address on the island but got a signal of "peace out" and she stopped calling. Then he stopped calling. Local taverns made neighbors mask to enter. And the government expected masks to be worn between sips, but the level of stupid stopped there and no farther, ignored. Responding to voicemails with texts, Peter didn't want to talk to anybody but his boss directing work.

He'd never been depressed before, but if looking around and seeing from every angle that you're fucked was the definition, then he was very depressed. He could survive for a few months without work, but if his parents asked him if he needed money then Corrine might have another friend to eulogize. Then he got sick, like a really bad cold.

"I wonder if you have COVID?" Corrine wondered.

He coughed and sputtered. "I never get sick, and even then my colds are pretty mild. But this one has been hanging on for over a week."

"I wonder if you should go get tested?"

"You do a lot of wondering." That made her laugh a little. "I don't know. What for? Just so they can say I should quarantine for two weeks? I'm doing that now." Peter coughed then spat into a tissue. "I haven't spoken to anyone for a few days, it seems. Is it peaceful on the island?"

As lousy as he felt Peter maintained some toughness and dignity, trying to, at least. The truth was that neither knew when they could see each other again, like real time spent together without risking her life. When work picked back up, he could never commute from the island. Corrine was stuck like a bug on flypaper. But if he did get tested and was negative and then quarantined until he could get onto a ferry?

Corrine had to wait another week before being texted that Peter found a place that would give him the swab. The next day he forwarded her the negative result. A way forward?

"Hey Peter, this is Owen," the voicemail said. "My gal is marrying me on Saturday, the fifth of June, at our place. We haven't talked in a long while. Call me back." There were going to be lots of Dolls in attendance.

Peter bought a quick suit from JCPenney and held a corsage as the ferry docked. Its motors pushed spray upon the pylons ever so powerfully, with a schedule to keep. Her truck pushed past quickly in line, then parked a block up the road. Cassie was so excited she was yelping and spinning between his legs. Cory gave him a hug when Peter got close, pulling his mask over his nose, really unsure. The boy wasn't wearing one, and his mom didn't tell him to.

Corrine dropped her mask, waiting a second for him to do the same and then kissed her guy. She looked so regal and buxom in a pink shimmering, satin dress, a sash across her chest. After the nuptials and the party at Owen and Queen Hot Rod's, they motored back for the day's last sailing. A sleepy boy needed to be put to bed. The Roadrunner followed onboard.

www.ingramcontent.com/pod-product-compliance
Lightning Source LLC
Chambersburg PA
CBHW050903130726

47900CB00015B/2009